Suzanne Wa[...] (handwritten)

Mary Balogh was born in Swansea, South Wales. She now lives in Saskatchewan, where she taught for twenty years. She won the *Romantic Times* Award for Best New Regency Writer in 1985 and has since become the genre's most popular and bestselling author. Recently she has begun to write historicals, which have received critical acclaim as well. Her most recent Regency is *Lord Carew's Bride* (Signet), and *Longing* (Topaz) is her latest historical.

Marilyn Campbell is the author of three suspense novels, two contemporary romances, six futuristic/time-travel romances, two novellas, and a screenplay. She resides in south Florida with her two children. Her most recent time-travel is *Just in Time* (Topaz).

Carole Nelson Douglas is the author of many romance, mystery, and fantasy novels. Her mystery *Good Night, Mr. Holmes* won a number of awards and was chosen as a *New York Times* Notable Book for 1991.

Emma Merritt is the bestselling author of thirteen contemporary and fifteen historical romances. Her historical romance *Viking Captive* was nominated for the RITA Best Book of the Year award in 1991.

Patricia Rice was born in Newburgh, New York. She attended the University of Kentucky and now lives in Mayfield, Kentucky, with her husband and her two children, Corinna and Derek. Ms. Rice has a degree in accounting, [...] tory, travel, and antique [...] latest historical (Topaz).

Angel Christmas

Mary Balogh

•

Marilyn Campbell

•

Carole Nelson Douglas

•

Emma Merritt

•

Patricia Rice

A TOPAZ BOOK

TOPAZ

Published by the Penguin Group
Penguin Books USA Inc., 375 Hudson Street,
New York, New York 10014, U.S.A.
Penguin Books Ltd, 27 Wrights Lane,
London W8 5TZ, England
Penguin Books Australia Ltd, Ringwood,
Victoria, Australia
Penguin Books Canada Ltd, 10 Alcorn Avenue,
Toronto, Ontario, Canada M4V 3B2
Penguin Books (N.Z.) Ltd, 182-190 Wairau Road,
Auckland 10, New Zealand

Penguin Books Ltd, Registered Offices:
Harmondsworth, Middlesex, England

First published by Topaz, an imprint of Dutton Signet,
a division of Penguin Books USA Inc.

First Printing, November, 1995
10 9 8 7 6 5 4 3 2 1

PUBLISHER'S NOTE
These are works of fiction. Names, characters, places, and incidents either are the
product of the authors' imagination or are used fictitiously, and any resemblance to
actual persons, living or dead, events, or locales is entirely coincidental.

Contents

Catch a Falling Angel
by Carole Nelson Douglas

London, 1821

"Adrian, you are madness incarnate! You are obstinate enough, I vow, to duel the very Devil to get into Hell."

Mr. Giles Covington seized the object of his admonitions by the greatcoat shoulders, resolved to keep the man he addressed from mounting the driver's seat of a daringly sprung perch phaeton.

Since Mr. Covington was a middling young gentleman with no particular skill in pugilism, any attempt to control his taller, more muscular friend was more a matter of form than of force.

For Adrian Ashworth, Lord Heathford, was in high holiday spirits, abetted by more than a cup of strong eggnog and several brimming glasses of mulled wine.

"Release my collar," his lordship ordered in the outraged articulation of a true dandy of the *Ton*. "Friendship does not permit crumpling my tailor's finest work."

"Friendship entails preventing disaster," Mr. Covington insisted, though he hastened to uncurl his fingers from m'lord's greatcoat. "'Tis after one in the morning, Adrian. You would do better to accept my escort home."

"And thereby delay the pleasure of trying out my

sensational winnings at the hazard table?" Adrian's large frame, made impressively broader at the shoulders by the many-collared greatcoat, sprang onto the driver's seat. "These beauties should gallop like the wind," he predicted.

The beauties in question were prancing matched gray steeds. Their flared nostrils hung wisps of fog like phantom wreaths on the chill December air. Beneath their polished hooves damp cobblestones gleamed bootblack-fresh in the glow of a mist-haloed street lamp, one of the newfangled lighting devices cropping up in London's more prosperous districts.

"Look at the lamps, man!" Giles fussed. "The fog's as thick as ghost stew tonight, with slick stones underfoot. And you have tipped more than a glass or two—"

"You dare to imply that I shall tip myself and these prize ponies into the gutter during the short course home? I may be obstinate, Covington, but *you* are clucking like a mother hen with a severe stutter. I abhor pointless repetition. My condition is utterly splendid, and so is the night for a fast turn through London. Now, out of my way."

Adrian wrested the slender whip from its brass socket, then snapped it above the grays' mincing flanks. They leaped forward as if stung, seeming to fly like Pegasus.

Mr. Covington wrung kidskin-gloved hands, then pulled the high-crowned beaver hat from his head and wiped a fog-and-fear-dampened brow with his coat sleeve.

He watched the grays' ebony hooves strike sparks from the wet pavement as they careened around the corner, the perch phaeton tilting precariously. The driver's fashionable figure leaned the other way to counter the motion. Despite the fog, every detail was as sharp as a silhouette picked out with embroidery scissors. Then elegant steeds, vehicle, and driver vanished around a corner into the utter dark.

"The Devil take you!" Mr. Covington muttered to the fading clip of hooves and a banshee screech of tortured springs. "I will not be held accountable for your survival this night."

Lord Heathford heard no such fainthearted protests over the clatter of his headstrong horses and the rush of cool night wind. His face felt flushed, of course, but that was from the thrill of winning these steeds, not from overimbibing wine, as that young fogy of a so-called friend Covington insisted.

Ah, he could feel the racing tremor of the new coursers even through his leather gloves, though the tips of his fingers tingled a trifle. A chill Christmas they would have, though his heart should be warm and his spirits high now that he had wrested Cartwright's prize pair from his foul grasp. What a Christmas present to himself this rig and coursers made! How Honoria, his mistress, should laugh at Cartwright's chagrin. After all, she had been *his* mistress before Adrian had lured her away with a nobler name, a larger private income, a more sumptuous town house, and more compelling personal attractions, which went a good deal farther than mere fine tailoring.

M'lord leaned his head back to gaze at the fog, which the eerie lamplight pierced like beams of moonlight. He felt the wind draw off his top hat, a fine beaver worth many pounds. Begone with it! He flew with the wind and M'Lady Whimsy, as did the ghostly gray manes and tails streaming ahead of him.

Not a soul was out and about. None would witness m'lord's high-spirited dash through Mayfair. He angled his head farther back to search for the moon, a jolly round face peeking through a muffler of clouds.

The perch phaeton tilted. Tightening the reins to correct the steeds' unbridled progress, he glimpsed a peddler's stand crouching at the corner. By Jove, his dashing new rig was headed directly for the wretched thing! How had his attention wandered, and more to the point, how could he have been so careless? He was a first-rate driver, as he was first-rate at every other pursuit in a life of pleasure and leisure, including a healthy dose of dissolution. He would hate like the Devil to prove that parson-in-training Covington right. . . .

Even as his hands fought the grays for control, the perch phaeton's right wheel ground into some unforeseen impediment. The vehicle lurched sideways while he desperately leaned the opposite way. Directly ahead, the mean shambles of the abandoned peddler's cart hunched like a troll lurking under a bridge.

Adrian's body was suddenly bathed in icy uncertainty. He could feel the vehicle's center of balance shifting hopelessly askew. No stopping it. Carriage and damn-fool driver were headed for a nasty spill. If only the horses came through uninjured! His last, selfless wish evaporated as the reins jerked from his gloved hands. Man and phaeton heaved sideways like a sinking ship. Then all was an upside-down clash of sound and fury.

Adrian glimpsed the faint circle of one of the new-fangled streetlamps hanging over him like a fallen moon. A reedy wail of wheels spinning protest pierced his ears. The shining black pavement flashed an odd bit of bright light in his eyes, blinding him for an awful instant. Something fell besides the pallid moon from the sky: himself, crashing to damp and darkness and hard, cold stone. Himself damp and cold and decidedly disheveled and likely losing consciousness. . . .

He next came to himself standing, surprised.

He awoke in fine fettle, feeling not a bruise or a throb. Lifting a hand to what should be an aching head, he was startled by the immaculate white frill of lace edging his shirt cuff. Looking down, he found that all his attire was equally clean.

He looked perfectly fine. He felt perfectly fine. In fact, he felt . . . nothing . . . at all. Neither hot nor cold, no particular state of being, such as hungry or hurt, anxious or satisfied, worried or calm. He simply was, as he had always been. The overturned perch phaeton could have been a dream. Had been a dream. But where the deuce was he, now that he was fully awake?

He eyed his surroundings, feeling neither panic nor curiosity. He was accustomed to mastering every environment he confronted, whether magnificent or mean. This setting was as familiar as family: the anteroom of some fine city mansion. A black marble floor reflected his lower limbs clad in mahogany brown leather pantaloons and Hessian high boots. No mud or ordure insulted either. He grinned at his damnable hubris in going to Brooks's in this shockingly informal attire, already garbed to drive home Lord Cartwright's prize horseflesh. And so he had. He would have smiled in remembered satisfaction, except that he felt strangely . . . unsatisfied.

This was no way for a man who had survived a perilous accident unscathed to feel! Why couldn't he . . . feel?

The discreet scrape of a soft sole on marble made him whirl to face the chamber's other end. A paneled door was hushing shut as soft as death behind a soberly attired footman.

Adrian smiled at the hopelessly antique figure in white powdered wig and silken hose, black satin breeches, and cutaway embroidered coat. Rather like an elegant monkey at a funeral, he thought.

"Your lordship," this manservant said, bowing slightly.

"I am expected," Adrian noted, surprised, for he did not yet know where he was. Perhaps the accident had addled his memory. He would recognize this domestic scene in a moment or two. No doubt he had been in so fine a house many times.

"Expected, yes." The footman's servile hesitation boded no good.

"Well, then? Is your master or mistress not at home?"

"The master is always at home." Another bow, this time at the mere mention of the absent master.

M'lord approvingly eyed this exemplary servant. Would that his own staff were so respectful. But where the devil *was* he?

"This is—What is your name, sirrah?"

"Pitt, m'lord." Yet another bow.

"Well, Pitt, would you kindly tell me the name of this establishment? I am still somewhat muddled from a recent mishap. And I may have a devil of a hangover," he added ruefully, "thanks to the Season."

M'lord was as famed for his hardheaded consumption of alcohol as for his equally insatiable taste for women. He expected a shrewd smile from this sober servant, who certainly would know of Adrian Ashworth's enviable reputation for self-indulgence.

"This is not a private home, m'lord."

"Then what the deuce is it?"

"A club, sir."

"A club. Ah. I see. I do not recall ever being here—"

"You are not a member."

"Even *I* cannot belong to every gentlemen's league in London! What is this one's name, and purpose, and who are its members? If I am suitably impressed, I may consider joining."

"Membership is not voluntary, m'lord."

"How intriguing. One must be invited, then. I assure you that I am welcome in the most discriminating houses and clubs of the land. Perhaps *I* will not be interested in joining when I view your membership roster. But, first, this so-exclusive enclave's name, if you please."

Pitt bowed again. Adrian began to think that some concealed mechanism plucked an invisible string at his nape every two minutes.

"The Yorick Club, m'lord."

"Ha! After the jester's skull Hamlet contemplated so morosely. I remember it well." Adrian took a turn on the marble floor, admiring the ghostly white-and-gray shades that comprised the decor. "A sober name for a subtle place. And what do they do here?"

"What they have always done, m'lord. Eat, drink, be merry." Pitt spoke in sepulchral tones quite opposed to the listed activities.

"And do they game here, Pitt?"

"Of course, m'lord. And wench as well."

"Well. Well, well! A club after my own heart." He rubbed his leather-gloved hands together. "I will join. But first I must examine your membership roster. A man cannot be too careful of his company these days."

"No, my lord." Pitt bowed away from the wall behind him to reveal a chest-high black marble pillar. Upon its flat top piece lay a massive book bound with blood red calfskin.

Adrian reached the pedestal in one long stride. By the flickering light of a candelabra he bowed over the book to peruse the names written in elaborate red script.

"The Earl of Bath, Lysander Bollingham, *Napoleon Bonaparte*? Isn't that carrying even peace too far? Although I have found the man a fair partner at chess— via the mails, of course," he added with a charming smile that was not usually lost on its recipients. It was now. Adrian read on: "Mainwaring, and Neversby . . . *Countess* Northshire? Women are permitted to be members? This is unprecedented."

"Not at the Yorick Club, my lord. You will find that it gives the proceedings a provocative new dimension. If you are accepted, of course."

"Of course I shall be accepted if I apply. Have you not heard of me, man?"

Pitt's smile was a bit too familiar. "Indeed I have, my lord. All of us here have."

Mollified, Adrian turned a heavy parchment page. "Lord *August* Hervey? Your roster is out of date. That is the father of the current Lord Hervey, whom I know well." He ran his gloved fingertip down another column. "And Howland has been dead these past twelve years . . . and Huddleston only this past fortnight. I say—!"

Adrian's gloved fingertip jerked back from the page's last entry. His gesture had smudged the red ink. Huddleston's name was now an unreadable blot, a bloody smear. He looked up.

Pitt was regarding him with a superior smirk.

"What is the date?" Adrian demanded.

"December twenty-first, eighteen hundred and twenty-one, my lord."

"That is correct. That is the day I left Brooks's and had my mysterious mishap, yet I am none the worse for wear, though"—Adrian went on with dawning horror, bowing over the book—"*all* of these names, all of these people are . . . quite dead."

"Indeed, my lord."

"Napoleon. I had not received a chess move from him since last spring, and I was far too engaged during the Season to read the gazettes."

"Five May," Pitt said, pointing to the book. "He entered without a qualm once I assured him that Josephine was not present."

"Then I myself must be—?"

Pitt bowed yet one more time.

Adrian sighed—how could a dead man breathe?—and manfully straightened his broad shoulders. His greatcoat was gone, he suddenly realized, as he also realized for the first time that he felt damnably cold, even icy.

"I will join your club then." He lifted a graceful right hand, ready to receive the inevitable. "A pen or quill?"

"A moment, my lord. We are not certain that you belong here."

"Of course I belong here. I am . . . dead, am I not, as are the rest of your members? These are exactly the sort of people I associated with in life, all the best society: gamesters, bluebloods, aristocratic trollops. Perhaps I should be comforted that there is some sort of an afterlife, after all, and that one is able to share it—whatever it is like—with one's peers."

"There is an impediment, in your case."

"What impediment? My breeding is impeccable, and my manners exquisite when I choose to exercise them. I am well tutored and tailored and worth—well, *was* worth—a king's ransom. What other qualifications could I have to recommend myself to any club I chose?"

"Your self-regard and arrogance are legendary, my lord, and speak highly in your favor."

"You need not insult me, Pitt, simply because I am dead."

"I spoke only praise, my lord. Selfishness is a sterling virtue here."

"Where . . . is here?"

"This is the anteroom to Gehenna, my lord."

"Gehenna? You mean . . . Sheol, Pandemonium, Tophet, Abaddon, Naraka—"

"Your lordship has had a splendid classical education," Pitt noted with another smile. "Also known as Hades and, most commonly as—"

"Hell!" His lordship paled to the Corinthian curls framing his handsome face as he stepped back a pace. "Good heavens!"

His expletive, however innocent, was a grave error. The candles suddenly flared, exhaling a sulphurous stench.

Adrian drew an immaculate, lavishly laced lawn handkerchief from his waistcoat pocket and muffled his nose. "You mean that I stand on the lip of the Pit itself, Pitt? Oh." The significance of the footman's name hit home as he stared at his aptly named companion, who possessed, he saw now, a dreadful pallor. "I am in the waiting room of Hell?"

"So some call it. We call it the Yorick Club, and we are very particular of our membership."

"This must be a dream!" Adrian's laugh echoed hollowly on the marble vault surrounding him like a tomb. "Hell is too nice to welcome me! Then I shall have to dash up to the other place."

Pitt actually snorted, most unforgivable etiquette. "They will not have the likes of you, my lord."

"Then . . . what will become of me?"

"Something you should have thought of while you were alive."

Adrian would once have described Pitt's thought-tented fingers as "prayerful." Now he feared that some vengeful imp would eavesdrop on the word in his mind.

"What have I done wrong?" he asked in a beseeching tone rare to him. If he was dead and still to have a consciousness, he suddenly feared what would happen to it.

"Not enough," Pitt answered sharply. "We find ourselves in a quandary. You are not quite . . . good enough for us, my lord, by virtue of not being bad enough while you were alive. For instance, you have not a single ruined virgin to your account."

"Good G—, er, Bad Beelzebub!" He waited, but the candle flames remained calm. "Virgins are a dreadful bore, Pitt—ignorant, shilly-shallying misses who whimper and wail. I prefer willing women who know what they are about. Surely fornication and the occasional amusing adultery suffice for your, er, membership qualifications?"

"I am afraid not, my lord. Misconduct with those equally debased is simply too easy."

"Well, what of Lashbrook?" He rushed back to the book and flipped the heavy pages to the "L's." "Here he is! I won all his lands and estates at Brooks's two nights ago. Ruined the man utterly. I understand that he died soon after."

"Indeed, my lord. He shot himself that very night."

"No! Shot himself? That did not get about." Adrian spoke in quite genuine shock, perhaps even regret. "'Tis not the done thing."

"The undone thing was done in this case," Pitt said acidly.

"Drove a man to suicide . . ." Adrian stiffened his shoulders again. "Surely such a dastardly deed is worthy of the Yorick Club."

Pitt's dour head shook. "The suicide was *his* deed. You were merely the excuse. Excuses do not qualify for membership here. If you had murdered him as well . . ."

"I did not think of it at the time!"

"No, my lord, you did not think, which is what made you such an excellent sinner. If only you had possessed the true profligate's lust for excess," Pitt said mournfully. "But you were too busy indulging yourself and your appetites to be truly wicked. You were merely self-satisfied and careless."

"I am to be condemned, exiled from my fellows, struck from the roster of my peers, merely because I did not sin diligently enough? Come, man, give me a chance!"

Pitt folded his white-gloved hands before him. Now that Adrian studied them, he saw that the fingertips were slightly smudged, as if by soot.

"Is it . . . hot in there, Pitt?" He nodded to the handsome double doors of polished cherrywood before which the footman stood guard.

"Hot, my lord? Whyever should it be? What on earth gave you that idea?"

"The . . . preachers."

"Oh, them. Ignorant ninnies. Now. There is a final, slim chance. We have never tried it before, but you are a promising candidate who might have entered easily had you lived but a while longer. You are, after all, only six-and-twenty. The Master is inclined to show mercy to such a promising miscreant as yourself." Pitt sighed.

The scent of sulphur in the chamber increased, yet

Adrian did not feel hot. If he felt anything it was even colder. Icy cold.

"And the Master is—?" he asked.

"Belial."

"Otherwise known as Asmodius."

"Or Apollyon."

"Or more commonly as—"

"Old Nick."

"Old Scratch."

"Beelzebub."

"Lucifer."

"Satan."

"The arch fiend," Adrian finished with some relish. At least he had drawn the attention of the top echelon. "The Father of Lies, the very Devil. So the Master himself approves this scheme?"

"The Other Place has attempted this occasionally." Pitt grimaced at so much mention of the opposition. "We could return you to the living world, which would afford you an opportunity to make bad, as it were."

"A chance?"

Pitt shook his powdered head in warning. "You would not have long, days at best. Within that short space of time you would have to perform one truly despicable act, one deed of such great wickedness that it would wipe your slate clean of any lingering doubts. We cannot, of course, guarantee in what earthly time or place you would arrive."

"Time? Or place? I could return to King Solomon's salt mines!"

"Or to the Queen of Sheba's boudoir." Pitt smirked

again. "You always did like the ladies, my lord. And the fall of the dice."

"And you are sure that the Other Place—"

"Would not touch you, my lord, with a nine-foot harp."

"There is no other alternative?"

"You could drift, forever, in some half-conscious state between Us and Them."

Adrian shuddered. "More than anything, I cannot tolerate being a nonentity."

"We thought not."

Adrian bowed his head.

"Wherever you will find yourself, my son," Pitt added in a softer paternal tone, "the date will be the same, if not the year. So you must complete your despicable act by that Day whose name I dare not pronounce."

"You mean . . . Christmas Day?"

Pitt hissed and cringed as if struck by flung acid. The burning candle wicks elongated into flaming serpents and joined their hisses to his.

"I must know the terms of my quest," Adrian said in apology. Obviously he had not been dead long enough, or evil long enough while he was alive, else such forbidden phrases could never leave his tongue.

"Begone!" Pitt ordered, narrowing like a snake into a sliver of himself.

The entire antechamber elongated, making Adrian feel he was shrinking. Walls shot up toward the dark, unseen ceiling. The pillar bearing the book was suddenly a towering obelisk. The marble floor beneath his feet shifted, its veins becoming writhing serpents, all hissing at him: *inadmissssssible.*

Cast out by Hell itself! He had never been so humiliated in all his life as after the end of it.

The gleaming cherrywood doors had become brazen barriers that loomed into the black fog wreathing the remains of the room. Everything was cold, hard, huge beyond comprehension and as remote as regret. Adrian felt himself becoming hard and cold, felt Death's icy grip seize and squeeze him into a lifeless puppet.

Then he was hurling again through black night, vague glimmers exploding at the hems of his vision. He hit the pavement with a bone-numbing crash. Colors reeled behind the blackness of his eyes. They must be shut. Again he heard the sickening collapse of the perch phaeton, the screams of falling horses, felt the lash of flailing reins.

Again? Was he to die again and again? Was that his punishment for being too bad for Heaven and too good for Hell?

Someone—Pitt?—seized his shirt to haul him up into the blinding light. A bolt of blue lightning reddened like blood before his eyes. The hateful noise in his head became the cacophony of a chanting crowd, its roar torturing his reviving senses. Sweat drenched his body, yet his skin felt clammy.

Adrian opened his eyes to the most terrifying scene he could imagine. He must have been tricked by the Father of Lies and hurled into the deepest pit of Hell itself. Why had he hoped that he could redeem himself and become fit for the upper hierarchy of Hell?

Again the very naiveté that had misled him into wasting opportunities for truly large-scale sin in his life had betrayed him, he thought bitterly. The Devil must have sensed his weakness, his regret for Lashbrook's self-inflicted death, must have known that he never meant to hurt anyone, only to please himself. What a miserable, niggling, *minor* sinner he was! How undeserving of the Yorick Club.

His captor dragged him into the bright light, rasping jibberish in his ear. "Buck up, Adrian, old chap. Thought you were a goner just now, for sure. Since you're up and about again, sneer for the people like a good bad boy. Come on!"

He was dragged to the edge of a pit writhing with doomed souls, whose wails heightened as he came nearer. Some held flickering candle flames. All swayed to the raucous rhythm of their madness, dressed in tatters that showed slices of flesh not meant for public view. Men and women mixed together in that unspeakable madhouse mob, screaming and stretching scrawny arms like tentacles for him.

Just below, a clot of nearly naked women struggled to crawl from the pit, only held back by beefy men who were shirtless except for leather vests, and attired in leather breeches.

"Get it together, man!" his captor screeched in his ear, propelling him to a tall silver-metal wand whose supporting base spewed narrow black serpents along the pit lip.

Adrian regarded the fiend beside him with wonder. Long, unkempt hair haloed his head and shoulders. Cryptic markings covered his bare arms and chest. Crude metal chains jangled around his neck.

The man leaned his mouth to the silver wand as if to

drink from it, still holding Adrian upright by some feat of strength belied by his lean, wiry body.

"Never let it be said," he shouted to the mob, "that Adrian Lord and Dark Angel don't knock themselves out for their fans!"

The meaningless words echoed back like loud weapons. Adrian put his hands to his ears as the mobs' screams rose to a deafening pitch and even the silver wand began to screech with them.

"Come on, man." At last! His captor dragged Adrian away from the pit of horrifying hordes.

Adrian glimpsed other unappetizing fellows on an upraised platform. He would almost call it a stage, had Hell such places as theaters. Awful sharp sounds and demonic drumming made the earth beneath his feet thrum. No, he trod a wooden floor. This was indeed a stage, albeit a queer one.

In moments the dark peace of the stage wings enfolded him. Yet even there equally ugly demons labored over massive sideboards lit by hellish lights and punctured by coiling cables of serpentine wires.

His heart was pounding, Adrian suddenly realized. He stopped walking, despite the urging of his keeper.

"I'm alive," he noted with further wonder. That is what he had *not* felt at the antechamber to the Yorick Club: the ever-present soft thunder of a human heart beneath his skin. "I'm . . . alive again."

"No thanks to you, dude." The man's custodial grip loosened. "Really bummed me out, man, when you kissed the floorboards after your final prance around. I figured you for an O.D., for sure. What are you tryin' to do, kill yourself in public? Luckily, the tour's over and you can do yourself in for the holidays on your own time. Merry Christmas. Better lay off treating the coke fairy to brandy chasers, though, if you want my advice."

Adrian blinked. Half of what the man said made no sense. Yet half of it did, which frightened him even more.

Apparently the shell he occupied had died not moments before, and its occupant, the chillingly named Adrian Lord, had sped swiftly to a welcoming Gehenna. Now Adrian would borrow his body long enough to commit a despicable act worthy of the same swift entry to Hell.

He studied the bizarre scene. If this was another time and place, rather than simply a vision of Hell, then despicable deeds would be child's play here.

He managed an uneasy grin.

His rescuer slapped him on the back, a liberty Adrian would not allow from King George IV himself, until last year known as the Prince Regent or, more familiarly, as that scandalous beau-about-Bath, Prinny.

Before Adrian could rebuke his guide, the fellow was gone. Another sour, unkempt sort took his place.

"You looked a deader, all right, Adrian. Still, it would have ended the tour with a bang *and* a whimper from your adoring fans. Think of the ink."

Adrian wrinkled his aristocratic nose as the Cockney tones of a fishmonger spewed from this odiously familiar fellow. The man tickled the piratical gold ring in his left earlobe.

"Got some good stuff for you, boyo. C'mon backstage."

Adrian knew too little about his new environment to

object. The moment he moved to leave the wings, the burly leather-clad men he had seen in the pit appeared from nowhere to flank him.

Screams were rising around him again, feminine in origin if not nature. He winced. As he entered an ugly, dark hall, the harpies from the pit appeared to tear at his clothes with their long, blood-dipped fingernails. No wonder these men's garb looked so disheveled, if this was what they were subjected to. The women were gaunt bags of unattractive bone, hideously displayed. He glimpsed alarming lengths of legs swathed in skin-tight sheer black veils, of bared torsos and even the swelling edges of breasts, yet these females were as seductive as the Greek Furies, those relentless and horrific seekers after vengeance. Was this where he was? Ancient Greece? The culture was famed for its dramas, if not for as much decadence as he saw before him. The women's eyes were rimmed in smoke or coal dust. Some had painted their fingernails and mouths the shiny ebony of bootblack, reminding him of the slick London paving stones on which he had met his first death.

Query. When his quest was done, would he have to die again to return to the Yorick Club? He shuddered, whether at the thought of a second death or the touch of the clutching females he could not say.

Another overfriendly pat upon the back. Had these people no manners? Of course not.

"Come on, mate. Jimbo will take care of you."

The lower-class tone grated on Adrian's sensibilities as it never had in Londontown, but then he had never needed to rely upon such a lowlife there. Here, he was helpless and went where led.

At last the tunnel of hideous humanity was behind him. He entered what was recognizable as a dressing room. There he met a man in the mirror over the dressing table—himself as he was now.

Adrian shook off his guide's arm to approach the glass.

His own clothes. He was wearing his own clothes. Then he frowned. Now his waistcoat was missing as well as his greatcoat. His leather driving pantaloons and boots were the same, though both clung with a taut smoothness that would seem to defy possibility, but his white lawn shirt gaped open to his waist. His bare chest (thankfully also bare of the sooty calligraphy the other men around him sported) nonetheless bore a collection of bizarre ornaments on gold chains. Genuine gold, though, by the weight and color.

And his hair! He stiffened with indignation. Still a striking shade of auburn, it hung loose and uncurled around his face. A shoulder blade-long section was tied back into an old-fashioned queue at his nape. Queues had been out of fashion for decades! Thank God his hair was not powdered, at least, or he would be taken for a footman! Thank . . . the Master, rather, he revised hastily. Still, despite the appallingly untended and uncut hair he looked quite his handsome, hale self, not like a man who had died twice.

Startled, he glimpsed a second self in the mirror. Turning to the opposite wall, he saw that a large, unframed painting on slick paper was affixed askew on the bare plaster.

His own image was the work's centerpiece. There he stood, legs splayed like a groom's, hands on hips, staring with admirable hauteur despite his unkempt condition, as if he owned the world. The words "Dark Angel" hovered over him like a half halo, and he was surrounded by these same unsavory men in cheap beads and tattered clothes, who bore odd instruments, perhaps musical in nature. His booted feet stood on the three-inch-high letters of his oddly altered name, "Adrian Lord." Beneath it he read the strange words: NORTH AMERICAN TOUR: HELL ON WHEELS.

He had to admit that this image of himself radiated a certain feral power and looked considerably better than his present state. He leaned closer to the mirror, seeing now that his skin had an unhealthy pasty pallor not due to powder. Too much brandy! His eyes—a much-admired whimsical shade of blue-green—were rimmed in unattractive red; his nostrils were ruddy with a catarrh. Adrian Lord had not been taken proper care of, he noted with disapproval. A gentleman's first obligation is cultivating an appearance that is elegant, pristine, and manly all at once. Here he was dressed—or undressed, rather—as a groom. He looked as if he had endured a five-day carouse with no valet to tend him.

"This'll fix you right up, mate."

Jimbo, wearing a dirty grin, held a rectangle of mirror crossed by a tiny dune of white powder under Adrian's nose. While Adrian hesitated, Jimbo hoisted another slice of mirror and eagerly inhaled the entire ridge of powder. What an odd manner of presenting snuff! And what odd snuff, Adrian thought next. These barbarians could not even afford, or appreciate, the elegance of an enameled snuffbox, properly bejeweled.

Still, Adrian was confused, weary, and a tad frightened. He could use a bracing sniff, no matter the source. He lowered his nose to the crude piece of mirror and inhaled a few grains, delicately.

A sally of celestial ecstasy seared his mind and surged down every vein in his body. He felt as if he were falling again, to earth, or rather to wet London paving stone. Yet he found himself instead prone upon the slick marble floor of the Yorick Club. He bowed over his own faint reflection like Narcissus, but it was hard to admire himself when Pitt's pallid face was hanging over his reflected shoulder like a vengeful Man in the Moon. Adrian shut his eyes as a fresh, soaring feeling gripped him. He was plucked away from the Lower Regions at sky-shattering speed and lifted into some airy, unheard-of height. Light radiated his closed eyes, so bright that he could almost see through his eyelids. Exploding flowers of sensation bloomed in his brain like fireworks, bringing warmth and ease and utter enjoyment. Seeking to view this implied paradise, he tried to peer through his lashes at the blinding light. Instead of viewing the Elysian Fields, he glimpsed the black-clad harpies still charging the guards at his dressing room door. Only now they were clothed in an absolutely angelic haze of bright, white fleshy beauty, the most desirable women on earth, or in Hell. . . .

Adrian thrust the mirror away, spilling the powder.

"Hey!" Jimbo cried, crawling under the dressing table like a foxhound to sniff up the elusive powder.

Adrian stood panting with disgust and fear. The powder's celestial vision of endless pleasure surely must be a heaven-sent lure meant to destroy his pact with Pitt. Anything that would make the repellent Furies at his dressing room door look appetizing, even snuff, was an impure delight he would not court. He may be out of his element, but he was no fool.

"A little late to reform, isn't it, Adrian?" The first wildman stood at the dressing room door, a crooked grin on his face. "Which ones do you want tonight?" He cocked a thumb over his shoulder at the writhing harridans.

"None!"

"No coke and now no women? What is it, a death-bed conversion? You don't want to give Dark Angel a bad reputation at this late date."

"I care not."

"Guys would kill for all these moaning groupies. They're screaming for you, man, just like the audience always does."

Adrian eyed the hopeful harpies jumping for his attention.

"Let them eat . . . coke," he said roughly. "I need a rest."

The man shrugged and led him past the hysterical women, who hurled themselves at the burly guards keeping them from their object. Adrian glimpsed Jimbo laying out rows of tiny mirrors and tracks of white powder with a demented grin. He had not meant his departing words literally, but he assumed that the miserable wretch would soon be enjoying Adrian Lord's leavings in every respect.

In the mirror, as he left, he had glimpsed some cryptic characters at the very bottom of the reflected painting. His weary mind worried at them while he was escorted down the hall to a mean alleyway and into a truly terrifying machine—long, low, and black like a locomotive steam engine, yet quiet and smokeless.

Seated in the dark, leather-tufted compartment that muffled any sense of motion and direction, he finally realized that he must reverse the backward letters to decipher them. Save they were not letters, but *numbers* . . . the numbers of the beastly time to which he had been transported: the year 1995. Was it possible? He was one hundred and seventy-four years in the future? Could humankind have descended into such degradation in so short a span? Apparently humanity had always underestimated the Master's work.

He had to give the Devil credit. This place and time were certainly rife with sin and dissolution.

The woman who greeted him at the huge, ugly, towering hotel to which he was brought was thin, but neatly if scantily clad. Her hair was an unearthly fair shade and her nails were the same long, bloody claws that had decked the so-called "groupies."

She apparently functioned as both secretary (shocking!) and maid. She greeted him at the door to his chambers with the words "What can I do for you tonight?"

"Draw me a bath," he responded, eager to shed these debased clothes and cleanse this sweat-abused skin.

She had gone immediately into a far room and soon he heard a roar of falling water. He edged into the proper room, which reminded him of the Yorick Club antechamber, so paved it was in white-and-black marble, including the sunken circle of foaming water at its center.

The woman was bending over to place a flute of champagne on the bathing tub's broad marble rim, her short kilt lifting to reveal her legs nearly all the way to . . . to Waterloo.

"Do you want me to stay?" she asked.

"No!"

She shrugged. "I noticed that the usual cheering section was absent. There are some papers you need to glance at tonight. Is there anything else you need?"

"Can you . . . find me a virgin?" he said suddenly. If the woman was willing to service him in place of the harpies (and she was far more appetizing), perhaps she could fulfill other needs.

She laughed, heartily. "Is that it? Long for the simple pleasures, do you, after all these years? Sorry, boss, but virgins are rarer than unicorns these days. You'll just have to find your own, and I imagine you'll give it all you've got. Just watch the age of consent. Even teenage virgins are hard to find, and anyone under eighteen is jailbait in the States."

He nodded, not really understanding, but relieved when her high-heeled boots clicked out over the marble. High heels, as in the eighteenth century, how grotesque! And on *boots*! He began stripping off his overworn clothes, turning to find the room ringed with mirrors. His borrowed body mimicked his own, and did not disappoint, though it was not as pale as it should be. He supposed that being in Hell would end all that. Despite the alien look of the enormous bathing tub and the sheet of water pouring from its gilded spigot, he stepped in quickly.

Ah, hotter than all the buckets heated belowstairs, if not Below. He sank until his horridly long hair floated on the foam, then he surfaced and used a bar of scented soap to wash off the stink of Adrian Lord. After viewing the groupies' forward behavior (and many of them were under eighteen, he would vouchsafe), he was not surprised that virgins were a vanished species.

He sighed and lay his head against a cool marble pillow. Perhaps this bathing chamber was a bit too reminiscent of a tomb for his taste, at the moment. Though the hotel's rooms were seriously devoid of decoration, they were commodious and comfortable enough. This marble-lined bathing chamber was indeed an improvement on certain matters in his time, especially the privy, as he found later after some anxious moments of investigation.

The chamber beyond the bath was also mirror-lined, and concealed an immense circular closet. Behind his vanishing images he found a wardrobe whose size would warm a Regency buck's heart, however dismaying the styles within. Half the space was devoted to garb of the sort he was used to wearing: high boots, tight trousers, and loose shirts. The other half was distinctly odder, especially bulky but lightweight canvas shoes that tied closed and an exhausting amount of blue denim trousers so humble that they were folded rather than hung. An extraordinary number had tears in the knees, yet were stored as if treasured.

Adrian shook his head as he shrugged into a dragon-patterned silk robe and returned bare of foot to the main room. The champagne-haired woman was waiting for him, unsurprised by his state of undress.

"The reviews just came."

She handed him a stack of printed pages still reeking of the printer's ink.

"How did you get these so quickly?" he asked.

"We have messengers waiting at the major papers and magazines." Her smooth features, painted about the eyes, eyebrows, and mouth, crinkled a little. "You've never asked before."

He glanced at the headlines: DARK ANGEL LAYS ON THE LICKS FOR FRENZIED SELL-OUT CROWD. The bottom one was larger than the others. BRIT ROCKER ADRIAN LORD COLLAPSES ON STAGE. IS HE ANGEL OF DEATH, OR DRUGS? He frowned. What did "Brit Rocker" mean? And "lay on the licks"?

"Yeah," the woman said, noting his bemusement at the newspapers. "The tabloids will go ballistic on your momentary swan dive tonight. What caused it?"

"I felt a bit . . . out of sorts. All is well now."

She handed him more papers without comment, contracts to sign. He could only comply. If the real Adrian Lord returned to this body, it might be committed to impossible terms, but that would be his lookout. He hesitated as his right hand lifted to sign. Was Adrian Lord right-handed? And what did his signature look like?

"Just your initials," his efficient factotum said, as if anticipating his hesitancy. "These are final changes. You signed already."

Relieved, he jotted "AL" at the myriad places indicated. The stubby fat writing instrument felt impossibly clumsy in his hand despite its enamel and gold touches. Oh, for a good slender modern metal pen!

The last item she handed him was a large gold-paper envelope. He pulled out a letter that was printed in type like a newsheet rather than handwritten, more printed sheets, and a large etching on shiny paper, in shades of gray-and-black on white. The last was a portrait of a pretty, soulful young woman, with something at the back of her dark eyes that quickened his interest. He sat up. Her eyes were not soot-rimmed, nor were her nose and ears pierced like those of some savage. In fact, she radiated the healthy, wholesome innocence of some Mama's most precious marriage bait in her first Season.

Ordinarily he would have snorted and cast away such an insipid image. Now his borrowed heart beat faster. Here's a virgin ripe for dispoilment if I ever saw one, he thought. Perhaps not all was lost.

Reading the typed papers was painful for one used to flowing penmanship. Adrian looked up after a while. "Wishfull Wings of Christmas Foundation?"

She seemed prepared to answer any query. "One of those do-gooder operations that grant seriously ill children's dearest requests for Christmas presents beyond their wildest wishes. You happen to be hers."

"This one hardly looks a child."

"In age, no. But she was hit by a drunk driver seven years ago. A terrible accident." The young woman shuddered in sympathy and so did Adrian. "Wiped her out, literally, for years. Memory, mobility. She's undergone endless, painful physical therapy; hospitalized and home-schooled all that time. Seems pretty much all right now, but her memory is still shaky. In her sixteen-year-old mind, she fixated on her favorite rock star: you. The foundation wants to you to visit her for Christmas. But obviously this last tour has been grueling, and after last night's incident—"

"I will go." He threw the papers onto the low, glass-topped table between them, glimpsing his demonic image reflected faintly, as through a very dark mirror. The girl's image landed face up, smiling. She couldn't have done much in hospital all these years. To despoil a tragic waif who idolized him would be an unforgivable sin. She would be his "open sesame" to the one and only true Hellfire Club. "How can I get there most speedily?"

"Chagrin Falls, Ohio? Do you have any idea how small a burg it is?" His decision had startled her, but she seemed well accustomed to whimsical notions on his part, and sighed. "Your jet. It'll take a few hours to arrange."

"Then you should be about it promptly." He smiled as he would at any faithful servant he wished to charm while spurring to action.

"Of course. Anything you want done here before I go?"

"My . . . music. I'd like to review it. Something was playing in the . . . vehicle that brought me here."

She waved a demonstrative hand tipped in bloody fingernails to a secretary faced with more of the bizarre protuberances and green-and-red glowing lights.

"Would you arrange it, please?" he asked. When she started at him, he added, "My . . . fall from grace last night seems to have muddled my memory." He smiled as if she were the King's valet. "Quite a lot, actually."

"I wasn't surprised that you wanted me to put on the CDs," she said. "I was just floored by your 'please.'"

Since he didn't know what "floored" meant, he said no more, merely asking for additional "papers" before she left. Thus he spent the rest of the night and most of the ensuing morning, interrupted only at breakfast time by a gentleman who called with a linen-clad cart bearing the oddest foodstuffs he had ever encountered.

He sipped a foul tobacco-dark brown liquid that was served cold while waiting for the coffee he had instantly demanded. Although it had no ecstatic effect on him, this wry liquid was evidently related to the powder of last night, for the server had called it coke and the name on the garish metal container was Coca-cola. Is this what a decent dish of hot chocolate had sunk to?

By watching the woman whose name he did not know, he managed to insert a succession of Dark Angel "seedys" into the machine. The so-called music that ensued indeed evoked the darkest caterwauling in Hell.

In time, he even learned to identify the tortured howling and growling that was "his" voice. By reading the newsheets from front to back, despite bizarre spellings and expressions, he learned several dismaying facts.

First the date in the year of their Lord 1995. December 22. His time was short. Second, the origin of the papers. New York. That could only be the once-Dutch community on the north coast of the upstart United States of America across the Atlantic. Most disturbing was the realization after much reading that this "America" was a global force in these times, and majestic Mother England (which had a queen now, imagine that!) a weaker ally. He began to taste the true bitterness of Hell: knowing how the mighty have fallen. But, after all, Hell was founded by fallen angels, and he supposed he was an apprentice fallen angel, as it were.

Finally he tossed aside the disheartening papers with their alien images and notions and let the seedy player sit silent. A set of changing red numbers on its face, he realized, ticked off the time minute by silent minute.

Adrian retrieved the portrait from the table. Her name, the letter had said, was Natalie Parks. She was twenty-three years old (well above the legal limit he had been cautioned to observe) and her dearest Christmas wish was to meet Adrian Lord.

He was willing to wager that this poor injured waif who had survived a recovery period of years was perhaps one of the few remaining virgins in the sadly degenerate United States of America. He was also willing to wager that she would get more than she bargained for from Dark Angel Adrian Lord. So much more.

Seducing a crippled virgin. A truly perfidious act, he thought, smiling and sipping the loathsome "coke." It was beginning to taste rather . . . spritely.

The hospital was nothing like the rambling public edifices of stench and disease for London's poor. A bland, boxlike building, it gleamed within of the silent-running machines so common to this future time. He no longer cared about the strange surroundings: nothing would amaze him after the long "flight" in the massive, droning metal dart fashioned like some avian automaton. A servant of the Abyss must tolerate great dangers. Still, he wondered what it would be like to fly on his own, and where Pitt's wings had been.

He had worn clothes similar to his own: leather boots and breeches; the indecently agape shirt and gaudy trinkets, casting on a long leather coat as a concession to the weather. He was becoming used to stares, and had already learned that they were admiring rather than amazed. It appeared that Adrian Lord was famous as well as infamous.

His secretary/servant, who the flying machine's hawkmaster had called Layla, led him to a hallway and a closed door. There he was accosted by a middle-aged woman clutching a bundle of papers to her chest. Even she wore shockingly short skirts, though her stockings were a sturdy and decent pale cotton.

"Mr. Lord! How wonderful of you to come. You're so . . . large—in person, that is. If you only knew how much Natalie admires you and your music. She clung to that one memory after the accident and all through therapy, almost as a talisman. Her doctors used it to motivate her. She had to relearn everything, you see: to walk, to talk, to remember. I don't care what they say about young people's music these days. If it can do what it did for Natalie, I want to shake your hand."

She pulled a pallid palm from the papers and extended it while beaming at him over her huge spectacles. He took the hand, then bowed and kissed it.

"Thank you, dear lady. But I am anxious to meet my admirer."

"Your greatest fan, I promise."

That word again. Why, wondered Adrian, should the

young woman want to be his fan, no matter how enamored? Only the most effete beaus carried fans in his latter days.

The woman swept aside and Adrian entered the room. It was as revoltingly pale and undecorated as the rest of the hospital. Bed, chair, table, window . . . and there at the window stood a shadow, the bright daylight beyond turning the figure into an unreadable silhouette. He heard the door shut behind him.

He advanced eagerly, anxious to assess his quarry.

"Stop!" she cried, putting a hand out to him.

A gentleman must obey a lady, so he did. He realized that she was drinking him in, and that the daylight exposed him completely, that he was as baldly lit as by the ranks of candelabra that raked a stage. He began to feel silly in his ridiculous impersonation. *I am not this loud, prancing lout,* he wanted to explain. *I am a far more superior sort than that.* But that kind of thinking would not unlock the doors of the Yorick Club, and he longed to quit this confusing new world where his mind was constantly challenged by some new oddity.

So he put out his hand, and she took it. Her fingers were icy, as if Death had held her in long embrace, and so indeed He had. As though leading her to a dance floor, Adrian drew her nearer, into the room, then gracefully reversed their positions, so his form was in shadow and hers in sunlight.

He was not displeased. At last, a young woman with some flesh on her bones and some resemblance to a gently bred female! In fact, she began blushing at his inspection, her pink cheeks enhancing her white, admirably even teeth, the soft brown hair that curled around her face and eyes of celestial blue . . . eyes of blue, at any rate. She hardly looked the rather advanced age of three-and-twenty.

Adrian's sigh of satisfaction was louder than he had meant. He had feared the accident would have deformed her, but she was perfect, delightful, no difficulty at all to imagine in his arms, his linens. He glanced to the hospital bed, a truly inhospitable furnishing, but realized that he must not rush himself, or her. After all, he had three days. Of course, the earlier he started, the more thorough would be her fall and his victory.

"I can't believe I'm actually meeting you," she said in a flatteringly breathy voice. A soft, pleasant voice.

Actually, my dear, you are not, his harder inner voice answered her, though his outer self only smiled.

"You . . . look just like your posters," she went on.

Posters? Was this some sort of portrait?

"Do you sound just like your CDs?" she added in a teasing voice.

"Worse," he answered quite honestly. A seduction was always most successful when baited with the truth.

She laughed. "I love your British accent. It's so, so Lord Peter Wimsey."

His eyebrows shot up inquisitively, a response he had found helpful when perplexed. People always explained themselves when interrogated by gesture rather than words.

"I've read a lot these last years," she explained shyly. "Couldn't do much else, besides therapy."

"Have you spent all those years here, in hospital, alone?" he asked gently. "No school, no games, no . . ."

What was that ludicrous expression he had read in the story about lost youth? Ah, yes. "No boyfriends?"

"I'm afraid so. I'm afraid I'm terribly boring and backwards, not at all like the women you know."

"Thank God!" He hoped the Master would forgive his hearty outburst, under the circumstances.

She had as much declared her virginity like the daughter of the proudest Earl of England. She was fit for a king, and certainly fine meat for a mere hellbound Lord. Even if his name was decidedly not Peter. So common a Christian name, what was the girl thinking of, mooning after this fictional Lord when she had a flesh-and-blood one before her? Well, an apparently flesh-and-blood one, for he felt his borrowed heart begin beating faster with triumph and with something else. That was reassuring. He had wondered if all of his, ah, *faculties* would survive the descent into Death and Hades, then his recent resurrection and reincarnation. The answer was, resoundingly, yes!

He eyed the bed again. Sad as it was to set his life's—er, death's—crowning moment on so pedestrian a piece of furniture, perhaps he should stop shilly-shallying around with this tender miss and make a mistress of her. Surely the Devil would not mind if he enjoyed his own perfidy. . . .

He drew her toward him and she came like a lamb to the shearer.

"You can't imagine," she said, "how long it took me to learn to make these few steps."

"You can't imagine how long it took me to get here to see you make them," he said, letting his voice grow deeper and more intimate.

She was beyond blushing, staring at him in wonder as though visited by a god. Lucky, lucky Zeus, who had made a habit of deflowering maidens. How had he been so foolish as to eschew this sublime sense of triumphant vanity before? Pity that he could only do it this one time. He was sure that, whatever they did at the Yorick Club, virgins were not involved.

He pressed her cold hand against his warm, bare chest, bowed his head until his damned long hair hung around them like a living veil. Still she stared up at him, helpless, mesmerized. He lowered his face to hers. . . .

And felt his head yanked back by the hair. Wrenching around, he blinked at the window's daylight, now more savagely brilliant than the noonday sun.

The light shrank and concentrated into a luminous figure, female and furious.

Again it yanked his hair, nearly snapping his neck. He glanced with concern to Natalie, but she was frozen in her adoring posture, gazing up at him, oblivious to this rude interruption.

"Who are you, madam?" he demanded of the apparition. "I suggest you leave instantly."

"Of course you would," it answered in a voice of sheer bronze, melodious but underlaid with iron. "You despicable demon lord! You think you can waltz into my time, my place, my responsibility, and despoil my own? Begone, would-be Satan. I see your dark wings. I know what the likes of you means. You shall not harm one hair upon her head, one lash upon her eyelid."

"What business is it of yours? And why can she not see you as I can, or hear you?"

"That you hear and see me proves your unnatural state, no matter how solid you seem. I am Natalie's guardian angel, and I did not save her from the drunken driver—and see her through more pain and heartache than a supercilious creature like you could know in seven lifetimes—to have her fall to one of Hell's own rakes."

The creature began to flail him with ropes of light, so he felt stung all over by bright lashes. Yet the guardian was incorporeal, and he was not. He was Adrian Lord, bad boy from Bristol, to read his own reviews, and she was . . . history.

How to defeat the angel's interference, though? He turned back to Natalie, who apparently was spared from witnessing any debate between angels dark or light.

With one forefinger he tilted up her chin, her eyes obligingly closing. At his back the sizzling disembodied attack hovered like a swarm of invisible bees, but he concentrated on Natalie, on the moment, and gazed intently down on her, so she would feel his regard through her closed eyelids. They fluttered, and her lips parted. The harrying sensation withdrew. A guardian angel could not defend that which did not wish to be defended.

He smiled, still feeling a last annoying tug on his hair. His kiss landed chastely on her forehead. And so they were found when the door opened. Layla and the woman from Wishfull Wings of Christmas stared in at them.

"What a delightful young girl," Adrian declared, smoothly stepping away. "I am most honored by her admiration. In fact, I have decided to fulfill her Christmas wish beyond her wildest dreams. She shall go home with me to New York. I shall take her Christmas shopping on, on—"

"Fifth Avenue," Layla put in, eyeing him knowingly. *You Devil,* her look said. *You have found your virgin, after all.*

Layla was a rather unwholesome female, Adrian decided, to so relish another woman's peril, and she an utter innocent at that.

"Fifth Avenue," he repeated dutifully. "And we will have all the Christmas trimmings to deck the, the—"

"Penthouse on Central Park," Layla explained to the Wishfull Wings of Christmas woman.

He turned to Natalie. "Come, you must pack. We must be off immediately if you are to experience the quintessential Adrian Lord Christmas."

"I can't." This time she stood frozen by her own amazement and uncertainty. Adrian saw a vague brightness growing at the window. "I wouldn't know what to do in a big city like New York. I've not left the hospital in years, never been anywhere. I have no clothes, no good clothes—"

"That is why we will visit Fifth Avenue," he told her. "To find good clothes, and we will have a splendid English Christmas with wassail and mince pie and plum pudding. Please, you must come—"

The window haze was blazing so bright that Adrian felt his eyes blinded to the room, the girl, the present, even to the feel of his own body, or Adrian Lord's own body. And Adrian Lord's body was not inclined to an insensate feeling at the moment.

"Please," he said in a whisper, bending all his persuasion, his much-practiced charm on one shy waif. "You have no idea how lonely Christmas is for me."

"For you too?" she asked.

He nodded, surprised by the sudden truth that it always had been so, which perhaps was why he gamed and wenched and wined and dined so damn much at that particular time. The window dimmed to its ordinary daylight, the buzzing at his ears subsided; he could live and breathe again.

She eyed the Wishfull Wings of Christmas lady, seeking support.

"You're a grown woman, Natalie, with no family to answer to," the woman said carefully. "You don't have to ask me. But perhaps—" She glanced at Layla, who looked perfectly respectable, if you considered the age and its customs. "Oh, go ahead. I wish I were so close to having a Christmas hope come true. You've earned whatever fate will grant you many times over, my dear."

And so it was done. Adrian Lord would have his Christmas wish granted as well. He was as good as in Hell's antechamber right now, walking through those cherrywood double doors to join his peers.

Layla proved to be a true devil's imp. She arranged everything, an amused smile hovering on her painted mouth all the while. That smile appeared whenever Adrian halted at an unfamiliar word or concept and she leapt in to provide the proper answer; it broadened whenever Natalie's dazzled gaze rested on Adrian to the exclusion of her.

On the "jet," Adrian and Natalie sat side by side on

the austere sofa, staring out the tiny windows and counting clouds. Or rather, Natalie counted clouds. *He* could barely stomach the sight of them, all fluffy and white and angelic. This great height unnerved him. His head felt as though a metal band were compressing his temples, and the sensation had worsened on the return journey, despite Natalie's disingenuous chatter. At least no guardian angel would be able to fly as fast as this machine, he thought, though the sensation of speed was oddly unsatisfying, not nearly as thrilling as his last wild and fatal perch phaeton ride. . . .

He winced and put a hand to his head. The pressure had become unbearable for an instant.

But it passed and soon they were on the ground, speeding in the low black engine through——Manhattan, Layla said—to the place he had been before. His penthouse.

Natalie marveled at everything along the way, and Adrian took comfort in her simple ignorance. She had lived in this time and was still intimidated. The strain was not as great around her; she greeted everything with wonder, though he began to feel a throb of jealousy at how easily she was impressed. Perhaps she was too easy a conquest, and beneath the attentions of a truly perfidious man. No, that was the point, to corrupt a true innocent, and she certainly was that. Though . . . why had an entourage as disreputable as Dark Angel entranced such an angelic child? Now, that was a conundrum. Perhaps it had to do with the times, he thought, and settled back into the seat of the . . . "limo." What words! By George, these people were hopping mad.

Once arrived, the ever-efficient Layla took Natalie in hand.

"You don't want to go shopping with us," she cajoled Adrian, "after your arduous tour. Remember your . . . stage accident."

At that cue, Natalie chimed in. "Oh, no, Mr. Lord. You must stay here and rest. I read about your illness this morning. That's why I never dreamed you would come for me."

"Hell could not stop me, my dear," he said between gritted teeth.

"We women will shop for women's things," Layla decided. "You stay here to supervise the arrival of the Christmas decorations and some other things I ordered while we were in the air."

"You are a treasure, Layla," he said quite honestly.

Her queer, knowing smile broadened. "Rely upon me, Adrian. I know exactly the right thing to do."

How correct she was, without realizing it. He had no appreciation of women's fashions in this debased time. Much as he hated to admit it, Layla was proving to be a fiendish accomplice. She seemed to revel in poor Natalie's being led to the slaughter . . . though entering womanhood via his own expert ministrations was hardly a fate worse than death. She was fortunate. In this dreadful age such an unnatural innocent might otherwise succumb to a clumsy oaf Adrian would not wish upon a groupie.

When the women were gone, with three-quarters of the day before them, he spent the time exploring the fifteen or so rooms. Some were more sumptuously furnished than others, such as a dining chamber paneled in beaten copper. The lighting throughout was equally bizarre but obedient to the turn of a dial. One room reminded him of a seraglio, with low cushioned couches and dim lighting, and more machinery that made noise and pictures. He suspected that devotees of the heady snow white snuff practiced their arcane rituals in this arena.

Of the bedchambers, his own was a mate to the Romanesque bathchamber, a sybarite's paradise surrounding a huge circular bed sufficient for entertaining a half-dozen groupies. Mob scenes did not attract him, in public or in private. He preferred a sensual partnership, which was why virgins had never appealed to him. His mistresses had been worldly, wise, and witty women, as adept at the arts of conversation as those of lovemaking. He recalled them for a moment with sudden fondness.

Seduction had been their mutual game, with little more at stake than pride. He had underestimated them, he saw, and himself. Theirs had ever been a civilized association, yet it had lacked . . . heart. Now that he totally lacked a heart, he could see that. Pity. But too late. They too would visit the Yorick Club antechamber in their times, and be judged worthy or wanting. He wondered if they . . . missed his company. Or his money.

He avoided the penthouse's many wall-sized windows, his sense of balance still askew from being so unnaturally high. He had glimpsed a vast snow-covered park far below, where bare dark trees blotched the albino landscape.

True to the miraculous Layla's prediction, a parade of goods came pouring into the penthouse all day. Adrian's composure did not shatter until the footmen bore in a tall fragrant pine tree severed below the branches, installing it upright in some sort of device. What a savage custom! A crew of garland strewers buried the rooms in scented boughs, gilt ribbons, tiny lights, and fat candles of fantastic design, though they left the strange and puzzling tree denuded. Picnic baskets that could have come direct from Fortnum & Mason arrived, overflowing with fruit, tinned meats, cakes, and wines, so no one need bother with cooked food for several days. Until Christmas was past at least. How convenient, he thought, beginning to feel at home.

Yet after the flurry of deliveries, time began to tell on him. He was unused to being alone, servantless. He poured himself a large brandy from a glittering selection of spirits in the main room, sipped, and felt a sublime warmth transport him almost as thoroughly as the white snuff.

He returned to read the bottle's label. Ah. No wonder. The brandy was as old as his former chess partner by correspondence; in fact, the label boasted of the connection. How comforting to know that the finer things endured. Would the Yorick Club serve Napoleonic brandy? Or was all that civility a facade? A trap? Was he really so anxious to find out?

Then he recalled the squeamish moments in transit between his own world and this. He envisioned spending eternity in that noxious state. Hell, even Heaven, would it have him, would be an improvement. He began to wonder what Heaven would be like, if Hell was so unlike his conception. Then he remembered Natalie's pernicious guardian angel, all prickly heat and light. Interfering ectoplasmic nanny! Thank you, no; he could never embrace such a state of postmortem meddling. No, Hell it was for him; a match made in Heaven.

Wandering to the windows, he watched a faint image of himself approach, trodding on air in the deepening twilight. He and Adrian Lord could have been twins, and both were fine figures of men in any time. What would it be like to "tour" before the raving crowds? Would one grow to like the acclaim, even need it? If he was a fallen angel in disguise, perhaps he could fly; he hadn't attempted it.

Below, the tiny lights that decked the stunted trees lining the city's ugly streets massed like fireflies over the dim park grounds. It was growing quite dark. Where were they? Alarm tightened his grasp on the brandy snifter. Suppose something had happened to them, to her, his deepest necessity? Another accident? No, not all this way for nothing!

A scratching at the distant hall door made him rush there. He had heard not a polite scratching for entry, but the scrape of the odd key cards that opened doors in this hotel. Layla's sardonic face peeked through the door's opening crack.

"Greeted by Himself! Were you worried we had absconded to Rio on your credit cards, boss? Nope, just stuck in Christmas traffic."

Natalie came behind, her face ducked in shyness, her dark hair dewed with melted snowdrops. Behind them trailed the uniformed footmen from the street door, garbed in burgundy greatcoats and bearing a regiment of boxes and parcels.

"Where's Natalie's room?" Layla asked. "You did intend for her to——?"

"'Of course." How fortunate that he had explored the premises. "Three doors down the passage, on the left."

"Right next to yours, how cozy for Christmas."

Layla marched off her shy charge, not before a girlish laugh escaped Natalie's lips. Adrian frowned. He could not bear giggles. This scheme would have its unpleasant aspects. Now Layla . . . he was beginning to appreciate her formidable virtues, not the least of which was tweaking his dignity.

She returned, threw off her own greatcoat, poured herself a small brandy, then began dispensing information.

"I told the crew to let you and your guest decorate the tree."

"Is that what that monstrosity is doing indoors?" he asked. "It is to be . . . garnished in some such way?"

Layla's yellow head tilted with disbelief. "You've forgotten what Christmas trees are for? You *have* been taking too many head trips, boss." She sighed. "Yes, ye olde Christmas tree is ritually strewn, adorned, trimmed with ornaments. The stuff is in those boxes." She pointed to the cluster surrounding the tree.

"As for your forgetting to buy any Christmas presents for Natalie, fear not. All taken care of. We maxed out three of your platinum cards, or rather, I did. The poor kid has been in hospital gowns for six years, so I figured she deserved a shopping spree. I must admit that she wanted to go a bit overboard, biker-chick stylewise, but Mama Layla prevailed. In some ways she's such a sixteen-year-old still. Hasn't seen much of the world but the back of its hand. Well"—Layla downed the remaining brandy like a thirsty subaltern—"the tree's up and the stockings are hung at the chimney with flair. Central Park is taking a snow bath. You've enough food and drink to last until Easter and I didn't lay in any drugs, as you seem to have gone on the wagon since your onstage nose dive. You're on your own. The staff was never engaged for this place for Christmas, since you were supposed to be in London now and I was supposed to be snuggling up with St. Nick at my apartment in Queens."

"Don't you have a family?" he couldn't help asking. Layla was the most fiercely self-sufficient female he had known in any world, and he wondered why.

"I did," she said, suddenly terse. "They're all dead now."

"For a long time, like Natalie's?"

"Yes." Her voice sounded forced as she turned to retrieve her coat. "For a very long time. Like Natalie's."

As she turned back to him he glimpsed pale eyes glittering with some odd emotion in her impervious face. "You do this right, buster," she ordered.

"Do what?" His innocent tone sounded fraudulent even to himself.

"You know what I mean. She deserves better than she's had so far."

"I haven't the faintest notion what you're talking about."

"Like hell!" Her abrupt laughter was loud and somehow threatening as she slung her heavy coat over her shoulders and strode for the door. "You're on your own for once. Don't blow it."

He may not have understood every idiom, but he got the message. He was on trial in her eyes, though he did not know how or why.

He turned back to the now ebony-dark window, cosseting his brandy snifter. He looked the spitting image of the Dark Angel, Adrian Lord. He was even beginning to feel at home in this world. Layla evidently realized his intentions toward Natalie, but she wasn't stopping him or warning the girl. And why was she demanding that he accomplish his seduction "right?" Didn't he always?

The twinkling lights in the dark below seemed to swirl into an eddy and swoop upward like flying embers. Or perhaps he saw a whirlwind of snow. It rose and gathered until it swarmed around his reflection, then shaped itself into a figure he knew too well—the guardian angel from Ohio he had hoped to outfly!

He stepped backward as if he had seen a ghost, which he supposed he had. The figure's angry radiance made him blink and lift an arm to his eyes, but the angelic form and face pressed against the window glass, blotting out his reflection, forcing him to see the holy conviction of her expression boring into his once-dead eyes, into his lordly nineteenth-century conscience, into his half-damned soul.

Adrian stumbled to the side of the window, found a cord, and did something he had never done before in his life: he drew the draperies closed with his own hands. Only these curtains were shiny metal slats that clanged like New Year's bells as they tangled shut on the dreadful December night outside and the avenging angel poised a half mile up in the night sky. He saw his own image again, wavering on the fragmented mirrored metal slats, cut into ribbons like a rent etching. He felt again the falling sensation of the accident, and his arrival here. Felt dizzy and disoriented and not himself at all . . .

He fell against the wall, shutting his eyes.

"Adrian! What's the matter? Are you ill again?" Natalie was at his side in a long emerald velvet gown, oozing angelic concern, sweet as baby's breath. Her hand on his forearm warmed him through the lawn shirt. "You shouldn't have put yourself out for me."

"Only a touch of ague." He pushed himself free of the wall's welcome support.

Her warm, sympathetic presence had banished the do-good demon outside the penthouse. He breathed deeply and smiled. "What are you wearing?"

She stepped back and drew her long skirts wide. "Evening culottes. Hard-core Laura Ashley, I'm afraid. Sweet as syrup." She made a charming face. "But Layla said you were a bit old-fashioned, and I did want to please my sponsor."

Despite the yards of fabric, he glimpsed the skirt's separated center and felt himself do another unheard-of thing. He began to blush. "*Culottes*. That is French for . . . trousers. It is not fitting for a young woman to wear such things."

"You *are* something of a fuddy-duddy! Layla was right." Her laugh was more than a giggle now, it was a tease. "I guess I was right to pass up the radical black-lace bustier and the vinyl miniskirt."

He didn't know what to say, not having the slightest idea what she was talking about.

"Did you eat while you were out?" he asked.

She nodded happily, her eyes shining. "Un huh. At Planet Hollywood. Cool. You must know those guys, Willis and Schwarzenegger."

"Er . . . I must. Well, then, perhaps we should garland the tree."

"I love the way you talk! Your accent, your expressions! It's . . . divine."

He winced at the word, but went to open the plain boxes, which were filled with garlands, glass globes, feathered birds and . . . angels of every description.

"Oh." She fell to her knees by the glittering hoard, some of the dazzle infusing her face with a delicate beauty he had not glimpsed before. "That Layla! She thinks of everything."

Her busy hands hoisted hosts of angels—crystal, silver, and gilt, dove-feathered—all winged and haloed and simpering like mad with the joy of the Season.

He felt weak again, and sat on the nearest low sofa.

"Look!" Natalie reverently lifted a different angel, one shaped from dark, smoky glass with hidden features and no halo, only wings. "A wickedly perfect likeness. Where on earth did she find it?"

He shrugged.

Natalie tilted her head, puzzled, then lifted another trophy. "There are two. Exactly alike. But there are a dozen each of the others. I can see why Layla would order one dark angel, but why two?"

He shook his head. "I don't know."

Concerned, she shuffled over to him on her knees, then sat on her heels like a child. "Are you all right, Mr. Lord?"

"You called me Adrian before. At the window, when you believed me ill."

Her eyes dropped. "That's how I thought of you, all those years." Her eyes narrowed and saddened. "Time stopped for me, but not for you. You must have been very young when I was first your fan seven years ago."

"Not so very young even then. I was born old."

"How old are you now?"

"Impertinence becomes you. Six-and-twenty."

" 'Six-and-twenty.' I think I fell in love with the way you talked, your voice, first." Her enthusiasm faded at the shock of her own expression. "I mean, fans are supposed to be fanatical."

"My voice." He laughed a bit bitterly. "I cannot understand why. I don't sing, I shout."

"But you have to, in those big arenas. If you sounded like Placido Domingo, you'd probably look like him too."

"How does this 'Serene Lord' sound?"

"Like a tenor cherub."

"And how does he look?"

"Short. And fat."

"And I look?"

She didn't hesitate. "Tall. And lean. And sexy as hell."

He didn't pursue the alien word that had preceded his would-be home, for as he gazed down at her sitting at his feet, her forearm resting across his knee, she looked amazingly like a lass from his own time, though no respectable miss would arrange herself so casually after childhood.

She had donned a velvet tiara decorated with green

velvet roses and some glittering stones. With the gown's puffed long sleeves and gentle décolletage she could have entered any London drawing room and been declared a stunner. Her skin was hospital pale, pure ivory silk, not the harsh, tawny leather color of the groupie women. Any paint she wore was as soft and subtle as the breath that stirred the shadow between her breasts.

Who was seducing whom?

He rose abruptly, letting her arm fall from his knee, and uncorked a bottle of rosy wine, pouring it into two crystal flutes with a frosted cut-glass design of . . . winged angels.

"Oh, these are beautiful! Lalique crystal." She turned the glass after he gave it to her, azure eyes aglow with awed enjoyment.

Adrian began to understand the meaning of the word purity, and to loathe it. He sat again, sipped a light effervescent wine unlike any he had ever drunk. "Tell me about your accident."

She looked up, alarmed. "It happened at the holidays. I try to forget that."

"At Christmas?"

She nodded, turning her glass to admire the angel's rosy wine-tinged face. "Such an old, common story. It happened at night. It was Christmas Eve and a drunk, driving too fast, lost control of his sports car. It crashed into our station wagon. My parents died at the scene, my little brother a few hours later in the hospital. I was flung free, despite my seat belt. Oddly, that's what saved me, they said. I landed on some"—her would-be brave laugh trembled on a sob—"old clothes. Piles of them left by the curb, a holiday collection for the homeless. Still, I managed to break a lot, mostly my head. I don't remember anything of the accident, nor months and months of my recovery. I still don't remember everything." She glanced up again through the angel glass. "That's why the staff wanted me to have a Christmas wish fulfilled, even though I'm ages too old for that sort of childish thing. The one thing I remembered at first was Dark Angel. You, I guess. Teenage girls need to have crushes on unattainable older men, you know."

"But Dark Angel is such a rude, dirty, tawdry pack of fellows! We leap and pose like demented wildmen, and yowl like wolves."

"You sound like a fundamentalist preacher complaining about evil rock and roll."

"I sound like a sane man, describing insanity. Dearest Natalie, there's no skill or grace in what I do. I might as well be a gladiator teasing lions. Why do you admire me so much for so little?"

She sipped the wine, then rose to her knees so her face was closer to his. "I told you. Because you're the sexiest thing I've ever seen." She smiled at his frown. "Don't tell me they don't use that word in England either?"

He took a quick swallow of the light wine for courage. She was too close. She expected something of him that he did not seem to have. He was not used to being deficient in his own eyes.

"Probably they do, but *I* don't. You see, I took a bit of a tumble myself of late. I can't remember . . . some things."

"Silly," she reproved gently. "I know."

"You know?"

"It takes one to know one. I saw immediately at the hospital how you were tiptoeing around names of things. Don't worry, you're getting better at leading people into cueing you. Has it been just since the other night onstage?"

"No. That was . . . different. Mine was a . . . vehicular accident too."

"Oh—!"

"Nothing like your true tragedy. I lost no one I loved. Perhaps because no one loved me. I was by myself, and soon myself again with barely a bruise. Save for my delinquent memory."

"Everyone loves you!" she said indignantly. "Except for the rock critics."

"What happened to the man who ran you down, ran down your . . . er, wagon, rather?"

"I try not to think about him. He was indicted, tried, served some time in prison for manslaughter. Not enough, a few months. He was young. It was a first offense."

"No, it wasn't," he murmured.

"What?"

"I mean that a man must be responsible for himself and what he does, especially when he is in an irresponsible state."

She smiled impishly. "Are you in an irresponsible state now?"

He took her hand, rose, and pulled her upright. "Yes. Let us trim this naked tree."

"All right." She swayed against him, warm human velvet in his arms, reminding him of the chill reception room of the Yorick Club to which he was hellbound to return. And she, her body, was the passkey, like one of those slick, hard rectangles that opened every door in this world. Only she would open the door to the Underworld. Only she. He had no time to procure—ugly word for an ugly deed—someone else. Perhaps there was hope for his career as a hardened sinner. The act he contemplated must be sufficiently despicable because he was coming to despise himself.

Time, he told himself, setting aside the wine that tasted like watered red vinegar, to fulfill his mission.

Her joy, her innocent attraction to him, nursed when she was young and vulnerable, as she still was, was all the spirituous liquor he needed that night. They laughed as they untwined tinsel garlands and twined themselves in strings of tiny glass bulbs that would blossom light.

"You've forgotten what an electrical outlet is?" she chided in mock amazement. And then crawled behind the tree with the cord and did something that made the dull forest green tree explode with an infestation of fireflies, like the trees outside.

He stood transfixed. This light lacked the acid burn of the guardian angel. It was pure, ultramodern magic. He touched a fingertip to one flame-shaped bulb, and found it cool as crystal.

"Careful!" she warned. "It'll get hot later."

Their glances crossed and the heat leaped between them and spread. He professed to be too bad to hang up the angel decorations—the "bad boy from Bristol," he reminded her—so she placed each one. He had to lift her to hang the highest ones, and was loath to let her down, lowering her along his body, her hands tangling in his hair, sliding down his arms.

They stood before the shining, light-swathed tree. She leaned her back against him, and he wrapped his arms around her. He could not ask for an easier, more natural seduction. His fingers played at the smooth skin of her neck, he inhaled a scent of freesias and for a moment was at his country home, young and foolish, with no mistress in his past but his nanny. He was not fashionable, or enviable, or cynical. He simply *was*, as she was. How long ago that had been, in his life and in true time.

"I can't believe I'm here," she said slowly, softly. "I can't believe I'm so close to getting my Christmas wish."

Something in the way she put it surprised him.

"This"—he looked around at the festive room—"isn't it? Weren't you to be satisfied with a mere meeting at your hospital room?"

"Oh, Adrian." In the glow of the tree lights, she looked at least his age and far wiser. "That was my sixteen-year-old wish. I'm much older than that now, with much more interesting wishes."

"Such as?" He smiled down at her, wondering whether he should kiss her first on the nose—a bit cousinly—or the neck. The neck, perhaps, and then the chin, the cheek, the cheekbone, the temple, the mouth, the shoulder, the breast. By then there would be no turning back.

"I want to seduce you, of course," she said fondly, as if speaking to a rather thick-headed child.

"You? Seduce me?"

"Don't sound so shocked. And don't tense up so. You were just relaxing nicely."

She wriggled closer, but his muscles had turned to stone. This was all wrong. He was the predator. He was the bastard out of hell, sworn to bring an earth angel down.

"You're shy, aren't you?" She was snuggling in his arms, insuring his utter stoniness in every part. "I used to be that way too. Sometimes the boldest pose covers a sensitive soul. You're so wonderfully funny and old-fashioned. I think I always sensed that. Don't worry. I find that sexy too. We can go slow."

Go. Slow.

He forced his hands from her back to her upper arms. Then he clamped them shut on the velvet and lifted her away from him, away from his still-too-human body.

"I don't understand," he said. "I shouldn't be touching you like this. I'm violating the most basic standards of decency, holding a girl who has faced such tragedy, who has no experience of men and the world."

"Listen, Dark Angel. I read, you know. I watch TV and movies. Especially the soaps. Whew!" She fanned herself with her fingers, a sign of these debased times when women were not properly accoutred for the stresses they faced, he thought. "I know what I'm missing," she went on. "I just want to make up for lost time in the most wonderful, exciting, safe way possible."

"I'm safe?" Now he was getting angry.

"No, not that way. You're fabulously dangerous in all the right ways. But you're not real like the boy down the street. You're bigger than life, and I know you've had, oh, hundreds of women. I don't want my first time to be all fumbling and apologies. I want to rock and roll!"

She hurled herself toward him like her annoying guardian angel. And, speak of the devil, where was the supernatural ninny when one needed her? He held Natalie back, which wasn't easy, and found himself again making a strong case against himself.

"Well, dozens of women, perhaps. And then you speak of safety. If I am such a woman chaser, what about this dread disease that's about?"

She paused in her loving assault, and there was no mistaking the expression in her eyes; however misguided, it was love. Her head tilted.

"I'm not afraid of that. Somehow I know, *I know* that you've never been exposed to anything deadly. I don't know if I believe that you'd be scrupulously careful, or simply that I've always sensed in some deep, spiritual way that you're no threat to me."

"Ridiculous," he said, snorting with panic.

For she was right. In his world the penalties for profligacy were minor compared to her terrible time. And though he had considered himself a seasoned man of the world, he understood now that the four mistresses he'd had in his lifetime would be a night's work for the likes of Adrian Lord, in person.

What a despicably selfish monster! He began to loathe the body he borrowed, though it was identical to his own.

"Maybe I should explain myself," she said penitently.

Lord, she was adorable when she was penitent! If he

were her husband, he would see that she sinned frequently, were that possible in the married state, and he thought that it could be arranged.

"Perhaps." He sat down on the sofa.

She sat on his lap like a naughty child.

"Pretend that you're Santa and I'm asking for my dearest Christmas wish. You." She grinned and ran her fingers down his chest, reminding him that Adrian Lord's shirts were unfastenable. Now he knew why.

"First," she began, "you must understand what it's like for a girl growing up in the United States. There's high school and the senior prom. I should have had a boyfriend by then, and we would neck—kiss and stuff—in his car and maybe he'd muss my clothes a little, but we wouldn't do much more, because I was raised to worry about being a good girl. Then I'd go off to college and meet somebody, a young man I really was crazy about. And we'd do more and swear eternal love and go our separate ways and I would never forget him, but I'd know he wasn't The One. And then I'd meet The One and that would be it. I'd be a woman of the world, and if we were very lucky and worked very hard at being honest, we'd be married to this day. And I'd have never met you, though I'd always remember my Dark Angel, like someone distant I had known and loved once."

"That didn't happen," he reminded her. "You're a virgin, aren't you?"

"Yes, and I hate it! At twenty-three! It is to die. Now I'm ready to go out into the real world, and—with all my therapists—no one has thought about how stupid and ignorant I'll feel, how I don't know how to judge men and the situation and myself. But ... if you are my Christmas wish, I'll know all I need to know, and I'll learn it from someone I really want, someone I always understood could not be for me in any permanent way. But for a moment—don't you see? You'll give me a great gift, because I know it will be easy with you, and we won't end up hating each other or ourselves, and you'll have taken pity on the poor crippled girl and I'll have my secret hero and no one will know the difference."

"What," he asked, "if we end up loving each other?"

She stared at him. "That's impossible. We're worlds apart. You'd find me boring after those wild women. I know I'm not your ordinary speed, but I am something different."

"Very different," he said thoughtfully. "I must think about it."

"Thinking is not what this kind of thing is about."

"Yes, it is. I have spent too much of my life not thinking. This may be my last chance."

He stood, lifting her in his arms. It pained him to think how long it had taken to bring her mind and body to this point, where she would commit the results of her agonizing recuperation to the stranger that was himself on a moment's notice.

"We must be careful what we do, because it's not so easy to forget," he told her. He had reason to know now.

"We both are fairly forgetful already," she jested.

"Because we've both been hurt. We don't want to compound the damage." He let her feet gently touch the floor.

"Loving and wanting aren't damage." She touched the side of his face. "Not having either is. That much I know."

He paced to the window. Sexy. Another untranslatable word. Did weary and confused perchance meet that definition? After all, he had Hell and her entire future to consider. If she was so willing, did it ruin her ruination? Or did her feelings, her participation not matter, so long as she was different than she had been, his victim somehow? Or was he hers?

He did not feel successful or triumphant. He felt responsible and troubled, both unpleasant states. And he felt . . . willing to have her at any cost, under any pretenses. Just once, as she had said. Once would be enough.

Would that terminal selfishness of love get him into Hell? Did he even care anymore? Which was the greater evil? To use her to serve his purposes? Or to need her despite his purposes?

He saw her dark figure hovering behind him in the glass. No angel was in sight now. They were both fully human. She was his angel. He eyed the emerald velvet gown, barely visible in the dark glass, and smiled. His dark angel.

He turned.

She waited, breathless.

He held out his arms and she walked to him, each step straight and steady, bought with years of terrible effort and will he would never understand.

The only thing he understood was that this moment was both pure Hell and pure Heaven and would always be both.

When he kissed her he was thrust back to the innocent age of sixteen. Like a raw youth, he shared her tremulous surprise, her eager adventuring. Nothing wrong could come of this.

Yet . . . lights flashed in the darkness of his mind, as if a Christmas tree blossomed in his brain. And pain came then, a sharp, disciplining crack like the whip on a horse's withers.

Lightning flashed in places deeper than memory. The Yorick Club's doors swung open, then shut. He glimpsed a cool, quiet garden, each flower on its graceful stalk showing the face of a pale, deathless angel. . . .

Then he was falling again, into night. Tumbling like a die. Dying. He heard the horses scream. Noble beasts, he would never even flick them with a whip now that he knew the touch of true pain. The night was again wet and chill, and dark as a deep December. Christmas was coming, but it meant only a round of carousing and escape from the utter loneliness of his drive through Londontown.

He was hitting the pavement, feeling his body vibrate to the vicious impact, his head strike stone. Lights flashed, a particularly bright white bolt illuminated the peddler's stand collapsing from the impact of the carriage.

Thank God he had taken no passenger along to join him in this great and fatal fall!

Yet something dark was crashing to the pavement by the stand even as something fiercely bright was wrapping . . . wings . . . around it.

The unnatural light brightened impossibly until it illuminated the object it protected—no, the person. A beggar girl, clad in rags!

His solitary accident had not been so lonely, after all. Another human being had witnessed it. Dear God, he had killed not only his own miserable self, but that poor beggar girl, whose face was even now turning toward him, shining in the angel's sheltering arms!

And it was hers. Natalie's. *She* was the victim of his cruel carelessness . . . until her guardian angel—the heavenly fury who had been bedeviling him, and rightly so—had snatched her to another time, another untenanted body wasted in another drunken accident, to permit her another chance at life, and yet another encounter with him.

He might as well have been the drunken driver that had killed her father and mother and brother and condemned her to seven years of amnesia and recovery. For the beggar girl's angel had "borrowed" the dying body of Natalie Parks to give her unhappy charge a chance at a better, brighter life than the London streets, just as his devil had infused him into Adrian Lord's drugged and dead body at the moment of the rock star's onstage collapse.

He himself was the man he had most come to hate in the world, in any world, be it his own or this one, be it Heaven or Hell.

She is clinging to him, her face wearing the same look of sad concern that her guardian angel's had almost two centuries before, the last sight he had glimpsed unknown as he lay dying.

"Adrian? Are you all right? Are you ill again?

69

She is looking at him with all those one-syllable words he had laughed at in life: hope, trust, love.

Now he, whose life was a paean to heedless pleasure, however fleeting, now he knows, for eternity, the weight of another person's pain. He has accomplished his mission and found true Hell, the one within himself.

Although he can hear her, see her, as he could not quite do the night of his accident, he still feels himself in that removed state, halfway between Heaven and Hell. He feels his corporeal body, shocked by emotion, sink under the burden of his incorporeal guilt. He watches it collapse, going down on one knee, as if from a distance.

She sinks with him, now truly terrified. "Adrian, what's wrong? Don't do this! Don't die. I didn't tell the whole truth about my Christmas wish. I don't just want to make love with you. I love you!"

Worse. As if the whip of his own evil had snaked back to lash him with demonic force. There is only one answer, the one he had been trying to give her in many different ways tonight. Adrian Lord did not deserve her admiration or love, just as his impostor deserved it even less.

"I am not worthy!" he cries out, loud enough that Heaven and Hell can hear him.

Hell certainly does.

In the penthouse, lights flicker and douse, even the tiny gentle lights wreathing the Christmas tree. Angel faces among its branches vanish. Her angel face, painfully distraught, also vanishes, and he knows what it is to die twice.

* * *

Cold. Icy. Like the marble floor on which he kneels alone, his head buried in his dead, chill hands.

"Disgraceful, my lord," a cold, dry voice says above him.

He looks up. Pitt is gazing down on him, the dour features graver still.

"I had no idea," he says, hearing his voice echo off the surrounding marble.

When he turns to see why, he sees an addition to the decor. A statue of a young woman in classical draperies—Natalie! Why is she entombed in cold stone in the antechamber of the Yorick Club?

"I didn't realize I had killed someone," he confesses in a dreadful daze.

"That is of no account," Pitt says briskly. "You have failed not because of anything you did in life, or in the leaving of it, but because of what you were about to do. The Yorick Club cannot sanction such behavior."

"I do not blame even Hell for condemning me."

"You are indeed unworthy of our company. You have not the constitution for true evil, which abhors common sentimentality. Had we not intervened, instead of seducing your prey you would have been down on one knee offering to marry the chit and committing fidelity. We cannot tolerate a person who would be such a bad influence in our club."

"Then send me to the aimless nonexistence you mentioned before. I will happily roam the half-world forever, but release her from that stony bondage in which you hold her."

Pitt lifts a hand, the lace at his cuff falling back to reveal a band of black, bruised flesh at his wrist.

Lightning flashes. The Yorick Club vanishes. Before Adrian can even move, before he has any sense of motion, he finds the scene has changed. He is in the cool moonlit garden he had glimpsed, no warmer than before.

This is more than the half-world, he knows, rising effortlessly to approach its dim perfection. Yet when he reaches for a flower, it remains just inches distant, as if he were not really there. His steps make no sound, and he senses that his impression of his own body is an illusion played upon him to keep his far-venturing mind sane.

Yet peace pervades his soul—he assumes that is all that exists of him now—and he walks the phantom garden with wonder, drawing some serenity from its solitary beauty.

Then he passes a moon-silvered hedge and enters a cul-de-sac. A statue stands in the middle—Natalie clad in pale white marble from a tomb, draped in robes one might call classical or heavenly, silent and still as stone.

"No!" he cries out, surprised to hear his thoughts echo as a voice; not any voice, his voice, wounded yet still strong enough to reach to the last row of an arena.

If this is the fringe of heaven, as he suspects, shown only to those who will never enter, then he has been allowed here only for his eternal pain. She should not be here! She had only begun to live again.

He stands there, transfixed with horror and a selfish joy as well, at seeing her one last time. When or how he knows he is no longer alone, he cannot say.

He turns to greet an almost motionless female figure, all in silver. As he watches, misty wings unfurl from her back, making her aspect grave and terrible. Her features are vague, save that they seem very beautiful, serene, and sad.

"You cannot stay, she says. "You should not even be here."

"Perhaps there was no place else to go," he answers, all emotions quieted. "I saw the statue . . . she is not—?"

"Dead yet? No. The statue commemorates her first brush with immortality. She would have come here directly, had I not pleaded with Heaven to give her another chance at life, poor thing."

"You—you are her guardian angel?"

"Indeed."

"You are so unlike the . . . self you showed me on earth."

"You are unlike yourself now also," she says, a smile in her voice. "Besides, you are no longer a danger."

"No. I am fully dead now." He holds out a transparent hand. "At least Adrian Lord will no longer make those abominable noises anymore. I assume I finished my collapse in the penthouse. How did she . . . take it?"

The angel's head tilts in consideration. He still can read no features. Perhaps that is what a halo really is, not a gilt circle above the head, but a radiant nimbus that swathes the entire figure.

"What shall we do with you, Adrian?"

"You need do nothing but release me to the outer emptiness I am told awaits me."

"So that is what they told you in Hell."

"I fear I did not get even as far as that. I saw only the antechamber."

"Saw only the antechamber? You mean that you have never actually been in Hell proper?"

"No. I assumed you knew that."

"Our prescience hardly ventures that far into the Dark, or our Light would diminish. How vexing. You are as much a problem on the brink of death as you are in the full flesh of life. I am not sure I approve of Natalie's choice, but I cannot argue with true love."

"What do you mean 'on the brink of death'?"

The angel floats off the moonlit ground in contemplation. "She is heartbroken, of course, at your apparent condition," she murmurs. "Such unhappiness might undo all her painful recovery. But dare I trust her to such as you?"

The angel sighs, a soft, soothing sound.

"I did not know angels could sigh."

"Oh, we sigh a good deal at the goings-on below. You present a problem."

"I am used to it," he says humbly if atypically.

Her laughter is as silvery as sleigh bells.

In the garden a glittering snow begins to fall, until he feels lost within a tiny glass snow dome. The air remains cool, not cold. Yet it is not warm, not as warm as the room with the sparkling Christmas tree and the woman beside it. Adrian feels his soul shiver. Hell is always within oneself, and now it has a new name: Memory.

"What to do?" the angel frets.

"Is all not preordained?" He is confused. Why torment him with visions when eternal loss is to be his only lot?

"Yes, and sometimes in such ways that even Heaven must bend the rules. You see, we cannot possibly accept you in either form: Adrian Ashworth or Adrian Lord. Yet this new . . . blend of the two presents unique problems, and opportunities. It is possible, and I should not have said this three days ago, that in time, with great patience and compassion and the love of a good woman—yes, that is a dreadful cliché but even angels must fall back on the hackneyed now and again—you might be rehabilitated enough to qualify for another look. You might even squeak into Paradise. To let you fade into limbo with no further opportunity to evolve might be regarded as . . . unkind. Unfair. Certainly not in the Christmas spirit."

Her hovering feet touch ground even as her folded wings spread into a great cloudy cloak above them both.

"You must return to your present body and present life to live it out as best you can."

"Return? To Natalie?"

"If she will have you, and I fear that she will. You can count your blessings this New Year, Adrian. Had you not found a Christmas angel who has won influence in Heaven, you would be broiling in Hell."

"Pitt said it was not hot there."

"And you would believe *him*?"

The angel sweeps toward him.

He quails, remembering the face of righteous indignation that had confronted him before. But he sees no face now, just a diffusing form of light and warmth that swaddles him in such delightful comfort and promise that he thinks he is again embraced by what the wildman had called the coke fairy.

He opens his eyes to find Natalie's arms around him, her breath on his cheek.

"Adrian! You were so still, so strange." She hugged him tightly, pressing her face into his shoulder, and the comfort, promise, and ecstasy were only human now, but entirely sufficient. "I thought you were ill again, or . . . dying."

"No," he told her, loosening her embrace only to draw her even closer for the long, earthly communion of a passionate kiss.

"Nothing wrong with you!" she commented when they finally parted. "Then why are you on bended knee?"

"Because I am an old-fashioned man, as you pointed out, and I am proposing marriage."

"You . . . you can't mean that! It's impossible."

An awful suspicion gripped his mind. He knew so little about Adrian Lord. "You meant to say that I'm already married?"

"Heavens, no," she said with a laugh. "I know everything about you . . . well, everything fit to print. I just meant that you can't marry a nobody from Ohio. It's unthinkable."

"This is the twentieth century, isn't it? Aren't even the Prince and Princess of Wales on the brink of divorce? These are evidently unthinkable times. If they can do that, I can certainly marry whomever I like. It's not as if I'm anybody but an exceedingly rich, famous, and insufferable rock star."

"And sexy," she added, demanding a return engagement on the kiss, which was even more ecstatic this time.

He ran his palms over the velvet gown, wondering what sort of fastenings to look for, when he felt the bright white shadow of an angel on his shoulder. Nothing was there, of course, but his conscience.

Better not jeopardize his second chance so soon.

He broke their embrace and kissed her forehead, this time intentionally. "Please marry me, Natalie, for my sake, my salvation."

"You are the most amazing man. Really too, too old-fashioned. I suppose our assignation is off until the ceremony."

The disappointment on her face delighted him.

"I fear so. But we can be married within a day or two in Gretna Green."

"Greta *where*?"

"What am I thinking of? I mean to say, ah . . . Los Alamos."

Her face remained sweetly blank while he cast his mind back at the many newspapers he had read. "Er, Las—"

"Las Vegas."

"The very place. I'll get used to these strange Colonial names yet."

"We haven't been a British colony for a very long time, Adrian."

"No." He grinned and began kissing her like a bridegroom again. "But *you* soon will be, and I don't intend

77

to emulate King George the Third and let you go. He was quite mad, you know."

"I'm beginning to think you are too, but I love it. Won't there be a lot of publicity?"

"Layla will take care of the arrangements," he answered confidently. "And I will take care of all the rest."

Layla returned the day after Christmas, observing the pristine order of the foodstuffs and the surroundings with a twisted smile.

"No pigsty left for me to clean up. Not your usual weekend orgy, boss."

"Not in the slightest," he said a bit stiffly. Adrian Lord had a lot to live down. "At least you can devote yourself to serious secretarial duties."

"Aye, aye, sir," she mocked with a salute. "What are your orders?"

"I want you to arrange for a quiet wedding as soon as possible in Las Vegas."

Layla laughed so hard she collapsed on the sofa and held her sides. "Quiet? Your 'accident' must have made you forget what Las Vegas is like. So who're you marrying? The piercing parlor model or the rap queen?"

"Don't be vulgar. Miss Parks, of course."

"Oh, of course." Layla stood, looking quite pleased. "Well, you can get yourself a new gofer, boss. I'm outa here."

He felt a surprising sense of abandonment. Who would be his guide to this bravura new world in which he had to find his way? Who knew Adrian Lord like a book?

"You can't leave me, Layla. I need you."

"Not anymore."

"I'll pay you anything you want."

"You already were."

"I don't know what to say."

"Listen, you'll have a wife now. You have a new right-hand woman. Congratulations. She's a very sweet girl."

"She's an angel," he corrected ecstatically, "but she knows nothing about my . . . profession." He paced away so she couldn't read his face. This hard-edged woman was an amazing judge of character. "I'm thinking of making a big change. I used to have a rather good baritone voice, years ago. Years and years ago. I'm thinking of trying some sort of real music."

"Going unplugged, huh? Dumping the Bowery Boys and doing a solo act? Not a bad idea, boss. I think you might be able to pull it off, now that you've got your personal act together."

Layla came close, put a clawed hand on his shoulder. "She's a lovely woman, Adrian. Do right by her."

"How could I do wrong? But, Layla, surely you can't mean it. You're leaving now just as I'm behaving like a human being."

"That's why I'm going. Don't you get it yet, Adrian? I'm your guardian angel. Case closed."

He blinked in confusion. "But . . . I was a candidate for H-h-h, for the other place. How on earth could I have a guardian angel?"

"Everybody does, Adrian. You were just a harder case than usual." She patted his shoulder. "I'm not needed here anymore, so I can't stay. I'm obsolete. I've just been replaced. Besides, after almost two hundred years on duty, I'm due for some R and R upstairs. I'll be watching you."

She walked away from him, heading not for the door, but the window. Once there, she paused, looked back, and winked.

Then she walked through the wall-to-wall glass into the broad daylight beyond.

He rushed to watch where she would go, but saw only a shimmering curtain of falling snow.

"Isn't it beautiful?"

Natalie had come to join him at the window.

"You know," she said, smiling at the swirling flakes, "when I was in the hospital, I couldn't go out and play, or do anything. I was like some sick twelve-year-old kid, bored and frustrated and so lonely. Then one day a woman in white, this nurse I'd never seen before, came in. It was snowing just like this, slow and soft so you could see every flake. And she told me that it wasn't just snowflakes fluttering past the window. Each one was a falling angel. She said that if I watched long enough, someday I would catch one." She smiled up at him. "And then one day long after, you walked into my hospital room, and for the first time I believed her. I've always wondered why she stopped by that day, and who she was."

He nodded at the gentle drift of snowflakes sharp as winter stars outside the window and pulled her into the warm, human circle of his arms. "Just another passing angel. I have a feeling they're everywhere that you least expect them."

Brush of Angel Wings
by Emma Merritt

1

At last he was home. Vince Carmichael stopped the pickup and gazed through the night shadows at the ranch house. In particular, he stared at the porch light, its dim glow illuminating the veranda that stretched across the front of the house. He had known the light would be burning. It had burned all night, every night for as long as Vince could remember.

His great-grandmother had begun the practice with her two children. Now those children had children who had children, and the light still burned at night. When Vince was a child, he had asked his grandmother if she was ever going to turn it off. No, she had replied, there would always be a child needing to find his or her way home.

A lump in his throat, Vince gripped the steering wheel. Tonight that child was him. The glowing porch light had been his beacon of hope, shining through the darkness of the past four years, and it had led him home. He couldn't count the times he had lain awake in the dark, thinking about home, about his grandmother and the porch light . . . and about Hannah, the only woman he had ever and would ever love.

In his youth and immaturity, he had been unwilling to make a commitment, and he had lost Hannah. She had turned to another man, Vince's cousin, James. Eventually Hannah and James had married. Six years later James had been killed in a motorcycle accident. Vince had lost his best friend and cousin, and he had been hurting. He could only imagine the grief Hannah had to be suffering. He had gone to her, to give solace and comfort, hoping for the same himself. She had refused, had told him to get out of her life and to stay out. She wanted nothing to do with him.

For the past four years Vince had honored her request. Not anymore. Time was passing too swiftly, and he loved her. He wanted her to be a part of his life. He had to see her, had to talk to her. He was fighting for a second chance, for a chance to live again. Hannah was that chance, that lifeline. Without her, he was incomplete.

Vince opened the door and climbed out of the truck. His boots thudded to the ground. In the distance a dog barked. He walked slowly; the closer he drew to the house, the more nervous he became. He lifted his Stetson and raked his hand through his hair. He resettled the hat on his head, tugging the brim. He brushed his hands down his leather vest.

He had done a lot of hard things during his thirty-three years, but tonight he was learning that coming home was the hardest. He stopped and contemplated leaving. But he couldn't. He had to lay to rest the ghosts and demons that had chased him for the past four years. There was only one place he could do that, here at home, here at the Guardian Angel.

The drapes and curtains were pulled in the den. Framed in the bay window was a twinkling Christmas tree. Standing in the middle of the room was Vince's great-grandmother, Charlotte Alison Carmichael. Even at ninety, Charlie—as she preferred to be called by her grandchildren—was a regal woman. Tall and slender, she swept her white hair from her face in deep waves and coiled it atop her head. Tonight she wore a mauve, long-sleeved dress. Her favorite color. Vince had missed her and wondered why he had waited so long to come home.

His great-grandmother was the only mother that he had. He had lived with her since he was eleven, after his parents and his grandparents, Charlie's son and daughter-in-law, had been killed in a car wreck. Kindly aunts and uncles and his other grandparents had invited him to live with them, but he had chosen Charlie and the Guardian Angel.

His stride easily took the flagstones that lined the way to the house. He climbed the steps to the porch, quietly moving until he stood in front of the oak door in the pool of faint light. He pressed the doorbell. The chime—just as he remembered—echoed through the house.

The door opened. Standing in front of him was a little girl, about eight or nine years old, clad in a long-sleeved shirt, jeans, and sneakers. Through green eyes alight with curiosity, she stared at him, and did not move aside to allow him to enter. Neither did she invite him in. She swiped a shock of auburn hair from her forehead.

"I remember you. You're my Uncle Vince. My daddy's cousin."

"Your daddy?" he asked.

"James Anderson."

No, they didn't look alike, Vince thought. James had been blue-eyed and blond-headed. Vince was the opposite with black hair and ebony eyes.

"You were his best friend," she said.

"Allie?" he murmured.

She nodded.

"You can't be!" he exclaimed. "You're . . . you were only five. Look at you! You've got to be—"

"I'm nine. How old are you?"

"Thirty-three."

"If my daddy was alive, you'd be the same age as him."

"Yes."

"He's gone to heaven," she said matter-of-factly. "He died in a motorcycle accident."

"I know."

The green eyes sparked with tears. "I miss him."

The innocent words cut deeply into Vince. Stepping into the foyer, he hunkered down and put his arm around her. "We all miss him," he said kindly.

"You used to come visit us." She tilted back to look at him. "But I never saw you again after Daddy died."

"I moved away." He took off his hat and laid it on the floor at his feet.

"I missed you. You could have called or written me a letter."

"Yeah, I should have."

He had wanted to, had often thought about it, but

he couldn't. He was responsible for the death of Allie's father, for the loss of Hannah's husband. He would never forget the look of horror on her face when she learned that James was dead. Vince hadn't outrightly killed James; no one had accused him of it, certainly not Hannah. They didn't have to. He blamed himself. If he had not insisted that James ride into El Paso with him as a passenger on the bike, James would be alive . . . not the casualty of a drunk driver.

"I used to ask about you," Allie said, "but Mama would start to cry. So I stopped asking."

"I'm sorry." Unintentionally he had hurt so many people, and didn't know if he could set it aright or not. He had to try.

Mercurial as only a child can be, Allie pushed out of his arms and smiled brightly. "But you're back now, and that's all that matters."

Vince wished life could be so simple.

Allie grabbed his hand and tugged. "Come into the den. I'll go get Charlie. She's out back, getting some jars of homemade jelly from the smokehouse."

Picking up his hat, Vince rose and watched the child dart across the foyer, through the den, and disappear into the kitchen. Hannah and James's child. She could have been his! And if he had not been such a fool, she would have been.

He pegged the Stetson on the clothes rack just inside the door. Hanging on the wall next to it was a cross-stitched sampler. It looked familiar and he stepped closer. Immediately he recognized it as the one Hannah had made for his grandmother about fourte years ago . . . when he and Hannah had been going together, when they had been planning to get married.

Inundated with memories, he touched the sampler's frame. When he and Hannah had first met, she was a sophomore in high school, he a senior. Immediately Vince had been snared by her slender beauty, by the green eyes, the shy smile, and auburn hair. But he soon came to realize that Hannah's beauty was deeper than appearance; she was beautiful inside. She had been a happy person, always laughing, always seeing the bright side of any situation.

Until the day he had walked out on her.

He had been such a fool to lose Hannah! She had been the magic that made every day a holiday for him. He had loved her but not enough. That's what ate at him. He had been too caught up in his own world, in his own dreams, to make the sacrifices necessary for commitment.

Hannah had wanted security and stability and thought an eight-to-five white-collar job guaranteed this. Vince had gotten his degree at Sul Ross University, but he hadn't wanted to be tied down to a desk job. He had wanted to rodeo. Hannah had refused to give him a chance; he had refused to see her side. Angry at the ultimatum he thought she had given him, he had walked out.

For a year, he had tried to forget her by living and playing hard, with other women, but it hadn't worked. No matter who he held in his arms, he held Hannah in his heart. He was possessed by auburn hair and laughing green eyes. By the time he decided to push pride aside and admit to himself that he had made a mistake, that the rodeo was a small sacrifice to make in comparison to her, Hannah announced her engagement to his cousin James.

A part of Vince had died that day. The rest of him died when Hannah had refused to let him give her comfort after James's death, when she had refused to give him the comfort he had needed.

The back door slammed.

"Vince," his grandmother shouted, "is that really you?"

"Yes, ma'am."

Long strides carried him across the foyer and into the den where he met her halfway across the room. He gazed into her gently wrinkled face, into blue eyes that sparkled with tears.

"Vince!" she whispered.

"Merry Christmas, Charlie."

She opened her arms, and he went into them. She was fragile, and he held her tenderly.

"Oh, Vince, it really is you!" She hugged him tightly, pressing her cheek against his chest.

"Yes, ma'am, it's me."

She pushed out of his arms but caught his shoulders and gently shook him. "It's been so long."

"Too long," he said. "It's all my fault, and I'm not going to let it happen again. Where's Stella?" he asked, referring to his grandmother's housekeeper. "I thought she was living in."

"She is," Charlotte replied, "but when I have company, I let her work during the day and stay with one of her daughters at night."

Her eyes sparkling, her face aglow, Allie skipped around the room.

"Is Hannah here?" Vince asked, looking around, eager to see her, apprehensive at the same time.

"No," his grandmother replied. "She's coming in day after tomorrow, on Friday. She let Allie come a few days early."

"Then I'll stay tonight."

"You'll stay through the holidays!" Charlotte declared. "You're in for a big surprise if you think I'm letting you leave so easily."

He cut his eyes over at Allie, who was picking up an ornament and replacing it on the tree.

"Charlie, you know how things are between Hannah and me. She hates me."

"I'm sure you've exaggerated her feelings," Charlotte said briskly.

Vince only wished he had.

Before he could argue further, the telephone rang.

"That's for me," Charlotte said, slowly making her way to the study. "Marv said he would call."

Vince knew the tall, lanky cowboy well. He had been foreman of the Guardian Angel since Vince could remember, and the two of them had become good friends during the years Vince had lived with his grandmother.

"Come look at the tree, Uncle Vince," Allie invited. "Charlie and I decorated it today."

Walking toward the bay window, Vince's gaze swept over the room. It hadn't changed since he'd been gone. A fire burned briskly in the stone fireplace, and the golden oak mantel, draped with tinsel garlands, gleamed.

A leather sofa and two overstuffed chairs were grouped in front of the fireplace and around a large coffee table. Close to the door leading into the kitchen was a large antique table for all occasions, from gaming to eating. Finally his gaze turned to the Christmas tree that glowed with lights and colorful ornaments.

"Do you like it?" Allie said.

"It's pretty," Vince said. "You've done a good job."

"All that's missing is the angel on top."

Vince nodded. The tree certainly needed the Carmichael guardian angel, but something else was missing. Hannah. Just as surely as she belonged in his life, in his heart, she belonged here with him in this house on this holiday. Christmas was her favorite day. When they had been going together, they had shopped every year for a special ornament to add to the tree. The last one he had bought was an angel because it looked like Hannah. He moved around the tree, searching until he found it. He cradled the small porcelain ornament in his palm.

"Uncle Vince," Allie asked, "what do you want most of all for Christmas?"

His gaze returned to the little angel in his hand. Most of all he wanted Hannah for Christmas. No, he wanted her for all time.

He shrugged. "What do you want most of all?"

"A daddy."

A swift, hard blow to the gut couldn't have hurt worse than the child's request. He released the ornament and looked at her.

"I'm sure that one of these days your mom will remarry," he said. He was tormented by the thought that she would and that he would not be the man of her choice.

"I hope so," Allie murmured. "I just wish it could be this Christmas."

He smiled indulgently at her. "Patience, kiddo."

"That *was* Marv," Charlotte confirmed as she slowly walked into the room. "The truck broke down today, and he had it towed in for repairs. Since you're here, Vince, I told him that he could use my car tomorrow. He has some ranch business to tend to." She looked at him. "Is that all right with you?"

Vince nodded.

"Marv's glad that you're home and said to tell you that he would see you when he came for the car tomorrow." Charlotte stooped and picked up a piece of leftover garland. "Now, let's get this tree finished."

As Charlotte dropped the tinsel into the large cardboard box at the end of the sofa, Allie dug out a smaller box and carried it to the coffee table. Carefully, almost reverently, she sat it down and opened the lid. She withdrew the Carmichael guardian angel.

Although it had been carved out of native pecan wood, it was delicate and beautiful. It had darkened with age, only traces of its original paint still in evidence. Ironically, it was a cowboy, dressed in broad-brimmed hat, western shirt, vest, jeans, and boots. Sweeping absurdly from his shoulders were outstretched wings, definitely incongruous to the Texas cowboy.

"Tex," Vince murmured. "It's been a long time since I've seen the ole boy."

Allie giggled. "He's not an *ole boy*. He's an angel."

Vince grinned. "That's right. The Carmichaels' guardian angel."

"He's my favorite angel in the whole wide world," Allie declared. She brushed her hand over the ornament and gave Tex a big kiss. "He's so beautiful."

Beautiful was definitely not a word Vince would use to describe the Carmichael Christmas tree angel. He looked at Charlie, her eyes alight with laughter, but her expression remained serious.

"Yes, darling, he is," her grandmother agreed.

"Santa Claus and the elves and flying reindeer are just legend, aren't they, Charlie?" Allie asked.

"That's right."

"They can't answer prayers."

"No," Charlie said pensively, staring at the child curiously, "I wouldn't suppose so."

"Angels can," Allie declared.

Earlier when Allie had gotten the boxes of decorations from the attic, she had told Tex she wanted a new daddy. And she wanted him pretty soon . . . in fact, on Christmas Day.

Tex hadn't answered her, but she knew he heard her. She had that special feeling—that wonderful warm feeling when you know you're not alone yet you don't see anyone. The feeling Charlie always described as the brush of angel wings. Charlie had always said Allie would know when she was brushed by angel's wings. Allie had. She knew Texas had heard her.

"Tex is going to help me get a new daddy," she said, extending her thoughts into words.

"God has to take a lot into consideration in answering that prayer," Charlotte said. "You see, you're not the only one to be considered. There's you, your mother, and your prospective daddy. In order for you to have a father, your mother must have a husband and your daddy must have a wife. This can be a little tricky."

"Not for God or Tex," Allie said. "Nobody in the whole wide world is stronger or wiser than they are."

"That's true," Charlotte conceded.

"Isn't God wise enough and strong enough to give Mama a husband who can love her and give me a daddy who can love me?"

Vince walked over to the tree and stared out the bay window.

"Yes, he is," Charlotte replied, "but as I said, we're not dealing with God only. Your mother has got to want a husband; she's the one who must use the wisdom to find a man who will love both her and you."

"Tex can help her. I know he can." Allie looked up at her grandmother. "I haven't seen Tex yet, but I've felt the brush of his wings."

Surprised, Charlotte asked, "How do you know?"

"I was standing in the attic, holding the box, and I was alone. Then I thought you or someone had come up. But you hadn't. And I wasn't alone. Tex was with me." She gazed intently at her great-great-grandmother. "You said I would know it when an angel brushed me with its wings, and I did."

"Yes," Charlotte said, "I'm sure you did."

Allie walked to Vince. "Would you put him on the tree for me?"

Vince caught her by the waist and swung her up. "How about doing it yourself?"

Laughing, she set Tex atop the tree, making sure he

was firmly in place and stood straight. For good measure she rubbed his wings one more time.

When Vince set her on the floor, she gazed up at him. Swiping the errant lock of black hair off her forehead, she asked, "Do you believe in angels, Vince?"

"Yeah, I believe I do," he replied.

He glanced across the room at the oak bookshelves, filled with his grandmother's lifetime collection of photographs. He strolled over and looked at them. His grandparents, Charlotte's oldest son and his wife. His mother and father. A photograph of him and James. Because both of them were only children, they had been as close as brothers.

They had even fallen in love with the same woman.

Vince gazed at the photograph of Hannah. God, but she was beautiful in the picture, and it did nothing to capture the essence of her, the spontaneity, the joy of living. He ran the tip of his finger around the frame, then around her oval face, over her full lips . . . kissable lips . . . over her eyebrows. She was the closest thing to an angel he had ever met. While he was . . .

"The devil's spawn," he murmured. That's what Hannah had called him when she had ordered him out of her life after James died.

"What did you say?" Allie called.

"Never mind," Charlotte said crisply.

The mantle clock chimed ten o'clock.

"Allie," Charlotte said, "it's time for bed."

"Yes, ma'am."

Charlotte glanced at Vince. "Time you went to bed too, young man. You look tuckered out."

"I am," he said. "I've been on the road since early morning."

Once he had made his decision to come home, he had driven straight through from Phoenix, stopping once for gasoline.

"You shouldn't have pushed yourself like that."

"I wanted to get home," he replied. "Where am I sleeping?"

"Your old room," Charlotte said.

"You are welcome to it," Allie aid. "I was going to sleep there, but yuk!"

Puzzled, Vince looked at his grandmother, who chuckled.

"I hired an interior decorator in November," she informed him, "and let myself be persuaded to make some changes in the house. Some I really like. Others I don't."

"And your room is one of the ones we don't like," Allie said. "It's like a hideous jungle. White wallpaper covered in green ivy. Leaves and vines everywhere."

"I told the decorator I didn't like it," Charlotte said, "but she begged me to keep it for a while. She said I'd get used to it."

"But Charlie hasn't," Allie chimed in.

"No, if anything, I like it less. I'm going to change it, but I decided to wait until after Christmas."

Allie went over and kissed her grandmother. "Good night and sweet dreams."

"Sweet dreams to you, darling," Charlotte said.

Allie wanted to give Vince a good-night hug, but she was too shy. When she walked by him, he smiled at her.

"How about me?" He held out his arms, and she ran into them and pressed her face against his chest.

"I'm glad you're home for Christmas," she murmured, her voice muffled. He was so big and strong and warm, and she could hear his heart thumping. He was comforting. And he smelled good.

He hugged her tighter. "I'm glad too, Allie."

"I just know that Mama is going to be happy too."

"Yeah," Vince drawled dryly, "I'm sure she will."

As Allie pulled away from Vince, she looked at Tex. He smiled and winked at her. Her heart skipped a beat. Tex winked at her! Allie knew for sure that Tex had heard her prayer and was going to give her a daddy for Christmas.

Vince awakened, covered in perspiration, his heart beating rapidly. The Harley! He and James were on it, one with the wind as they clipped over I-10 headed for El Paso. The ride was so smooth, Vince would have sworn they were sailing. Then he had seen the car on the wrong side of the expressway, headed for them.

Horns blared; brakes screeched; metal clanged against metal. When Vince had regained consciousness, he had a deep cut on his face, a few broken ribs, a sprained ankle, and bruises from head to toe. James had died instantly . . . they told him.

Vince rolled over, slung his legs over the edge of the bed, and cradled his forehead in his hands. James was dead, and he was alive! Vince had never forgiven God for that; Hannah had never forgiven him.

In the dark he rose and dressed in jeans, shirt, and loafers. Leaving his shirt unbuttoned, he walked into the study and poured himself a glass of whiskey. He didn't often drink, but tonight he wanted something to relax him.

He walked outside to sit on the front porch, something he had frequently done when he was a child growing up and wanted to think. The bulb yet burned, soft light glowering over the porch. The night was brisk, typical weather in Texas at Christmas, but he didn't mind. The coolness might clear some of the cobwebs from his mind.

Leaning back against the porch column, he slowly drank his whiskey, letting its warmth seep through him. He was glad to be home. He had missed Charlie, and a telephone call once or twice a week had not been fair to either of them. Yet she had not once faulted him for leaving, for staying away. She had seemed to understand his need to be away from the Guardian Angel . . . away from Hannah.

Vince had come home to confront some of his ghosts, and he had fully intended to see Hannah. But he had not planned to see her so soon. He had wanted to choose the time and the place . . . to set it up so it would be perfect.

Gazing at the moonlit lawn, he rose and walked to the end of the porch. He stood for a long time, finishing off his drink. Then he set the empty glass on the banister. Still he made no move to go inside the house.

He didn't want to dream again, not so soon.

Breathing deeply, he inhaled the peacefulness that surrounded him. He had forgotten how tranquil it was here. He gazed at the silver blue sky, aglow with star- and moonlight. God, but he was glad to be home, glad to be at the Guardian Angel. Wide open spaces, unpolluted and unspoiled by man. This is where he belonged, not shut up in an office, prisoner of modern communications, designer of computer software.

He knew and understood computers, had been accused by his friends of working magic with them, and could create programs before people knew what kind of programs they needed. But it was something he did well, not something he loved.

Rodeoing and ranching were his loves. When he was younger he had followed his dreams along the rodeo circuit. After losing Hannah, he had thrown himself into his work, winning several national championships, earning a great deal of money, and spending it as quickly as he earned it.

But he was smart enough to know when to quit. Deciding to put his college degree to work and begin a *respectable* career, he had taken his meager savings and invested in a budding computer software company. Always in the back of his mind was the dream of being a full-time rancher. Now that dream was about to become a reality.

If only the rancher could take a wife . . . and that wife could be Hannah.

In the distance on the road leading to the house he saw the dip of headlights—a sight he had not forgotten—and knew someone was driving up the lane toward the house. He glanced down at his wristwatch. Close to one in the morning. Who would be out at this time? Knowing the Laramie was parked out of the way, he waited and watched.

The lights came closer. A sleek modern car. He

couldn't make out what kind in the dark. It stopped; the headlights flicked off. The door opened, and the dome light glowed softly, illuminating a woman. She held her head up, and through the windshield he saw her. Hannah Anderson. The only woman Vince had ever loved, and the woman whom he had hurt so irrevocably that she could never love him.

A part of Vince wanted to rush to her and help her with the suitcases, but he knew better. He curled his hand around the pillar and stood where he was. He didn't want to frighten her. If she knew he was here, she would probably leave. He didn't want that.

They needed to settle their past, so he could have a present, could plan for a future. But he had a sinking feeling. If she was not part of his life, he had no present . . . no future.

He moved closer to the edge of the porch so he could see better. The years had been kind to her; she was older, more mature, but she was still beautiful. Her jeans and shirt fit snugly, revealing her slender curves. Her auburn hair fell around her shoulders, framing her face. He couldn't see her eyes, but he didn't have to; he remembered their color and could see them as clearly as if he were looking into them. They were the most vivid shade of green he had ever seen.

Hannah locked the car, picked up her suitcase, and started walking toward the house. Vince knew he should leave, but he couldn't make himself do it. He wanted to be close to her, wanted to see her in the porch light. He needed to see her. She had filled his dreams for so many years. When she stepped onto the porch, he slid further into the shadows. His hand accidentally grazed the glass

he had set down a little while ago. It fell to the porch
. . . shattering at his feet.

2

Glass splintered. Hannah spun around.

"Don't be frightened," said a masculine voice she immediately recognized.

Vince!

Her heartbeat accelerated, and her breath caught in
her chest. She trembled so much she set her suitcase
on the porch and put her hand on the door frame to
steady herself. The past wrapped its suffocating tentacles around her and squeezed.

"What are you doing here?" she asked.

A stupid question! James and Vince had been cousins; Charlie was their great-grandmother; this was their
ancestral home. But Hannah had not expected to see
him . . . not tonight.

Nonetheless, he answered. "Home for a visit."

Vince stepped out of the blackness, a shadow slowly
taking form. He was taller than she remembered, his
shoulders wider, his chest more muscular.

"Charlie didn't tell me you were coming home for
the holidays." She forced herself to speak calmly.

"She didn't know."

His voice was raspy and deep, just as she remembered; it sent shivers of anticipation through her. It always had. She still felt guilty that he affected her like this, in an elemental way that James never had.

Vince hitched his thumbs in his jeans' pockets. "I surprised her too."

"I'm—I'm sure you did," she said, for lack of anything better.

A breeze touched his shirt, lifting one side of it. In the pale glow of porch light, Hannah gazed at the thick black hair that pelted his chest and swirled beneath the waistband of his jeans. They rode low, too low for her comfort. They resurrected memories; they stirred old familiar sensations. She closed her eyes and breathed deeply.

After a moment, he said, "Charlie said you weren't coming until day after tomorrow."

"I had some days I needed to take before the end of the year."

"Are you still with Alamo City Educational Institute?"

She nodded, then added, "I'm up for a promotion, a directorship."

"Congratulations," he said.

"I haven't been selected yet," she said.

"You'll get it," Vince said. "You've known what you wanted from the time you were a junior in high school."

"Or what I thought I wanted," she replied softly. After a moment, she added, "Sometimes, Vince, I wish I could turn the clock back and we were in high school again."

He nodded, leaning against the porch column. "We had some wonderful times, didn't we?"

"Some of the happiest of my entire life."

"Five years we went together," he said. Then he added with a smile, "If you could call it going together."

She laughed softly.

"You were still in high school. I was at Sul Ross University."

"I lived for the weekends and holidays," Hannah said.

"So did I," he murmured. "Harley and I—"

Mention of his motorcycle jolted her, brought her back to the present. She shook her head. "Vince, we can't go back; time moves forward . . . or it ceases entirely. What we had is over. Dead. Buried."

No sooner had she uttered the words than she threw her hand over her mouth and gasped. *James!*

"Dammit!" Vince muttered.

Would James forever come between them?

"Don't worry," Vince said. "I'll be leaving tomorrow."

"You can't leave on my account," Hannah protested. "This is your home, Vince. If anyone leaves, it should be me."

"Don't go," he said. "Charlie will be hurt. She considers you as much a member of this family as I am." After a pause, he added, "And there's Allie."

"You've—met her?"

"Yeah. She's quite a girl, reminds me of her mother."

"The green eyes and auburn hair?"

"That, and her spirit. When she's excited, her eyes sparkle like yours."

Hannah would be staying. She would risk being hurt

herself before she would hurt either Charlie or Allie. She would stay because she wanted to be with Vince; she had missed him, had hurt for him. He had always been in her heart, even when she had been married to James. She would never forgive herself for having married James on the rebound, for being unable to give him what he deserved and wanted the most: her love. But she couldn't give him what she no longer possessed, what she had given to Vince.

He moved closer, into the spill of light, and she saw his face clearly. She didn't have to see it to know what he looked like. She carried the picture of him in her heart.

He was darkly handsome, his rugged features dominated by ebony eyes and black hair. A scar ran from the corner of his right eye to his temple, the one he had gotten in the accident that had claimed James's life. The features had not changed so much as the soul behind them had changed. Vince had matured. Hardness had replaced his youthful vulnerability.

"I'm—tired," she said.

"I can imagine. It's a long drive from San Antonio."

"I think I'll go to bed."

"The door's unlocked."

"Where are you sleeping?" she asked.

He arched his brows suggestively and grinned, that one-sided gesture she had always found so endearing. Heat rushed into her face.

"My old room," he answered. "It has new wallpaper in it. Ivy. Dark green vines on all the walls. The bedspread and quilted blanket are ivy also. It sort of gets to you real quick like."

Hannah smiled.

"You're in the lilac. It was lilac before, and it's lilac now."

The room next to his. She needed more than a wall between them.

"I'm not guilty," he said. "Allie and Charlie made the room assignments."

She reached for her suitcase at the same time that he did, his hand closing over hers. His touch sent fiery shards of desire through her. She looked into his face and saw the same yearnings reflected in it that she felt. For a moment she considered not turning the handle loose. She loved Vince, always had and always would.

He had been her first lover, had sweetly taught her the joy of making love. She remembered the magic the two of them had created with their touches, their kisses. The dreams they had spun; the promises they had made.

But the dreams hadn't come true; the promises weren't kept. Vince had chosen the rodeo over her.

"Vince—" Her voice was ragged. She pulled her hand away. "Please don't do this to me."

"I didn't mean to."

"I—I can't stay."

"Please, Hannah." His voice was low. "I know this is going to be hard on you. It's going to be tough on me also, but let's not make everyone suffer because of us."

"No," she said quietly. "I won't."

He pulled open the screen and walked into the house. She followed. As she passed the den, she stopped. The porch light dimly illuminated the tree.

Remembering how much she loved the holidays with all its decorations and trimmings, he brushed past her and flipped on the switch. The room was cast in the soft glow of twinkling lights.

Leaning back against the door frame, she gazed at the tree. "It's beautiful," she breathed.

Vince stood next to her. "Yes, it is."

Feeling his eyes on her, she turned her head. "The tree," she said.

"The tree." He smiled, and so did she.

The muted light softened Vince's countenance and brought back more old memories, warm and sweet ones she had thought long since over. For four years she had insulated herself against pain, had refused to allow anyone but Allie to get close to her. She had determined that she would never be hurt as deeply as she had been when James was killed. Yet Vince had been back in her life only minutes, and already her resolve was slipping.

"I've missed you, Hannah," he said. "A day doesn't go by but that I think of you."

"Don't, Vince." Hannah blinked back the tears, irritated with herself for being so emotional, for letting him get to her so easily.

He brushed a strand of hair from her face, his fingertips grazing her cheek, again making her acutely aware of his touch. Heat curled through her body.

"I've always loved you, Hannah," he said. "And I still do."

"Don't!" Hannah turned and walked from the den, across the foyer into the hallway. Carrying her suitcase, he followed her. When she opened the door to her bedroom, she turned. "Nothing has changed, Vince." She kept her voice low. "Nothing."

"No, it hasn't," he said slowly. "You're still feeling guilty because the man you loved lived, and the man you were married to is dead."

Hannah slapped him. They stared at each other. Tears threatened, but she held them at bay. She refused to cry in front of him. She saw the red imprint of her hand on his cheek and regretted her childish reaction, but she did not apologize.

"Hannah, if each of us can get past the guilt, maybe we can have a future together."

"I can't, Vince." Anguish underlined her words. "Don't you think I would have if I could?"

The guilt gnawed at her day and night. She had loved James as a cousin, a friend, but not as a woman should love her husband.

"Good night, Vince." She shut the door on him. She had to; it was her only escape. She couldn't shut the door of her heart to him.

After Vince left, Hannah paced back and forth beside the bed. She couldn't stay here, not since Vince had come. She would stop, pick up her suitcase, and head for the door. Then she would return and set it down.

She couldn't ruin Allie's holidays. Being with Charlie was all Allie had talked about for months. Besides, if she and Allie left, they would have to spend the holidays by themselves. Hannah's parents, knowing that she and Allie were with Charlie, were on a Christmas tour in Europe.

To save Allie's holidays, Hannah was going to have to

sacrifice hers. She had to stay, but she did not have to stay at the Guardian Angel. She would drive back to Bethlehem, the nearest town, and stay at the motel.

Yes, that's what she would do! Charlotte and Allie didn't know she had arrived yet. She could slip out without them knowing the difference. She needed space so she could think, so she could marshall her emotions, and plan her strategy.

Picking up her suitcase, she eased out of the room, careful not to disturb Vince. She tiptoed down the hall, glad the tree lights were still on and casting a rosy glow over the foyer. She closed her hand on the doorknob.

"Where are you going?" Vince demanded.

She gasped and dropped her suitcase. Her heart pounded so heavy, she thought she would pass out.

"How dare you, Vince Carmichael!" she whispered.

She turned to see him sitting in one of the leather chairs. His shirt was still unbuttoned. One leg was curled beneath him; the other was propped up, an arm resting on his knee.

"I know you, Hannah," he said softly.

"Not as well as you think," she retorted, keeping her voice low.

"Better than you think."

She said nothing.

"Hannah, you have no reason to run."

"I was going to Bethlehem," she said. "To the motel."

"No room at the inn," he said. As he had driven through the small West Texas hamlet, he had glanced over at its one and only motel/hotel, called the Bethlehem Inn. The green neon sign beckoned to travelers with its flashing ROOM AT THE INN.

Puzzled, she stared at him.

"I saw the sign as I drove through." He smiled, a slow upcurving of his lips.

"I did too," Hannah retorted, then added a little more kindly, "You're not above lying."

"Exaggerating," he said. "And I'll use any tactic I have to to get you to stay here. I want to talk with you, Hannah."

"My staying at the inn won't keep us from talking."

"You're going?"

She nodded.

"Then I will too." He grinned wickedly. "Think how the tongues will wag."

"You wouldn't."

"I will," he promised. Then he added, "Admit it, Hannah, you and Allie will have a much better time if you stay here."

Silence, as well as the truth, hung heavy between them.

"I was routing through the pantry for some of Charlie's jellies and look what I found." He held up a bottle of wine. "Your favorite, if I remember correctly. And I should." A wicked smiled glimmered on his lips. "I bought it and put it there."

She looked at the label. It was her favorite.

"If you hadn't come out," he said, "I was going to come get you. There's no need for us to be angry with each other. By no ulterior design on either of our parts—"

She hiked a brow.

He grinned. "We're here together. Let's make the

best of the situation and give both Charlie and Allie a wonderful Christmas."

She stared at him.

"And us too, Hannah. Let's have a good holiday."

Both of them knew she would be staying.

She laughed shortly and shook her head. "If anything, Vince, maturity has made you even smoother."

"Or has let me know what's really important in life." Through hooded eyes, he stared at her.

Refusing to make a comment, she walked into the den and sat in the chair across from him. "I'll have a glass of wine," she said. "I need it. Then it's bedtime for me."

"Here or at the inn?"

"Here." She took the wine from him and leaned back in the chair. "But we'll talk tomorrow, Vince. No more heavy stuff tonight."

He held his glass up. "To a new beginning, Hannah."

She hesitated momentarily before she tipped her glass against his. "To old and bittersweet memories, Vince."

"Not what I wanted, but for now I'll settle for what I can get."

After several sips, Hannah curled her legs beneath her. "Are you still rodeoing?"

"I go to them, but I don't compete anymore."

"You finally outgrew them?"

"Grew too old for them."

His hand rested on the end of the sofa armrest. His silver ring with the turquoise setting—the one she had given him when he graduated from college—glinted in the glowing light.

"The bones don't mend as quickly or as well," he went on.

She couldn't take her gaze from his hand, from his strong fingers. Because he had worked the ranch all of his life, his hands had been callused and rough, and she had liked to feel them. They were big hands, strong and protective. She had enjoyed twining their fingers together. Then he would bring them up to his mouth and kiss each of her fingers one by one, slowly and breathlessly soft.

She looked up; their gazes locked.

"Your hands were always so soft," he said, as if he had been privy to her thoughts.

He caught one of them and held it, turning it over, rubbing his thumb first over the palm, then over the inside wrist. She shivered as pleasure shot through her body.

"They still are."

She tried to pull her hand from his, from the fire of his touch, but he held it tightly. He ran his fingers around the gold wedding band. "You still wear James's ring."

She nodded.

"Will we forever be ensnared by the past?" he asked bitterly.

She nodded. "But I wear the ring mostly because I don't want to be bothered with men."

"What about me?"

She smiled. "You're a cowboy."

With a shrug, he said, "Yeah, I guess I am." He glanced at her, his eyes sparkling mischievously. "I tried being a man. I gave respectability a whirl, Hannah. The three piece suit. White shirt. Tie. Eight-to-five regimen. The whole nine yards, as Charlie would say."

"Did," Hannah said, "as in past tense?"

"Yep." He held out his glass and watched the play of light through the wine. "When I quit the rodeo, I invested my meager savings in a software company in Phoenix."

"You always were good with computers."

"Yeah, I'm good with them, but being good with something and liking to do it are two different things. Working there suffocated me. I sold out my interest, and as of right now am gainfully unemployed. I don't have a roof over my head, and my only possession at the moment is my new Laramie SLT."

She took several sips of wine before she said, "You don't have a motorcycle anymore?"

He drained his glass. "Yeah, I guess I do. The one I got as an insurance replacement. It's in the barn if no one has moved it." He set the glass down. "I was here when they delivered it, but I never rode it. I couldn't. I had them wheel it to the barn."

He leaned back into the cushions and closed his eyes, but he knew from past experience it did not shut out memories.

"What are you going to do now?" Hannah asked.

"Ranch. The Holcomb boys finally put their dad's place up for sale." He spoke of property adjacent to the Guardian Angel. "I'm going to see about buying it."

"Does Charlie know?"

He shook his head. "We haven't talked. It was late when I got in, and both of us were tired."

"She's going to be happy. She's missed you." Hannah

leaned forward and placed her glass next to his. "It'll be like old times."

"No, Hannah," Vince said softly, sadly, "it won't be, and I don't want it to be. I . . . want you and me to create new times together."

Rising, she crossed the room and stood in front of the tree. Her back was to him.

"We're grown now, Hannah, matured."

"Too much is between us."

She heard him approaching. He faced her.

"Nothing we can't work out," he said.

He caught her hands in his. She tugged, but he didn't release her. Then she stopped trying and let the warmth of his hands infuse hers; let his strength wrap around and support her.

"I once looked at the world through rose-colored glasses," she said. "But when you left me, you shattered them. Some things can't be worked out, Vince, no matter how much we wish they could."

"They can, Hannah." He pulled her, and she went into his arms, resting her face against his chest. He brushed his hand over her head. "Please believe me."

"I did, and you left me."

"I'm not going to leave you again."

Not wanting to frighten her away, he continued to hold and to comfort her. He brushed his fingers through her hair, finally cupping the back of her neck. He held her, savoring these sweet moments they were spending together, wishing they could go on forever. He promised himself that he would make them last that long, hopefully longer.

"I love Christmas," she murmured.

"I know. I remembered."

"Allie could hardly wait to come," Hannah said. "She turned down a Christmas tour to Europe with my parents so she could be here. All she could talk about was Tex."

Vince thought about Allie's conversation earlier in the evening, her confession that her dearest wish for Christmas was a new daddy, but he didn't mention it.

"Yeah," he drawled, "she's like the best of us Carmichaels. She really believes in the ole boy." After a pause he added, "And I guess she should. He's been a family member for about one hundred twenty-five years. Ever since this line of the family began. Ever since Grandmother Vicentia and Grandfather Jonas married. And he's always had a place of honor on top of the Carmichael Christmas tree."

"The Carmichael Christmas love story," Hannah said softly. "One of the few I know that has a happy ending."

Both of them grew quiet as they thought of the story, so familiar that it needed no retelling.

Young Vicentia Garcia was on her way from San Antonio to El Paso to spend the Christmas holidays with her grandparents when outlaws attacked the stagecoach. She was seriously wounded and left for dead. Then she heard someone. Thinking it was one of the bandits returning, she was frightened. It *was* a cowboy, but not one of the outlaws. This man was gentle and kind. He calmed her fears and promised that he would take care of her.

She had asked him his name. Before he answered, she lost consciousness. When she came to, she was at the ranch of Jonas Carmichael. He always claimed that a drifter came and got him, leading him to the massacre. Vicentia and Jonas both agreed that a cowboy had indeed saved her life, and both of them had seen the man. But Vicentia firmly believed the cowboy whom she had seen was an angel, not a drifter. She remembered the glow she had seen around him, and he had wings. She called him her guardian angel, hence the name of the Carmichael ranch.

According to the story, the minute Jonas saw Vicentia he fell in love and determined to marry her. He sent word to her parents and grandparents where she was and invited them to his ranch for Christmas. When they arrived, Vicentia announced she was in love with Jonas and they were wed on Christmas Day. Jonas's Christmas and wedding gift to Vicentia was the carved angel, named Tex. And Tex had topped the Christmas tree ever since.

Breaking the silence, Vince said, "Tex isn't the only angel on the tree."

Pulling back, Hannah gazed up at him. He put his arm around her shoulder and guided her across the room to the tree.

"Ours." He pointed to the porcelain angel.

Memories warmly washed over her.

"Do you remember it?" he asked.

"Yes." She brushed the tip of her fingers over the wings. "She was so expensive."

"Only twenty dollars," Vince said.

"*Only twenty!* It was our last twenty," Hannah exclaimed with a laugh. "And we had nothing left to buy dinner or go to the movie."

"But she was worth it."

"You might not have thought that if Charlie hadn't had a refrigerator full of leftovers and there hadn't been a good show on TV."

"If I remember," Vince said softly, "we didn't watch TV."

"Yes, we did."

Shaking his head, he said, "We came into the den, turned the set on, and curled up on the sofa . . . together." He lowered his voice. "But we didn't watch the show."

Warmth infused Hannah's face, and Vince chuckled. "Do you remember what we did?"

She didn't answer.

"Hannah?" he taunted.

"I remember," she whispered.

"Hannah—"

"A memory is all I want it to be, Vince." She stepped away from him. "Do you believe in angels?"

"I believe in Tex."

"Allie does too," Hannah murmured.

"Yeah, she told me."

"She thinks Tex is going to get her a daddy by Christmas."

"Maybe he will."

"I doubt it."

"You don't believe in angels."

"I don't believe in men." A sad smile played on her lips. "Or maybe I don't believe in myself. I've made so many wrong choices."

"Did I do that to you?"

"No."

"Hannah." He moved closer to her. "I'm so sorry. I wish there was some way I could undo the past."

"I do too." Her voice was husky with tears.

They were inches apart, caught in the magical glow of twinkling lights. She raised her head; Vince lowered his. Their lips touched in a light and wonderfully sweet kiss. Her lips trembled beneath his, and he wanted to deepen the caress, wanted to take her into his arms and hold her tightly. Old yearnings clamored for relief. He wanted to make love to her. Only her love would cleanse him of the guilt he had carried for the past four years; only it would give him a present. But he restrained himself. He would move slowly and gently. This time, he promised himself, he wouldn't lose her.

She stepped back. "Good night, Vince."

"Good night, Hannah."

3

Vince stirred, opened his eyes and shut them; then he burrowed his face in the thick, downy pillow. It couldn't be morning yet; he wasn't ready to get up. The bed was warm and comfortable, the room filled with familiar sounds and smells. He breathed deeply, the aroma of bacon, eggs, and coffee tantalizing his taste buds.

Three loud knocks sounded on the door.

"Uncle Vince," Allie called. "Are you awake?"

Sleep was over.

He grinned and brushed his hand through his hair. "Yep."

"Are you dressed?"

"No, but I'm covered."

The door opened, and Allie walked in. She smiled brightly and held out a cup, wisps of vapor curling in the air. "Coffee," she announced. "I made it myself."

"Just what I wanted." Grabbing a pillow, he slid it up against the headboard and pushed into a sitting position.

"Black and hot," she said as she handed him the cup. "Just like you take yours."

"How do you know?" He took a careful swallow.

"Mama."

He almost choked; then a sweet feeling washed over him. Hannah had not forgotten how he took his coffee.

"She's here," Allie announced. "She came in late last night and slipped in without waking me up. I wanted to wake you up, but she said no." Allie sat down on the foot of the bed. "She didn't want me to wake you up now, but I wanted plenty of time to talk to you before we left."

"Before you leave!" Vince jerked straighter on the bed.

Allie nodded. "Ms. Stella called Charlie this morning, and they decided to drive into town to do some last-minute shopping."

He settled back down.

"Then Charlie and I are going over to Bitta's house—"

She paused. "You know Bitta is Ms. Stella's youngest daughter?"

He nodded.

"Well, we're going over there for Gena's birthday party."

"Gena?" he asked.

"She's Bitta's daughter, and we're going to have a slumber party. We get to have one every year. That's one of the reasons why I love coming here for the holidays. We have Gena's birthday party, then Christmas." Her eyes sparkled. "We're going to have lots of fun, Uncle Vince. We really are."

"Is Charlie going to join the slumber party?"

Allie laughed. "No, Ms. Stella will bring her home after the party."

"Allie," Charlotte called from the kitchen, "if you want to help with the biscuits, you need to get in here."

"Coming," she replied. Then she said to Vince, "Homemade biscuits. We're baking them especially for you. I've got to go now." She slipped off the bed, but didn't leave the room. She kept looking at him. "If I had a daddy, I'd bring him coffee in bed, just like I did for you."

"The man who gets you for a daughter is going to be a mighty lucky one." Vince set his cup on the night table and held out his arms. "Why don't you give me a hug to carry me through the day?"

She rushed into his arms, half lying across the bed, half across him. She pulled back, grinning at him. "You've got a dark beard, Uncle Vince." She rubbed her hand over his cheeks.

"The better to beard you with." He gently nuzzled her face.

She giggled and squirmed.

"Allie," said Hannah from the doorway, "your grandmother has been calling you."

Allie turned her head, and Vince looked up. Hannah wore navy blue slacks and a yellow sweater. She had tied her hair back in a pony tail with a blue and yellow scarf. Even though her face was shining and had no makeup, she was beautiful.

"Good morning," Vince murmured.

"Mama," Allie called, "Uncle Vince was—"

Smiling, Hannah nodded. Her lips trembled; her eyes sparkled with unshed tears. As if she were protecting herself, she crossed her arms over her chest. Vince curled his hand into a fist. He couldn't bear the thought that she was frightened of him, that she was trying to insulate herself against him.

Allie slipped off the bed, innocently pulling the cover so that it rode low on Vince's stomach. As Hannah had done the night before, as if she had never seen a naked man before, she stared at him, at the broad expanse of muscled chest that bore a few scars from his rodeo days.

Allie threw her arms around her mother and hugged her tightly. "Uncle Vince said the man who became my daddy would be a *mighty lucky man*."

Still looking at Vince, Hannah said, "He will be, darling. Now, run along to the kitchen and help your grandmother."

As Allie disappeared down the hall, Vince tugged the sheet a little higher. "Are you going with them?"

Hannah nodded.

"Coward."

Again she nodded. "Also I'm furnishing the car. Marv is borrowing your grandmother's while the truck is being repaired, and Stella loaned hers to her daughter."

"Maybe I'll come with you."

She grinned. "There's safety in numbers."

Allie raced down the hall and bounced back into the bedroom. "Uncle Vince, Charlie said if you want her to cook your breakfast, you'd better get up right now."

"Well, now, I'm a growing boy, and—"

Hannah's gaze went to his lower body. When she looked back at him, he was grinning at her. Her cheeks burned, and she averted her gaze. Not before he winked.

"I do need my breakfast," he finished. "If the two of you will step out of the way and close the door, I'll get up, dress, and join you in the kitchen."

Without a word, Hannah closed the door. His soft chuckle followed her down the hallway to the kitchen.

Happy that he had returned home, happier that Hannah was here, Vince threw back the covers and climbed out of bed. In short order, he shaved, showered, and dressed. Then he joined the rest of the family in the huge, old-fashioned kitchen, by far the largest room in the house and the one most used. At one end was a stone fireplace, chairs and sofa grouped in front of it. At the other was the kitchen itself. Separating the two was a dining table.

"Coffee?" Charlotte asked when he walked into the room.

He nodded, sitting down at the table laden with

food. Eggs, bacon, and grits. Biscuits. Gravy. Syrup. Jellies. He reached for a biscuit.

"Baked those fresh this morning," his grandmother said. "I knew you'd be wanting some of my biscuits."

"I could make a meal off these alone," Vince told her.

Charlotte chose to sit on the other side of the table, and Allie darted in beside her. Hannah reluctantly slid in beside him, Vince noted. He put his coffee to his face to hide his grin.

As they filled their plates with food, Charlotte said, "Allie told you about our plans for today, Vince?"

He nodded.

"Had I known that you were coming and that Hannah would get here early," Charlotte said, "I wouldn't have committed myself, but if we don't have this party, Gena gets slighted because her birthday is so close to Christmas."

"And I want to go to the slumber party," Allie said.

"Allie tells me that you're not going to stay for the slumber party," Vince said to Charlie. "So what time shall we expect you home?"

"The party ends at five," Charlotte replied. "I expect Stella and I will be back here about six-thirty."

"Charlie and I are going to have fun today, Uncle Vince." Allie grinned. "We're going to buy some gifts."

"Maybe I'll join you." Vince ladled gravy over his biscuit.

He glanced up to see Charlotte's pensive gaze on him and Hannah.

"You can't, Uncle Vince," Allie said. "You and Mama do something else today."

The suggestion sounded good to him.

"Allie's right," Charlotte said. "She and I have business that doesn't include you or Hannah. I'll just have to see what I can do about getting us a car."

"I don't have to go," Hannah said. "Go ahead and take mine. I trust Stella's driving, and besides I have things I can do around here." She grinned at Allie. "I've already done my shopping. All I need to do now is wrap the gifts."

Allie's eyes widened. "Did you get me the computer game I wanted?"

Hannah laughed softly. "You'll have to wait and see."

"How about you, Uncle Vince?" Allie asked. "Have you bought all your gifts yet?"

"Nope. I need some help. I'm not sure what to buy all you women."

"Was that why you wanted to come with Charlie and me?"

He looked at Hannah. "One of the reasons."

Allie's face brightened. "Uncle Vince, why don't you and Mama go shopping? She knows what Charlie and I like." Then her enthusiasm died out. "But you would still be in town at the same time we are."

"I think your plan will work, Allie," Vince replied. "I want to go over to the old Holcomb place as well as do some shopping. By the time Hannah and I wrap the gifts, visit with George Holcomb, you and Charlie will have finished your shopping."

"Yes!" Allie jabbed her fist in the air.

"What do you want to see George about?" Charlotte asked. "I don't remember the two of you being friends."

"I'm thinking about buying the old ranch property."

"Buy the Holcomb place?" Charlotte murmured, staring at Vince. She added, "You're home to stay?"

He nodded.

A tremulous smile curved her lips. "I'm so glad." She reached across the table and laid her hand over his. "Welcome home, Vince."

"You're going to live here all the time, Uncle Vince?" Allie shouted gleefully.

"If I can buy the property," Vince answered.

"I'm so glad!" Allie jumped up and ran around the table. Standing next to his chair, she threw her arms around him. He slipped his arm around her waist.

"You ought to be able to get it for a good price," Charlotte said. "It's been vacant for the past six years since John died, and the boys have let the place go to ruin. All the buildings will have to be rebuilt." She took a swallow of her coffee. "In fact, there's not a building on the place that's fit for you to live in."

"What about my renting the old house until I'm able to build?" he asked.

Surprised, Charlotte sat back. "The adobe? The one that Jonas was living in when he and Vicentia married?"

Vince nodded.

"It's been used as a line shack for so long," she said doubtfully.

"It's been kept up," Vince pointed out. "And it's close to the Holcomb place. With a little determination, money, and elbow grease, I could transform it into a temporary home."

"A little rustic for my taste," Charlotte said, "but if it suites you, who am I to complain? I like the idea, Vince. I like it very much."

They heard the dogs barking, and a car approaching.

"May I see who it is?" Allie asked. When her mother nodded, she scooted out of the chair and raced to the window. "It's Ms. Stella." She turned around and shot across the room. "I'm going to get my suitcase, Charlie."

"Don't forget your coat," Charlotte reminded her. "A northerner is blowing in this afternoon."

"I'll give George a call and see if we can make an appointment," Vince said. "The sooner I can get the ball rolling, the better I'll feel."

"Don't forget that Marv is coming over for my car," Charlotte reminded Vince.

After Charlotte, Allie, and Stella left, Vince disappeared into the study to put through his call to George. Hannah straightened up the kitchen. By the time Vince returned, the dishwasher was going, and Hannah was on the back porch hanging out the kitchen towels to let them dry naturally, something Charlotte insisted on. She tolerated dishwashers and washing machines, but she wasn't sure about dryers.

Opening the door, he walked to the edge of the small screened-in room. "It's getting colder," he said.

Clipping the last towel to the line, Hannah moved around the two oak rockers to the kitchen safe. She closed and latched one of the doors.

"We have to be at George's by eleven," he said.

One by one Hannah straightened the mason jars and lids that Charlotte used in her canning. Her back to him, she said, "Vince, I stayed home today because of

Allie. She wanted to shop for you, and I didn't want to spoil her day."

He turned, leaned against a porch column, and crossed his arms over his chest.

"I didn't intend for us to spend the day together," she went on.

"As I said," he murmured, "it's getting colder."

He straightened and stepped toward her. She backed up, but she was against the wall.

"Do you really still hate me?" he asked.

"No." She opened the door and slid past him into the house. "I never did."

He followed her into the kitchen. She stood in front of the sink, leaning against the counter, looking out the window.

"I hate myself." She gripped the edge of the sink so tightly her knuckles turned white. "I shouldn't have married James."

"He gave you what you wanted," Vince said softly.

"Yes, Vince!" she shouted and spun around. "He gave, and I took. But I never gave him what he wanted the most. My love." Tears coursed down her cheeks, spiking her lashes. "But I couldn't because I'd already given it to you."

"James was happy," Vince said.

"No, he wasn't. He just didn't want you to know that his wife loved you."

"Hannah, James didn't walk into the marriage blindly. He knew about you and me."

"I didn't know how much I loved you," she said. "He certainly couldn't have. I thought, Vince, that I'd get over you. But I didn't." She brushed a tissue against her cheeks. "For a year I had been talking to James about a divorce, but he wasn't listening to me. That night I told him that I had hired an attorney and had started the proceedings." She reached over and yanked another tissue from the box. Dabbing her eyes, she said, "I had expected anger. Accusations. But he was quiet. Looked at me, smiled, and told me that everything would be all right. We'd work it out. We'd talk about it when he returned from El Paso that evening."

She looked up at Vince, her eyes swollen, her lashes glimmered with tears. "He was acting so strange, I think I had pushed him over the edge. All because—" She started sobbing.

Vince crossed the room in long strides and caught her shoulders. She twisted out of his grip and stepped away. Tendrils of hair escaped her scarf and wisped around her face.

Leaning back against the counter, she said, "You're not to blame for James's death, Vince, and I never thought you were. I am. I drove him to it. I'm a murderer."

"No, you didn't!" Vince caught her shoulders again and held them firmly. He didn't let her twist away. "Both of us have got to stop carrying around this guilt, Hannah. Neither of us is responsible for what happened. James chose to ride into El Paso with me. The driver of the car chose to be drunk."

Crying as she had not cried since James's death, Hannah melted against Vince, gladly welcoming his embrace, gladly letting her grief and anguish pour out.

Later when the tears had dried to sniffles, he said,

"James and I were close, but he never told me about you wanting a divorce."

"It wasn't a reality to him," Hannah said. "He kept telling me that time would take care of our problems."

Vince rubbed his hands up and down Hannah's back, comforting and reassuring her.

"Were you going to come back to me, Hannah?"

Tilting back in his arms, she gazed at him through tear-glazed eyes. "No. I had hurt the three of us enough."

"I love you," he said.

A tear slipped down her cheek. "I love you."

He lowered his head, his lips touching hers, lightly at first, then heavy and demanding. Moaning softly and giving herself to the kiss, Hannah pressed fully against him and wrapped her arms around his neck. Desire swept through them, engulfing them in its flames. In a matter of seconds inhibitions, years, absence, all was eradicated.

Vince's hands slid lower on her back, until he cupped the gentle curves of her buttocks. He pulled her closer to his hardness and slid his hands beneath her sweater, touching her hot skin. She trembled, and he breathed in deeply.

"Oh, Hannah," he murmured, his lips brushing against hers as he spoke, as he touched her and reacquainted himself with the sweetness of her body. "I've dreamed of this for so long."

"Yes."

She pulled his head back down and locked their mouths together. The kiss deepened as she stroked his lips, as they opened to receive her tongue, as she received his.

He lifted his mouth from hers, his eyes glazed with passion. "Hannah, I want to make love to you."

"Yes," she murmured, "I want you too."

He caught her hand and started toward his bedroom. She held back; he turned to look at her.

She shook her head. "But I can't."

He stared at her in disbelief.

"Not right now," she said. "Both of us are too vulnerable right now, Vince. We think we know what we want, but we're not sure."

"I've never been surer of anything in my life!" he exclaimed. "I've loved you since I was in high school. You've loved me as long. And James has been dead for four years." He looked at her scornfully. "I don't like being played with."

"I didn't mean to."

"Didn't you?"

"No. Like you, I was so caught up in our passion that for a moment I went back in time." Her eyes pleaded for understanding. She touched his arm; he flicked her hand away. "Vince, you said we needed to talk. But we need more than that. We need to listen and to understand. Or maybe you really didn't mean talking," she said softly. "Did you just want to get me in bed?"

"I want to get you in bed," he admitted, "but I want us to talk. To listen . . . and understand."

"I'm frightened, Vince," she confessed.

"I don't want you afraid of me."

"Not of you. Of myself," she replied. "When you

begged me to go on the rodeo circuit with you, I should have."

"No, Hannah, you were right." Vince plowed his hand through his hair. "You deserved better than that kind of life."

"I didn't consider your feelings at all," she said. "If I hadn't pushed you, hadn't forced you to make an ultimatum, maybe we would be together today."

"I was a fool!" Vince said.

"We were young and immature." She smiled at him. "Let's give ourselves some time, Vince, to explore our emotions, to really know what we want out of life."

"We've already explored our feelings for each other, and I know what I want out of life. I want you, Hannah. That's why I came home."

"I want you too, Vince," she said, "but want is not strong enough to be the basis for a relationship. Not now, not at this time in my life. I have Allie to think about."

"She wants a daddy for Christmas."

Hannah sucked in her breath. "Marriage?"

He nodded. "That's why I'm here, Hannah, why I'm going to buy the Holcomb place."

Hannah rubbed her forehead. "That's another problem."

Surprised, he asked, "You don't want me to?"

"Vince, I don't live in Bethlehem anymore. My job, my home, my life is in San Antonio. No matter what I might feel for you, I can't give up everything I've worked for."

"Another ultimatum?" he asked.

She shook her head. "No, I just didn't expect you to return to my life so quickly. I need time, Vince."

He walked over to the screen door and stared out. "You were right, Hannah. Nothing has changed. This sounds like the same discussion we had twelve years ago. You're not going to be happy unless I live up to your definition of what a husband should be."

'No, Vince, you're a cowboy, a man of the land. And this is your land. Like it, you're wild and untamed."

She crossed the kitchen and stood beside him.

"It seems that this time, Vince, I'm the one facing the ultimatum. And I don't know that I've changed much during the last twelve years. I don't know that I can give up the security of my job, of my life to become a rancher's wife."

He closed his hand in a fist and softly hit the door frame.

"This is a big decision for me, Vince, especially since I'm up for the directorship of curriculum."

An unsettled silence lengthened between them. Finally he stepped back from the door, careful not to touch Hannah.

"Let's wrap those gifts," he said. "Then I'll head on over to George's."

"May I go with you?" she asked.

He shrugged. "If you want to."

"I want."

As they wrapped gifts on the floor in front of the Christmas tree, Vince kept Hannah talking about her life. He listened but he also wondered if they were destined to be star-crossed lovers. During the eight years that Hannah had been at the educational institute, she

had steadily moved up the ladder, from teacher/
coordinator to assistant director. Now she was being
considered for a full directorship. He could understand
her needing time to think, to sort through her feelings.
If she married him, she would be giving up a lot.

Before they finished, the doorbell chimed.

"Marv," Vince said, pushing to his feet and walking
into the foyer. When he opened the door, a tall middle-
aged man stood there, decked out in a fleece-lined
jacket, jeans, and boots.

"Howdy, Vince." The foreman held out his hand.
"Good to see you home, boy."

"Good to be home, Marv," Vince replied.

They hugged as they shook hands.

Stepping back, Vince said, "Come on in out of this
cold."

"Hello, Marv," Hannah said.

He took off his hat.

"Howdy, Hannah. Good to see you."

She inclined her head. "How about some coffee?"

"Sounds mighty inviting," Marv replied, "but I'd best
be getting on my way. I have an appointment with Ed
Mitchell in a couple of hours."

"Let me get the keys," Vince said.

As soon as Vince had put on his jacket and hat, he
accompanied Marv to the garage to get the car.

"Tell Charlie I sure do appreciate this," the foreman
said.

Vince nodded, holding his head down against the
wind.

Marv asked, "Have you seen your bike?"

"No."

"Maybe it's time you did."

Vince shrugged.

"I've been keeping her revved up like you asked me to."

"Thanks," Vince murmured, not really wanting to talk about the Harley.

"Taken her out on a few little spins," Marv went on. "She rides smooth, Vince. Real smooth." He paused, then said, "Try her out. Remember what I taught you about riding."

Vince grinned. "Yeah, you got to climb back on after you've been thrown."

"Time for you to climb back on."

After Marv drove off, Vince started back to the house, but he stopped and looked over at the barn. His feet, as if they had a mind of their own, began to move in that direction. Soon he was standing in front of the dull red building. He remembered the last time he had been here: the day the motorcycle distributorship had delivered his bike.

He opened the door and walked in, the sweet smell of hay greeting him. He stood for a moment, getting accustomed to the dim interior lighting. His gaze swept through the building, and he saw it. Wearing a protective covering, the Harley stood at the back of the barn. Vince's boots crunched the hay as he made his way to it.

When he reached it, he stood, looking at it. He was surprised that old demons were not squalling. Strangely, since he and Hannah had talked, they were gone. Regret and sorrow was there, but not the haunting demon of guilt. Feeling a peace within himself that he had not felt since James died, he caught the covering and pulled it off.

He gazed at the dazzling beauty of the Sportster. He brushed his fingers over the handlebars. Ordinarily his helmet would have been hanging from them, but it had been destroyed in the wreck.

"She's beautiful, isn't she?" Hannah said softly.

He had been so engrossed that he hadn't heard her enter. She was bundled up in her overcoat.

"Yeah." He walked around the machine, running his hands over it, stroking, caressing. "What made you call it a 'her'?"

"You always referred to your bike as 'her.'" She ran her fingers over the handlebars. "I used to feel like I was competing with *her* for your love and attention. She's a femme fatale. Beautiful and deadly. But in the end the motorcycle wasn't the siren's song that got to you, it was the rodeo."

Stopping beside her, he put his arm around her shoulder and pulled her against him.

"Are you thinking about taking her out for a ride?" Hannah asked.

"Would you ride with me?"

"No!" Then she quickly added, "I'm sorry. I just can't. I hate them, Vince."

He gave her shoulder an understanding squeeze. "Do you remember how to drive?"

"Yes."

When they had been going together, he had taught her how to drive the motorcycle, believing that the more she learned, the less she would fear it. Reluctantly she had learned, but she hadn't gotten over her fear of the cycle. And that fear had been compounded when Vince and James were involved in the accident four years ago.

"Do you think you'll ever ride again?" she asked.

"Yes."

He walked over to the pegged workstation and snagged a set of keys. He slid his leg over the Sportster, inserted the key into the ignition, and turned it. The engine sputtered, then glided into life, purring as smoothly as Vince could have wanted. He revved the bike, excitement rushing through him. His hands closed around the handlebars. He flexed his fingers; he got the feel . . . no, he'd never lost the feel. He would be taking her out soon. Looking up, he smiled at Hannah. Then he turned the key and slid off.

After he rehooked the keys, he flicked his wrist and looked at his watch. "Time for us to leave if I intend to meet with George."

When he reached her side, he caught her hand in his, twining them together. He brought them to his mouth.

"I'm glad you're going with me." He kissed across the tips of her fingers.

She stared into brilliant ebony eyes. "Me too."

4

By the time the tour of the ranch was over and George Holcomb had driven off, the northerner was blowing in. Black clouds hung low, and a bitter wind blew. Vince and Hannah walked away from the dilapidated old building that had once been the Holcomb homestead. Glad for a reprieve from cold, they hurriedly climbed into the truck. As Vince turned on the engine and heater, Hannah shivered on her side of the seat and pulled her coat tightly about her.

"It's getting colder." Her teeth chattered.

"Then come over here and let me warm you up." Vince caught her hand and tugged.

Willingly, she moved over, and he wrapped his arms around her. She snuggled up to him, laying her face on his chest and inhaling his aftershave.

"Obsession," she murmured.

"What?"

"Your aftershave."

"Yeah."

"Because of me?"

He nodded. "Christmas twelve years ago."

"I still have the lamp."

"Our Aladdin's lamp?" He remembered the day they

had been shopping in El Paso and had seen it in the window of an antique shop. "That had to be the grungiest lamp I've ever seen."

"But look what lay beneath the grunge," she replied.

Vince laughed. "Talk about elbow grease. How long did we polish that thing?"

"Well, we didn't exactly polish straight through. We took several breaks."

He laid his cheek on top of her head. "That was part of the joy of having gotten it for you." He paused, then said, "I'll never forget the way your face lit up when we had it completely restored. Your eyes sparkled." His arms tightened about her. "That was a wonderful Christmas."

She agreed, and they lapsed into silence; holding each other was enough.

"Where are we going shopping?" she asked at last.

"Are you still game to go with me?"

She nodded her head, loving the feel of his jacket against her cheek. "Bethlehem or El Paso?"

"We can get one gift I want in Bethlehem, but I'm not sure about the others. What do Charlie and Allie like or want?"

"For Allie we need a computer store with plenty of games."

"She's really into computers?"

Again she nodded. "I bought her a new one for Christmas. It'll be waiting for her at home when we return after the holidays."

While the engine was warming, they sat and talked about computers, about the games that Allie enjoyed, the way she utilized the word processing program for her schoolwork.

"She and I will get along swell," Vince said, then launched into an explanation how he could show her some added features of her games. He even sounded excited when Hannah described Allie's computer and began making plans for utilizing and expanding it.

Finally Hannah braced her hands on his chest and pushed away. Grinning at him, she said, "You'll have to continue this conversation with Allie. I know the programs I use on a computer, and that's all."

"Then, Hannah, my love, Allie and I have our work cut out for us. We shall have to teach you."

"I don't need to know any more than I know right now."

"You never can tell." He brushed his lips across her forehead, down to the tip of her nose. "What if you married a rancher and he needed you to help him keep up with his operation?"

Her heartbeat accelerated and his arms tightened around her.

"To be honest, Mr. Carmichael, until today I had not given a thought to being married to a rancher."

"Does this mean that since today you have been giving it thought?"

"Maybe."

His lips closed over hers, and they kissed, deeply, hotly . . . hungrily. When he finally lifted his face from hers, the windows of the truck were frosted. With her fingertip she traced his thick brows, his nose, his mouth.

"One thing I haven't given thought to," she murmured, "is making love in the front seat of a truck."

He laughed, the raspy sound wrapping seductively around her. "Might be interesting."

She laughed with him. "At our ages, I would say so, and in this weather."

"Shall we head for the house?"

"My heart says yes, but my head says no."

"Which one are we going to obey?"

"For the moment my head."

He caught her hand and held it close to his mouth. "I think I like the route of the heart best."

"I have a feeling that we'll be traveling it."

He took her finger into his mouth and gently caressed it, running the tip of his tongue around it. Hannah sucked in her breath. She felt as if her entire body were being consumed with fire. Never had she been so hungry for a man's touch . . . no, for Vince's touch. Inhaling deeply, she pulled her finger from him. He shifted his position in the seat, and she glanced down to see his hardness. When she looked back into his face, his eyes smoldered with passion.

"You do this to me, Hannah."

"I know. You have the same effect on me."

Tucking her chin against his chest, Hannah still snuggled against him. He flicked on the defroster, and they watched as the frosty boundary of their magical world slowly evaporated.

"Where to now?"

Puzzled, she stared at him.

He grinned. "Does Bethlehem have a computer store?"

"Oh," she murmured; then: "Oh, yes!"

"And for Charlie," he said. "Can we get her something in Bethlehem too?"

"For her I would suggest a new pair of house slippers. She was complaining about hers the other day."

"Bethlehem it is," Vince said.

He put the truck in gear and slowly pulled away from the Holcomb property. As they drove down the narrow dirt road, Hannah looked around.

"It's in bad condition, isn't it?" she said.

"Not as bad as I thought it was going to be, considering it's been neglected since John died."

"Oh, Vince, there's not one building intact," Hannah said. "They'll all have to be rebuilt. And the land. It's been overgrazed."

"That's why they're asking such a low price for it," he returned.

"The price isn't low if you consider the financial outlay ahead of you."

The pickup thudded over the cattle guard.

"Are you trying to talk me out of it?" he asked.

Was she? Hannah honestly didn't know. "I don't want you to make a hasty decision."

"I'm not. The price is right, Hannah," he said. "I'm thirty-three, and for the first time in my life I know what I want to do, and I'm going to do it." He pushed the brim of his Stetson back and flashed her a quick grin. "Remember, I'm a cowboy."

"Yeah," she murmured, "I remember."

"Rhinestone cowboys live in cities. Cowboy-cowboys live on ranches."

Laughing with him, she slipped her hand across his chest and played with the buttons on his coat.

"Can *this* cowboy—" she gently punched his chest with her finger—"afford *this* particular ranch?"

"It'll take most of my money for the purchase," Vince replied, "but I'll have enough left over for operational expenses for several years. If I live frugally in the old house."

It started drizzling, and he turned on the windshield wipers. "The weather is getting worse."

Hannah's gaze ran across the blackened horizon. "It's so dark you would think it's evening time."

"I haven't experienced a Texas blue northerner in a long time," he said.

"Four years." She continued to play with the button on his coat. "Vince, I'm sorry about the way I treated you after James's death."

He squeezed her shoulder.

"At the time I was so caught up in my own grief and guilt that I didn't think about how you were feeling."

"We both had some demons to exorcise," Vince said, "and now that we've done that, we're going to look to the future."

"Yes," Hannah murmured, but deep in her heart, she wondered if looking would be all they did. So much lay between them. But for the moment she didn't have to think about that. She had the day with Vince, and she was going to enjoy it.

The afternoon was wonderful. Hannah and Vince had lunch at a local restaurant, then went shopping in the mall. Their first stop was the computer store, where they bought Allie a new and exciting computer game. Hannah laughed as Vince sat down at the display computer, inserted the demo diskette, and played the game for her. Before she knew what had happened, she had the joystick and was going for a ride through cyberspace.

Laughing, they had departed the store and strolled down the mall toward Dillard's. Along the way they window-shopped, spending a long time at the jewelry store. As they looked at rings, Vince knew which ones Hannah would like. Both of them stared at one in particular. Her birthstone. An imperial topaz surrounded by diamonds.

"It's beautiful," Hannah murmured.

They had gone inside, and Hannah had tried it on.

"And expensive," she whispered to Vince when the saleswoman moved down the glass counter, seeking more merchandise.

She held out her hand, and they stared at the ring.

"It looks like you," Vince said. "Maybe someday I'll have the kind of money it takes to buy one of these, and it can be your Christmas present."

"It's all right," she replied. "Just trying it on"—she looked into his face—"just being here with you is enough, Vince. This is all the present I need."

For Charlie they bought a pair of leather house slippers lined in fleece. Soft and warm. They bought Allie a new pair of pajamas. For each other they bought perfume and aftershave. This time moving from Obsession to Passion. Reveling in the joy of rediscovering love and happiness, both felt it more closely related to their present emotional state.

"What about a housecoat?" Vince asked as they strolled through the lingerie department.

Hannah stopped in front of one of the display racks and flipped through the robes. "This one would be nice." She stopped shuffling them, and pulled out a hanger. Holding it up to herself, she said, "In fact, I could use one."

Vince leaned close to her and whispered, "That's not quite what I picture you in."

She looked up. He reached behind him and pulled out a skimpy lace teddy from the rack. Hannah felt the heat rush into her face. Vince grinned and returned the hanger to the rack. To cover her embarrassment, Hannah quickly returned the robe to its rack.

Laughing softly, Vince capped her shoulders with his arm. "Now, Hannah Anderson, it's time for us to separate."

Puzzled, she stared at him.

"I have some shopping of my own to do."

She grinned. "Sure you don't need me to help you?"

"Nope." He kissed her lightly on the lips. "I'll meet you back here in a hour. Then we'll head home."

By the time they arrived home, the drizzle had thickened. The wind howled around the buildings and swirled twigs and debris through the air. As soon as they were inside, Vince carried their gifts into the den and set them on the floor in front of the tree. Taking off her coat, gloves, and muffler and hanging them in the hall, Hannah moved through to the kitchen, where she prepared two cups of hot chocolate, frothing with marshmallow creme.

"Humm, these look good." Walking up from behind, Vince caught her by the waist and drew her back against him. He nuzzled her throat. "And so do you."

She turned her head and brushed her cheek against his.

"You have five o'clock shadow," she murmured, lightly dragging her fingernail across the stubble. She turned around in his arms, and slid her hands up his chest. "Oh, Vince, I love you so much."

She tilted her face up to his, and they kissed. Although Vince had kissed her many times, had taught her to kiss, a feeling such as he had never known came over him, a feeling of infinite tenderness. He wanted to love Hannah, to protect and take care of her. Passion waited; it was enough to hold her. To know that she loved him.

"Vince," she said as he began to stroke her back, "I've been thinking about us."

She touched his face again, brushing her fingers over his lips. He captured one of them, kissing it.

"I want there to be an *us*."

He stared at her for a moment before he asked, "Are you sure?"

She nodded and caught his shirt in both fists. "I'm sure, but I'm a little scared."

His eyes darkened. "Of what?"

"I—I haven't been with a man since James died."

A smile eased across his troubled features. "I wish I could make the same confession—"

"It's not a confession and not meant to question you about your past. I just wanted you to know," she whispered.

"Oh, Hannah!" He held her tightly, not knowing which of them trembled the most. "At first, there were lots of women in my life. I was searching for you. Then one day I realized that I would never love another woman, would never find satisfaction with one. For the past six months I've thought of no one but you. I've been with no one."

She pressed against him, and they held on to each other, onto the tiny but strong thread of love that had spanned the years to bond them together.

"Does this mean that you're going to marry me?" he asked.

"Yes."

He swept her into his arms and carried her to the bedroom, kicking the door shut behind them. He set her down and kissed her long, hungrily. Then they separated and divested themselves of clothing until they stood naked.

"You're beautiful," he murmured. "More beautiful than I remembered."

He caught her hands and guided her to the bed, both of them stretching out together. Untying the scarf that held her ponytail, he dropped it to the floor and brushed his hands through her hair.

"I've dreamed of doing this for years."

He placed kisses all over her face, her eyebrows, the tip of her nose, her chin. When he kissed her breasts, she threaded her fingers through his hair.

"You're not the only one who dreamed," she whispered. "I did, too."

His mouth was warm, his lips unbelievable tender as he caressed her.

"Vince," she whispered.

He moaned low in his throat, and the sound excited her because she was pleasing him. Then he claimed her lips in another long, drugging kiss; his mouth was warm and moist and sweet.

He raised his head and stared down at her with eyes that were dark with passion. "I love you, Hannah, and I'll never give you up again."

"I love you." She cupped his head and brought it down again, their mouths locking.

With a fierceness that took her breath, he joined his body to hers. For the first time in fourteen years, she felt complete. She was filled by Vince, one with him, part of him.

He plunged into her; she arched up to receive him.

She began to spin out of control. She wanted to hold back, wanted to prolong the moment of ecstasy, but she couldn't. Four years had been too long.

"Yes!" His voice was raspy, his breathing ragged. "Oh, yes!" His body surged over hers; his arms tightened about her.

With a low and passionate cry, Hannah gave herself to the flames that he had lit in her twelve years ago, that he now rekindled.

Vince covered her face with kisses, and held her until her breathing evened.

"I feel so young and innocent," she whispered, kissing his chest.

He felt her tears.

"So loved."

"You are loved," he murmured.

"Vince"—her voice was so low he could hardly hear

her—"I honestly thought I could make myself love James because he loved me."

"I know." He hugged her tightly.

"But you can't make yourself love someone no matter how hard you try."

"It's okay."

"No, it wasn't," she said, pushing up on an elbow and leaning over him. "I made life miserable for you and me . . . and for James."

Vince brought her head down again, holding her cheek to his chest. "It's over, darling. Now, you must forgive yourself."

They lay there for a long time before they got up and went into the bathroom, where they showered together . . . and made love again. Replete, they returned to bed and lay there, holding each other, basking in their newly rediscovered love. Then the telephone rang and shattered the idyllic world they had created.

Vince stirred. "Shall we ignore it?"

"If we were at home, I'd say yes," Hannah replied. "But it might be an important call for your grandmother."

He kissed the side of her face.

"Or it could be her calling."

Vince swung his legs over the side of the bed, slipped into his jeans and padded into the study. In a few minutes he returned to the bedroom with the cordless.

"For you."

Surprised, she pushed up on an elbow and took the receiver from him. "Hello," she said.

"Hannah, this is Jeff. Sorry to bother you on your holidays."

My employer, Jeff Reardon, she mouthed to Vince. He turned and walked to the window, staring out.

"No problem, Jeff," she said into the mouthpiece.

"The board met this morning."

"But I thought—"

"I know. They took me by surprise too. They weren't supposed to meet until next Monday to go through the preliminary list, but an emergency came up. Since they had to meet today, they went ahead and discussed the directorship."

Hannah gripped the telephone so hard, her fingers hurt. Out of the corner of her eye she saw Vince dressing.

"It's down to you and Vela Hendrickson," Jeff said. "They've been locked up for the past two hours discussing the two of you. Last break you seemed to be the strongest contender."

"When will you know?" Hannah asked.

"Hopefully today," he replied. "I wouldn't have called, but I'm so nervous." He paused, then said, "Here they come. Wait."

Looking over at Vince, Hannah said, "I may have gotten the directorship, Vince. They're coming out of the meeting, and—"

"You got it, Hannah!" Jeff shouted. "You got it. You're the new director of curriculum."

"Yes!" Hannah exclaimed.

She and Jeff talked a little longer. Then she hung up.

"Oh, Vince, this is wonderful." She jumped off the bed and quickly put on her clothes, repeating her conversation with Jeff. She laughed; she spun about; she sighed deeply. When she was dressed, she flung herself into Vince's arms. "This couldn't be a more wonderful Christmas. Maybe I do believe in angels. Allie is going to get her daddy. I'm going to get you and my promotion."

"You accepted," Vince said quietly.

She pulled back. "Yes," she murmured, "I did."

"You gave them your answer without discussing it with me."

"I'm sorry. For four years I haven't had to discuss my decisions with anyone. I didn't . . . think." Her voice trailed into silence.

"Hannah, have you been listening to me?" He caught her by the shoulders and held her, staring into her eyes. "I'm buying the Holcomb ranch. I'm going to live here. I thought when you agreed to marry me, to make love with me, that you understood. That you had agreed."

"Yes, Vince, I understood," she answered. "And I don't see a problem. We can still buy the ranch. We just don't have to live there right away. We can live in San Antonio for a while and both of us work. We can slowly build up the ranch."

"I don't want the ranch as a hobby, Hannah. I want to live here, to work here."

"Vince, I've worked so hard for this. I just need a little time. A year or two as director will look good on my resumé."

"Sounds like we're having the same argument that we had twelve years ago, Hannah."

"It's not, Vince. We're older, more mature—"

"Older for sure, but I don't know about the mature bit."

"It'll take you at least two years to reconstruct the buildings," Hannah pointed out.

"You and I can make sweet, sweet love, Hannah, but I don't know that we can make a marriage," Vince said sadly. "It's been twelve years since we broke up, and both of us claimed to have changed. In reality neither of us have. Each of us still wants our own way."

The mantel clock began to strike the hour.

"Earlier you told me that you were the one who had to answer the ultimatum. But you didn't give me a second thought when you told Jeff that you'd accept the job."

"I can still talk to him, Vince," Hannah said. "And I explained to you that it's going to take time for me to readjust my thinking. I've been by myself for so long."

When the last bong of the clock silenced, Vince held up his arm and glanced at his watch. "It's five," he announced. "I've got an errand to run."

"Vince, we're not finished talking," Hannah said.

"For right now we are," he said.

"No, Vince—"

He laid a finger over her mouth. "Each of us needs time, Hannah. Even if you don't, I do." He walked out of the bedroom, down the hallway to the foyer.

Hannah rushed after him. "I'll go with you. We'll talk in the truck."

"No." He slipped into his jacket and fastened it down the front. "I'll go by myself." He settled the Stetson on his head and pulled on his gloves. "I'll be back later."

A darkness she had felt only once before in her life, when Vince had left her to go rodeoing, descended again. She followed him onto the porch and watched as he walked across the flagstones. He stopped at the truck and looked toward the barn.

The Harley! He was going to take the Harley.

Disregarding the rain and the cold, Hannah rushed off the porch over to where he stood. "Don't take it, Vince," she begged. "Please don't take it." Tears mingled with the rain that washed her face. She shivered but it was from fear not the cold.

"Get inside," Vince said gently, putting his hand in the center of her back and pushing her toward the house.

"Not until you promise me that you're not going to take the Harley. It's too dangerous to be on it, Vince. You haven't ridden in four years. You aren't familiar with the changes they've made in the road. You—"

He swept her into his arms, cutting off her pleading, and carried her over the flagstones, up the steps, and over the porch into the house. He set her down in the foyer.

He smiled sadly as he brushed dampened tendrils of hair from her forehead and temples. "I won't take the Harley. Now you dry off and stay here."

"You're coming back," she said.

He nodded. "We have to decide what we're going to do."

With a heavy heart she watched him stride out of the house to the truck. Earlier today she had felt that too much lay between her and Vince for them to make a commitment of love and marriage. She had wondered if looking would be all they did. But at the time she hadn't had to think about it. She took the day.

Now the day was gone, and she wondered what was going to happen between her and Vince. She knew beyond any doubt that she and Vince loved each other, but she also knew that sometimes love was not enough. She prayed to God that this wasn't so for them.

5

A couple of hours had passed since Vince had left Hannah. He had driven into town, picked up the gift he had placed on hold for her, and was now headed back to the ranch. The only sound inside the truck was the swish of windshield wipers. Fog hung oppressively in the air, eating up the beam of the headlights, isolating Vince from the rest of the world, making him feel alone and vulnerable. He had to admit his feelings for Hannah also contributed to his vulnerability.

He glanced over at the package on the seat. A crystal Christmas angel, a special hanging ornament for the tree. He had seen it when he and Hannah had been shopping. Since it was the last one, he had asked the saleswoman to hold it for him. He told her that he would be back later to pick it up. He was going to give it to her and Allie on Christmas Eve. When he had bought it, he had dreams of Hannah, Allie, and him hanging it on the tree together, of their being a family.

A horn blared, and a truck flew by Vince. He shook his head and murmured, "Fools!"

He reached into his pocket and closed his hand around the small box. He had also returned to the jewelry store and had bought Hannah the imperial topaz ring. It had been expensive, had taken a chunk of the money he had put aside for the ranch, but he wanted her to have it. He planned to give it to her on Christmas Day.

During the past two hours, he had been doing a lot of thinking. At first he had been angry with Hannah, but he wasn't anymore. He was disappointed that she hadn't talked with him before she told Jeff she would take the job, but he no longer faulted her for taking it. Her career was as important to her as his was to him.

And in this instance compromise was easier for him to make than for her. As she had pointed out, they could still buy the ranch and work on it. It wasn't as if he would lose his dream altogether. She would be.

Mostly, Vince had decided that life without Hannah wasn't worth living. He had never envisioned the ranch without her. She had always been an integral part of it. He wasn't going to deny her the chance for promotion.

Although he wasn't traveling too fast, he saw an indistinguishable blur straight ahead of him on the road.

"What the hell!" he muttered.

Then he realized that it was stopped; it wasn't moving. He threw on the brakes and skidded over the asphalt. Taillights flashed on ahead of him, and he saw a truck—the one that had whizzed past him earlier—spin out. Vince sat there for a minute, accelerated slowly, and straightened out the Laramie. He started moving again.

He hadn't gone far when he was once again behind the truck. It was creeping along. He pulled into the left lane to pass. When he was even with the truck, the driver picked up speed. The faster Vince went, the faster the other truck went. He looked over. The driver, a teenager, grinned. Two other boys sat in the car, waving liquor bottles and shouting at him to drag.

Vince slowed down; they slowed down. He speeded up; the driver let him get by. Then he pulled out and drove up on the left side of Vince. By now Vince was getting a little nervous. It was obvious the boys in the other truck were drunk and were looking for excitement of some kind, and he seemed to be their promise of excitement. If not dragging, a fight. Neither of which Vince looked forward to.

When he continued to ignore them, the truck dropped back and Vince picked up speed. With a little luck he'd be at the turnoff to the Guardian Angel before they caught up with him again. Then out of the fog-hazed darkness he felt the jar as his truck was grazed on the left. The screech of metal against metal. As he fought to control the truck, he looked over and saw the teenagers. They were laughing and cheering.

Vince continued to struggle to keep the Laramie on the highway, but the attack had taken him by surprise. He tried to outrun them, but their souped-up truck was fast. They were dangerous. They plowed into Vince again. He hit a pool of water, hydroplaned, and spun out of control, flipping over and over as the truck rolled across the flat Texas desert.

Hannah, he kept thinking. The angel. He heard the paper sack rattling as he tumbled. He slid his hand into his pocket and clutched the ring.

"Hannah," he murmured as he sank into blackness, "I love you. I'm not going to leave you . . . ever."

Vince felt the soft brush of air against his face. The sweetest softest brush of air he had ever felt. He gasped, inhaling it. Then he opened his eyes. He hurt, hurt all over. His head was splitting. He tasted blood. He was hanging upside down in the truck, suspended by the seat belt. Never had Vince experienced quietness like this that surrounded him now.

"It's okay, son," a masculine voice said. "I'm going to get you out of this."

Vince peered through the haze and saw a cowboy hunched outside the shattered window.

"Marv? Is that you?"

"No, I'm not Marv," he replied.

The man's voice was the kindliest Vince had ever heard, and he glowed. Glowed! Glowed around his shoulders as though he had wings.

"Who—who are you?" Vince demanded. Through swollen eyes, he stared at the stranger. But he was growing dimmer. Vince was getting light-headed again, spinning . . . spinning. . . .

Hannah was curled up on the bed in Vince's room, on the bed where they had recently made love. She had called Jeff back and told him about her and Vince. She requested time to think about the directorship. Jeff had been disappointed, but he understood and told her that she wouldn't have to give him an answer until the office reopened in January.

She had known even as she spoke to him that she would not take the position. She had lost Vince once because of her demands, because of her beliefs about security. She wasn't going to do it again. Life without Vince would be mere existence, and that was no life at all.

He had said he had an errand to run, that he would be back, but Hannah was afraid that she had run him off a second time, that he wouldn't come back.

"Oh, Vince," she cried, "please, darling, don't leave me again. I love you so much."

Hannah felt a brush of sweet air around her. Someone was in the room with her. She opened her eyes. Through the light that filtered in from the hallway, she looked around the room. She saw no one.

She had imagined it. She closed her eyes again.

"Hannah," a soft masculine voice said, "Vince needs you."

Hannah bolted up. "Vince?" she cried out.

"He's been in a wreck and needs help," the voice said.

Hannah slid off the bed and moved around the room. "Who are you?" she demanded. "Where are you?"

Out of nothing a man materialized. A cowboy. A cowboy with wings.

"Tex," she murmured.

"Follow me," he said, "and I'll take you to Vince. We have no time to lose."

Without rationalizing what was happening, Hannah

ran into the foyer, donned her overcoat and raced out of the house. She was at the garage when she realized she had no car . . . no truck. How was she going to get to Vince? She looked at the barn. The Harley.

"Hannah," the cowboy prompted, "hurry."

"I can't," she cried out. "I can't ride the Harley. Not with this weather." She was shaking her head and wringing her hands.

"You have to," the voice instructed. "You're the only one who can save Vince. If you wait much longer, he'll die from exposure. He'll freeze to death."

"Will you go with me?"

"Yes, I'll be with you, but I can't do it for you."

Slowly Hannah walked toward the barn. With stiff, cold hands, she opened the door and walked through to the motorcycle. She yanked off the covering, moved to the pegged workstation and lifted off the keys. As if she were guided by a force outside herself—and she truly believed she was—she slid onto the roadster and turned the key in the ignition.

The next thing she knew, she was flying, following a glow of light ahead of her. The fog was heavy and greedily lapped up the headlights, but as long as she had Tex guiding her, she didn't need them. She felt the wind slice through her. But she never took her eyes off the glowing light. Mile after mile clicked off, and she drove.

Her only thought was Vince.

Then the glow she was following turned off the asphalt, off the highway onto the flatlands, and she did too. She no longer feared the Harley, no longer feared for herself. She thought only of Vince.

She lost the light she was following. She slowed the bike, looked around, then saw it again. As she drew nearer she realized that it was a different kind of light. Headlights! Vince's truck.

Hannah stopped the Harley, leaped off, and ran toward the lights. "Vince," she called. "Vince, can you hear me?"

The truck was sitting on top of the cab. Vince was suspended by his seat belt. Lying on the wet ground, Hannah touched him, touched his face. It was cold, but she felt his breath as it fanned across her hand. He was alive.

"Vince," she cried. "I've got to get you out of here."

She pulled on each of the doors, but none of them would open; they were jammed. She clawed around the belts, trying to unfasten them, trying to free him so she could pull him out of the truck.

"Hannah," he mumbled.

"Vince," she cried again. "How bad are you hurt?"

"Is that you, Hannah?"

"Yes. How bad are you hurt?"

"I'm not sure. My head aches, my chest."

"Your arms and legs," she said. "Can you feel them? Can you move them?"

She heard some shuffling, and the truck rocked.

"Yes, they seem to be okay," he replied. "My chest and stomach. That seems to be okay too."

"Undo the seat belt," Hannah instructed. "That's the only way we're going to get you out of here."

Together they worked until they had the belt unfastened. Painfully Vince shifted inside the cab and slowly, carefully crawled out the broken window. When he was fully out, Hannah raked her hands over him, again and again, feeling, examining, assuring herself that he was all right, glad that he had suffered only superficial cuts. She didn't care that he was bloody; she strewed kisses over his face and held him tightly.

"Oh, Vince, I was so frightened."

"How did you find me?" he asked.

"I'm not sure," she replied. "I was lying on the bed, my eyes closed, thinking about you, about how much I loved you, and I felt something."

"A rush of sweet air," he said.

"Yes, that's it exactly. Then I heard this kind voice speak to me and warn me that you were in danger."

"He told me not to worry, that he would get me out of this mess," Vince said. "And he did."

"Tex?" Hannah said softly.

"Grandmother Vicentia would say so," Vince replied.

"What does her many-great grandson think?"

"I think it was the ole boy," Vince replied.

"I do too." She gently pulled away from him. "We'd better get out of this weather."

"Where's your car?" Vince asked.

"Charlie and Stella still have it," she answered.

"How did you get here?"

"The Harley." She led him to the Sportster, faintly visible in the gleaming headlights of the overturned truck.

"I can't believe you rode it," he said.

"I would have ridden anything to get to you," she replied. "I wasn't going to let you go this time."

"I wasn't going to leave."

They smiled, their love shining in their eyes and on their faces.

"But since you don't seem to be too badly hurt," she said, "I'm going to be the passenger on the return trip."

Vince drew her into his arms and gave her a long, satisfying kiss. When he raised his head, he said, "Let me get yours and Allie's gift out of the truck."

His boots crunched over the iced terrain as he made his return to the truck and knelt at the driver's window. He felt around until his hand closed over the shopping bag. He pulled it out, rose, and walked to the front of the truck to stand in the beam of light. He opened the bag and withdrew the white tissue paper. Carefully he unfolded layer after layer until he reached the ornament . . . perfectly intact.

"An angel," Hannah murmured.

"A crystal angel for you and me and Allie to hang on the tree on Christmas Eve," he said. "That is, if you and Allie will have me."

"We will," Hannah said, "and we'll have the ranch too."

"As you suggested, I'll buy the land," Vince said. "In the meantime we'll live in San Antonio and give you a chance to further your career. Perhaps when the time comes to move, you'll be able to find a comparable job here in Bethlehem. Or maybe you can set up your own agency."

"I like those possibilities," she said, "but I meant it, Vince, when I said I'm willing to give everything up. You're more important to me than anything else."

"I think, Hannah Anderson, that you and I are going to have our cake and eat it too."

"When are we going to tell Allie?" Hannah asked.

"How about Christmas Day?" Vince said. "Then our miracle will be complete."

On Christmas morning, the house was filled with the aroma of food. The turkey and dressing. Cranberry sauce. Pies and cakes.

Allie rose and rushed into the den. Her gifts were piled high and she was ready to open them. She dashed into the kitchen to give her grandmother a hug and kiss.

"Uncle Vince!" She slid to a stop when she saw him standing at the sink, mixing the fruit salad. "I didn't know you were a cook."

"A cook of sorts," he answered. "Your mom was up early with the turkey, and Charlie and I sent her back to bed for a few extra winks while we did our share."

"Everybody's gonna be coming in soon," Allie said.

"That's right."

"And I'm going to show them the angel we put on the tree last night, Uncle Vince." She spun around. "Oh, Charlie, this is the best Christmas ever. Tex saved Uncle Vince, and taught Mama how to ride a Harley." She danced over to Vince. "Tell me about it again, Uncle Vince. It's so-o-o good."

"I will later," Vince replied.

"I would imagine you'll be telling the story for the rest of your life," Charlie said with a smile. "Well you should, it's worth retelling."

Allie gave her grandmother a big hug and kiss.

"How about some breakfast?" Charlie asked.

"In a minute." Allie ran back to her mother's room

and knocked lightly on the door. When Hannah answered, Allie cracked the door. "Merry Christmas, Mama."

"Merry Christmas." Smiling, Hannah held out her arms and Allie sailed into them.

"This is one of the very best Christmases I've ever had," Allie repeated. "Uncle Vince is great, Mama."

"You like him?"

"I love him, Mama. I'm so glad he's back."

"Yeah," Hannah said, "so am I."

"He's cooking."

"I know."

"Are you ready to open the gifts?" Allie asked.

"That's what I was going to ask," said Vince from the doorway.

He gazed fondly at the mother and daughter who lay on the bed. . . . soon to be his wife and child.

He grinned at Hannah. "Do you think you can get up, sleepy head? Or do you need some help?"

"Yeah," Allie said, joining in the teasing. "It's time to get up, sleepy head."

Soon all of them were seated in the den, opening their gifts. Festive paper, bows, and ribbon lay scattered all over the floor. Allie happily examined her new computer games and her new jeans, boots, and the Stetson Vince had surprised her with. She jumped with glee when Hannah told her about the computer that awaited her at home.

They oohed and aahed over the other gifts, the sweater Vince had bought Hannah, the leather vest Hannah had bought him. Hannah turned red when she opened the box with the teddy in it; Vince chuckled softly; Allie giggled, and Charlie looked pensively from Hannah to Vince and back to Hannah. Then she tried on her new robe and slippers, liking them so much she decided to wear them through breakfast.

"Now," Vince said, "for the second to last gift." He reached into his pocket and withdrew the small blue box. "Hannah, this is for you."

"Oh, Vince," she whispered. She took the box, opened the lid, and gazed down at the twinkling imperial topaz surrounded by diamonds.

"Whoa!" Allie exclaimed. "That's something else!"

Charlie moved closer and peered at the ring.

"Yes, Allie, I would say so myself."

"You shouldn't have, Vince," Hannah said.

He took it out of the box and reached for her left hand.

"Mama," Allie said, "Daddy's ring is gone."

"Yes, I took it off," Hannah replied.

"So I could put this on her," Vince said.

"Another Carmichael love story that has a happy ending," Charlie murmured, a pleased smile on her face.

Looking at Allie, he said, "May I be your father?"

Her lips trembled, and tears spiked her lashes. "Oh, yes, Uncle Vince. Yes, you can."

She threw herself into his arms and hugged him tightly. He picked her up and spun her about the room.

"Tex answered my prayer," she shouted. "I got a new daddy for Christmas."

She looked over at the Christmas tree, at the Carmichael guardian angel.

"Thank you, Tex."

He doffed his hat and winked. Allie laughed. Tex doffed his hat and winked at her! She winked back.

The Trouble with Angelina
by Marilyn Campbell

1

BAM! The crashing sound reverberated through the guardrail next to Angel Chadick, warning her to look up in the nick of time. Barreling down the sidewalk directly toward her was a tire the size of a Volkswagen. She dove onto the grass and rolled away with a second to spare, then watched in horror as the wheel careened into her bicycle. The collision caused the bike and the wheel to ricochet into the air. With a sickening crunch of metal the bike landed again, only to receive another powerful body slam before the mindless attacker continued on its way along the sidewalk.

Her chest clenching with residual panic, Angel's stunned gaze flew from the scene of destruction to the wheel, now wobbling to a stop on the grass, then back to the direction it had come from. Over a quarter mile away, on the opposite side of the street, she could see a man setting up orange hazard cones around a truck with a lopsided forklift on its flatbed. Apparently the wheel had come off the forklift, negotiated three lanes of moderate traffic and a considerable length of sidewalk, without coming in contact with a single thing except the guardrail ... and her poor bike. Cars continued whizzing by, but no one stopped. Hadn't they witnessed the impossible happening, or didn't anyone care?

The realization that *she* could be the mangled remains on the sidewalk instead of her bike had her body trembling as she forced herself upright. It never occurred to her that being a crossing guard could be life threatening.

As she brushed dirt and dried leaves off her dark blue polyester uniform, anger replaced her fear. *Someone* was responsible for almost killing her. A few minutes earlier, a pack of children with bikes had been jammed together in that spot. There was no way they could have all escaped the danger as she had. Determined to vent her fury on the responsible someone, she marched to the truck as soon as the last of the children were across the intersection.

The driver, a slightly built, older man, looked more frightened than she had been. The name Garcia was embroidered on his gray work shirt, above the words, SHAMROCK CONSTRUCTION CO.

"You . . . okay, officer, ma'am?" he asked with several head bobs and a hopeful expression.

"No, I am not okay. Did you see what happened to my bike? You totaled it! That could have been me!" He was beginning to look ill, but Angel was beyond caring for his welfare. "Now I'm going to have to walk home. That's over a mile away! And it's ninety degrees out here. Do you realize how hot this uniform is? I may die yet today—from heat stroke!"

The man's mouth moved from side to side. Finally,

he shrugged and said, "*Lo siento*. No speaky *Ingles* so good."

"O-o-oh," she groaned and threw up her arms. Stomping around to the back of the truck, she pulled a paper and pen out of her pocket to make a note of its tag number. Somebody at Shamrock Construction was going to be very sorry they crossed her path today!

It had to be a zillion to one shot, a highly improbable accident, but not for Angel. The trouble was things like this happened to her all too often. Ever since she first heard her mother refer to her as *an accident,* the word hovered around her life. But this time, she positively could not be held responsible. The cause of her mishaps was usually because she was too high-strung. The more nervous or excited she got, the more likely an accident would occur. It wasn't so bad once she learned to expect the impossible and deal with it efficiently when it happened.

It was the eighth of December, but in Coral City, Florida, it felt more like the Fourth of July. Only the big red bows on the street lamp poles and the silver-and-gold garland wrapped around the royal palm tree trunks gave evidence that Christmas would soon be here. Thirteen years in the tropics had accustomed Angel to the year-round heat, but the long walk home under the blistering sun had her head pounding like a steel drum. At least she could be grateful that her Italian heritage, which cursed her with a body too short to carry her full figure, also blessed her with skin that tanned instead of burning as her redheaded friend Becky's did.

* * *

"Shamus O'Grady! I saw that."

With a sheepish expression, Shamus looked up into the stern face of his boss. "Ah, now, Your Holiness, ya know I've tried all the reg'lar tricks ta git me boy Sean and that little colleen together and nothing worked."

"I know," Gabriel said with a sympathetic nod. "But endangering lives and destroying property are hardly angelic behavior. We have discussed this mischievous streak of yours before, Shamus, and I warned you—"

"Yes, yes, but ya know how much it means ta me ta see me grandson happy, an' 'tis already the second week o' December . . ." Shamus knew he had the old archangel on that one. No angel's wish could be refused at Christmastime.

"Hmmph. All right. You may proceed. But I'll be keeping a watch, so no more dangerous stunts. Angelina is a particular favorite of mine, and she has enough trouble getting through her days as it is."

Shamus crossed his heart. "Ya got me solemn word, Your Holiness, sir. I'll be playin' it by the book from here on." *Me own book, that is*, Shamus added to himself, knowing his boss would be too busy in the next three weeks to look over his shoulder the whole time.

For the last ten months, since Angelina had caught his eye, he'd done all the little things an angel was permitted to do to assist an earthbound soul. He was absolutely certain she'd be perfect for his grandson and vice versa, but no matter how he meddled, they failed to notice each other. They were both so busy and so determined to maintain their unmarried status that they'd passed one another a dozen times without a glance.

Since he had no doubt the two of them would be blissfully happy together, he felt justified in doing whatever was necessary, even if it meant bending a few rules.

Two hours after reporting the accident to the police, hauling her twisted bike home in her car, and taking a shower, Angel's body had cooled down, but her temper still raged. Becky had come next door for a cup of coffee and some gossip, but got an earful of Angel's anger as a side dish.

Angel's red, white, and blue kitchen complimented her vibrant personality. It was a big, happy room that encouraged friends to stay and visit . . . when she wasn't on a rampage.

When Rolf, the black Labrador that was more child than dog, began whining with his tail tucked between his legs, Angel softened her voice and stroked his large head. "I called the police and they took a report—in between fits of laughter—but they said it wasn't technically a crime, so they couldn't actually arrest anybody. In fact, they said it wasn't even a real traffic accident." The peal of the doorbell interrupted her complaints.

Remaining in the kitchen, Becky added her two cents as Angel walked through the dining room toward the front door. "At the very least you should sue that construction company to get your bike replaced."

"Oh, the bike was an old clunker anyway. What I'd really like," she called over her shoulder as she opened the door, "is to see the owner of that forklift flogged!" She turned her head back to greet her visitor, and found her eyes leveled at a man's chest—a nicely developed one, packaged to perfection in an aqua knit shirt.

Tipping her head back to get the full picture, she discovered a dream of a man with sun-streaked blond hair and gray eyes—the clean-cut boy next door grown to a mature man. With one eyebrow lifted, his mouth twisted in a way that suggested he had heard her wish and wasn't certain whether to laugh or run for cover. He conducted a brief, but very masculine scan of her person that made her bare toes automatically curl under in response.

"Mrs. Chadick? I was told you had a bicycle accident."

His voice stroked her with rich, velvety tones, like that of a disc jockey on an easy-listening radio station. "Yes, that's right, but how . . ." She stopped as she realized he looked familiar. A television anchorman? No, that's not it. He was explaining something about the police giving him her address, but she was trying to place his face. A newspaper picture? Possibly.

". . . and my driver said—"

"What did you say?" Her brain raced to catch up with her ears.

"My driver—"

"No. Before that. Something about you owning the truck and the forklift."

"Yes, I'm—"

"The man responsible for demolishing my bicycle and endangering thousands of innocent lives!"

"Who-o-oa. You want to slide that by me again?"

The horrified expression on his face forced her to re-word her accusations. "All right. So no one was critically injured, but only because I've got great reflexes. However, I am suffering from an extreme case of traumatic shock. And you should see my bike!"

"That's one of the reasons I'm here," he replied with sincerity.

"Fine. Follow me. I don't know why I bothered to put it in the garage. It belongs in a trash heap now." As they entered the kitchen, Rolf rose, wagging his long, thick tail and panting anxiously for an introduction. He had never learned he was supposed to protect her from bad guys. Becky, on the other hand, just panted. Angel frowned at the glowing smile her friend bestowed on the villain behind her. "This," she said with a jerk of her thumb, "is the man who owns the truck that was hauling the forklift that lost the wheel that wrecked my bike."

"Who lives in the house that Jack built," he finished in a singsong voice. "Sorry. You sounded so much like that old nursery rhyme, I couldn't help myself."

Angel glared at him, but her extended sentence echoed in her head. The man was struggling so hard to look contrite that her mouth rebelled against her bad mood. Her reluctant grin allowed him to smile in return. "I may have let my temper get the best of me."

"Not at all. You have every right to be upset, but maybe we could start over. The police told me how to find you, and that no one was hurt, but I wanted to make sure. Naturally, we want to make amends, and I really am sorry about your trauma. As soon as I get back to the job site I plan to investigate how that wheel came off. If it was due to someone's negligence, I promise I will have the individual responsible flogged as you requested."

Her eyes widened in surprise, then sparkled with humor. "I'd prefer to wield the cat-o'-nine-tails myself, if you don't mind."

"Such a pretty lady to be into deviant behavior," he shot back with a distinct twinkle in his eye.

"Excuse me," Becky interjected, glancing from one to the other. "This conversation is taking a decidedly intimate turn, and I haven't even been introduced yet. I'm Becky Hays, Angel's next door neighbor."

"Angel?"

The disbelieving look he gave her suggested he was thinking of a character from the other end of the spectrum. "Short for Angelina," she explained with a laugh. "Sorry, I guess I was too busy attacking to catch your name."

He smiled again and held out his hand to her. "How do you do. I'm Sean O'Grady, owner of Shamrock Construction."

Her hand was already enveloped by his when the name registered. She withdrew her hand and took a step back. Now she knew why he looked so familiar. "*Mayor* Sean O'Grady?"

He nodded, taking in her crossed arms and stern face. "Now what? Was my last opponent your brother?"

She considered keeping quiet for about two seconds. "No. As a matter of fact, I voted for you. I was too busy with my children and everything else to check out your record. I won't make that mistake again."

Instantly, he clutched his chest. "Wow! Direct hit.

Before they bury the body, do you mind expounding a little?"

"Not at all," she said, raising her chin a notch. "This was a nice, small town before you took office five years ago. I don't approve of the direction it's gone since then."

His smile disappeared completely. Of course, she thought, he owns one of the construction companies making money on the overdevelopment of Coral City.

Sean glanced from Angel to Becky and back, taking their full measure before he spoke. "Let me ask you this, Mrs. Chadick. You said you voted without researching the candidates. Have you ever attended the monthly city council meetings? I'm sure I would have recognized you, and you, me, if you had."

"Well, no. I'm the den mother of a Cub Scout troop that meets on that night."

"Don't you think you owe it to yourself to get involved in the city government before you criticize it?"

Becky laughed out loud, breaking the growing tension. "If this woman got involved in one more thing, God would have to add a few hours to every day."

Angel turned away from him and walked to the garage door off the kitchen. "You said you wanted to see the bike."

"Geez!" was all he could say when he saw it. "Thank heavens you weren't on it."

"Yeah. I'm lucky like that."

Returning to the kitchen, he said, "Look, there's no question about my buying you a new bike, but I'd like you to pick it out yourself, to make sure it's one you'll be happy with. If you have time now, we can go right over to the bicycle shop on Baldwin Drive."

Angel shook her head. "Can't. My son Christopher has soccer practice in a half hour. It's my turn for the car pool."

"After practice?"

"Uh-uh. Parent-Teachers' Association meeting. I'm the chairperson for the Book Fair."

"Tomorrow afternoon then."

Another negative head shake. "Josh and Jeff—my twins—have dental appointments."

"Tomorrow night?"

"Cub Scouts."

His tone became incredulous. "Thursday?"

"St. David's carnival committee heads are meeting here."

"Good grief, woman! I thought I was busy."

Becky couldn't resist enlightening him further. "Yep, she's Coral City's very own Sicilian cyclone. Besides all that, she volunteers in her children's classes every Monday, and has her own business, too. You should have come around last football season when she filled in for the Optimists' cheerleading coach."

"You have a daughter also?" he asked incredulously.

"No, but no one else was willing to make a fool of themselves."

Sean was at a momentary loss for words. "And what does your husband do when he wants to see you? Make an appointment?"

Angel swallowed once before answering. "My husband died two years ago." His regretful expression looked quite genuine this time.

"I'm sorry. I didn't mean to be flip. Let me try one more. How about Friday evening?"

Angel opened her mouth, but nothing came out. She walked over to her wall calendar and stared at the clean white square for the day in question. How could this be? She had nothing scheduled, not a single excuse to refuse to accompany him.

"*Bzzt,*" Becky sounded, mimicking a game show buzzer. "Round one goes to the persistent man in the blue shirt. I was planning to take my boys out for pizza and a movie then anyway. I'll take your three also."

Angel stared daggers at her to get her to stop being so helpful, but Becky ignored the silent threat of violence.

Sean grinned victoriously. "Great. I'll pick you up at six, we'll go to the bike shop, then get something to eat."

"No!" Angel said quickly. "I mean, I appreciate your replacing my bike, but dinner's not necessary."

"Consider it my apology for your traumatic shock."

"A verbal one is more than sufficient."

He pondered her answer for a moment, then smiled. "Not even if it means a golden opportunity to take a crack at me and my platforms? I'll give you my solemn promise to discuss every one of your complaints."

Darn him. She really would like the chance to tell him how she felt about what was happening to Coral City. "Well . . ."

"*Bzzt,*" Becky sounded again. "Time's up, kiddo. Round two goes to the smooth-talking politician."

Angel rolled her eyes at her friend's foolishness, and Sean let out a husky laugh.

"You know, Becky," he said with pretended concern, "maybe you should hire a sitter Friday and come along as our mediator."

"What? And give up a chance to referee five boys on sugar highs? Not a chance!"

He confirmed the arrangements and left before Angel could think of a valid reason to change them.

As soon as he departed, Becky let out a whistle. "Can you imagine cuddling up to that every night?"

"Tch. Tch. What would Larry say if he heard the mother of his children talking like that?"

"I wasn't referring to myself. You're the one with the vacancy in your bed."

"And it's going to stay that way, so just give it up." Angel took a sip of lukewarm coffee and shuddered with distaste.

"How can you be in the same room with a man like Sean O'Grady and not think about sex? He's absolutely gorgeous . . . and *single*."

"I really don't care."

Becky leaned forward in her chair, always ready to pass on a little gossip. "A woman sitting next to me in the beauty salon was telling her stylist about a friend whose sister—"

"Becky, please!"

"Anyway, he's definitely a bachelor, and she's pretty sure he's straight, but no one's ever heard of him dating anyone. The rumor is, he was engaged to be married when his fiancée died, and he never got over it. Can you imagine how romantic it would be if you were the first woman he'd been attracted to in *years*?"

"I'm not listening." To emphasize her conviction she

took Becky's coffee mug over to the sink and began noisily emptying the dishwasher.

But Becky saw an opening for her favorite Angel lecture and steamrolled through. "It's been two years since Warren passed away. Nobody expects you to live like a nun anymore. The trouble with you is sexual frustration, pure and simple. That's why you stay so busy. I bet Sean could slow you down to a snail's pace."

"You're doing it again, Becky. Just because you believe sex is one of the basic necessities of life, doesn't mean that's true for everybody. I'm perfectly happy with my busy schedule, my boys, my friends, and my business. That's good enough for me."

"Boo, hiss on good enough. You're only thirty-one years old, your sexual peak. *Good enough* is good enough for an eighty-year-old. You should be going for *great*. And speaking of great, did you notice the fit of his slacks? Probably custom-made. What do you think?"

Angel groaned loudly. "In the case of Sean O'Grady, it is not a question of what he does or does not have in his pants. I was almost mutilated today because of him."

"Baloney. It was an accident, and you know it. You can't hold him personally responsible."

"Then there's the small matter of his being the politician I would most like to see run out of office; a man with whom I am in complete disagreement."

"So? You'll work that out over dinner. You've heard the saying about politics making strange bedfellows."

At the reminder of dinner, she felt the flutter in her

stomach that usually preceded a bout of clumsiness, but she ignored it.

"Why do I keep letting you in my house?" With that, she balled up the dish towel she had been using and pitched it at her friend. Instead of hitting her target, it caught the edge of the wicker napkin holder, which then flew over the edge of the table, causing its paper contents to go floating throughout the kitchen. Angel immediately began scrambling around the floor, picking up napkins, but Rolf thought it looked like playtime. His big front paws landed on her back and she ended up sprawled flat on her stomach. Rolf barked twice, licked her cheek, then lay down beside her.

"You're right, Angel. Who needs a man when you've got the mutant puppy to make you feel loved?" Becky picked up a handful of napkins and put them on the table as Angel peeled herself off the floor.

Before Angel could respond, her eight-year-old twins burst in through the back door with tempers flaring.

"Ma-a-aw!" Josh cried out first. "He kicked me right in the privates."

"Did not," Jeff retorted even louder. "He got in the way of my foot." He tried to grasp a handful of his brother's auburn hair, but Angel grasped his wrist before he could do any damage.

"Stop it, both of you. If you fight, you get hurt. The end. Now, wash your hands and faces while I call Chris. We're going to be late for soccer practice again."

"Are you happy, Shamus? I behaved like you instead of me."

Ah, but how could ya resist such a foin bit o' fluff?

Occasionally, when Sean was particularly bewildered or frustrated by some problem, he imagined himself talking it out with his dearly departed Irish grandfather.

Of all the dumb things to do, asking out a female constituent ranked in the top ten. A date could turn into a relationship, which would end in hard feelings when she discovered he wasn't looking for a wife. And there was no telling what a disappointed woman might say about the man responsible. When the man was a political figure, it could ultimately damage his career. Of course, Shamus never understood the need for so much logic, especially if it involved an exceptionally pretty lass, like Angelina Chadick.

Sean had truly loved Grampa Shamus and had spent every childhood summer with the laughing Irishman, listening again and again to his tales of The Little People and hidden pots of gold. It often crossed Sean's mind that Grampa was an overgrown Leprechaun himself.

After Grandma passed away and Alzheimer's disease began to erode Grampa's mind, Sean didn't hesitate to offer his help rather than put the beloved man in a home. Shamus's children, including Sean's father, all had homes and businesses in other states, while Sean had been roaming the globe without any goals, in the aftermath of personal tragedy. Eight years ago, he moved into Shamus's Coral City home, to care for him and take over the management of Shamrock Construction.

Even in the late stages of his disease, Shamus's eyes occasionally twinkled with mischief. He wanted to see Sean having fun with his life, but Sean had not felt lighthearted since the day his dreams turned to dust. Shamus also wished to attend Sean's wedding, and to bounce Sean's children on his knee before he died. His grandson had not been able to grant those wishes either. Perhaps that was why Sean sometimes imagined hearing his grandfather's voice prodding him to do and say things he wouldn't, or shouldn't, as the serious, most respectable mayor of Coral City.

But a date with Angel Chadick? Sure, she was a *foin bit o' fluff*, with her flashing eyes and lush body. But she also had an irrational temper, a total lack of political savvy, and a life-style that only a masochist would elect. So, why didn't he simply call her back and cancel the engagement?

'Cause ya need ta be sure, now don't ya?

Yes, he needed to be sure, because he hadn't felt that kind of instant attraction since he was ten years old.

Vicky had been in third grade and he in fifth the first time he asked her to marry him, and she accepted. Their love for each other withstood every storm life tossed at them in the years that followed. They firmly believed they would still be holding hands when their grandchildren got married.

She was only twenty-three when Sean got the call. He hadn't even been in the same state as she that day. A car accident, his mother told him, with tears strangling her throat. Vicky had been passing through an intersection when another driver ran a red light. She was in critical condition. Hurry home.

He had hurried home on the first flight he could get. He arrived in time to watch her die through the glass window in the intensive care unit. He couldn't even say good-bye.

"I heard he's a gigolo."

"Christopher!" Angel scolded her ten-year-old son. "Where do you pick up words like that?" She continued folding the laundry at the kitchen table.

"He probably heard about all the money Dad left you. He'll marry you, then kill us all off. He'll probably even move right into this house."

"That does it. No more TV. It's pickling your brain. Mayor O'Grady is a very nice gentleman, and I think he has a lot more money than we do. Your father left us comfortable, but we're hardly rich enough to be killed for it. This isn't even a date. I already explained that to you. He owes me a new bike, and he's letting me pick it out myself. We are then going to have a meeting . . . about Coral City."

"But Scott said he's taking you out to dinner." Christopher accented his whining voice with a pout.

Scott said. How many times a day did she have to hear those words? Becky's son Scott was Chris's best friend, but sometimes she wished they'd never met. "People often have meetings over a meal. Here," she directed, handing him a stack of folded clothes. "Put your things away, then go play so I can have some peace."

As he stalked off, grumbling all the way, Angel gathered up the rest of the laundry. Christopher had taken Warren's death so much harder than the twins. That had to be why he objected so vehemently to her going out with men. She had only accepted a man's invitation to dinner once in the last year, and Christopher got so upset she decided not to try dating again for a long while. She was being honest with him when she said tonight's appointment was not a date.

Every one of the hundred times over the past four days, when she picked up the phone to cancel, she repeated that litany to herself. *This is not a date.* Then why wouldn't her stomach settle down? And why was she worrying about what she would wear? The answer was logical. This evening was important . . . to the future of her hometown. He promised to discuss her complaints, and she was going to see to it that he heard her point of view.

Two hours and three dress changes later, Angel was as ready as she would ever be. Her straight black skirt and tailored, white silk blouse gave her the businesslike look she thought appropriate for the situation. The fluttering in her stomach had multiplied tenfold, warning her that she would have to be extra careful until she relaxed a little.

Becky was in the kitchen waiting for her when she came downstairs.

"Oh, hi," Angel said with forced cheerfulness. "I was going to send the boys over there in a few minutes."

"I know. But His Honor isn't due here for about twenty minutes, and I wanted to give you a little present to commemorate your first date." She handed Angel a dress-size box prettily wrapped in silver foil and purple lace ribbon. "You're so out of practice, I figured you needed some help."

Angel took it and carefully removed the wrapping.

"So help me, Becky, if this is a sexy black negligee, you can take it right home and wear it for Larry."

"I swear—" She stopped short as they both heard the doorbell.

Suddenly a chorus of boys' voices yelled, "I'll get it," and a fight broke out in the foyer.

"It's my turn!"

"You got it last time."

"I'm the man of the house. I have to check him out first."

Angel dashed from the kitchen with the box still in her hand. At the same moment, Rolf joined the fray by the front door. Beyond the boys' shouts and the dog's barking, she vaguely heard Becky demanding she give back the box.

Angel never saw which boy got to open the door, because just then Rolf's big head jerked up under the box, knocking it out of her hand. When she tried to catch it, the lid flew off and the box turned upside-down in midair, tumbling the contents all over the slick tile floor.

Sean caught the tail end of Angel's juggling act as the door was yanked open and the noisemakers all took off in the face of certain punishment. Without hesitation, he joined her on her knees and began picking up the items on the floor and returning them to the box.

Suddenly their hands froze as they each realized exactly what those items were. While Angel held a box of fluorescent condoms, Sean had possession of a black lace brassiere with the cup centers cut out. Contraceptive foam, K-Y Jelly, and a can of oysters were the other objects Sean immediately recognized. There was also a variety of paraphernalia, some of which he couldn't identify, but he had no doubt about the kind of store that sold those things. Becky had mentioned that Angel ran her own business. . . .

He folded the lingerie and placed it gingerly in the box. "I know I'm a bit early, but it looks like you're, uh, all set."

2

"Good heavens," Angel muttered after the first shock wave subsided. As if her fingers had abruptly caught fire, she threw the nasty box away from her and bolted to her feet. "Becky! You're a dead woman!"

Becky knew a sincere threat when she heard one. On her way out the back door, she yelled, "I think I hear the boys calling. See ya."

"Excuse me," Angel said with as much dignity as she could gather, then took off down the hall and ducked into the bathroom.

Sean gathered up the remaining items on the floor and put the lid back on the box. He realized his comment had pushed Angel's blush from pink to crimson, but he had been unable to stop himself. This really was a unique way to greet a date. The box of goodies probably had nothing to do with her business. Otherwise, she wouldn't have looked like she had just encountered a werewolf. When Angel didn't return after a few minutes, he followed the path she had taken and stopped by the only closed door.

"Angel? Are you all right?"

A few seconds passed before she mumbled a reply. "No. I . . . I don't feel well. We'll have to make it another time." Like when hell freezes over.

Sean stared at the closed door. She was probably right. He should leave; sign a note at the bicycle shop to pay for whatever she picked out on her own time. But he imagined hearing Shamus's reaction to a retreat.

Don't ya be shamin' me now. When I was a lad I could charm a lass roit oot o' 'er pantaloons. Surely ya can charm this one oot o' the necessary.

"I'm not leaving, Angel. It could be another month before you have any free time again, and I want to get this matter of your bicycle cleared up."

Charmin'. Truly charmin'.

"Angelina?" He thought he heard an acknowledgment. "I gather Becky had something to do with that, uh, collection. And that there was a private joke involved." This time he heard a definite groan. "I promise, if you'll come out of there, I won't ask what the joke is. In fact, I'll erase my memory of everything that happened from the moment your front door opened until now."

The door opened slowly and she stepped out. "I can't believe I just hid in the bathroom. My ten-year-old handles himself better than that." She lowered her lashes so she wouldn't have to see the laughter in his eyes.

True to his word, however, he dropped the matter. "You look very"—his gaze skimmed the prudish blouse buttoned snugly around her throat—"nice. Shall we go?" He gallantly offered his arm to escort her down the hall, but she quickly stepped away.

A few minutes later, she had located her purse and locked up the house. Her heartbeat had returned to normal, but she could still feel an abnormal amount of heat in her face and her stomach felt like she'd swallowed a tankful of eels. When they reached his dark blue, American-made sedan, he opened the passenger door and held out his hand to assist her into the seat. Still preferring to avoid his touch, she tried to duck her head and step inside in one move.

Thud! Her forehead rammed against the edge of the roof. Flashes of color burst behind her eyes as she rebounded back into Sean's chest.

"Geez! Are you all right?" he asked, turning her to face him. He tugged at the hand she had reflexively pressed to her head, then inspected the injury. "I'm afraid you're going to have quite a goose egg. We'd better go back inside and put some ice on it."

"It's not that bad. Let's go." All she wanted was to get the evening over with as quickly as possible.

After several minutes of silent driving, Sean attempted to draw Angel into a conversation about the merits of dressing casually in south Florida. She assumed it was his way of explaining why he was in a short-sleeved sports shirt instead of a jacket and tie. Their opposite choices of attire gave evidence of how differently each had approached the evening. Fortunately the trip to the bicycle shop ended shortly after they exhausted the scintillating topic of the weather.

"I must look like Cyclops," she said when she saw the sales clerk staring at her forehead.

"Nonsense," Sean assured her. He moved a few hairs of her bangs back and forth. "No one can see it with your hair like that. Besides, it could have happened to anyone."

Angel gave him a skeptical look. She knew differently, but she couldn't explain about her little problem without letting him know how nervous he made her.

Although he steered her toward the most expensive, state-of-the-art touring bicycle, she saw the one she wanted on the other side of the store—an old-fashioned, pedal-brake, with fat safety tires, and a comfortable seat. The only thing fancy about it was the candy apple red color of the framework.

When Sean was convinced she was not simply trying to save him money, he paid for it and gave the clerk instructions for delivery. He had the feeling the type of bike she chose told him more about the lady than she would willingly reveal. Perhaps beneath her conservative black-and-white exterior, there was a little candy apple red dying to get out.

The restaurant he had chosen was not the big, family type, nor could it strictly be termed cozy and romantic. A white tree trimmed with blue and silver ornaments—the traditional south Florida Chanukkah bush—had been added to the lobby, all the help had on Santa Claus hats, and the planters surrounding the booth they were seated in were filled with bright red silk poinsettas. As soon as they had both ordered, she was ready to get on with what they had come here for.

"Well now, Mayor O'Grady, as . . ."

"Sean. Call me Sean or I don't have to listen."

She narrowed her eyes at him. "You didn't say there were any conditions to our discussion."

He raised an eyebrow at her. "I didn't say there weren't either."

"I see. All right . . . Sean. As I told you, there are several issues facing Coral City that I'm very concerned about."

"Another condition is that you must wait until after we've finished our dinner. Political discussions tend to flatten the taste of a good meal."

"Hmmm. Are there any other conditions I should know about?" The light from the hurricane candle on their table gave his eyes a silvery glint. His mouth wasn't smiling, but his eyes said he was definitely thinking of something humorous.

"I'll let you know as I think of them. Tell me about yourself. Do you usually fill every minute of every day with some kind of activity?"

She shrugged. "I've never thought about it like that. I do whatever has to be done. The police department needed a crossing guard at that busy intersection for an hour in the morning and the afternoon, and no one applied. So I offered to do it. By spending time in the boys' classes, I always know how they're progressing. My volunteer work at church is a way of paying back what the church provides for us. The neighborhood boys wanted to be Cub Scouts, but none of the other parents had the time . . ."

"So naturally, you offered to be the den leader. Do you ever do anything for Angel?"

"Well, certainly I do," she answered defensively. "I have my business."

"Oh, yes, Becky mentioned that. Are you going to tell me or should I start guessing?"

The silver glints flickered again. Was it a telltale sign that he was suppressing his mirth? What kind of business could he be thinking she had? "I make hair ornaments called Angel's Haloes. You know, ponytail holders, headbands, barrettes, and so on. I converted the laundry room into my work area."

Sean shook his head. "I don't know how you find the time for all of it."

"I make the ornaments while the kids are in school or after they're in bed. A few stores are regular customers now, so there isn't much selling involved; except for the occasional craft show. Actually, it's just a matter of being very organized. Warren was a stickler for organization."

"Your husband?" When she nodded, curiosity nudged him. "How did he . . . Sorry. You don't have to talk about him."

"No. It's not so difficult anymore. He died of a heart attack a little over two years ago. He was quite a bit older than me, and after the children were born . . . well, he worked much too hard, and . . . it was all too much."

Sean could hear remnants of sorrow and something else he couldn't quite identify. Thinking to comfort her, he reached over the table and placed his hand over hers.

The heat of his touch shocked her so much that she jerked her hand away from his and right into the full wineglass at her place. Pink liquid splashed all over the white tablecloth between them. Without missing a beat, Angel moved the candle aside, sopped up the extra liquid with her linen napkin and continued the conversation as if nothing unusual had happened.

Sean started to signal to the waiter, but stopped as he realized she would probably rather not have more attention drawn to her. He righted her glass, refilled it, then handed her his unused napkin. "Losing a loved one is never easy."

The quiet way he said the words let Angel know they were expressed from personal experience. She couldn't help but recall what Becky had said about his fiancée dying.

In between courses he asked her about what sports the boys played and how they did in school. She never had any trouble talking about her children.

"Josh and Jeff are doing fine now that the school agreed to let them remain in the same class. Normally they split twins, especially identical ones, but mine became so withdrawn and uncooperative when they were separated, the principal agreed to make an exception. Twins are unique children and should be treated as such. I'm certain they read each other's thoughts, even if they're not aware of it yet. They fight, like all kids do, but they're also extremely close. Outsiders rarely come between them.

"Christopher's the one I worry about. He gets straight A's, excels in every sport, and seems to get along with other children. But he doesn't smile very often. I'm afraid he really believes Warren left him in charge of the family."

"Has he told you that?"

"Not in those exact words. He won't talk about his father at all. I keep hoping the day will come when he'll want to share his feelings with me."

Sean's forehead creased with concern. Remembering how hard Vicky's and Shamus's deaths were for him to accept as an adult, he could not fathom how little Christopher felt about losing his father. "Maybe something will happen to force him to express his feelings. If not, you may want to consider counseling."

Angel's chin lifted defensively. "My child does not need counseling. He just needs time and a lot of love."

Sean knew when to defuse a bomb. "We would probably all be better off with a little of that remedy. It's a shame you didn't have one girl. I'll bet three boys can really keep you on your toes!"

Mollified, she entertained him with a few of her favorite kid stories, but she remained prepared to change the subject to politics the moment he swallowed his last bite. When he ordered coffee for them both, she excused herself "to powder her nose."

She was congratulating herself for only spilling one glass of wine and not getting a single drop of food on her white blouse, until she caught sight of herself in the mirror. There, in the center of her forehead was the biggest, bluest golf ball she had ever seen.

All through dinner Sean's gaze had skittered around the room or focused on his food. She had wondered why he kept asking her questions yet didn't meet her eyes when she answered. Now she knew he had been doing his best *not* to look at her. He probably would have burst out laughing.

Darn. The eels were back, and on a full stomach too. It didn't matter. She intended to say her piece, he would take her home, and this whole night could be forgotten.

Weaving her way back to their table, she reviewed the points that needed to be covered. Her thoughts took flight when a young waitress stepped into her path carrying a huge tray of dirty dishes.

"Excuse me," the girl blurted out at the same instant Angel bumped her arm. Glasses jiggled. Plates rattled. But the waitress's excellent balance prevented a disaster. Angel was about to heave a sigh of relief when the girl directed her attention to the floor.

As Angel's gaze followed the waitress's, she noticed several patrons turning their heads away from her. Then she saw the reason for the furtive smiles. Caught on her high heel and trailing behind her was at least ten feet of toilet tissue. The withheld sigh escaped now, but it was one of pure exasperation. She bent over, removed the tissue from her shoe, and balled it all up as quickly as possible. Dropping the tissue on the tray, she thanked the waitress as she continued on her way.

One look at O'Grady's mouth working hard not to smile told her he had witnessed this latest embarrassment. She wondered if there could ever be a fitting comment for such a situation, and decided denial was still her only reasonable option. Sliding into the booth, she cleared her throat and began her prepared speech.

"Mayor . . . Sean, you did promise that I—"

"I'm all ears."

His smile looked real, but his eyes still didn't meet hers. They focused on her mouth instead. Angel found that rather unsettling, and when he leaned toward her, she automatically inched back a bit and straightened her spine.

"There are two issues I wanted to talk to you about. I will admit that I may not have been as involved in the local politics as I should be. However, I do know I don't like what I see happening to Coral City.

"The development of vacant land is an atrocity. There should be much stricter controls on what is being built and where. Someone broke ground last week for another shopping center, but the new one two blocks away is still half empty. And those little matchbox houses on the corner of Shelton Road are bound to bring the market value of the community down. You're letting the developers do whatever they please with this town. I realize construction is your business, but I don't think that should affect your decisions."

She took his serious expression and slow nod as understanding, if not agreement, and went on. "Also, the children desperately need a neighborhood sports field." His head tilted a bit and his one brow lifted, as if with curiosity, but the silver glints in his eyes had turned to shards of glass. "Well?"

"Well, what?" he asked in a flat tone of voice.

"What do you have to say?"

Sean stroked an imaginary beard on his chin. "Let's see. As to your complaint about the development, I'll have to give you a brief lecture on city planning. Thirty-three years ago a master plan was laid out for Coral

City. Parcels of land were designated for certain uses at that time.

"If a developer buys a piece of property that has an existing commercial zoning, the city cannot prevent him from building a shopping center on it. We can only discourage him by charging a prohibitive fee for the additional impact that the new construction will have on the city's utilities. We do have the power to turn down a request to *change* a zoning on a parcel, and if you had taken the time to investigate the matter, you would have learned that the present council has not approved a single variance request that would have increased the development originally intended."

Angel felt her cheeks flush. As an interested citizen, she should have known how the system worked. She swallowed hard and made herself meet his eyes. "Oh," she said softly, her embarrassment evident, but it didn't spare her from the rest of his lecture.

"Realizing just how uninformed you really are, I should probably ignore your insinuations against me personally, but why stop now?"

His voice had raised a notch with annoyance. Angel glanced around, but all she saw were plants, and diners concentrating on their meals. She wondered if anyone would notice if she simply slid under the table and crawled out of the restaurant.

"Please note that the mayor is a voting member of the city council. I am *not* omnipotent. What powers we have were given us by the voters . . . like yourself. And lastly, I am not required to do this, but in order to prevent anyone from accusing me of a conflict of interest,

Shamrock Construction *never* bids on a job within the city limits.

"The mayoral election is in March. If you have any other questions about my record or my platform for re-election between now and then, please don't hesitate to ask. Now, unless there's some other accusation you want to sling at me, I'd just as soon call it a night."

Already having paid the check, he slid out of the booth. His manners prohibited him from walking out ahead of her, but he didn't bother to offer her his assistance as she rose.

The drive back to her house seemed endless. A thunderstorm had erupted outside, but the tension crackling between the two people inside the car competed with that of the lightning. Neither attempted to speak until they were parked in Angel's driveway.

"I apologize," she said as he turned toward her. "I do things like that all the time—get worked up over something, then go off half-cocked without always having all the facts. I should know better by now, but . . ." She shrugged, not able to think of a reasonable explanation. "I'm sure you've been a very good mayor, and I'll probably vote for you again in March. Thank you for the bicycle. And dinner." As she fumbled for the door handle, he slid to the center of the bench seat. Capturing her hand in his, he halted her exit.

"Wait," he said softly, much too close to her ear. "You'll get drenched. It'll probably slow down in a minute and I want to say something." And he meant to, but he couldn't think of anything except how good she smelled. Her face turned toward his, and a flash of lightning revealed more than a hint of nervousness in her big dark eyes.

Give it up, me boyo. Ya've wanted a taste since first ya seen 'er.

A roar of thunder muffled Angel's gasp as Sean's lips touched hers. A kiss was totally unexpected, completely inappropriate. He must have thought the same thing, because he abruptly pulled back and scrutinized her face as if it were the first time he had seen her.

Angel felt the hand that had been holding hers graze its way up her arm, stroke her cheek, and cup her neck. The masculine eyes that had shown momentary confusion softened and warmed in their appraisal of her. Angel wondered at the heaviness filling her body, preventing her from doing the rational thing. *Move,* her mind demanded. *Stay,* her body argued. *Again,* her eyes requested.

He complied.

Where his mouth pressed to hers a tingling sensation began as a spark and intensified as it coursed through her limbs and exploded in her fingertips. To ease the odd feeling, she molded her hands to his shoulders and soon found it got even better when she stroked his neck and hair. His lips slanted over hers and she tucked her head in his arm to accommodate them both.

An unfamiliar liquid heat energized and drained her at the same time. The desire to explore, to discover more, overcame any last remnants of rationality. She just wanted to feel all there was to feel. Immediately.

His tongue begged access, and she granted it without hesitation. When his hands moved over her, too urgently to do more than relay his need to get past the barriers to bare flesh, she dragged one knee up over his lap. A murmur of approval escaped her throat as his fingers slid beneath her skirt to caress her stocking-covered thigh.

Flash! The high-intensity security light over the garage door glared through the car's windshield like an evil eye, and Angel's sanity returned with a jolt. Sean's took a few seconds longer.

"Good heavens," she whispered, then repeated the words with considerably more volume as she pushed against his chest.

"Angel . . ." His palm teased the outside of her thigh on its way out from under her skirt.

She couldn't think of anything intelligent to excuse her incredible behavior, so she did the only thing she could think of—escape. Oblivious to the pouring rain, she shoved the car door open and bolted out. But she didn't get far. Her high heel caught on the seat belt strap and broke off with a loud crack. The sudden release of her trapped foot threw her off-balance, hurtling her forward like a rock from a slingshot. The next second she was facedown in the soggy grass.

By the time Sean reached her, she was back on her feet, holding the remains of the shoe in one hand. Soaked to the skin and smeared with dirt and leaves, she lacked the energy to stop Sean from helping her hobble to her front door.

The door flew open as they approached. Seven pairs of eyes stared at her in shock until Christopher broke away from the group. With all the strength his seventy-eight-pound body could muster, he walloped Sean in the stomach.

"You creep! What'd you do to my mom?"

3

Angel switched on the lamp next to her bed, then picked up the novel she had started the previous night. Sleep was clearly out of the question.

After convincing everyone that she had merely had another little accident, she had sent Sean and Becky on their respective ways.

Becky's curiosity would have to wait until daylight to be satisfied . . . after Angel figured out what had happened herself. And Christopher! He shouldn't have hit Sean, but should she punish him for being protective of her?

Of course, Christopher's attack hadn't been nearly as awful as her own. Even if she had been justified, which she now knew she hadn't been, her disapproval of Sean could have been voiced in a more cautious, tactful way. But those two adjectives had never been associated with Angelina Santieri Chadick. Words like impetuous, hot-tempered, and passionate suited her much better.

Passionate? She mulled the word over in her mind. Yes, she had always considered herself passionate when it came to a cause she believed in. When she cared about something, energy built up inside her like a volcano until it spewed the fire and lava from her system.

Unfortunately, fire and lava burn. Usually she only hurt herself, in the form of embarrassment or little mishaps, but occasionally someone else got singed. In those cases she always made a sincere apology immediately after she regained her composure . . . as she had with Sean.

Was it a crime to care so much about her community that she felt passionate about it?

Passionate. Her Italian heritage strikes again. She doubted that either of her parents would willingly accept responsibility for her ludicrous behavior in Sean's car. Perhaps the evil spirit of some demented nymphomaniac had taken over her body. There, now that's rational thinking. She could write the mayor a letter and explain that supernatural forces had been at work.

She would have liked to put the blame entirely on him; he started it. But she not only encouraged him, she had been all over him like a kid let loose in a toy store. How could she have done that? She didn't even know the man.

What she did know was that he made her lose control, and that made her extremely uncomfortable. One didn't have a lifestyle like hers without a tremendous amount of discipline. When one was juggling as many responsibilities as she, one couldn't afford to relax even for a second, or else everything would come tumbling down at once.

Chemistry—it was the only possible answer. Naturally, she had heard, and read, about the phenomenon, but firsthand experience had eluded her all these years. Never would she have imagined that it could indiscriminately strike its victims without any prior warning, nor did she realize it could transform a straitlaced mommy into a world-class hussy. Out of a lifetime of little embarrassments, this was the first one she was certain she would never overcome.

What she had felt with Warren was the way it *should* be between a husband and wife: comfortable, secure, respectful. One month after Angel graduated from high school, she and a girlfriend declared their independence. Suffering through countless New York winters helped them select Fort Lauderdale as their destination. Within a week they had secretarial jobs and an apartment outside the resort city.

Warren Chadick, the senior vice president of a national credit card company, was her first boss, her first male friend, and a year later, her first, and only, husband. He was a dynamic businessman who regularly put in seventy-hour work weeks. She was a bright, highly skilled whirlwind who found him and his work more interesting than the dating scene her roommate endorsed.

When Warren's wife divorced him, his friendship with Angel flowed beyond the office. She was nineteen and he, forty-five, when they married. Stress and chain-smoking had begun to take its toll on him even then. His once auburn hair was nearly all gray and worry lines permanently marred his pale complexion.

Angel gave him her virginity as a wedding gift, not so much because she had carefully protected it for her future husband, but because none of the boys she had dated during her teens had stirred any desire in her.

For that matter, neither had Warren. From the beginning their relationship was built on respect and friendship. That didn't change too drastically after they shared a bedroom . . . except on Saturday night. Then, after the lights were out, Warren would occasionally join her in her twin bed for five or ten minutes.

Though he had no desire to father more children since his were grown, he knew how much Angel wanted them, and he wanted to give Angel everything she desired. Although their couplings were neither frequent nor earth-shattering, they were effective. Christopher arrived two years after their wedding day and, as planned, she had her tubes tied following the twins' birthday eighteen months later. After that, Warren shared her bed less and less often, and she hadn't given that more than a fleeting thought. Their life had seemed so perfect, until the morning Warren didn't wake up when the alarm clock went off.

The encounter with Sean O'Grady explicitly demonstrated another way she had been less than an ideal wife for Warren. She had never stirred his passion. Discovering she was capable of acting like a sex maniac with a virtual stranger made her more aware than ever of how selfish she had been.

Had she been as considerate of him as he always was of her, if she hadn't added to his stress by having three rambunctious children, perhaps he would still be alive. She couldn't go back and change what had happened, but she couldn't seem to get rid of the guilt either.

Sean truly did not want to rehash the events of the past hours. Why bother? None of it had happened. Someone like Angel Chadick didn't exist in real life. All evening he had expected to see a cameraman filming the situation comedy they must have been acting out.

He couldn't remember anyone ever putting him through such a kaleidoscope of emotions in so brief a time span. Even without Shamus's imaginary goading, he would have had a devil of a time maintaining his mature, gentlemanly image. It had been a monumental struggle not to laugh out loud at her *little* accidents, to argue at the top of his lungs over her twisted, uninformed opinions . . . to share hot, urgent sex with her in the back seat of his car.

The trouble was, she made him want to do it all over again!

Shamus watched his grandson tossing and turning on his bed and smiled. Finally. It had taken a lot of energy to whip up that thunderstorm, but it had been worth it.

Sean and Angelina had kissed. The rest would be a walk in the park!

"You turned him down? How could you!" Becky made it sound as though Angel had betrayed all of womankind with her refusal.

Angel tried her best to meet her friend's glare of disapproval, but ended up watching Rolf's tail slap the kitchen floor. "I can't imagine why he even called this morning. After last night he should have had his fill of the entire Chadick family. I certainly have no intention of going through that kind of torture again. It was the most humiliating experience I have ever had. And for me, that's saying a lot. Anyway, wouldn't I have appeared too available if I had been free for dinner again tonight?"

"Hmmph. I can almost understand you putting him off for the next couple of weeks because of Christmas, but what was your excuse for New Year's Eve?"

"I promised the boys they could each have a friend sleep over."

"I'd bet my grocery money the boys haven't heard that good news yet. Listen, kiddo, playing hard to get is fine when you're twenty, but . . ."

"Ha! Listen to yourself. The other day I was at my peak at thirty-one, and today I'm too old to turn down a date."

Becky clucked her tongue. "Not just any date. Sean O'Grady is, oh, never mind. If you can't see what a catch he is, nothing I say is going to open your eyes. Since you're so indifferent to his charms, how about letting me enjoy them secondhand. I demand a minute-to-minute account. *Something* good must have happened."

"After your cute little joke box, you don't have the right to demand anything." She shook her head in disgust. "Let's just say it went downhill from there, and I don't want to recall a single minute of it."

Angel may not have wanted to recall any of her encounter with Sean O'Grady, but he simply refused to stay out of her head no matter what she was doing. It didn't help matters that he called again on Sunday afternoon.

"How's the busiest lady in Coral City?" he asked as if they were old friends.

"Up to my elbows in ribbons and lace and hours away from completing an order I promised to deliver by tomorrow morning," she answered in an equally friendly, but hurried tone.

"I thought I'd check your schedule again. Any chance you're free this evening?"

"No. Sorry."

"Then how about tomorrow night? I'd like to take you to dinner and *not* talk politics. I'll pay for a sitter for the boys."

Angel took a deep breath. "I'm sorry. I can't."

"Angel? Are you seeing someone?"

"No," she responded quickly, surprised that he leapt to that conclusion, but it helped her come up with her excuse. "No, it's not that, really. I'm afraid I'm just not . . . comfortable about . . . going out. I still . . . well, Warren . . . and then Christopher gets so upset . . . I just can't. I hope you understand."

Understand? He hadn't understood a single thing since he met her, but he recognized rejection when it hit him between the eyes. "Sure. I was only trying to make up for causing you so much . . . *discomfort*. Don't forget the city council meeting Tuesday night. If you can rearrange your Cub Scouts for one night, maybe you'll pick up something interesting."

Angel waited for the relief to wash over her after she hung up. He wouldn't be calling anymore. She wouldn't have to jump every time the phone rang. There would be no more fretting that he might talk her into being alone with him. Wasn't that terrific?

When it took her more than a heartbeat to answer herself, she decided that, although she wanted to attend a council meeting, maybe she would wait until January, or February. Or after the election. Sometime after the memory of his hand beneath her skirt stopped making her blush.

Good, Sean told himself. She's definitely not interested. I can get on with my life. Before he even finished the thought he imagined hearing Shamus's sarcastic retort to that.

Not interested, ya say? That's a wee bit 'ard ta believe.

How could she not be interested? Kissing her had been all the proof he'd needed to know that his attraction to her was out of the ordinary. There was so much chemistry between them, it was a wonder his car hadn't blown up.

But damned if he was going to beg. He would simply have to put her out of his mind.

Shamus rubbed his chin through his thick gray beard. Obviously, understanding the way a colleen's mind works wasn't one of the powers granted him when he became an angel. The kiss had been enough to push Sean into the proper frame of mind, but not Angelina.

It looked like a bit more meddling was called for after all. Considering the fact that there were only twelve days left till Christmas—twelve more days to take advantage of his extended powers and Gabriel being too busy to watch him every second—Shamus knew he had to come up with a humdinger of a plan.

But what more could he do?

Like a bit o' magic, he recalled the political discussion the couple had had over dinner, and an idea popped into his head. All he had to do was whisper a few words in the right ears. . . .

"We need a show of support from the parents. Please, Angel, say you'll be there."

Angel sighed. Perhaps it was time to enroll in a "How to Say No" class. This was hardly the first time the president of the Parent-Teachers' Association had asked for help, but it was the first time she needed to refuse.

"I'm sorry, Pam. I have the Cub Scouts tomorrow night."

"No problem. The boys can earn a badge in civic awareness or something. Get their parents to meet you with their boys at city hall. The issue isn't on the agenda, but if enough of us are there the mayor won't be able to ignore us. We want some answers."

Angel knew her priorities. The children's welfare always came before her own fears. She couldn't say no, as usual. "All right. I'll bring the troop." She disconnected, then started making the necessary calls.

She would attend, but this time, Angel swore she would get all the facts before she opened her mouth. No one, especially not His Honor, was going to accuse her of being uninformed again.

"Shamus! Is that your doing?"

Shamus smiled innocently. "Why, Sara, me darlin'. You're lookin' lovely t'night."

"Don't try to charm me, you old rascal. I've been working for a month to give my granddaughter Pam a peaceful Christmas, and you've gone and gotten her involved in another cause. That vacant land issue wasn't supposed to come up until late January."

"Now ya know as well as me that your Pammy is happiest when she's all stirred up over somethin', an' ya've got me solemn word that the whole thing will be over with afore Christmas gets here." He hung his head in shame. "I know 'twas wrong, but I couldna come up wit' another way ta get me grandson a sweetheart. I guess I'm just an old romantic fool."

Sara clucked her tongue at him, but her expression softened. "All right. You're forgiven. This time."

Shamus partially lifted his head to peek at her. "Then ya won't be tellin' Gabriel what I done?"

"No," she said, then grinned. "But you owe me one, you old coot."

Tuesday night, seven of her twelve scouts showed up with their parents at city hall. Pam's telephone network had been so effective, Angel's group had to stand along the back wall. She wished she could have sat, preferably behind a very large person. Perhaps he wouldn't notice her. In her sneakers she was barely five foot two, and she could scrunch down a little more. Besides, it was a fairly large room; maybe he was nearsighted.

She heard his voice calling the meeting to order and decided to hazard a glance toward the raised platform in the front of the room, while he was busy doing whatever mayors do. The only acknowledgement to the season in the entire hall was a garland of plastic holly tacked onto the front of the dais.

As the reading of the minutes droned on, she took the opportunity to study the people who represented her and made a startling discovery. All four members of the council were over the age of sixty. Sean was younger, but had no wife or children. How could these people understand the needs of a young family?

Her gaze clung to the one person she had intended to ignore. Why did he have to be so darn good to look at? The floodlights illuminating the dais also enhanced the paler streaks in his thick blond hair. The somber dark suit he wore was tempered by a powder blue dress shirt and a handsome tie. He had the kind of lean build that carried a suit well. When her wicked mind automatically progressed to thoughts of how those shoulders had felt beneath her hands, she forced her eyes back to his face.

He was intently listening to the city manager's report, and his head was turned to the side. What a marvelous profile. He could have been a model. She couldn't tell from that distance whether his tanned face was freshly shaved, but she recalled the light brush of stubble against her throat when he . . .

Caught! His gaze latched on to hers and clung with velvet hooks. One eyebrow raised, an imperceptible nod of his head . . . Was he greeting or taunting her? She felt a wave of dizziness sweep over her, and realized she had forgotten to breathe. Inhaling sharply was her next mistake. He couldn't possibly have seen the movement, but his slow grin implied he had. His ego must thoroughly relish the knowledge that he could unnerve her so easily.

For over an hour Angel managed to avoid looking at Sean and concentrate on the proceedings. The boys applauded the part where one of their classmates received an award for the best bicycle safety poster. The endless series of variance and business license requests, however, had them begging to go home.

She sensed his gaze return to her again and again, but only verified her instincts once. When she did, the same light-headed feeling filled her. It had to be a trick of some kind. He was sending suggestive messages with his eyes and making her think about . . . about things that didn't belong in her head while her children fidgeted at her side.

Finally the floor was opened to any other new business and Pam popped up with hers.

"Mayor O'Grady, we heard a large piece of property has been deeded to the city. Would you tell us what plans have been made for its disposition?"

He smiled and turned his sexy eyes on the PTO president. "Your information sources have beaten me to the punch again, Mrs. Kaplan. But it's a bit premature. For those people who haven't heard about the land grant, let me give you some background. Last year we passed a resolution regarding new development in Coral City. Because of the impact that additional residences or businesses have on the city's utilities and services, the developer must now pay a fee. The expenditure of that fee must go toward public improvement.

"In the case of the developer that recently broke

ground for a shopping plaza, we agreed—just yesterday—to accept a parcel of undeveloped land in lieu of a portion of the fee due. The members of this council haven't had time for more than a preliminary discussion, but the land will probably be best utilized as a passive park, leaving most of the property untouched."

Angel pressed her clenched fists to her sides. She wanted to speak out, but her vow not to open her mouth again until she had all the facts, combined with not wanting to bring his attention back to her, kept her silent. Thankfully, one of Pam's other supporters picked up the ball.

"I heard the property contains over ten acres, more than enough for a sports field. We already have one passive park. The people, the *children,* of Coral City need a field much more."

A third parent stood without being called on. "Right now they have to be driven all the way over to Petrie to share their facilities. Both towns have grown so much that scheduling the fields there for games for all the teams has become next to impossible. Just because children can't vote doesn't mean you should ignore their needs."

Voices of approval rose around the room, but Angel could hear the grumbles of dissension as well. She surveyed the dais and was dismayed to see the elderly council members frowning and shaking their heads. It looked like they had already decided firmly against a sports field. Mayor O'Grady's smile remained fixed, but Angel felt certain his mind was already made up as well.

When the noise level in the room rose to deafening proportions, the mayor pounded his gavel, then said. "I see this is going to be more sensitive than we anticipated. If the council agrees, I suggest we hold an open forum on this issue. A public notice will be posted and the forum can take place at the end of January's regular council meeting. Mrs. Kaplan, you'll recruit one person to present the case for the sports field, I'm sure I'll find someone to do the same regarding the passive park."

The meeting was adjourned soon afterward, and Angel herded the boys outside without another glance toward the dais. She had a lot to consider, like how she could actively support the group demanding a sports field without having to be in the same room with Sean O'Grady.

Sean lost sight of her dark hair amidst the sea of taller exiting citizens. Had he honestly thought he could simply forget her? How could he possibly forget a woman who could put him in a semiaroused state from across a roomful of people? Her passion had literally reached out and excited him. He had felt her straining to get on her soapbox. Why had she held back? Surely their encounter hadn't frightened her speechless. Impossible. There had to be another reason for her reticence.

Mayhaps ya were roit afore. She's just not interested in ya.

Sean flinched as though someone had just elbowed him in the side. He had imagined hearing Shamus's voice from time to time since the dear man's passing, but lately it had seemed like he was standing right beside him full-time.

Not interested, huh? He had willed her to look at him throughout the meeting, but she had done a fair job of pretending she didn't notice. After the first visual contact, he knew her avoidance of him was not due to lack of interest. She practically devoured him with her eyes.

So, what d'ya 'tend to do aboot it?

One thing was certain. He couldn't let it drop just because she wasn't *comfortable* around him. Hell, comfortable wasn't the way she made him feel either, but their mutual discomfort took them each in opposite directions. At the very least he believed they should spend one more evening together to see if they had anything more in common than spontaneous combustion. And if the next date should head in the same explosive direction the first had, he would make sure they were somewhere a lot less cramped and infinitely more private.

He would call and politely ask her out once more. If she refused again, well, he'd simply have to launch a campaign to wear her down.

By noon the next day, he had her refusal.

"Why not?" he asked merely to hear what excuse she would come up with this time.

"I already told you."

"I didn't like that explanation. Are you afraid of me?"

"Don't be ridiculous."

"Then meet me for lunch. Someplace full of people, completely unromantic. We need to talk."

All she could think of was how little the roomful of people had mattered the night before. "No."

"We'll talk politics, I promise."

"You've used that promise already, Mayor. I really don't have time to talk now. I have an order to get ready."

"You know, Angel, maybe I just need a clearer explanation about why you don't want to go out with me. Tell me that you can't stand talking to me and that kissing me completely turned you off, and I won't bother you again."

She tried. She opened her mouth to insist that she wasn't the least bit attracted to him, but lying had never been easy for her. All that came out was a frustrated sigh.

"All right, Angel. I accept your challenge."

"I am *not* challenging you. I just want you to stop calling me."

"I don't believe that. And I'll tell you something else you won't like to hear. You should have accepted the lunch invitation. Now I won't stop until I've gotten everything I want."

"What are you talking about?" Angel's voice sounded far braver than she felt.

"Surrender, Angel. Total, unconditional surrender. And that's a promise you can count on." He let the receiver drop into its cradle. He hadn't planned to be so melodramatic, but she may as well have thrown her gauntlet at his feet. He felt the adrenaline pumping through his system and laughed to himself. Damned if he wasn't having the most fun he'd had in ages.

During his college years, he discovered he had a strong aptitude for political science, with a particular fascination for analyzing successful campaigns. Running for mayor of a small town had not taken a genius of campaign strategy, but the knowledge remained with him.

Angel had initially thought she didn't like him because of his record as mayor, but she had admitted being wrong about that. She said she didn't want to go out with him, but she couldn't deny that she had liked his kisses. If he could seduce her into his arms again, he was certain she would also admit she was wrong about not dating him.

'Ave ya considered a good old-fashioned blind side, Mr. Know-It-All wit' your fancy education?

Not a bad thought. He knew most of her crazy schedule. He just had to figure out which activity he could infiltrate.

Angel hustled her boys out to the car as soon as the dinner dishes were cleared away that evening.

Within ten minutes of walking in the house after the meeting last night, Pam Kaplan had called. She was having a meeting the next evening at her house to help organize a campaign for the sports field and she knew Angel would want to be involved.

Pam's living room was already packed with supporters when Angel and her boys arrived.

"Oh, good!" Pam exclaimed when she saw her. "Now we can get started. Boys, go on to the family room. The kids are having some sort of video game contest." That was all they had to hear to leave their mother's side. Pam called the impromptu gathering to order a few seconds later.

"For any of you who missed last night's meeting, let me review the situation."

Angel had never mastered the art of speaking in front of large groups, so she truly admired how Pam held everyone's attention and spoke with such authority. In no time, she had given a summary of the land deal, mapped out a strategy, and asked for volunteers to work on various committees.

This being such an emotional issue, hands immediately went up to help with door-to-door canvassing and telephone calls. There were petitions to be drawn up and signatures to be solicited, research to be done to acquire solid statistics, and someone had to get the information into the newspaper.

Angel repeatedly raised her hand, but Pam passed her over every time. She began to wonder why Pam had even asked her to come if she didn't want her help on any of the committees. And she definitely wanted to help. Not only because of the strong need for a sports field, but also because it was the opposite of what Mayor Sean O'Grady wanted.

After his nonsensical call that day, she kept trying to think of what she could say or do to convince him to leave her alone.

"Well, Angel, what do you say? Will you do it?"

Angel blinked at Pam. What had she been asked to do?

"Someone has to do it. And it should be someone with a familiar, friendly face, like the city's favorite crossing guard. Someone who everyone likes, regardless of which side they're on. I'd do it, but I tend to rub some people the wrong way."

That caused a ripple of jovial laughter throughout

the room which turned into encouragement for Angel to accept the job.

"What exactly would I need to do?" she asked cautiously, hoping no one could guess she'd been daydreaming.

"Just be your concerned, caring, passionate self. Everyone else will do the legwork and gather statistics. I'm sure someone would be glad to help you prepare the actual speech." Several voices instantly offered their assistance. "You see? All you'd have to do is be the official spokesperson for the group and present our case at the next council meeting."

Angel's eyes widened in shock. "*Spokesperson?* I'd have to get up in front of everyone and talk?"

Everyone in the room seemed to think she was the perfect choice . . . except her. She wanted to help, she really did, but wasn't there something else she could do? Something less noticeable? Pam's usage of the word *passionate* echoed in her ears. Lately, that personality trait was getting her in more trouble than usual.

Suddenly it occurred to her that if she could overcome her fear of public speaking, this would be the ideal way to turn off the persistent mayor. He couldn't possibly want anything personal to do with the spokesperson of the group going against him on such an important issue.

Without giving it another thought, she announced, "I'll do it."

4

Angel didn't normally work on Saturday morning. At least one of her boys always seemed to have a sports event at that time, and she felt it was important that she always be there to cheer them on. It may have been different if their father were alive. He might have gotten interested in their activities now that they were older. *May have. Might have.*

She shook her head and sighed. Warren had been on her mind a lot lately . . . ever since a certain someone's hand had crept under her skirt. She gave her head another shake. "Enough!" she said aloud.

The reason she was at home instead of at Chris's soccer game was because of the large order she had unexpectedly received from a ladies' accessory shop at the mall. If Angel's Haloes did well there, it could mean a lot more orders. Although Warren had left them comfortably fixed, she wanted to be self-sufficient. It was a matter of pride, and neither memories of Warren nor thoughts of that other man were going to distract her from getting her work done.

She heard Rolf barking several seconds before the doorbell rang. She considered pretending she wasn't home, since she normally wouldn't have been, but that would have been like telling a lie. Besides, it could be a neighbor who just needed to borrow something.

"Quiet down, Rolf," she ordered as she walked to the door and pushed the big dog out of her way. His tail was wagging happily, and his bark had been one of recognition. She didn't hesitate to open the door.

"Good morning," Sean said with a wide grin.

Angel frowned and made a mental note not to trust Rolf's barks and tail wags ever again. A lifetime of good manners forced her to reply, but not to smile. "Good morning." She kept one hand on the door and stood in the opening, the way she would if he were a stranger.

Sean recognized the defensive stance and wondered again if he could be mistaken about the mutual attraction.

Not a chance, laddie. Git on wit' it.

"I heard you're going to be the spokesperson for the group in favor of the sports field."

"That's right," Angel said stiffly, without opening the door any wider or moving aside to let him in.

"After the meeting Tuesday, I got to thinking that it wasn't really fair for the council members to have access to more information than the concerned parents. I decided right then that I would make a point of passing along any facts we have to the parents' spokesperson, whoever that turned out to be. Since that person is you, I just thought I could stop by and discuss the matter with you this morning."

Angel grimaced. She needed all the ammunition she could get to help their cause. What if he knew something that the sports field group didn't? "That's very considerate of you, Mayor. I'm listening."

He arched an eyebrow in disbelief. "Don't you think you could invite me in to talk?"

She had a few choices. She could tell him the truth—that she was all alone and didn't trust herself to be alone with him. Or she could lie—say she didn't care to hear what he had to say. Or she could let him in as if she were a mature adult, perfectly capable of controlling her emotions. "You're welcome to come in, but I'm filling a rush order at the moment. I need to get it done before the boys get home. Do you think we could talk in my workroom?"

"No problem," Sean replied with a smile, and stepped inside before she changed her mind. He gave Rolf a vigorous ear scratch that further endeared him to the Lab. "Where are the boys?"

"At Petrie's Sports Field. Chris is playing soccer, and Josh and Jeff went to watch. Of course, they had to be driven there, whereas if we had a field here in Coral City, they could have ridden their bikes to and from the game."

"Don't the parents go to watch the game anyway?" Sean asked, not grasping her point.

As soon as they arrived in the work area, she sat down in front of her table and motioned for him to take the metal folding chair Becky used when visiting. "No. Unfortunately, not all parents have the time or inclination. Under those circumstances, the children are cheated out of a chance to play because they don't have transportation."

"Car pools?" Sean suggested.

She shook her head. "The parents still have to be willing or able to drive every so often." She chose several narrow ribbons in varying shades of purple, nimbly tied them together in the middle with a wire, then squeezed a dollop of tacky glue onto a ceramic tile. As her fingers created a satin bouquet of rosettes and attached it to a plastic barrette, she reiterated the other points that had been made at the council meeting, such as the overcrowded schedule at the Petrie field.

Sean's gaze moved back and forth between her face and the hair ornament she was working on. She was fairly sure she was getting through to him, which should have given her a sense of confidence, but with each passing minute she was growing more nervous.

She shouldn't have brought him into her workroom. There simply wasn't enough air in there for two people. Becky was okay, but the room was much too small for someone his size. She finished the purple rose barrette and started on a mate for it. "Your turn," she said when he had no further questions on anything she'd related.

For a heartbeat he couldn't comprehend what it was his turn to do. He'd been intently watching her hands and fantasizing about having those talented fingers threaded through his hair again, roaming over his body and bringing parts of him alive the way she turned a few strips of ribbon and wire into a thing of intricate beauty.

"The way you do that is fascinating. Do you mind if I get a closer look?" Before she could refuse, he scooted his chair next to hers and leaned forward so that he could better watch each movement of her fingers.

She swallowed hard and did her best to keep working. His warm breath wafted over the back of her hand

and a smell that she already recognized as part Sean, part aftershave, filled her senses. Only the fact that she had made this particular barrette hundreds of times allowed her to finish it.

"Beautiful," he said, looking into her eyes. "Do another one."

Pride in her work had her choosing to create a more complicated bow, but his nearness was making her hands tremble. Twice, she had to start over.

"Would it help if I held this part together while you gather the other pieces?" he asked innocently as he wrapped his fingers around the part she was still holding. The movement brought his arm along hers, his chest against her shoulder, and his other arm casually moved to rest across the back of her chair.

Angel felt the temperature in the room increase by several degrees and fought to maintain her composure. "That's not necessary. I have a clip to do that." She picked one up and clamped it around the netting she'd been fumbling with. "I should have done that to begin with." She waited for him to ease his body back to a safer distance. He didn't. Instead, he turned her face toward his and moved even closer.

His mouth had almost touched hers when she jerked back from him. "I thought you came here to give me information."

Sean noted the flush on her cheeks and the way she licked her lips. "What are you afraid of, Angel?"

She straightened her shoulders, but only accomplished drawing his gaze to her T-shirt-covered breasts. "I'm not afraid. I told you, I'm not comfortable—"

"With dating. I know what you said, although I still

don't understand your reasoning. At any rate, I wasn't trying to *date* you just then, I was trying to kiss you."

"Why?" she asked, eyeing him suspiciously.

He wasn't sure what answer she expected to hear, so he stuck to the truth. "Why? Because kissing you once was too good not to repeat." The flush that had begun to fade came back to assure him she had thought the same thing, but her words contradicted what was in her eyes.

"I don't believe that's the reason at all. I . . . I believe you have a whole plethora of young, beautiful women you could call up who'd be glad to share kisses with you."

"A *plethora*?" he repeated with a chuckle.

"At least a plethora," she answered seriously. "You have to have some ulterior motive for pursuing some-one like me!"

He became as serious as she. "What do you mean 'someone like you?' "

She got back to busying her hands so that she didn't have to look at him as she spoke. "You know exactly what I mean."

"Sorry. I don't have a clue. The first time I saw you I thought you were attractive. Some weird things happened that night we went out, but I admired the way you handled yourself no matter what went wrong. Kiss-ing you turned me inside out. And now I know you're not only devoted to a whole *plethora* of worthy activi-ties, you're incredibly artistic as well. Why wouldn't I want to pursue someone like you?"

She clucked her tongue and took a slow, deep breath. "Because . . . because I'm such a *mom,* and you're such a . . . a *playboy*." That made him laugh, but her next accusation hit a nerve. "And I'm beginning to realize that you're an even smoother politician than I first thought. I see what this is about now. You didn't come here to give me information. You came to get it.

"Or worse, maybe you came here to seduce me into giving up the fight for the sports field. Either way, I haven't heard one word of helpful information from you, and you've been here for"—she looked up at the wall clock—"almost an hour!"

He opened his mouth to defend himself loud and hard, then closed it again as he realized what she'd just done so skillfully. When putting herself down didn't discourage him, she attacked him and effectively cooled his desire for another kiss. She was a rather smooth operator herself! He leaned back in the uncomfortable chair and crossed his arms. In a level voice, he said, "Considering the fact that you took up most of the hour to tell me your opinions, that accusation is completely unfair. I happen to have a lot of important information to share. But if you're going to get nasty, maybe I should keep it to myself."

Angel didn't trust him, but she didn't want to give up the chance to obtain vital facts either. "All right, prove you came here this morning with a legitimate purpose."

Sean considered kissing her a very legitimate purpose, but he held his tongue and mentally congratulated himself for turning a touchy situation back in his favor. He had half expected her to throw him out.

"Fine," he said, crossing one leg over the other and leaning forward a bit. "To begin with, it would behoove you to know that the primary argument against the sports field is the expense. A passive park could be left close to its natural state and would require minimal maintenance. A sports field would have to be created and constantly maintained. Bleachers, bathroom facilities, and a concession stand would have to be constructed.

"All of it would take full-time upkeep as well as management. That means employees on the city's payroll. Who's going to pay for all that? We have a large number of retirees on fixed incomes in this community who already resent paying school taxes when they haven't had children in school in twenty years. It wouldn't be fair to expect them to take on an additional tax burden for something else that would be strictly youth-oriented. We owe our elderly all the consideration we can give them."

Angel could see this was no rehearsed campaign speech of his. He truly felt very strongly about what he was saying. She listened to the rest of his arguments in favor of the passive park and made mental notes of points she'd have to discuss with Pam and the other parents. The expense was definitely a problem to which they'd have to address themselves.

When he had given her all the reasons he could think of not to have a sports field and told her what costs he was aware of, he sat back and crossed his arms again.

"Thank you very much," Angel said as graciously as she could after accusing him of trying to take advantage of her.

Giving her an *I-told-you-so* grin, he replied, "You're very welcome. And now that the business is out of the way"—he uncrossed his leg and leaned forward—"I think we need to settle another matter." He took the hair ornament out of her hand and set it carefully on the worktable. "Look at me, Angel."

What she wanted to do was run and hide in the bathroom again, but instead, she turned back to him.

"Why don't you want me to kiss you?"

The way he stared at her mouth caused such a flurry in her stomach it took her a second to answer. "Because kissing—the kind of kissing you do—leads to . . . other things. And I'm not ready for . . . *that*."

Again he sensed a half-truth, but this one he couldn't let stand. "I'll make you a deal, Angel. If you'll kiss me one more time, I promise I will not ask you for a date again until after the park issue is settled."

Angel's eyes opened in surprise. She didn't want to risk kissing him again, but the thought of him backing off for a whole month tempted her. Surely by then he would have lost interest in her. "Okay," she said on a sigh. "One kiss." When he made no move toward her, she angled her head at him.

"The deal I offered was for you to kiss me."

"Oh." She took a deep breath, leaned toward him, and pecked him on the mouth.

"Uh-uh. That doesn't count."

With a slight frown, she placed her lips on his and applied a little pressure.

"Sorry," he said. "Still not good enough."

Clucking her tongue, she determined to be done with this nonsense once and for all. She moved to the edge of her chair, wrapped her arms around his neck, and brought their mouths together with a vengeance.

She meant to make him sorry he bullied her into the kiss, sorry he didn't accept the peck and be gone. But the heat that had been slowly suffocating her since they'd entered the room, increased a hundredfold, engulfing them both in an all-consuming furnace of need.

She felt a surge of relief when he pulled her onto his lap and their bodies were no longer separated. But when his tongue swept her mouth, desire flamed hotter.

She couldn't keep still. Her hands needed to feel every inch of him. Her body craved more intimate contact. When his palm scraped up her denim-clad thigh, over her hip and stopped at her ribs, she moaned and shifted to invite him further, and he accepted with her next breath.

Sean knew he'd died and gone to heaven. And an Angel had taken him there. Her fingers were doing all the things he had fantasized about and more. Her mouth was sweeter and hungrier than he remembered. Her full breast filled his hand and seemed to beg for more attention. He wanted to be rid of the layers of clothes and to feel her skin against his, but he didn't dare take more than she was willing to give. He could only hope, for the sake of his mental and physical well-being, that she'd be more willing very soon.

"*Mom*! Hey, Mom, we won!"

Christopher's exuberant voice shattered the spell in the small workroom. It took Angel a mere heartbeat to jump off Sean's lap and back onto her own chair.

"Did you hear me?" Chris asked, skidding into the tiled room in his socks. His joyous smile vanished the instant he saw Sean. His expression darkened even more when he looked at his mother. "What's the matter? You look all funny."

Angel forced a smile despite how badly her insides were quaking. "Nothing's the matter, honey. Mayor O'Grady and I have been discussing the sports field I told you about."

"You said you couldn't come to the game because you had a big order to do." He turned and ran off before either adult could say a word.

Sean reached for Angel's hand, but she pulled it away. "Angel, I—"

"Just leave. Please."

Sean had no choice but to quietly accept her dismissal. On the way home he reviewed his strategy. Seduction was definitely effective in wearing down her defenses, but it was obviously going to take a lot more than hot kisses to convince her to let him into her life on a permanent basis.

For his part, that second kiss was more than enough to convince him to keep up his campaign. His heart might be a bit rusty from lack of use, but he still recognized all the symptoms of love when they were upon him.

This time, however, he wasn't going to wait until it was too late.

"Got any brilliant ideas, Shamus?"

Count on The Little People, me boyo. They always show up to help when an Irish lad's got 'imself a wee bit o' trouble.

Shamus watched Christopher run as fast as his young legs and stockinged feet could carry him, away from the house, across the street, and down the canal bank. Given time, the boy would adjust to the idea of his mother having another man in her life, but Shamus didn't have that much time. And it was very clear to Shamus that Angel would not accept Sean if her children didn't.

Luckily, the twins were ready and willing for a father figure to join their family, so he could concentrate on their older brother. He had tried whispering positive thoughts about Sean in Christopher's ear, but the boy was holding in too much resentment to hear him. It was quite obvious that he was going to have to pull out all the stops.

Shamus had never tried to assume corporeal form, but he had seen others do it, so he knew he could if the need was great enough. With his mind focused on his wish, he pictured himself as he was, before the illness robbed his health and his memory. It took much more energy than he'd expected, but a few seconds later, he was standing on the canal bank behind Christopher. He blinked and two fishing rods, already baited, appeared in his hand.

As Christopher hurled another rock into the water, Shamus said, " 'Tis much easier to catch a fish wi' one o' these." He sat down on the grass beside the boy and held one of the rods out to him.

Christopher looked sideways at him. *Never, ever talk to strangers,* his mother's voice echoed in his head. *And never accept a gift from them.*

He's just a lonesome old man looking for someone to talk to, another voice countered, and with it a sense of security flowed through his body.

"I don't know how to fish," Christopher admitted with a glance at the rod that said he wished he did.

"Nothin' to it," Shamus said and placed the rod in the boy's hand. Remembering the day he taught Sean to fish, Shamus gave Christopher his first lesson. They sat in comfortable silence for a while until Shamus felt the boy calming down.

"It must be mighty hard on ya," Shamus began.

Chris glanced up at him. "What do you mean?"

"Why, bein' ten years old and havin' the whole world on your shoulders." Chris gave him another suspicious look, so Shamus elaborated. "We old folks don't have much to do but gossip, and your ma's a purty well-known lady. 'Tis a pure shame, ya bein' so young an' ya've got ta take care of her, and those twins must be a handful."

"They're not so bad. They kinda look out for each other."

"But I'll bet ya still have ta keep an eye on 'em. Your ma's probably too busy to bother."

Chris turned and glared at Shamus. "My mom's never too busy for us. She does stuff for us all the time!"

"Oh?" Sean turned to face him. "And what do you do for her?"

"Lots of things. I help a lot. You can ask her."

"Because you're the man of the house, right?"

"Right."

"Why didn't your da ever take ya fishin'?"

He shrugged. "He had a very important job. He didn't have time for nonsense."

"Nonsense, ya say? Why, fishin's one o' the necessities in a man's life. Keeps us balanced, ya know."

Chris gawked at him. "It does?"

"Absolutely. Take my friend, Sean O'Grady. There's

not a man around with more responsibility, but he always finds time ta cast a line or two. I can't help but notice that face you're makin', laddie. 'Ave ya got somethin' sour in your stomach?"

"Naw. It's your friend that gives me a stomachache."

Shamus looked shocked. "Is that so? An' here I thought he was such a good man."

"He keeps botherin' my mom."

"Ah, I see. An' ya don't want your mom havin' no men round but you and your brothers, right?" Chris narrowed his eyes, and Shamus let him think about that for a moment. "Tell me, who's your best friend?"

"Scott," Chris answered easily.

"Okay. What if Scott moved away? Forever. Ya'd probably miss him a lot at first, and there'd never be anyone else ta take 'is place in exactly the same way. But sooner or later, ya'd get lonesome or bored and want ta find another friend ta keep ya company. Would ya not?"

"Maybe," Chris slowly admitted.

"Sure ya would. 'Tis the same for your ma. She needs ta make a new friend, one ta make up for the empty spot your da left." Shamus couldn't be certain he'd made his point, but at least Chris was listening. "Ya know, if your ma had a man friend, ya might git ta enjoyin' his company, too. 'Specially if he liked ta fish and go camping."

"Camping?" Chris asked with wide eyes. "My dad wouldn't take us camping. He said it was a waste of time."

"A waste of time, now, ya say? Why, if me friend the mayor heard that, 'e'd 'ave a foin argument wit' ya, 'e would."

"The mayor? You mean Mr. O'Grady likes to camp too?"

Shamus laughed as he felt the boy's interest rising. "Almost as much as 'e likes goin' ta Disney World." He felt his energy fading and knew he had to go. He reeled in his line and got to his feet. "It doesna look like the fish are bein' fooled by our bait t'day, so I think I'll be headin' home."

When Chris tried to give him back the rod, he waved him off. "Ya hold on ta it for now. I 'ave a feelin' ya'll git a lot more use oot o' it than I will."

"Wow, thanks," Chris said with surprise.

"But in return, I want ya ta think aboot something. If I was your da, sittin' up in heaven lookin' down on my family, I'd be wantin' ta see ya havin' some fun like a boy should instead o' actin' like a little old man. I'd know that ya hadn't forgotten me just 'cause ya be smilin' once in a while. An' I'd want your ma ta find a good man to keep her company, so she wouldn't be so lonely all the time."

"You think my mom's lonely even with all the people around her?"

"I know she is, boyo. An' if ya'll open your heart ta her needs, the way your da would 'ave, ya'll know she is, too." Shamus placed his hand on the top of Christopher's head and applied just a wee bit of pressure. "God bless ya, son. An' may the luck o' the Irish be on ya."

Angel found Christopher exactly where she knew he'd be, but it surprised her to see him casting a fishing line into the canal instead of a rock. Her surprise increased tremendously when he looked up at her with a world-class little-boy smile. It was enough for her to forget everything she'd intended to say to him.

"Hey, Mom, look what I got. This neat old man gave me one of his rods and showed me how to fish."

Angel was completely bewildered. It was more than the fact that Chris was smiling, his whole personality seemed to have undergone some sort of metamorphosis. If she had known a fishing rod could make this much of a difference she would have bought one a year ago.

"Here, try it," Chris said, holding up the rod.

She sat down beside him and let him show her what to do. Fishing had always been one of those hobbies she never understood the allure of, but as she curled her fingers around the grip, a sense of peace came over her.

Chris seemed content to let her hold the rod for a while as he lay back on the grass and stared up at the clouds. "Have you ever gone camping?"

"No, but I wouldn't mind trying it if you wanted to. The troop's been invited to the weekend jamboree in May. We could all do that."

"But who would show us what to do?"

Angel smiled at her little worrier. "I'm sure someone would come to our aid."

"Mr. O'Grady knows about camping."

Angel was certain her ears were playing tricks on her until Chris went on.

"I been thinkin'. Dad wouldn't want you feelin' lonesome forever. I don't think he'd mind if you, you know, like went to the movies or somethin' with Mr. O'Grady."

Angel scrutinized the rod in her hand, wondering if it had some sort of magical powers. How had Christopher gone from being jealous of Sean to accepting the idea of her going out with him in one hour? And why in heaven's name would he think Sean knew about camping?

She remembered suggesting a camping trip to Warren shortly before he died. She'd thought it might help him relax. Instead, the mere thought of such an adventure nearly did him in. Throughout most of their marriage, she managed to restrain her energy and youthful impulses, knowing how much more sedate he was, but occasionally it got the best of her.

There were times that she just felt like busting loose, skipping rope with the kids, racing them to the car . . . going camping.

Sean would do those things wit' ya.

Angel turned to Chris, thinking he had spoken, but he was busy following an ant's progress up a blade of grass. Her ears *were* playing tricks on her. It wasn't fair to compare Warren with Sean.

What had Christopher said? 'Dad wouldn't want you feeling lonesome forever.' How odd.

He wouldna want ya feelin' guilty neither. He passed on 'cause 'twas 'is time, not for anything ya did or didna do.

Now Angel knew her brain had slipped off track somewhere between the house and the canal. Hearing little voices in her head was perfectly natural, but none of them had ever had an Irish accent before. Despite the voice, however, she knew Warren had worked himself to death trying to provide for his young family.

Pshaw! The man worked 'isself ta death 'cause 'e loved ta work. He knew ver' well what 'e was takin' on by marryin' a girl 'alf 'is age. An' if 'e didna want the children 'e could 'ave done something ta keep from fatherin' 'em!

So, what's your point? she asked the foreign voice in

her head, as if it weren't her own subconscious talking to her.

Me point is this, 'tis time ta let go o' the life ya had wit' Warren an' git yourself hitched ta Sean. Now there's a young stud who'll be able ta keep up wit' the four of ya!

Angel dropped the fishing rod on the ground as if it had burned her hand. She had no idea why she was arguing with herself in a man's Irish-accented voice, but to tell herself to marry Sean, whom she barely knew, proved that there was something very weird happening to her.

Shamus scratched his whiskered cheek and decided he'd done as much work on the two of them as he could at the moment. Angelina wasn't completely convinced yet, but he figured another nudge or two would do it. At least he hoped so; there were only five days left to Christmas.

After what happened between them Saturday morning, Angel assumed Sean would start badgering her to go out again, despite his promise not to until after the park issue was settled. Considering Christopher's drastic change of attitude, she had even decided, if Sean asked nicely enough, to agree to a date at some future time, after the holidays perhaps.

She had also given a lot of thought during the night to everything the weird voice in her head had suggested. Although she had never heard of such a strange thing happening during self-analysis, it seemed to have worked for her. She definitely felt better about herself when she woke up in the morning.

But Sunday flew by, then Monday, and Sean still

hadn't called. Not that she had time to talk to him in the midst of Christmas preparations. She barely had time to talk to Flora Gelbert, the sweet lady from the Senior Citizens Auxiliary, who called to invite her Cub Scout troop and their parents to their Christmas party Tuesday night. When the boys heard there would be refreshments and Santa Claus would be there with a gift for every child who attended, every one of the scouts promised to show up.

By Tuesday afternoon, she accepted the fact that Sean wasn't going to call again. He had simply gotten tired of being turned down and moved on to his next quarry—probably someone younger, thinner, taller, prettier, blonder, and without children who punched him in the stomach—someone not at all like her.

The rec center was filled with people when she, Becky, and their boys arrived that evening. Flora Gelbert was at the door to greet them.

"Thank you so much for inviting us," Angel said. "This is the first year you've done this, isn't it?"

"Yes, but we've already decided to make it an annual event. Sean thought it was high time that the seniors and the children of Coral City do a little mixing."

"Sean?" Angel asked needlessly as Becky gave her an elbow in the ribs.

"Sean O'Grady, the mayor."

"Is . . . is he here tonight?" The mention of his name triggered a hot flash within her.

"Of course, dear. That's him up there."

Angel scanned the crowd, but couldn't see his blond head.

"Don't you think he makes the most adorable Santa Claus you've ever seen?"

Angel's mouth dropped open as her gaze lit on the jolly, fat man situated center stage in the red suit with the dressed-up little girl on his lap. *Sean was playing Santa Claus?* While she tried to absorb that, Becky took off after the boys before they could inhale the refreshment table, leaving Angel to converse with Flora alone.

"Of course, our Sean's adorable no matter what he's doing. Everyone agrees that he's the best bingo caller we ever had. Never gets his numbers backward the way Charlie used to."

Angel wondered if her mind was back to playing tricks on her again. "Did you say Sean is a bingo caller?"

"Oh yes. Every Wednesday night. Why do you look so surprised, dear?"

Angel shook her head in wonderment. "I guess I just don't see him as someone who would, uh, spend his evenings like that."

"Then you don't know our Sean very well. Whenever any of us seniors needs anything, he's right there with a helping hand. He not only organized the senior transportation corps, he's one of the main volunteer drivers." When Angel looked at her curiously, Flora explained. "A lot of the elderly in our city don't or can't drive, so when they need a ride to the grocery store or the doctor's office, all they have to do is call the transportation line in the mayor's office and a volunteer driver is sent to that person's house. It's a wonderful program."

"Yes, it certainly is." Angel was too shocked by her own ignorance to say more. "I'd better go help Becky with the boys. Thank you again for inviting us."

How could she not have known about the programs for seniors? Easy. She was always totally occupied with the programs for children. Why hadn't Sean told her about his volunteer work? Easy again. He didn't need to boast about what good deeds he did any more than she would.

How did he do it all? Mayor of the city, owner of a construction company, volunteer? He must not have any free time to—

She stopped cold as the realization hit. He wasn't much different than she was, filling every minute of every day with some sort of activity. Could it possibly be that they had something in common? Could he possibly be as lonely as she? Her mind flew back to the rumor Becky had tried to tell her the day after he first came to her house. Someone he had loved had died. Could it be—

"Angel! Have you gone deaf?" Becky said, laughing. "I want you to come take a picture on Santa's lap with me."

"Oh, no. Please, Becky, I can't." In spite of her protests, Becky managed to drag her all the way to the stage, but that was as far as she would go. Santa's blue eyes met hers and she knew there was no way she could sit on his lap in front of all these people.

Becky gave up on her, and had a photo taken with her boys instead. After the picture was taken, Angel watched Santa pull Becky close and say something to her that made her laugh and give him a thumbs-up sign. But when Angel asked her about it, Becky insisted it was just a joke. No big deal.

The joke, however, was apparently on her, for when it was time to leave, Becky and all five boys had vanished.

"Will you accept a ride home in Santa's sleigh?" Sean murmured from behind her, causing her to jump. He had gotten out of his costume, but he still had a twinkle in his eyes.

"Hmmm. How lucky for me that he hasn't left yet. I just happen to be stranded."

"I noticed," he said sympathetically, as if he weren't the one who conspired with Becky to put her in that position. "It's quite convenient actually, since I wanted to talk to you about the park issue."

She was relieved that he gave her a legitimate reason to be pleased about having to go home with him.

As they said good night to the group of seniors on cleanup detail, she noted that every one had a beaming smile for Sean and called him by his first name, but more important, he was able to do the same with each of them.

"I'm impressed," she admitted once they were on their way home.

He grinned at her. "Shows you how dumb I am. Here I was trying to impress you with kisses when all I had to do was put on a Santa Claus suit."

"And call bingo numbers every Wednesday night, and be the hero of most of the people over sixty in Coral City."

He shrugged and made a face as though he didn't do anything special. "It makes me feel good."

"I know. I feel the same way about the kids. Oh, you missed the turn," she said as he drove by her street.

"Only temporarily. I want to show you something." He drove for several minutes then pulled off the road. "This is the property."

"Oh! I had no idea it was this close." She got out of the car to get a better look, and he came around to her side. "I hope you didn't bring me here to convince me that this land should be kept in its natural state, because, even if I have changed my mind about you, I—"

His head dipped down and his mouth cut off the speech she was prepared to make. If only his kisses didn't make her feel quite so good, she might have protested his ploy to quiet her. With only the lightest touch of his hand on her back, he stimulated every nerve in her body, making her both agitated by the minimal contact and anxious for more.

His mouth moved softly over hers in an undemanding, yet thoroughly seductive manner. She could no more resist opening for him than she could stop breathing. Her tongue caressed his as he deepened the kiss and their sighs of pleasure drifted into the sounds of the night.

Without braking the hypnotic kiss, he repositioned their bodies so that he was leaning against the car and she was standing between his spread legs. Angel instinctively responded to the urging of his hands sliding down her back to draw closer to his heat. When those same guiding hands covered her bottom, pressing and lifting her more intimately against him, their kiss abruptly turned hungry.

He had kissed her like this before, stroked parts of her body, even caressed her breasts, but none of that had prepared her for the shock of what it would feel like to have his desire teasing hers. It was electric and exciting and frightening, all at once. The utter novelty of the sensation, however, also jolted Angel back to awareness.

"Wait," she gasped, turning her face from his. "Please. I . . . I'm not sure—"

"Easy, love," Sean whispered, quickly moving his hands up her back to change his hold on her from desperate need to a comforting hug. "I'm sorry. I didn't mean to go so far. I was only hoping for a few kisses, but you have a way of making me forget my good intentions."

She tipped back her head to meet his gaze. "I thought you said you wanted to talk."

"I do."

"That wasn't talking."

Sean brought her hand to his mouth and licked the center of her palm. "I didn't say I *only* wanted to talk."

She narrowed her eyes at him, but failed to keep a straight face. "Tell me, *Mr. Mayor*, are your campaign promises worded as trickily as your personal ones? Or am I just extra lucky to be on the receiving end of your smooth talk?"

"You know, Angel, if I wasn't so sure we'd be good together, your continuous put-downs might actually hurt my feelings. But since you asked, I'm always very careful about how I word any promises I make, whether political, business, or personal. I'm sorry if you think I've tried to trick you, but you haven't given me much choice."

"I just don't understand what you want from me."

Sean stroked her cheek. "It's not so difficult to understand. I want you to give us a chance. Can you honestly say you feel nothing when we kiss?"

She shook her head. "No, I can't. You know very well what happens when you touch me. But I'm not the type of woman who can casually give herself to a man."

"And I'm not the type of man who would ask you to.

Despite evidence to the contrary, I would be perfectly happy to practice celibacy until our wedding night."

Angel's eyes opened wide. She blinked twice, but he was still standing there, smiling at her like she was the most beautiful woman he'd ever seen. That settled it. She'd entered the Twilight Zone.

"Of course," he continued, "I realize we need to give your boys a chance to get to know me, but that shouldn't take too long. How does St. Patrick's Day sound? My grandfather would have liked that."

"Sean! I don't think this is funny."

He stopped smiling. "I'm perfectly serious."

"But . . . but we hardly know each other."

"Getting to know each other will help us keep our minds off what we'd rather be doing for the next, um"—he used his fingers to count—"seven weeks. I can see I've caught you unprepared again, so I won't insist on your affirmative vote tonight. Instead, I'll tell you my news. Before the party tonight, the president of the Senior Auxiliary told me their group had an emergency meeting about this property."

Angel's mouth turned down in anticipation of what he had to say.

"It's not what you think. They're excited about the idea of a sports field. It turns out there are a quite a number of seniors who would like to play softball and a lot of others who would like to get involved on a volunteer basis to be umpires, referees, coaches, scorekeepers, and so on. They wanted me to know that they're in favor of the idea, and would support a bond issue to pay for it if we put it on the upcoming ballot."

Angel was so surprised it took a few seconds for it to

sink in, and when it did, she gave him an exuberant hug. "That's wonderful!" A few seconds after that, she realized what else that meant. "I won't have to give a speech! That's even more wonderful. I can hardly wait to tell everyone."

She started to move out of his arms, but he held her still. "I know exactly how you feel, and it would be my pleasure to help you spread the news, however, I would like another kiss before I take you home. That is, if you can promise not to crawl all over me."

Angel gasped, but his smile and the twinkle in his eye let her know he was teasing. She shook her head and sighed. "Has it occurred to you that there's something very strange about how we came together?"

Sean pulled her close. "I heard angels can wish for anything they want at Christmas, and they can't be turned down."

"So you think I wished for you?"

"Who else?"

Who else? Shamus repeated as he watched his grandson and future granddaughter-in-law kiss. *Who else, indeed.*

Tin Angel
by Patricia Rice

October, 1855

"I don't care what party he claims to hail from, Palmerston is a damned dictator! We're up to our fool necks in a war we have no business to be in in the first place, and they elect a power-hungry jackal to run it! Asses! The whole country is full of bloody asses."

The speaker slammed his glossy high-crowned hat down on the table, grabbed a tankard of ale from a waiter passing by, and flung himself into a booth across from the recipient of this tirade. He propped his elbows on the table and glared at the half-empty tankard after he drank from it.

"Bulls, actually." The speaker's fair-haired companion already had several empty tankards lined up in front of him and signaled for another as he spoke. "John Bulls, Beefeaters, solid, complacent, narrow-minded isolationists. What else did you expect?"

Jeffrey, Viscount Darcourt, lifted his glare from the tankard to the man across from him. "What else, indeed?" he asked sarcastically. "We are a nation of illiterate peasants, grasping shopkeepers, and bloodthirsty, stupid asses. The aristocracy is supposed to have more sense than this! That's why we're the ruling class. I tell you, the Americans have the right of it. Educate the masses and let them vote. Someone out there has to have more brains than those blithering idiots back there."

"Educate the masses, he says!" The fair-haired gentleman hiccuped and drank deeply from his fresh tankard, slapping the waiter's hand away when he attempted to clear the table of empties. "Palmerston would have them chained to the land, if he could. Education reform is beyond our reach, old boy. Keep 'em ignorant and we can all live to rule another day."

Darcourt gave his companion a look of disgust and drained his cup. "Don't just keep them ignorant, send them to war. Fill the trenches with blood and bone for a stinking war for foreign Turks. I've had it, Henry. I'm tired of fighting the apathetic, the greedy, and the stupid. There isn't a single man in government today worth supporting. And the public is so damn fool ignorant to put them in there, they're not worth fighting for. I'm getting out, going home, and to hell with them all." He rose from his seat and returned his hat to his thick dark curls.

"Can't do that." Speech slurred, Henry barely raised his head from where it had fallen on his crossed arms. "Got to stay for the Season, find a wife. You're the only heir now."

Jeffrey's face darkened and his words were curt. "Good. The line can die out and there will be one less ass to run the country into the ground."

He practically ran from the tavern into the chilly streets. Even the London air repulsed him. Huge chimneys belching black coal smoke littered the skyline. In this part of town, the smell of offal didn't intrude, but he had traipsed the narrow, crooked streets of St. Giles and knew there were parts of the city no better than pigsties. Actually, a modern pigsty was more healthful than the crowded, filthy streets where pestilence bred in open sewers. He jammed his hat more tightly on his head and hurried toward his town house.

He wished Henry hadn't mentioned his duty as heir. It only served to remind him of George. He didn't want to think of his younger brother on a day when he was already furious with the world. George had died in those foreign trenches, slaughtered like a sheep for carrying out the orders of a criminally incompetent officer. George should have been the one who stayed home. George loved his country, loved the people on his lands, loved his wife. George had an infinite capacity for love and patience. And now George was no better than pig fodder.

Jeffrey refused to give in to the tears burning his eyes. He'd consumed too much ale. He was too furious to be coherent. His passions didn't tend to be the gentler ones of love and patience. Temper and arrogance ruled him. He missed George devilishly, but he was furious with him for dying. He had no business over there. His business was here, creating an heir with his lovely wife. His widow now.

As if just the thought of George's wife conjured her in front of him, she stepped from the carriage in front of his town house. Jeffrey cursed his blindness in not noting the carriage earlier. He could have escaped down a side alley. Now it was too late. His mother and sister were climbing down, assisted by a footman.

Bloody hell, he didn't need their interference on a day like this one.

The women greeted him cheerfully, and he growled in return. He waited impatiently for them to enter the house, but acres of skirts and crinolines and half a town full of packages had to be maneuvered up the stairs and through the doors. Their birdlike chattering drove him to the brink, but he gritted his teeth and endured with the hope of encountering a warm fireside and a bottle of brandy in the solitude of his study.

The discovery that he had been nominated to escort his female relations to the opera destroyed what remained of Darcourt's composure. He supposed all women weren't silly chits, but this particular flock apparently had no sense at all. They had no understanding of the elections, of the war, of the incompetence surrounding them. They chattered of clothes and operas while George lay in a muddy grave on foreign soil and children starved and died in filthy streets just around the corner. He couldn't bear another minute of it, but thirty years of training prevented him from screaming his fury.

Instead, in carefully controlled tones, Darcourt disabused them of his availability.

"I intend to go up to Dorset this evening, Mother. Send a note around to Uncle Martin and see if he might go with you."

"Dorset!" Shocked, his mother turned concerned eyes to him. Jeffrey felt the full brunt of those bruised violet eyes, but he resisted. "Whyever would you need to go there? The harvest is in fine hands. You have an excellent steward. You have your seat in Parliament, Jeffrey. You can't go to Dorset now."

"I can, and I will, Mother," Jeffrey stated firmly. "As a matter of fact, I have no intention of returning here or taking my seat. If I never hear another blithering idiot again, I will be perfectly content. And you will be much better off without me to dampen your spirits."

"Jeffrey!" she wailed, but he was already halfway up the stairs.

December, 1855

Darcourt sat before the dying fire, sipping at the glowing brandy in the crystal snifter. All around him rose richly paneled walls and towering bookcases, shadowed in the light of a single lamp. The room gleamed of wealth and security, as did the rest of his Dorset estate. He had acres of arable land and fields of livestock, enough to support him and his family for the next few generations without lifting a hand. He should be feeling snug and comfortable, away from the squalid poverty of the city, the strident arguments of Parliament, the frivolity of society.

Instead, he felt frustrated and miserable. He wanted to smash the crystal snifter against the wall and bellow with rage. He wanted to pace the expensive Oriental rug and rant and rave. He wanted to smash things. He'd never been allowed to smash things. He'd always kept his temper pent up inside him, where it lashed at his insides instead of flailing at its cause. Right now, he'd be hard-pressed to decide on a cause.

A footman tiptoed into the room bearing an awkward

burden. At the sight of Darcourt glaring at him from the fireside, the servant visibly quailed, but resolutely, he proceeded to the corner library table. Darcourt watched as he set up a pail full of sand from which a freshly cut evergreen tree protruded.

"What do you think you are doing?" he inquired in falsely calm tones.

"A Christmas tree, my lord," the servant stammered. "The family will be arriving shortly, and my lady insisted we must have a tree. She always likes one in here, my lord. She says they are too messy for the salon."

Darcourt sank into a gloomy silence as the servant straightened the tree and added more sand. He couldn't very well counter his mother's orders. This house had always been hers, even if the ownership belonged to him now. There hadn't been Christmas trees when he'd been growing up, but his mother had introduced the idea the year after his father's death. They had been all the rage in London, and it had made her happy to hang trinkets and invite the village children. She'd needed a little happiness back then. Undoubtedly, she'd hoped to have a half-dozen grandchildren of her own by now to entertain with the tree. Her wishes weren't going to be granted in the matter of grandchildren. He couldn't object to her wishes on the matter of the tree.

Stoically, Darcourt refilled his snifter and watched as the maids tiptoed in and scattered a few ornaments among the branches. His mother would bring more trinkets from London, but over the last few years they had gathered a few oddments that had meaning to various members of the household. And his sister had taken to collecting the brightly colored tin ornaments that came stuffed with sugarplums, a different one for each year. There had been the year she had adorned the tree with jolly elves, and another when she had fancied drums. The sugarplums were gone, distributed to the village children, but she had kept one of each box to hang on the tree every year.

Whispering among themselves, the maids wired the tiny candle holders to the tips of each branch. They treated the tree reverently, as if it were a thing of magic. Jeffrey grunted cynically. Instead of a thing of magic, it would be dropping pine needles all over the carpet in a few days. Pine sap would drip on the table and require hours of scrubbing. Nothing magical about that mess. It was a bloody nuisance.

He supposed he would have to forgo his fire and find another room to sit in for the evenings or the blasted thing would dry out even faster. He didn't know why they were putting it up so early when his mother wasn't expected for days. He didn't know why they were putting it up now, when they could have done it during the day. He supposed the dragon lady of a housekeeper had insisted they keep to their regular duties and they were doing this after hours. He didn't know much about the running of the household. As long as he was fed and warm and had clean clothes, they could all go to perdition for all he cared.

Jeffrey returned his gaze to the book he was trying to read, but the words blurred together on the page. He'd drunk too much brandy again tonight. That would have to stop. He couldn't keep drinking himself into a stupor every night. But as long as he was half seas over anyway, it wouldn't hurt to have another sip before he went up to bed.

Somewhere between the book and the brandy, he must have dozed. When next he opened his eyes, the maids had gone. The fire had died down until the Christmas tree was little more than a shadow against the night. The air was already redolent of evergreen. Darcourt reached for his snifter, but found it empty. He contemplated pouring another drink, but a trick of firelight made him glance back at the tree again.

A single tiny candle gleamed among the branches.

Darcourt stared blankly. Did the maids mean to burn the house down around their heads? The whole bloody tree could catch fire if that candle burned down, left unattended like that. What did they mean lighting a candle now, anyway? They never lit the candles until Christmas Eve.

He couldn't make himself stir from the chair. A wintry chill filled the room as the fire died, but he had enough brandy in him to combat the cold. The flickering candle held him fascinated. It gleamed off one of Susan's sugarplum boxes. He couldn't make out which one in the dark, but he could see flashes of white and gold. He wondered what would happen if he let the candle burn down to the branch. Would the tree catch fire immediately, or smolder awhile? If he fell asleep, would he even notice when the flames swept across the room? Perhaps he was cold enough that he wouldn't even feel the heat. He had enough brandy in him to go up in flames like a plum pudding.

"That's a revolting way to die," a crystalline clear

voice intruded rudely on his wandering thoughts. "Not only would it be painful, but the disaster left behind would destroy the lives of everyone in the household. The whole place would undoubtedly burn to ashes, throwing dozens of servants out of work just at Christmas. Your family would be utterly devastated. They would have no means of coping with such a disaster. Unscrupulous lawyers would come in and milk the estate beyond retrieving while searching for the next heir. Your sister would probably have to marry some wealthy Cit to keep herself and your mother from starving. And your sister-in-law would no doubt have to become someone's mistress, since she is entirely dependent on your generosity and has no portion of her own."

Darcourt began to laugh. The image of his silly little sister doting on some fat wealthy Cit was bad enough, but the doom-filled dramatics of this little speech smacked so much of the ridiculous that he couldn't help himself. Even in his blackest glooms he had never imagined such a fate for the bevy of foolish women in his life. He'd seen them all well provided for in case of his untimely demise. They were more likely to go on much happier without him.

Not until he had laughed off the foolish melodrama did he stop to wonder who had spoken it. The brandy had addled his wits beyond redemption. Feeling a little more in humor, he reached for the decanter and searched through the darkness for the cynic who had read his thoughts.

Read his thoughts. Damn, but he was more pickled than he realized. He returned the decanter to the table and scanned the darkness. "Who's there?"

A frustrated sigh answered his query. An irritated mutter drew his attention in the direction of the long library table in the center of the room. Although it was some feet from the glittering candle of the Christmas tree, he noticed an odd glow shimmering over the polished mahogany. He squinted into the darkness, and the glow seemed to take shape. He blinked, and the shape seemed to become a little more solid. He could still see the shelf of books on the far side of the table, but he seemed to be seeing it through the ghostly shape of a woman—wearing wings.

He rubbed his forehead, glanced at the embers of the fire beside him, then glanced quickly back to the table again. She seemed to be slumped forward with her elbows on her knees. The wings formed a graceful curve at her back. She didn't even look at him.

"Are you satisfied?" she asked sullenly. "I'm not very good at this, as you can see. And I feel regularly ridiculous with these things flapping at my back."

Maybe he ought to have a little more brandy. But he couldn't seem to lift his hand. He kept staring at the ghostly shape fading in and out in the faint light of the tree. He couldn't see colors. He couldn't tell if he saw blond hair or red, but he could definitely tell it was a she. Although now that he looked, he couldn't say why. Flowing robes disguised any trace of a figure.

"Not very good at what?" he asked, parroting her words rather than trying to think.

She turned her face enough to give him a look of disgust. He could see that much, even if he didn't hear it in her voice.

"At this angel business. I'm not much good at anything up there. So I thought I'd come down here and try to be useful. It gets boring doing nothing but studying and watching all the time. I like doing. At Christmas, they need the extra help up there, so I accepted the offer. But look at me! I can't even make a decent showing. Shouldn't I be splendid with gold and glory so I can shock you into believing?"

Amused, Darcourt crossed his hands over his chest and watched her twinkling shimmer. If he meant to lose his mind, he'd found a most pleasant way of doing it. "Why me?" he inquired, humoring his idiosyncrasy.

Even if he couldn't really see her face, he felt the flash of her smile, a sudden mischievous grin, and he grinned back at her reply.

"I liked your curls."

"That's not a particularly angelic thing to say," he pointed out, reasonably . "And you're beginning to fade out again."

She muttered something obscure and shook her wings until they ruffled slightly. The image became a little more solid, and she gave him a glare of defiance. "These things take time. One can't learn to be an angel in just a day."

"Quite true, I'm sure," he agreed affably. "Are you only an angel when you come down to earth?"

She turned her glance with interest to the Christmas tree. "It looks that way. The rest of the time I'm supposed to be reading and observing and trying to improve myself, but I never was much good at that." She gave a little puff, and the candle flickered out.

The ghostly shape gleamed silver against the darkness, then faded. Darcourt decided his hallucination had ended, and he felt a peculiar disappointment at the thought. It was rather like waking up from a particularly interesting dream and wishing he could go back to sleep again and take up where the dream had left off.

"This is better." The voice came from the direction of the tree. "If I can't be splendid, there's no point in wasting my energy. It looks like I'll need all my resources with you. Next time I'll choose a starving orphan who needs a mother."

Jeffrey chuckled. A tin angel on the tree swung loosely on the branch where the candle had gone out. He didn't remember Susan collecting a tin angel, but he could just see the gilt paint trimming its gown. The voice's cynicism perversely appealed to him. He was no doubt mad. If anyone wandered in here, they would see him in Bedlam, but no one would come in here at this time of night. Relatively few things in life amused him anymore. He couldn't see any reason why he shouldn't talk to a tin angel. No doubt in the morning he would feel differently, but that was then and this was now.

"I should think an orphan would be a much better recipient of Christmas tidings than I am," he offered when she said nothing more. "I have everything a man could want." He gestured to his wealthy surroundings.

She made an inelegant noise that could almost be a snort. "You have nothing but material goods, and you're wasting them wickedly. You're worse than a little boy who takes his ball away when the other children won't play the game his way."

"That's ridiculous." Her reply stung, and he answered with curtness. "If that's the best you can do, you definitely are an incompetent angel. Maybe you'd better go back and find someone with a little more experience."

"Oh, yes, incompetence! One of your pet peeves, I've been told. Were you never incompetent? How lordly that must make you feel. You can strut down the street and hear people cry, 'There goes Lord Darcourt! There isn't anything he can't do.' It must be pleasant to be so certain of one's self."

"Don't be foolish! Of course I can't do everything, but I can do what I'm supposed to do, which is more than you can say."

The tin angel tinkled slightly in the breeze, although there didn't seem to be any other ornament close by to cause the chiming noise. "And just what is it you're supposed to do?" she called, from what seemed to be a distance.

Somehow, he knew the question was rhetorical. She was no longer there.

Darcourt woke with a thundering head and a sunbeam piercing his brain through his closed eyes. Groaning, he turned over, and his hand lashed the bedside table. A distinct rattle of something hitting the floor ensued, and he grimaced, trying to remember what he could have left sitting there last night. With difficulty, he pried open one eyelid and glared down at the floor.

The garish tin angel glared back at him.

He almost laughed, but his head hurt too much. Bigad, he must have been drunk as an emperor last night, seeing angels and talking to them! That he'd carried the damned ornament upstairs with him was testimony enough to that.

He groaned as the ornament reminded him that his family would arrive any day now. He'd have to send someone into the village to pick up something in the way of gifts. Susan was easy. He'd just have someone craft the most superb sugar-plum fairy they could make up. Maybe his mother would like one of those fancy shawls the women in town knitted and sold this time of year. He didn't know what to do for George's widow; he didn't even want to think about Helen.

"She wants a marriage proposal, but she'd settle for a string of pearls."

Jeffrey jerked upright and stared around the room. Sunlight peered through the cracks between the draperies, and he could see every corner of the spacious chamber. No one was there.

Disgruntled, he threw his legs over the side of the bed. He'd sent his valet off to bed early last night, and he apparently hadn't managed his shirt buttons well enough to get his shirt off. The wrinkled linen fell to his knees, and he cursed. Jasper would give him holy hell for wrecking the shirt like this.

"Drat! Now I suppose I'm going to have to materialize again so you remember I'm here. It's that or get a rather interesting initiation into the male anatomy."

Jeffrey nearly jumped off the tin angel lying on the floor between his feet. Cursing, he grabbed the ornament from the floor and set it back on the table.

With laughter, the voice said, "Well, at least I know I'm quite competent at making myself heard."

Jeffrey grabbed the ornament and flung it against the farthest wall. The tin halo bent forward over the angelic face, the wings crushed awkwardly against glittering skirts, and the angel fell in a mangled heap to the floor. With satisfaction, he pulled the bell rope to summon his valet.

"I rather liked that little toy," the voice said sadly. "You have a vicious temper, you know."

The ephemeral winged figure glittered briefly from the edge of his bed. Jeffrey stepped backward, but he couldn't tear his gaze away. Could alcohol continue to affect the mind the day after?

"You don't have a problem with alcohol yet," the angel replied carelessly. "You will in the future if you continue as you are. I suppose that's one of the things I'm supposed to prevent."

His valet appeared and the shimmering image vanished. Jeffrey wondered viciously if she was still there, taking lessons on male anatomy, but he refused to admit that the hallucination was real. He stripped naked and proceeded to wash while his valet hurried about the room, gathering his clothes. Finding the damaged ornament, Jasper gave his employer an odd look, then set it carefully on the bedside table.

Before he went down to breakfast, Jeffrey grabbed the bent angel and shoved it in his pocket.

He set it in front of him as he breakfasted on coffee and toast. His pounding head had eased somewhat, but he was taking no chances on his stomach. He'd best stay off the brandy for a while.

He studied the tin angel as he ate. The halo now dipped rakishly over one shiny cheek. The wings spread out to the sides as if she meant to take flight. He blinked when the halo seemed to straighten itself.

"A proper mess you've made of it, but I suppose a

tinsmith could straighten it out." Complacently, his own particular nemesis shimmered enough so he could see her sitting boldly on the table, her legs—or her gown, if she didn't have legs—swinging back and forth.

"You're a ghost," he accused her. "You mean to haunt me."

She tilted her head thoughtfully. "Now that's an interesting concept. I'll have to take it up with someone more learned than I am. But I think ghosts tend to stay earthbound. I have to leave by Christmas."

"That's a relief," he said wryly, draining his coffee cup. "What do you mean to do in the interim?"

"Lots of things, I hope," she answered with enthusiasm, once more swinging her legs. "I haven't been down here in forever. There's so much I want to see. Will you take me with you into town?"

"Do I have a choice?" he muttered, then realized he'd had no intention of going into town.

"Well, no, you don't really." She leapt off the table to examine the abominable oil landscape over the sideboard. "Some habits die hard, apparently. I was always used to asking politely."

"No doubt you were an angel of decorum in another life," he said sarcastically.

The footman entering to clear his plate gave him a startled look and glanced around to see to whom he was speaking. Jeffrey gave him a glare, and grabbing the tin angel from the table, walked out.

"Very well done," she mocked from somewhere over his head. "Just glare them into retreat. So very polite of you."

His fingers wrapped around the toy in his pocket,

nearly crushing it, but no protest came from his nemesis, and he eased the pressure. Even in his madness he realized the toy had little or nothing to do with the voice.

He grabbed his hat and greatcoat from the butler as he stalked out. If he meant to converse with thin air for the rest of the day, it had best be out of sight of others. He had the curricle brought around and refused a groom's accompaniment. Let the damned angel look after the horses while he shopped.

"They're beautiful animals, but I don't think I'd have much control over them," the voice replied doubtfully from the seat beside him.

He glanced over at the empty seat but saw only a slight waviness to the air, as if heat waves rose from it. "You showed up better this morning," he said grumpily.

"It's the light. Sunlight tends to fade everything. Will you stop to see the vicar on the way in?"

Jeffrey had a dozen questions he wished to ask, but the thought of questioning an apparition stilled his tongue. Besides that, she kept bombarding him with impossibilities until his head spun. It was all he could do to keep up with her questions and demands and silliness. "Why would I visit the vicar? I see him in church every Sunday."

He might not be able to see her clearly, but he felt her scathing look.

"His daughter is dying," she reminded him, her voice laden with irony. "You might stop to inquire as to how she is and if there is anything you might do. The poor man has already lost one child and a wife. He will be all alone if this one dies. Your compassion would make his day brighter. He is easily pleased."

"Why in hell would my compassion make a difference to him? Sympathy never made it easier when George died. Dead is dead. Nothing anyone can say will make it different."

"Oh, I forgot. Lord Darcourt knows everything. Of course you know all about grief and pain and how one deals with it. Just visit the vicar and quit being such an obstinate jackass."

Jeffrey could swear the shimmer beside him glowed brighter with her anger. He could respect her temper easier than her platitudes. For whatever reason, he gave in to her judgment. Seeing the vicar's vine-covered cottage ahead, he eased the curricle to a standstill in front of it.

The older man had just stepped outside when Darcourt came up the stone path between the overgrown rosebushes. He looked up in surprise and pleasure at the approach of the young viscount. "Lord Darcourt! How good to see you. What brings you here today? Is there something I can do for you or your family?"

The vicar seemed to have aged tremendously since Jeffrey had last noticed him. He wasn't given to observing the man in his pulpit, but faced with him like this, he could see the threads of gray in his fading blond hair and the way his shoulders bent with the weight of his many burdens. The man couldn't be much older than fifty, but he had the wrinkled lines of age about his eyes and mouth.

"I came to ask after Clarissa. Is she doing any better?"

The vicar shook his head sadly, patted the viscount's back, and led him back into the cottage. "Come and have a cup of tea. It's chilly out here and you are in an open carriage. You must look after your health, my son. You can never be too careful."

Jeffrey thought he felt the rush of wings as he stepped across the portal, but he ignored the notion. He let the older man call for tea and took the seat offered in the best parlor. His mother usually did the visiting. He looked around him with curiosity, noting the volumes littering the tables, even though he knew this would be the room reserved for entertaining guests. Apparently the vicar's idea of entertainment was to produce volumes of text.

"My health is quite strong, sir. Females are more tender. Is there anything I can do to help?"

The vicar shook his head sadly and took the cup of tea served by his housekeeper. "The physician says he has done all he can. It is up to her now, and she doesn't seem to wish to live."

The gossip came back to him now, and Jeffrey nodded with understanding. Clarissa's fiancée had been killed in the same battle that had taken George in the Crimea. She had grieved this past year as if she had been his wife in truth. But unlike Helen and his mother, she apparently hadn't been able to put the death behind her. He sipped his tea and sought polite words to say.

"Perhaps if we found stronger medications, and

brought Christmas to her?" he asked tentatively. "A tree and candles? Children singing?"

The vicar wiped surreptitiously at his eyes behind his wire-rimmed spectacles. "You are generous, my lord. I am willing to try anything. The physician says the infection is in her lungs, and he has no medicines to make them stronger. He says sometimes patients recover on their own, but mostly he has no control. He believes it is hopeless. But I will try anything. I will ask the choir to sing for her."

"And I'll see that she has a tree and candles." Jeffrey stood up, satisfied that he had done as much as he could. He remembered Clarissa as a quiet, unobtrusive spinster, very different from the fine-feathered birds of society. He thought he might genuinely regret her illness.

"Would you like to see her?" the vicar asked anxiously. "She sleeps most of the time now, but perhaps your voice will remind her of this world."

The last thing he wanted was to walk into the sick chamber of a woman he scarcely knew, but trapped, Jeffrey nodded agreement.

He tried not to look too closely at the sleeping form beneath the blankets as he entered the darkened chamber with the vicar by his side. The face on the pillow was pale and lifeless, as if death had already overtaken her. The only thing alive about her was the glorious crown of burnished chestnut hair spread across the linen. Apparently someone took the time to keep it brushed.

He had no idea what to say, but the voice whispering in his ear prompted him and he repeated what he heard. "She is too lovely to die so young, sir. I will see the tree delivered tomorrow. Perhaps when she wakes and sees it, she will have renewed interest in the world."

The figure in the bed convulsed with a racking cough, and the vicar hurried him out. With a few hasty words of farewell, Jeffrey found himself on the way to his curricle again.

"There! See, even if she does not get well, you have made a difference. You have given him hope, made him feel less helpless and alone, and renewed his faith in people. Everyone needs that occasionally."

Jeffrey growled irascibly and contemplated throwing the tin angel into the shrubbery. "What good is hope if she dies? I have only made it harder for him."

"You are a stupid wretch, do you know that?" she asked angrily, shimmering beside him again. "Didn't you see the tears of gratitude in his eyes? He was feeling lost and alone and you showed him that someone cared. Can you imagine what it would be like to lose your entire family? His faith in God can only waver at such a time. You have given him strength."

"You have, maybe," he snorted. "I haven't done a damned thing but offer him a tree. Why can't you make her better if you have heavenly powers?"

"I can't make her want to live if she's chosen to go to the other side. Her betrothed is waiting for her, and she senses it. There is little enough I can do for her. It was the vicar I wished to help."

"So no matter what I do, she's going to die. What a charming Christmas that will be for the old man. I was supposed to learn a lesson from this? All I learned is that I'm helpless to change anything. I already knew that."

She made a noise of impatience. "Men! They must always have concrete results. It is not enough that you have made him happy and given him a little hope and faith. You must ask for miracles, too. No wonder your mother prays so hard for you that I've been sent down here to look into the matter. You are further beyond hope than that girl back there. At least she believes she is going to a better world."

"I certainly hope there is a better world than this one. If this is all I can hope for, I would just as soon put a bullet through my brain now and get it done with."

"My word!" She stared at him in astonishment. "What do you have to complain about? You've already admitted you have everything. Shall I arrange for you to be sent back here as a street urchin begging for scraps of bread?"

"Never mind." He brushed her off impatiently, no longer finding it odd to be talking to more than a shimmering wave of air. "What other fascinating lessons have you to teach me on this glorious day?"

Since the sky loomed leaden with rain and the air was so moist as to be mist, his sarcasm was evident. Miffed, his angel didn't reply immediately. Grabbing his chance in this unexpected silence, Jeffrey inquired, "Do you have a name?"

That caught her off guard. He felt her glance at him in puzzlement. "Name? I suppose I must, but it hasn't been important."

This was more interesting than learning lessons in

behavior. Jeffrey took the long road into town. "I ought to call you something. I don't believe the Bible mentions any female angels. Will Mary do?" She made what he assumed was a shrug of assent, and he continued, "Well, Mary, do you not remember who you were? How you died? Anything?"

She sat silent for a moment, a rare silence, he was coming to realize. "No, not actually. Those things aren't important once you leave earthly matters behind. I may have been many people at different times. I can't really say. I am told that character is all we retain. We are supposed to observe and learn and improve our characters."

"And your character is so improved that you have been sent here to instruct me in how to improve mine?" The sarcasm was strong again.

"Oh, I don't believe my character is all that strong," she answered airily. "I'm fairly young as these things go. I am easily bored and impatient. You irritate me immensely sometimes. I suppose those flaws will be corrected with time, but they are far less than your flaws. Even in my ineptitude I can see that you are a self-pitying man who cannot see the world around you through anything but your own selfishness."

"Thank you. I appreciate that," he replied harshly, whipping the horse to a greater pace. "I have worked to pass bills that would educate the masses, relieve the poor, provide sanitation for slums. I suppose it is due to my character flaws that all these bills were voted down."

"You aren't the only flawed character in this world,"

she said with irony, "as much as you might think you are the only person in the world."

"I don't believe I wish to hear any more of this adolescent inanity. I am beginning to believe you must have been a spoiled child and you have come down here just to amuse yourself by promoting your own silly notions. Go find an orphan to save. At least you will be accomplishing something."

A long sturdy brick building loomed into view. Instead of continuing the argument, Mary inquired with interest, "What is that?"

Jeffrey shrugged. "A carriage factory." He felt her glance of inquiry. He had become much too good at reading her thoughts. Perhaps she was just an extension of himself, after all, except that he knew what a carriage factory was. "Carriages are increasingly popular. There is a need for less expensive models. The village seemed to have a number of young men unable to follow in their father's professions, and we have several fellows who've been disabled from the army. I just put the two needs together. They pretty much run things on their own now. It's quite a nice carriage they build, if I do say so myself."

He felt her staring at him again. With irritation he asked, "What is it now?"

"What would have happened to those young men if you hadn't built that factory?"

He shrugged irritably. "How am I to know? Isn't that your department? They would have gone off to London, I suppose. There's always work there."

"But you allowed them to stay here, close to their families. You kept them out of the gaming hells and slums of the city. If it hadn't been for you, they could be roaming city streets now, starving and stealing for a living. You have changed lives. You can do so again. Can you not see that?"

"I can do nothing," he declared angrily. "Money built that factory. My mother could have done it. Anyone could have done it. It brings in a tidy profit. It does not save those children in St. Giles. It does not prevent the young men in other towns from going to London and losing themselves. It changes nothing."

"Do I have to throw a child in front of runaway horses so you can rescue her before you will recognize your importance?"

Her tone bordered on the furious, and he felt the distinct flutter of wings as he brought the curricle to a stop in front of the tinsmith. To hell with her. He would have Susan's present made. And then he would go next door and inquire about that shawl. Hallucinations be damned.

Jeffrey cursed as he pulled up the drive and recognized the coach and carriages halted in front of the stairs. His family had arrived. Somewhere in the long weeks of boredom, he must have lost track of time.

He stumbled over trunks and satchels in the foyer as he entered the front door. The high-ceilinged, spacious hall seemed filled to overflowing with chattering women in billowing skirts and crinolines, fat sausage curls bouncing as they all tried to hug him at one time. There seemed an inordinate amount of baggage and crinoline for three women, and as he impatiently allowed his mother to buss his cheek, he realized why. They'd brought along a fourth female.

He recognized Emma Wittingham at once, and his first impulse was to flee. His second impulse was to strangle his mother.

Before he had time to do either, a male voice intruded upon the happy homecoming.

"By Jove, that's a fine billiard room you have, Darcourt. The table needs refurbishing, however. I know just the fellow to do it. I'll send one of your grooms to fetch him first thing in the morning. Did a fine job on my father's, and his didn't have half the weight of yours."

Davenport! What in hell was Davenport doing here? Instead of strangling his mother, Jeffrey thought he might just leap all these trunks and throttle the intruder. He was contemplating the effort involved when the younger man apparently stubbed his toe on something in the hallway and went down, arms flailing, taking with him a centuries-old suit of armor.

Above the clatter of metal, the wails of women, and the rush of footsteps to the downed man, Jeffrey thought he heard a waspish voice saying, "Rotten company you keep, I must say." He glanced swiftly around and saw the brief shimmer of his taunting angel at the top of the towering armoire on the far wall. Mary gave him a mischievous grin and disappeared again.

Well, he had to grant she knew how to judge character. Rodney Davenport was a penniless bounder who lived off his father's title and his friends' generosity. His blue blood with a hint of royal purple gave him entrance to all the best homes, but it didn't pay his bills.

Apparently the leech had been invited to suck Darcourt's blood for a while. He wondered which of the foolish women in his life had made that decision, and didn't have to guess long when he saw his younger sister weeping and holding the fallen man's hand.

Damnation! He strode across the foyer and jerked her to her feet, pushing her into his mother's arms. "Damned clumsy of you, old fellow," he declared unsympathetically to the downed man. "Suppose you know a blacksmith who puts armor together too?"

Davenport dusted himself off, striving not to look sheepish as he pulled his legs back under him. "Don't know what came over me. One minute I was up, the next I was down. Best have that floor looked at, Darcourt. Could be a flaw in the flagging."

Darcourt rather suspected a flaw in the character of a certain angel, but he had sense enough not to mention his assumption. He held out a hand to help the hapless young lord up. "Just stay clear of Susan and you'll not come to any harm, Davenport."

With that brusque declaration and ignoring Susan's wail of protest, Jeffrey stalked out of the foyer in the direction of his study. The door was too heavy and too old to slam, but its firm closing notified the rest of the inhabitants that his lordship had no desire to be disturbed any further.

He found himself waiting for his nagging angel to scold him for his behavior, but she remained ominously silent. Perhaps she had given up on him and gone to find a deserving orphan. He hoped so. His overdeveloped conscience had seen him scorned and laughed at enough in the halls of government. Now that he'd de-

cided to write off the rest of the world as too foolish t
reform, he didn't need an arbitrary angel acting as a s
cial conscience for him.

Jeffrey went into dinner that evening grimly brace
for feminine chatter and Davenport's inanities. His dis
position did not improve as he watched Susan givin
the handsome cad adoring looks. His sister might no
be the brightest example of the feminine gender, bu
she was a good-hearted girl, far too good for a rake wh
would only spend her money and break her heart.

"If you'd been in London where you belonged, yo
could have kept that coxcomb from getting anywher
near her."

Darcourt gritted his teeth and glanced surreptitiousl
around. The tin angel ornament had found its way ont
the sideboard. Its bent halo made the figure look as i
it were bowing its head, either in devotion or laughte
He didn't intend to discover which. He decided to tr
ignoring her. He certainly wasn't in any position to re
spond to her challenge.

"Well, what festivities do you have planned for th
holidays, old boy? A Christmas ball? A New Year'
hunt? I haven't been on a good hunt in a devilish lon
time. Looks like you've got good country for it aroun
here." Davenport drained his wineglass and motione
for the footman to fill it again.

Jeffrey hovered between signaling the footman not t
waste any more good wine on their tasteless guest or a
lowing the clodpole to drink himself under the table
He settled on the latter as the simplest solution. Sip
ping at his own glass, he responded irritably, "We ar
only just out of mourning, Davenport. A ball would b

a trifle disrespectful, don't you think?" He raised his gaze to the ceiling and muttered under his breath, "Of course, you don't think. How foolish of me."

A soft giggle sounded in his ear, and he almost smiled to himself. He rather liked having his angel agreeing with him for a change. It put him considerably more in charity with the world around him.

As Davenport started to respond to his host's cutting speech, his wineglass tilted. A cascade of fine burgundy spilled down the young fop's immaculate linen and splashed across his garishly embroidered waistcoat. He stared down at himself in amazement, while everyone watched him with polite interest.

A footman hurried to hand him a napkin. Choking, Davenport shoved his chair back and dabbed frantically at the obviously expensive waistcoat. Jeffrey continued contemplating the ceiling, while the women made consoling noises about his valet surely being able to get the stain out. Davenport continued to sputter.

"Ghosts!" he declared, feverishly wiping at his clothes. "Haunts. Didn't do that myself. Hand pushed. Know it." He gave his host an enraged look, but Jeffrey was too far away to be the man behind the accident.

"So sorry, old fellow," Jeffrey said innocently. "Sometimes the family specters take a dislike to someone. I can understand if you want the carriage brought around."

Davenport glared.

"Ghosts?" Emma inquired warily. "You have ghosts?" She scanned the room as if expecting to see them walking out of the walls in procession.

"One or two," Jeffrey drawled at the same time as his

mother said reassuringly, "Of course not!" She turned and gave her a son a glare which quelled any further conjecture before going on, "The house is scarcely that old. The armor is just an eccentricity of Jeffrey's grandfather."

"Oh." Emma succeeded in still looking uncertain but she smiled tentatively at her host. "You are quite right about the ball, Lord Darcourt. It would be most inappropriate. It is good to know that there are still a few people in this world conscious of what we owe the fallen."

Darcourt nearly choked on his wine at this prepared little speech. Arbitrarily, he responded, "I thought a few dozen guests for New Year's would be pleasant."

Emma's eyes brightened. "Of course. You are exactly right. A few good friends to remind us of all that we have to be thankful for."

Idly, a smile of derision tugging at the corner of his mouth, Darcourt said, "Of course, this is much too short a notice. I think I'll ask the vicar to give us a service on remembrance that evening."

Before Emma could make a complete cake of herself and agree with this inanity also, Lady Darcourt intervened. "We'll do no such thing. Poor Mr. Cooper has enough on his hands with his daughter so ill. I think a gathering of the neighbors will be more than suitable. The girls and I will undertake the preparations so you needn't put yourself out, Jeffrey."

Well, his mother had never been entirely stupid. Bowing his head in acknowledgment of her better judgment, Darcourt retired to his study as soon as was decently possible after dinner. Let Davenport and the ladies make plans for the holidays. He needed to decide if he should plan for committing himself to an institution if he continued imagining all mishaps could be laid at the feet of his imaginary companion.

"I'm not imaginary," Mary said irritably, materializing near the Christmas tree. "Shall I rearrange this room to prove it to you?"

Sitting in his favorite leather chair, drawing on his cigar, Jeffrey contemplated the vision flickering in front of the evergreen. He could still discern very little of her face, but he could sense her mood well enough without seeing her expression. That was an insane thing to think about something that couldn't be real, but he had already accepted his growing insanity. It relieved the boredom, in any event.

"I've always wanted that desk turned to the window, but it's too heavy to budge. Would you mind seeing to it for me?" he asked idly, more out of curiosity to see how far his insanity would go than because he really expected her to do it.

"If I move something, it will have to be for a better reason than that. I'm not a magic fairy come to grant you three wishes. What are you going to do with that overgrown popinjay? Christmas is a sentimental season, and it is already obvious that your sister has formed an attachment. She's quite likely to accept his offer."

"I'm quite likely to bounce him out on his ear if he dares ask," Darcourt responded complacently. "He'll get the picture soon enough and hie his way off to greener pastures."

Mary groaned and rolled her eyes heavenward, disappearing in the direction of the tin angel now residing

on the mantel. "Lord Darcourt knows it all again! G
out there now. Open your blasted eyes and use you
brain for something besides pickling."

The shimmering image disappeared. Jeffrey contem
plated the ornament on the mantel for a while longer
He didn't have to go to the salon if he didn't want to
and he most certainly didn't want to. He tolerated the
company only because it was the holiday and he
couldn't very well keep his family out of their ancestra
home. Beyond that, he had no desire to keep them en
tertained. It was much more peaceful entertaining him
self. A good book, a good cigar, and a warm fire, that'
all he needed. The nagging inner voice that added
good woman in his bed would be welcome didn't come
from his angelic visitor.

Cursing under his breath, he found himself putting
out the cigar, shoving the angel in his pocket, and
strolling down the hall in the direction of the sounds o
music. Someone played the piano while his sister sang
one of the old Christmas carols. The sound soothed hi
irritation somewhat, until he walked into the room.

Susan sat unnecessarily close to Davenport on the
piano bench. She looked at the popinjay with wide
eyed attention as she sang, and he smiled down at he
with all the charm and sweetness he could muster. Jeff
frey wanted to gag. Before he could interrupt this fas
cinating little scene, the lid of the hideously expensive
grand piano suddenly slammed shut. The two musi
cians yiped and jumped, startled. Music sheets flew
into the air and scattered about the room. Emma and
Lady Darcourt looked up from their sewing with wid

ened eyes. Both caught sight of Darcourt standing in the doorway at the same time.

The pair at the piano turned and looked accusingly at him, but he was much too far from the instrument to have caused the incident. He smiled and strolled into the room, hands in pockets. "Better watch it, Davenport. Our resident ghost has taken a definite dislike to you."

"There is no such thing as ghosts, Jeffrey," Susan declared bravely. "You must have someone come and look at the instrument at once. There must be some flaw in the structure."

Did he imagine it, or did he hear the hints of an angelic chuckle? He responded with more humor than he might have otherwise. "I think Davenport must be the flaw in the structure then. Suits of armor and wineglasses and piano lids never had a tendency to fly about before."

Rodney scowled as he rose from the bench and bent to examine the fallen lid. "I don't appreciate your levity, old boy. Susan could have been hurt if she'd had her hand in here. Something needs to be done."

For once, Rodney was quite right. Darcourt squeezed the ornament in his pocket until he heard a muttered, "All right, all right," and walked across to examine the instrument. The women immediately crowded around him to look over his shoulder. He gave them a look of irritation which made them step backward slightly. Then raising the lid, Jeffrey set the prop under it again, and tested its sureness. Since his insanity told him that his rebellious angel had caused the accident, he felt secure in announcing that a maid must have loosened the base while dusting. He made a show of securing the prop thoroughly, then wandered to the mantel to allow the amorous duo to return to their music.

"Can sinners reform?" he murmured sotto voce, although why he bothered to speak at all, he couldn't say. Mary seemed to hear him even when he didn't say the words aloud.

"They make a pretty pair, don't they?" His invisible companion sighed wistfully. "True love is supposed to be a wondrous thing. I suppose it could transform even a fool, if he loved her."

"She's pretty well cap over heels already," Darcourt said gloomily. "She'll be miserable whether I throw him out or not."

He heard the unspoken "I told you so." She was right. If he'd been in London where he was supposed to be, he could have warded off this unhappy occurrence. Why in hell hadn't his mother seen what was happening? He glanced in the direction of the women, who had returned to their sewing and knew the answer without his angel telling him. Because his mother wanted Susan to be happy, and Rodney had a pretty face and nice manners. He sighed in exasperation. For that same reason, she had brought Emma Wittingham with her. She imagined herself finding him the ideal wife and filling the nursery with grandchildren.

"Marry that witless peahen and you'll regret it forever," the voice in his ear said remorselessly.

"I don't need another conscience," he answered in irritation.

"What's that, Jeffrey? Did you say something? Don't stand over there muttering. Come sit with us and tell us what you have been doing." His mother looked up and smiled at him pleasantly, as if she hadn't baited the trap and left it open.

"Just business as usual, Mother. I'm certain you wouldn't be interested. Now if you will excuse me, I still have some matters that need to be completed before morning. I wish you good evening." He nodded curtly to his family and guests and strolled out, trying not to appear as if he had a hive of bees after him.

He'd left only a low lamp and the fire for illumination in his study, so he didn't immediately discern the figure by the darkened Christmas tree. When he did, he cursed himself for not noticing that Helen had left the salon.

His sister-in-law looked up sadly at his entrance, then returned to her contemplation of the tree. Jeffrey hastened to light another lamp and turn up the one by his chair.

"George used to hide a special present for me in the branches," she explained quietly, not quite disguising the quiver of tears. "He would bring me down here before everyone else and begin lighting the candles until I found it."

"The explains the blackened wicks. I'd blamed the servants," Jeffrey said cynically, taking his chair.

She ignored his lack of sympathy. "George was always so full of joy. I cannot believe all that love and laughter is gone. I simply cannot."

Darcourt braced himself uncomfortably for the bout of tears. He wasn't at all certain that he could withstand them himself, and he had no desire to appear ridiculous. He poured himself a brandy and took a swift drink before replying, "He was the better man."

Helen sent him a quick look over her shoulder. A petite woman with silky blond hair, she presented an enticing picture in her midnight blue gown. Jeffrey couldn't tell if she was aware of that or not. Her reply didn't seem to be coquettish.

"George was simply a different man. That did not make him better or worse. You are a much more responsible sort than he. Do I remind you too painfully of him, Jeffrey? Am I wearing out my welcome? I don't wish to, you know."

He wanted to say he wished she would find someone else and get the hell out of his life so he didn't have to remember how much George had loved her, how happy George had been with her. But his remorseless angel listened, and he couldn't have said something so cutting in any case. Resignedly, he shook his head.

"You are part of this family now, Helen. I know someday you will find someone even better than George, but you will still be one of us. You are Susan's sister, the other daughter my mother wanted, the wife my brother treasured above all else. You will always be welcome."

He didn't think he sounded insincere, but she looked at him skeptically anyway. "I will take your words at face value now because I cannot bear to do otherwise. But I'm certain you realize that your mother is hoping we might make a match of it, and you must wish me in Hades."

"Isn't there something illegal or sacrilegious about marrying a brother's wife?" he asked facetiously, reaching for a cigar and the clippers.

She smiled then, a weak smile, but it erased the

tears. "Then your next choice is Emma. I wish you well of her."

She slipped quietly out the door, closing it firmly behind her. Jeffrey felt the breath go out of him and realized he had been holding it.

"Well, she is the practical sort," the voice from his angel said.

Jeffrey went to remove the ornament from his pocket, but it already rested on the mantel. Apparently Mary had a fondness for overseeing her territory from a height. "I never thought of her as such, but I suppose with a husband like George, she had to be."

Her materialization this time was much stronger than previously. Mary looked at him through wide eyes of sadness, and Jeffrey felt himself drawn to the understanding he found there. He almost lifted his hand to touch her before realizing the foolishness of the notion. Still, his fingers tingled, and he clenched them tightly in his coat pockets.

"I'm not very good at this at all, am I?" she asked softly. "You're not arrogant. You're lonely and trying to hide it. I've been a fool."

He blinked in astonishment. She disappeared before he could reply.

Cursing his aberrant imagination, Jeffrey threw down the cigar he'd never lit and made his way up to his bedchamber. This had been a damned long day and the morrow threatened to be worse. Maybe a decent night's sleep would chase away this nagging conscience he seemed to have developed.

As his valet undressed him for bed, Jeffrey surreptitiously scanned the room for any sign of the tin angel he had deliberately left in his study. Her remark about learning male anatomy this morning made him self-conscious now. He had no desire to inquire if the memory of physical attributes disappeared with death or if she had died innocent. He supposed angels simply didn't know anything about human flesh. That seemed the most reasonable assumption.

But this flesh of his was all too human. He ached for the comfort of a warm, willing female in his bed. He had been bombarded with perfumes and feminine voices and graceful figures all day. Like a child's dreams of sugarplums, they danced through his head now as he lay upon his pillow. If he could just reach over and bury himself in welcoming arms, he might be able to drive out the memories until morning. As it was, he was doomed to lying stiff and cold, staring at the ceiling.

"I'm sorry," a soft voice whispered out of the dark. "I wish I could help. I wish I could be what you need."

The voice echoed the agony he felt, and he relaxed slightly. "The physical part passes," he assured her. "It's the emptiness that hurts the most. I've been so long without decent companionship I'm coming to crave the sound of your voice. I don't suppose you could find me a woman who can converse with the same wit as you?"

Her laugh tinkled through the night air. "A woman who nags and berates you and tells you when you're wrong instead of agreeing with everything you say?"

He grinned. "Heaven deliver me from the Emma Wittinghams of this world."

"You won't like a nag any better."

He screwed up his face in thought. "If she had a

278

sense of humor, I might. It's a pity you don't remember your past life. Maybe you have a sister somewhere."

"You *can* be charming when you choose, can't you? Go to sleep. I'll go look for a nagging female for you."

He laughed and slowly drifted into dreamless sleep.

"Why in hell didn't I send one of the grooms to do this?" Darcourt muttered as he pulled the wheels of the cart out of the mud for the third time. "It's freezing out here."

"If it were freezing out here, the mud would be frozen," Mary pointed out relentlessly. "And the grooms might not get just the right tree. It has to be of a size to fit on the table, and it has to be absolutely perfect so when she wakes, she looks at it in wonder."

She walked alongside of him, examining a holly tree with interest, reaching out to pluck a few choice branches and add them to the cart. He couldn't see how nearly invisible fingers could break holly twigs, but she seemed to have no trouble in doing so.

"Don't you feel the cold?" he asked, consumed with curiosity.

She didn't quite reach his shoulder when they stood next to each other like this. When she turned to look at him, she had to look up. He liked that feeling better than having her always staring down at him.

"I think I am noticing it more than I did before," Mary answered with a degree of puzzlement. "It's quite invigorating. I've obviously forgotten the feeling of warmth and cold, or the smell of evergreen or spices. Your cook must be creating something delightful. The house smelled so delicious this morning, I almost felt hungry."

"I suppose humans do have physical pleasures to counterbalance their emotional distresses. I suppose heavenly bodies are above pleasures of the body."

"I think I rather miss it," she said wistfully. "As I told you, I'm not very good at this. There are so many things to be seen in this world, it's difficult to concentrate on the problem."

"Well, thank you for that," he answered jokingly. "This problem prefers your entire attention."

She laughed. "Oh, you have that, all right. Did you know you are very handsome when your hair falls down and curls on your forehead like that? You ought to come outside more often. It adds color to your cheeks."

He gave her a startled glance, and she laughed, shimmering a little more brightly. "We are almost at the vicar's. You'll have to quit talking to what's not there before someone sees you."

He would second that motion. The carter coming down the road was already looking in his direction, no doubt wondering why Lord Darcourt pulled a cart filled with evergreens through the field. If he saw him talking to the evergreens, he'd back off quickly. Somehow, that idea wasn't as appealing as it once might have been.

Jeffrey nodded in the carter's direction, then turned off on the path to the vicarage. The carter raised his hat in greeting and rolled on by.

The vicar ecstatically ushered him in, calling to his housekeeper for hot chocolate, offering to take Darcourt's wraps. Jeffrey brushed him off politely, hauling the fat tree onto his shoulder and into the house. Mr. Cooper looked too frail to lift even this small specimen.

The vicar hastily gathered up the angelically gathered

holly branches and hurried after the viscount down the hall to the sickroom. Together, they set the tree in the bucket of sand already prepared. The housekeeper came bustling in, murmuring suitable exclamations of awe. The invalid slept through it all.

Jeffrey finally doffed his coat and accepted the hot chocolate as they began fastening the candles he'd carried in his pockets. The closed room filled with the fresh scent of outdoors, and the vicar whistled a carol beneath his breath as he reached for the higher branches to wire on the candles and entwine holly among the boughs. Jeffrey watched in wonder as the older man's face seemed illumined from within as he worked. The gray lines of worry temporarily faded as hope replaced anguish.

He didn't know if he was doing the right thing. The girl in the bed seemed beyond these festivities. She looked even paler and weaker than she had the day before. Her breathing appeared more labored. He was raising the good vicar's hopes for naught.

When they had the last candle fastened and the last holly twig tucked in, the tree still looked bare. Jeffrey stepped back and looked at it disapprovingly. The vicar and housekeeper looked at it with expressions of wonder, but he was accustomed to the gaily decorated tree in his home. This one didn't appear to be the glorious miracle that would waken a dying woman to the world's beauty.

His fingers closed on the tin angel in his pocket. He clung to it for a minute, then with firm resolve, he drew it out of his pocket. It was naught but a child's toy. His insanity had to end sometime. It had been nice having a laughing, nagging, challenging delusion to keep him company, but it would be better if he returned to reality. With gentle care, he propped the angel on the very top of the tree, where it could look upon the invalid in her bed.

The gold-painted halo seemed to straighten of its own accord. The shining white wings looked ready to take flight. The painted face smiled radiantly, even within the dim confines of the sickroom. The vicar and his housekeeper made quiet exclamations of joy.

"It is magnificent, my lord," Mr. Cooper whispered as they tiptoed out of the room. "I must admit, I thought it a pagan enterprise to bring trees into the house, but it cannot be wrong to admire the Lord's handiwork. Clarissa will be delighted. She has long approved of your family's Christmas celebration."

The vicar's excitement and gratitude carried Darcourt out of the house, but his words didn't warm him as he began the walk to the village to pick up Susan's gift. He felt a peculiar melancholy at giving up the fantasy of a guardian angel.

The door closed after the vicar and the viscount, throwing the sickroom into darkness again. From her perch atop the tree, Mary wriggled and stretched a little, contemplating the impossibility of the task she had been assigned, while watching the dying girl in bed with a little more than curiosity.

Jeffrey Darcourt possessed a stubborn character, she decided. She admired his intelligence, and she knew his heart was in the right place. He just needed to be hit over the head with a brickbat upon occasion to bring the two together.

That wasn't right either. She had tried those methods, and they hadn't pierced his stubborn determination to let the world go to hell on its own. No, what Jeffrey Darcourt needed, she couldn't easily provide.

If only that silly Emma Wittingham or even the widowed Helen could be the kind of companion Jeffrey needed, she could arrange for him to fall into their arms and love would begin to heal the gaping wounds in the viscount's soul. He needed tenderness and understanding and companionship—and an occasional slam over the head with a brickbat.

Mary giggled lightly at the thought and again contemplated the woman in the bed. With a little care, Clarissa Cooper could be a lovely young woman. She didn't seem to lack for intelligence either. Unfortunately, her soul was quite firmly attached to that young man who had gone before her. Even if she interfered and forced Clarissa to stay here on earth, the vicar's daughter might make Jeffrey a capable wife, but she would never be able to love him as he deserved. It just wouldn't work.

A rather naughty thought entered her mind, and Mary teased it around awhile. She thought she might be able to do it, with a little cooperation. She would be taking a terrible risk. She didn't know if she was ready to take that kind of risk yet. But the more she thought about it, the more tempting it sounded. Of course, the path to hell was paved with good intentions and temptation had little to do with heavenly desires. But she just might be able. . . .

She wriggled some more and popped out of the tin angel. She had to give this more thought. She needed to work on Jeffrey just a little more, see if she couldn't accomplish her task with more orthodox methods.

Show him ghosts of Christmas past? Show him the future? Set an orphan on his front step? They all sounded dreadfully difficult for a junior angel.

She found the viscount walking down the main street of town, a package firmly grasped under one arm, his boots muddy from his traipse across the fields. Darcourt's arrogance had little to do with his wealth, she could see. He didn't need a fancy carriage and prancing horses to impress people with his consequence. He had a firm sense of his place in the world. He had just chosen to deny it.

Whimsically, Mary perched atop the swinging wooden sign announcing a tavern called the Fox and Hounds. She sensed the impending fracas to come, and she wanted a ringside seat. Human nature fascinated her, and she suspected had she been walking in Clarissa's shoes, she would not be allowed the opportunity to observe this next spectacle.

Sure enough, as soon as the two combatants were thrown into the street outside the tavern, the good ladies of town scattered in different directions, hurrying to hide themselves from unseemly conduct. Mary propped her chin in her hand and watched with interest as the younger of the two combatants scrambled to his feet with a curse and tried to walk off. The elder was a bit slower in gaining his balance, but he grabbed his adversary's coat by the back and jerked him around.

"If I catch you near Betty again, I'll beat you into mincemeat, I will!"

A peculiarly unpleasant threat, Mary decided, but she did nothing to interfere as the younger man dodged the blow thrown at him. The viscount was almost upon them. He had a black look on his face that didn't bode well for either combatant.

"You can't stand between me and Betty, you old goat!" the younger man shouted as he shoved at his opponent, striving to break the grip on his coat.

"She's my daughter and I'll have a say who she steps out with! She's too good for scum like you. I'll send her to her cousin in London before I let her have aught to do with the likes of you."

The battle escalated and both men rolled in mortal combat through the mud of the street by the time Jeffrey came upon them. Mary watched eagerly as the viscount grabbed the youngest by the collar and signaled for a nearby observer to grab the elder. The bystander hastened to obey the young lord. Near the corner, she saw the cause of this fracas, although she wasn't at all certain that Jeffrey recognized the fact. Young Betty had a pretty face currently wrinkled with anxiety as she wrung her hands and stayed out of the way.

"He's a rapscallion, my lord," the older combatant yelled. "Seduced my daughter, he did! Then won't make an honest woman of her."

"You bloody damned fool!" the younger man screamed. "You don't have to tell half the world! Betty deserves better than me. I can't provide for her. But she deserves better than a damned idiot like you too!"

Mary found human passion to be a trifle terrifying, but fascinating too. The two men looked as if they might throttle each other should Jeffrey order them released. The pretty young woman on the corner broke into tears and ran down a side street in shame. If someone didn't do something soon, this little scene would end in utter disaster. Mary bit her lip and clenched her hands, trying to refrain from interfering, urging Jeffrey to rely on his better instincts rather than turn away in disgust.

She held her breath as he dropped the younger man's collar and removed his gloves to beat the dust off them. He didn't look at the bystander still clinging to Betty's father. Without official permission to release him, the other man resolutely clung to his struggling prisoner.

"You work at the factory, don't you?" Jeffrey asked offhandedly, drawing his tight leather gloves back on again.

The young man nodded surlily. "It's good work, but it don't provide a house."

"You still live with your parents?" Jeffrey asked.

At the young man's reluctant nod, the viscount turned to give a perfunctory signal to his assistant. The other man released Betty's father, whose struggles had ceased once the young lord had showed his interest.

"Evan, you still have young ones at home, don't you?" Jeffrey's tone was still offhand, as if they merely discussed the weather.

The older man nodded even more reluctantly than the younger. The two didn't look at each other but focused on the man who was responsible in one way or another for nearly all the wealth of the village.

Jeffrey picked up the package he had dropped and returned it firmly under his arm. "Then the problem is easily solved if the young couple could find a place of their own?"

The young man responded sullenly, "It isn't easy as all that, your lordship. There's not a place to be had that don't cost more than I make. I won't be askin' Betty to move in with me parents. It's not fittin'.'"

Considering she had a clear picture of the young man's home from his thoughts, Mary had to agree with that. He should be commended for wanting better for himself and his wife. But she had also read the girl's thoughts before she ran away. She was not only ruined, but pregnant. Should she tell Jeffrey?

"There's the cottage out past the factory," Jeffrey was saying, looking as if he meant to be on his way. "It's small, but it shouldn't be costly."

Now was the time for that brickbat, Mary decided. Was the man deliberately obtuse? Or couldn't he add two and two? Surely he knew the workman's wages, and since he owned the cottage, he knew the rent. Yes, the young man could afford it, if he didn't eat. In a fit of irritation, she flung a pinecone at the viscount's shiny high hat. Being invisible had a few advantages— not many, but a few.

Looking surprised, Jeffrey caught his hat and glanced around. When his gaze settled grimly on the swinging wooden sign, she wondered if maybe he saw her better than she knew. She rather liked the idea that he knew where she was and what she was thinking. She swung her legs and made the sign creak. Jeffrey picked up the pinecone and disrespectfully threw it back at her. She laughed, although the men standing around watching stared at him as if he were crazed.

With more aplomb than seemed reasonable after making such a spectacle of himself, Jeffrey dusted off his gloves again and settled his gaze on the younger man. "The cottage has been empty too long. Obviously,

my agent has set the price too high. I'll speak with him
before I leave town today, but I expect to hear the
banns read in church on Sunday."

The young man looked as if he had been given a reprieve from death. Mary watched with interest as he
grabbed the viscount's hand and shook it so hard it
should have come off. When Jeffrey managed to disen-
gage his hand, the young lover tugged on his forelock in
respect and almost made a bow in his excitement. Betty's father still looked a trifle dazed, but he wasn't protesting any longer. They both ought to be running after
Betty to prevent her from doing anything foolish. With
a gesture of impatience, Mary shoved the young man in
the right direction. Jeffrey certainly didn't need to be
made to feel any more superior than he already did by
the young fool's obsequiousness. The young man didn't
need further urging. He ran off in Betty's direction.

Mary waited until Jeffrey had stopped at his agent's,
then picked up his final few packages before trudging
along beside him as he turned back toward home.

She couldn't tell if he ignored her or if he truly didn't
know she was there. "You saved at least three lives today," she said casually, just to see if he listened.

"I wondered how long you could hold your tongue."
He kept on walking, eyes straight ahead, not questioning her statement.

"That's not a very polite thing to say." Offended, she
contemplated leaving him to his own cynical thoughts,
but her duty was to wake him to his responsibilities,
not disregard her own. "Betty was pregnant. She would
have run off to London to try to rid herself of the baby.
You know what happens to girls who try that. Both

men would have been driven by grief if she died. They would have taken it out on each other and no doubt done their best to kill one another. You made a difference in this world without even trying."

"What difference?" he asked cynically. "Had they all died, what difference would it have made? What difference does it make that George is dead? The world still goes on."

Brickbat time again. Mary wished there were a good snowbank to fling him in. She contemplated conjuring one up just for the pleasure, but she wasn't totally certain of her abilities. She needed what strength she had for more productive activities.

"Perhaps it is you I should have tripped and flung into the suit of armor," she replied pleasantly. "Even young Rodney has more sense than you. That young man back there could invent some cog or part that will make the invention of the horseless carriage come much sooner. Or Betty could give birth to a child who will someday pass a reform bill in Parliament. Or they could just eternally remember your kindness and pass it on every day in every way, making other people's burdens lighter, causing them to make the world a little better. Maybe kindness will spread like a contagion. Perhaps it isn't your place in this world to make a name for yourself by bettering the living conditions of the poor. Perhaps your place is just to make little changes so that one day someone else can make the difference."

Jeffrey kicked a pebble in his path, then scanned the clouds piling on the horizon. Finally, as they reached sight of the house, he conceded, "I wanted the glory too much, didn't I?"

She felt like singing. Maybe this would earn her a harp. With a thrill of joy as she watched his handsome face lose some of its cynical hardness, Mary applauded enthusiastically, then disappeared. She had given him enough to think about for the time being.

Still feeling quite proud of herself, she sat on the study mantel later that evening, watching Emma Wittingham with curiosity. Tomorrow was the day before Christmas. Mary didn't have to leave until midnight of Christmas Eve. She enjoyed this sojourn into the world too much to give it up prematurely. She had to make certain her case had truly learned his lesson. Admittedly, she wasn't ready to leave Jeffrey. She had this foolish notion that someone needed to brush the curl out of his face once in a while, and she hadn't found that someone for him yet.

Emma Wittingham very definitely was not that someone. A proper lady wouldn't be surreptitiously lying in wait for a gentleman in a darkened room all alone. True, the servants had kept the fire burning for their employer, and one lamp burned dimly on the table beside his reading chair, but the room was large and cast deep shadows. Someone had hung a kissing bough on the side of the room near the tree. Presents had begun to gather on the table. Sugarplum boxes in the shape of fairies now adorned the evergreen branches. She could see the special box made for Susan on an upper branch where Jeffrey had placed it after his shopping trip. Susan hadn't seen it yet. Emma hadn't even looked. She was busy watching the door.

The woman's expression didn't bode well at all. For a frivolous little twit, she bore a devilishly determined look.

As an angel, Mary wondered if it was proper for her to whisper naughty things in the woman's ear and drive her screaming from the room. It didn't sound like a very angelic thing to do, but Emma didn't mean well, she was certain. Perhaps she could tie her shoelaces together.

She almost put that thought into action when the door opened and Jeffrey walked in. Mary wished she'd been a little swifter on the shoelace tying when Emma immediately dashed into the viscount's arms. Jeffrey looked stunned, but he was too gentlemanly to turn away a woman who broke abruptly into tears.

"Oh, my lord, I've been so frightened! Thank heaven you're here. It's so dreadful being a woman alone in this world. Please tell me what I should do." She clung to his lapels and wouldn't release him even though he caught her wrists and tried to pry her away.

"Miss Wittingham, you must release me. Nothing can be as bad as all this. We'll sit down and discuss it sensibly over a cup of tea, shall we?"

Emma clung to him more persistently, burying her face in his shirtfront, holding her scrawny body as close to his as humanly possible. "Oh, I can't discuss it! It is not at all proper, but I don't know where to turn. I need a strong man to advise me, but my aunt would be horrified!"

Unaccustomed to thinking in worldly terms, Mary hadn't noticed the low cut of Emma's dinner gown until it began to fall loosely from her shoulders. Her wriggling against Jeffrey's front didn't help the bodice's precarious perch. It didn't take any angelic mind-reading to understand the woman's intent. Jeffrey looked more resigned than panicked. He hadn't quite divined the woman's treacherousness yet.

"Your aunt undoubtedly ought to be with you, Miss Wittingham. I'm certain she can advise you if you will but confide in her. Or perhaps my mother can stand in her place if the matter is not of too confidential a nature. Won't you take a seat while I send for some tea?"

The bodice slid even lower, revealing a hint of one pink-tipped breast. Emma's side curls fell artfully loose over one ear. Along with her flushed complexion, the scene appeared very much like one of seduction. Jeffrey looked a bit more distraught as he caught a glance of his companion's disarray.

"Oh, don't leave me now!" she cried in great distress. "Your arms are so comforting. I am sure I will be fine in just a minute. Just give me time to calm myself. It is so comforting to have you holding me. A woman needs a man like you to help her. And a man must need a woman occasionally, is that not so?" Her look was almost coquettish as she glanced up at him through lowered lashes and rubbed herself suggestively against him.

"Balderdash!" Thoroughly disgusted with this blatant display of asininity, Mary leaped from her perch. Emma had apparently decided her breasts were her best asset. Obviously, her intelligence and moral character weren't. With relish, Mary set her foot on the long train of Emma's velvet gown and said blithely, "Step backward, my lord. See what happens should she try to follow."

Looking as much irritated as relieved, Jeffrey did as told. Catching Emma's wrists, he stepped as far away from her as his lapels would allow. When she pushed against his hold, trying to follow, the train of her skirt stayed put. An ominous rip tore through the silence.

Emma looked startled but determined. When Jeffrey relaxed his hold somewhat, she shoved forward once more, apparently attempting to pin him against the wall. Her skirt didn't budge, and her bodice slipped to follow the skirt.

"Oops!" Mary giggled as the bodice slid downward even farther, revealing not only a corset but a bust improver. "That didn't help much, did it?"

Jeffrey sent his irritated look in the direction of her voice but refrained from answering as he finally pried Emma's fingers loose by pointedly staring at her undergarments. Emma gave a slight shriek and tried to hide her revealing "improver." Voices in the hall caused her to give him a sly look of triumph however. She immediately began a loud wailing and weeping as she frantically clutched at her clothes and ran for the door.

"Oh, my, naughty little witch, isn't she?" Because Jeffrey was too gentlemanly to do so, Mary held out a dainty invisible toe and allowed Emma to trip over it. She supposed pulling the carpet out from under her feet would have had the same effect, but she preferred the personal touch. For good measure, she gave Emma's nearly bare back a shove.

Emma shrieked and went flailing facedown into Darcourt's most modern acquisition, a thick imported Aubusson carpet. The voices outside became excited and sounded considerably closer.

"A fine guardian angel you make," Jeffrey said in disgust, reaching to pull up the fallen woman. Emma resisted and began weeping frantically into the carpet.

Her skirt was torn at the waist, her bodice down, and her hair falling about her shoulders. Only one conclusion could be reached when the door flew open to reveal Rodney and Susan.

Mary didn't think it a particularly reasonable conclusion, but the shocked expression on the newcomers' faces made their opinions clear. She made a moue of disgust as they gave Jeffrey shocked looks and bent to help Emma from the floor.

"He attacked me!" she wept. "I tried to resist. I truly did! Oh, what you must think of me." And she broke into another bout of tears as they hauled her to her feet.

Jeffrey just shoved his hands in his pockets and watched the scene contemptuously.

"I say, old boy, this isn't like you." Even Rodney had sufficient sense to retain some skepticism as Susan wrapped Emma in her arms and led her away.

Mary's opinion of the dandy rose considerably, but she could do little enough at this point. She'd already done too much. She should have quit while she was ahead.

"Of course it isn't like me," Jeffrey said coldly. "The woman attacked me, then tripped over her skirts while trying to rouse the dead. If she thinks to coerce me into an offer, she has sullied her reputation for naught. The woman is not only an ass, but an immoral ass."

Rodney appeared suitably shocked and departed swiftly on Susan's heels. Mary sighed and settled back on the library table as the door closed behind him.

"I've done it this time, haven't I?"

Jeffrey grimly reached for the brandy decanter. "You just helped her along. Her intent was the same either way. I was the fool too stupid to see it."

"What will happen now?" Morosely, Mary swung her legs. The Christmas tree no longer looked so grand as it had. She had liked the idea of being an angel of mercy and splendor, a heroine. She didn't like being a bumbling fool quite so well. It didn't seem at all odd to her that Jeffrey could see her whether she materialized or not. She felt a little too close to human right now.

"If she's a complete fool, she will press charges." Jeffrey took a deep swallow of the liquor. "From all appearances, she's a complete fool."

"What will she gain from ruining her own reputation?"

"She will hope to extort an offer from me. She can press for breach of promise, possibly. It will do her little good to take a case of assault to criminal courts, but she can have her solicitor suggest a large sum of money placed at her disposal might disincline her to press charges. If I don't go upstairs and make an offer, it will become a rather nasty little business in which neither of us will come out untarnished."

"Which will affect your family," Mary added without being told.

"Which will affect my family," he agreed. "I could strangle the woman."

"If it weren't a sin, I would do it for you." She sighed and swung down from the table. "I think this calls for a little help."

"I think you have given me all the help I can need. I'll handle this on my own," he said coldly.

Mary had envied Emma's position in Jeffrey's arms. She wondered what it would be like to lean against him and absorb some of his strength and the security he radiated. And she thought it might feel a tiny bit good to hug him back and reassure him that everything would be all right. He needed the reassurance of someone who loved him right now. Despite his cold arrogance on the outside, he hid an ocean of turmoil on the inside. Briefly, daringly, Mary brushed the viscount's cheek with her fingertips. His jaw muscle jerked, but he didn't say anything.

"I was afraid I couldn't feel you, but I can feel your warmth. You're a good man, Lord Darcourt. You deserve a good woman. I wish I could have found one for you."

For a moment, his gaze fixed directly on her, even though she made no effort to appear. Then he looked through her again, in the direction of the door. "They say the good die young," he answered gruffly.

She laughed shortly at this. "But we have already decided that I'm not very good, haven't we?"

He shrugged. "I scarcely think an angel is what I need. All that perfection would be a trifle terrifying."

"Well, then, perhaps I am just a ghost. I'm certainly not perfect. Most of us on this side aren't. We're just learning to be better. I think I have a long way to go," she added a little sadly.

That got through to him. He reached to touch the place where she stood, but of course, his fingers couldn't feel her. He curled them fiercely into his palm and dropped his hand. "Why can't you inhabit human bodies instead of tin angels?" he asked with irritation.

"Most human bodies come supplied with souls," she reminded him gently. "It would be a little difficult with two of us in there."

He made a grunt that might have been amusement.

"You would no doubt be dangerous in any case. I'd best go upstairs and meet my obligations."

"Don't be in any hurry. Liars have a way of being revealed."

With a whisper of wings, she disappeared.

"She claims Lord Darcourt attacked her, my lady." Rodney held his hands behind his back. His expression looked almost sheepish as the matronly woman on the settee gave him a cold stare. "Her gown is torn, and she is in some disarray," he added, trying to hide his embarrassment.

"I'll send my maid in to her. She can repair the gown. The woman is more a fool than I anticipated. Imagine, expecting us to believe Jeffrey did any such thing! My heavens, she must be out of her mind. Perhaps we ought to return her home and recommend she be given some restorative medicines and a long rest. Obviously, she has become obsessed." Lady Darcourt shoved her needle through her embroidery with considerable vigor.

Helen rose to take the bellpull. "I'll see to her, my lady. I cannot imagine why she would believe we would think such things of Jeffrey. Everyone in the household knows he does not wish to be disturbed when he goes to his study. He was in the salon with us after dinner and Miss Wittingham was not. It can only be concluded that she lay in wait for him. I cannot think of any good reason a woman would do such a thing."

Rodney's head turned from one woman to the other, and he looked a little more relieved. He moved his shoulders more easily beneath his tight dinner coat. "I suppose she could have tripped on the carpeting. It is quite easy to lose one's balance on these old floors."

Lady Darcourt gave a sniff of disapproval. "If I were Jeffrey, I would have shoved her out the door. But I suppose you're quite right. He's much too polite to have shoved her. She no doubt tripped in her hysterics. Or fell deliberately. Jeffrey's character is without question."

Rodney nodded even more eagerly now. "You have hit upon it exactly, my lady. Lord Darcourt is known widely throughout society as an excessively honorable man. The whispers about Miss Wittingham have kept her on the shelf for years. You are precisely right. I shall go reassure Susan, if you do not mind. She is young and impressionable, but she is certain to come about once this is explained to her. Shall I tell the footman to notify the stable that a carriage will need to be brought round in the morning?"

"Just so, Mr. Davenport. An excellent idea." Lady Darcourt nodded approvingly as the young man turned to depart. He nearly collided with Jeffrey, who stepped out of his way and allowed him to pass without comment.

The viscount's gaze settled directly on his mother. "You do not expect me to offer for Miss Wittingham?" he asked in disbelief.

"My heavens, I should think not!" Looking shocked, Lady Darcourt stared at her son. "I cannot believe such behavior. I would never have thought her so weak-minded. I apologize for being such an appalling judge of character, Jeffrey. I thought her a modest, retiring sort. This is all my fault, I realize. I truly did not mean for you to be assaulted in your own home. I've quite learned my lesson. I'll leave you to your privacy from now on."

A hint of a smile quirked the corner of his mouth as he gazed affectionately down on his mother. "Not entirely, I hope, Mother. The holiday would be unbearably lonely if you and Helen and Susan chose to celebrate it elsewhere."

She looked up at him with relief, then seeing the smile tugging at his lips, she rose and hugged her intimidatingly tall son. Strong arms clasped her shoulders for the first time since George's death.

When Helen rose to politely leave this family scene, Jeffrey reached out to encompass her in the hug, pressing a brief kiss to the top of her head. "You will see to Susan? That young dandy is likely to trip over his own tongue trying to explain."

She looked up at him laughingly. "He is not beyond witless, you know. He's just in love and not certain how to handle it."

"You could have fooled me," he said dryly, releasing her to go his sister's rescue. "But you're the one with experience in these matters. I'll rely on your expertise."

Both women gave him wide-eyed stares at this admission, but he had already turned his back on them to summon a servant to bring his brandy upstairs.

Mary watched this family scene with teary-eyed wistfulness. She didn't know that she could claim responsibility for Jeffrey's acceptance of his family. He had too much good in his heart to pretend for long that they didn't exist. She couldn't say that she had awakened his realization that they weren't entirely weak-minded fools, either. Perhaps she had opened his heart just a little so he could do it on his own.

As Susan rushed in to hug him, Mary drifted reluctantly from the room. She had behaved childishly in her assigned task and almost ruined a good man. She had to admit that she had a lot to learn about life and human behavior yet.

She threw one last wistful look over her shoulder to the family scene in the salon. The Darcourts laughed merrily over some shared joke. They had shed the black of mourning for the holidays, and they looked like any other festive family in their silks and satins. The room had been strung with swags of evergreen and holly adorned with silver ribbons and interspersed with pinecones and shiny berries. Another kissing ball hung near the doorway. Jeffrey's dark curls brushed dangerously near it, and she longed for the ability to take advantage of the proximity, to brush his angular cheek with her lips and feel the rough bristle of his jaw.

The time to make her decision was now. She didn't even have the luxury of waiting for Christmas Eve. The opportunity was opening even as she lingered. With a sigh of regret, Mary closed her eyes on the touching scene and disappeared.

Jeffrey waited for a gloating comment on her success, but none came. He looked for a shimmer of light and listened for a flutter of wings, but saw and heard nothing to suggest his angel's presence. He'd learned to find her with just the slightest of hints, but search as he might, he couldn't find her anywhere.

He wandered to his study and examined the Christmas tree. Without his slightly twisted tin angel to adorn the branches, it no longer seemed as grand as he remembered. He retired to his chamber, but when he lay between the sheets regretting the emptiness of his bed, she didn't come to laugh and reassure him. He lay there feeling hollow, wondering if he would ever feel whole again.

He supposed she would tell him that time healed all wounds or some other such nonsense. She might even be right. It just didn't help much right now, here in the present, when he still felt lonely and uncertain. His family wanted him to return to London and politics in the spring, but he'd at least learned that lesson. He could do as much quietly, behind the scenes, as he could accomplish by staging dramatic speeches in the halls of government. The persistent application of time and money could accomplish great things, if not sweeping reform. Some things just required time.

He supposed the same principles applied to looking for a wife. If he applied time and determination to the search, he could no doubt find a woman somewhere who could match him in intelligence and character. He just didn't know if he could find one with the same mischievous sense of humor and wry wit as his angel. Where would he find a woman as willing to find fault with herself as with him?

He chuckled to himself. Only in heaven, he supposed. Perhaps he was better off looking for a more mature wife, one who didn't pride herself on tripping fools. A man in his position couldn't very well have a wife who threw pinecones and shoved ladies. He needed someone sedate and respectable. And boring.

Well, he didn't have to start the search immediately. After the New Year began would be soon enough.

* * *

Christmas Eve day dawned gray and snowy. Dark clouds scuttled across the sky and an icy wind cut through layers of clothing, but Rodney and Susan laughingly ran out to test the pond and taste snowflakes on their tongues. Jeffrey shook his head at their extreme youth as he watched them from the mullioned window in his study. He would never be that young again.

When he saw the dark figure wrapped in a wool coat and muffler bent against the wind as he walked the drive, Jeffrey's heart caught in his throat. The vicar. Something must be amiss with Clarissa.

Calling for a footman and his wraps, he hurried down the hall to greet the man before he could knock on the door. One look at the vicar's anguished face told him the worst.

"We haven't even lit the tree!" Jeffrey exclaimed as the footman came racing up with the required coat and hat.

"I've sent for the choir. The doctor says it is just a matter of hours. I want those to be happy hours. I've come to see if you might join us." The vicar stood shivering on the doorstep, his face once more gray with worry, but his eyes reflecting an inner serenity that hadn't been there before.

Jeffrey pulled on his greatcoat and turning to the footman, reached for his hat. "Tell everyone I've gone to the vicarage. If they wish to join us there, we're having a Christmas celebration with Clarissa."

The footman nodded in understanding. Everyone in the village knew of Clarissa's illness. He hurried to tell not only the family, but the rest of the household. Everyone in the area knew the vicar's beloved daughter, and the tragedy of the vicar's losses.

Jeffrey hurried beside Mr. Cooper as they traveled down the increasingly snow-covered drive. He had no words to express his sorrow. He wished his angel would return to supply them. Never before had he felt so empty and useless.

"My wife and Elizabeth died so suddenly, I did not have time to do aught but grieve at what I had left undone. At least the good Lord is giving me this chance to show Clarissa how much I love her," the vicar said staunchly as they approached the house.

"I think your family knows how much you love them by your actions every day," Jeffrey replied, certain of something for a change. "Your wife and daughter died knowing how much you loved them."

"Maybe so. And maybe they are watching over me now and can hear me say it. But I would have Clarissa know it now, while she is still with me. She has ever been the quiet, dutiful daughter. I have never heard a word of complaint cross her lips. I can understand why God would call her while she is still young. She has naught left to learn of this world. She will be happiest on the other side, with her young man. I understand that. It is just a matter of learning to accept my own loneliness."

Understanding from experience, Jeffrey nodded agreement. Accepting loneliness was not an easy task. It required a certain degree of skill and patience that he had not yet acquired. The vicar was no doubt better at it than he.

Members of the choir approached the vicarage from

all directions. A hay wagon sat in the yard, apparently already having dispersed a number of young participants. Mostly they were solemn and quiet as they hurried into the house, discarding woolen mittens and long scarves and knit hats across the furniture. The housekeeper made no attempt to keep them orderly but ushered them down the hall to the back bedroom as they arrived. At the viscount's tall presence, she nodded respectfully but continued on her way without offering to take his beaver hat.

Jeffrey dropped his overcoat on the growing stack and followed the vicar down the dim hall. The dark clouds outside stole all the light from the windows. It might as well be the night before Christmas in truth.

The choir had assembled in some kind of rackety order around the far wall beyond the bed. A candle burned beside the bed, but no one had bothered to light the lamps. The woman in the bed tossed feverishly, gasping for air. She didn't seem entirely aware of their presence. Someone had washed and tied her glossy hair into a long, thick braid. She wore a frilly bed jacket that was undoubtedly a Christmas present. It didn't seem the sort of thing the quiet, serious Clarissa would have chosen for herself.

The vicar handed Jeffrey one of two tinderboxes, and together they started lighting the candles. Lady Darcourt, Susan, and Helen slipped in quietly just as the candles closest to the top came to life. Small trinkets and toys had gradually gathered in the bare branches, gifts from visitors over the last days. Someone had placed a carved wooden rocking horse near the angel. Ribbons in red and gold glittered at the ends of the branches. A tin drum and a shiny gold horn swung together, making a tinkling music. A rosy-cheeked baby doll nestled on a bottom branch, and sweet-smelling candies strung with a colorful variety of ribbons decorated the places in between. Two of Susan's prized sugarplum boxes hung gaily in positions of importance. Jeffrey suspected the empty boxes had been filled with sweets before being placed there. He gave his young sister a smile of approval as the vicar lit the last candle at the top of the tree, near the tin angel.

As the two men stepped back out of the way, a whisper of awe circled the room. Dozens of tiny tapers illuminated the glimmering tree and all the upturned faces around it. Cheeks rosy with cold shone like miniature lanterns in the splendor of the little Christmas tree. Dark eyes sparkled with wonder and delight. It scarcely took a signal from the vicar for the children to erupt in song.

Jeffrey felt tears streaming down his face as the first refrains of an angelic carol soared through the room. He could believe in heavenly hosts just listening to these childish voices, even had he not experienced his mysterious visitation from heaven. He could feel her here, dancing with love and delight, from that radiant angel on top of the tree. She was here. He had found her. Closing his eyes, he offered his prayer up to God while the choir sang around him.

A quiet sound from the bed scarcely drew anyone's attention, but the housekeeper had been watching. She made an excited noise, and the vicar instantly kneeled at his daughter's bedside. The choir stumbled and lost their places as eyes turned to the invalid, but the vicar made an impatient gesture and they quickly found their places again.

Jeffrey was afraid to look. He had never truly faced death. George had died in a distant country. His father had died when he was off at school. He didn't know if he could bear to see a pain-ravished face or acknowledge that life could be here one minute and gone the next. But it wouldn't be gone entirely. Mary had taught him that.

Determinedly, he turned to stand beside the vicar. He had not been aware that he was the only other man in the room until now. The burden of standing beside the vicar in his grief extended to him. Resting his hand on the man's shoulder, Jeffrey stared down at the now quiet woman in the bed. Behind him, the candle in front of the tin angel flickered and went out.

Childish voices rang out in imitation of angelic choirs. The lovely harmonies filled the room, echoing around her with life and joy. She absorbed the sound into herself, finding strength in it. She loved children, she discovered. She loved the carol they sang.

Excitement rose in her even as the pain in her chest pressed down. She could feel the pain. She could feel the smooth linen sheets beneath her fingers. She could smell evergreens!

Terrified of opening her eyes, she searched her surroundings with her senses. She felt immeasurably weak. Her mouth was dry and her skin felt feverish. Layers of blankets pressed her down into a mattress of feathers. Her fingers tightened in the linens. She had done it. She couldn't remember precisely what she had done, but she knew she had accomplished something miraculous. The body around her felt light and strange, but it had feeling. It could reach out and touch the people beside her.

The people beside her. She smelled the warm scent of pipe smoke and chamomile that was her father. Her father. She smiled slightly as she worked her thoughts around that discovery. Her father, the vicar.

She sensed a stronger presence, one not so familiar but at the same time, as familiar as herself. That mystery puzzled but didn't worry her. She could feel his sadness, smell the faint aroma of his shaving lotion, and knew the feel of his strong hand in hers even though they didn't touch. Dying did extraordinary things to the senses, it seemed.

She lifted her fingers from the covers and reached for the man's hand resting near her. It wasn't the one she remembered, but it was familiar, just the same. She squeezed gently, unable to find the strength for more. Her father's voice rang with joy as he talked of love. Restlessly, she continued to search for that other presence, the one who had brought her here with his desperate needs.

Gathering all her resources, she forced her eyes open.

The room seemed ablaze with light. The children's voices rose higher in glorious noise. Her spirit rose with joy. She had found heaven, at last.

Her gaze swerved to the looming presence behind the kneeling figure at her bedside. His face appeared carved of stone, so stiff and solemn did it seem. But a dark curl had tumbled across his forehead, and she remembered . . . She struggled to locate the memory that had just slipped through her mind, but it eluded her. It didn't matter. She knew him, and she smiled.

He looked momentarily stunned. Perhaps she wasn't supposed to smile at self-important young lords. She smiled even more at that thought. She sensed her father looking at her strangely, but her gaze could only fasten on the tall man with the curl in the middle of his forehead. She remembered a nursery rhyme about someone with a curl in the middle of their forehead. Something about when they were good, they were very, very good, and when they were bad, they were horrid.

She wasn't aware she had uttered the words until an expression of utter shock crossed the viscount's face. Much to the surprise and enchantment of their audience, the young viscount fell to his knees beside her, reaching for the hand the vicar had released. He studied her face acutely, but he said nothing.

"I may never learn to hold my tongue," she whispered through parched lips.

"Mary?" The word was both anguished question and disbelieving hope.

She studied the desperate hope in the deep blue of his eyes and felt the solid pull between them. She had chosen rightly then. Closing her eyes, she whispered, "You may call me that."

She heard the exclamations of joy and wonder a little while later as the doctor rushed in to declare her fever broken, but her fingers clung firmly to a strong male hand.

* * *

"Surely you're not going to place that tatty tin angel at the top of that glorious tree," a feminine voice teased from behind him.

"I most certainly am," he declared firmly, reaching to see that it sat properly where it belonged. Once assured it was secure, he turned to take his lovely wife in his arms.

She smelled of cooking spices and lavender, and he grinned as he buried his face in the thickness of her silky chestnut hair. The bulk of her burgeoning pregnancy filled his hold, and he reveled in the intimacy of holding their child between them. Amazing, how just a year wrought such changes. He no longer desired to bury himself away from friends and family but embraced the warmth and familiarity of their presence. The reason for that rested contentedly in his arms now.

"I love you," he whispered, "even if you did sell my brandy decanter at the Christmas auction."

"You don't use it anymore," she answered serenely, "and the squire paid a handsome sum for it. The orphans can use the money more than you need a decanter."

"Your father says your sister Elizabeth used to sell his best pipes at the auction. Am I going to have to glue everything to the tables so we have something left for our golden years?"

"What good are things when those children need food in their stomachs and a roof over their heads? We have all we need right here between us." She turned in his embrace to rest her head against his shoulder, and sighed happily when he rubbed the place where their child kicked vigorously.

"You've been talking to the angels again," he accused with a hint of laughter.

"That's your province, my love," she answered dreamily, closing her eyes in enjoyment of this briefly peaceful moment. "I just shove you in the right direction once in a while."

No finer truth had ever been spoken. Smiling, Jeffrey lifted her into his arms. "Nap time, Clarissa," he whispered into her ear.

Snuggling closer against the masculine fragrance of his wool vest, she smiled to herself. "That means you're going to make love to me," she said smugly. "You call me Mary when you're really angry."

Angry wasn't precisely the word. Exasperated, overwhelmed, and amazed came much closer. But his lovely, very human wife didn't seem to understand or remember anything about an angel named Mary who threw pinecones and had a penchant for tripping people she didn't like. Clarissa merely laughed when he caught her behaving badly. At least, to this date, she hadn't tripped another soul.

And the vicar was so thrilled with his daughter's recovery that he didn't even notice when she behaved more like an adolescent than the serious woman she once had been. The sound of her laughter and the roses blooming in her cheeks overcame all else.

As the young couple laughingly left the room, the tin angel on the treetop tilted slightly to the side and seemed to bob its head in approval.

Guarded by Angels
by Mary Balogh

By midafternoon on the day before Christmas Eve all the family and guests of the Duke and Duchess of Dunsford had arrived at Hammond Park, their country seat, except for the two most anxiously awaited. Not that anyone would admit to feeling anxiety, or even great curiosity. Even the duke himself did not refer to either of them by name when he remarked with hearty good humor at tea in the drawing room, rubbing his hands together as if washing them, a characteristic gesture with him, that the gathering would be complete by dinnertime.

"And Christmas will begin," the duchess said, clasping her hands to her bosom and beaming at her guests. Nothing pleased the duchess more than having a houseful of guests, and she always made quite sure that it happened at Christmas. The family came and a large number of friends besides. The nursery was always crammed with children, who tended to spill over into other areas of the house once the serious business of celebrating began on Christmas Eve.

"The weather is clear and mild," the duke added, turning almost everyone's attention to the window as if his pronouncement needed to be confirmed. "There will be no trouble at all on the roads."

Almost all of them had been traveling on those roads either yesterday or today and indeed there had been no trouble. It had been a treat to find the weather so much in their favor, though there were those among them—as well as most of the children abovestairs—who looked hopefully and in vain for signs of snow.

The two people still to come were Elliott Nichols, Viscount Garrett, the duke and duchess's grandson and heir, and June Nichols, Viscountess Garrett, the duchess's great-niece, or *step*-great-niece, if there was such a relationship. She was the daughter of the man the duchess's niece had married. And she was Elliott's estranged wife. They had been married for five and a half years—and separated for five and a quarter years.

Since they were both independently members of the duke's family, they both belonged at family gatherings. But it had become understood that they would not attend together. And so it became customary to invite them alternately.

Until this year.

This year the duchess had reached and passed her seventieth birthday and the duke, to the alarm of his family, had suffered a series of chest pains during the summer. He seemed well over them now, and his physician had assured him that he might live another twenty years if he was sensible. But they had been reminded, the two of them, of their mortality. And they had been reminded of the unhappiness of their beloved grandson and his wife. And of the fact that they might not live to see the birth of *their* heir. There might never be an heir of that line.

And so this year the duchess had suggested playing Cupid. It was June's turn to come. Why not invite Elliott too, she had suggested at dinner one evening in late November. They could suggest to him, without openly lying, that June was not coming this year after all.

The duke had hemmed and hawed and muttered about deceit being deceit and about interference between a man and his wife. But he was inclined to agree nonetheless. What did Martha think?

Lady Martha Nichols was their youngest daughter, the only one who had chosen not to marry though she had had a number of suitors during her youth. Martha was the religious one of the family, though she was never stuffy. Children of the family always adored Martha and dragged her into activities in which they would not have dreamed of involving their parents.

Martha had thought carefully before answering. But she had smiled her customary placid and kindly smile eventually and directed it at both her parents.

"Yes," she had said, "it is time. June was too young when they married and Elliott was too soon home from the wars. But they should be together now. They are bound together for life even if they never again set eyes on each other. And they both need companionship and love and—well, and children. But they may never get together unless someone pushes them into it. Yes, Mama, I do believe you are right in what you suggest."

"You do not think it is—wrong, dear?" the duchess

had asked, all conscience now that it appeared she was about to get her way.

"No." Her daughter had answered quite firmly. "Nothing that is done out of love and concern for the lasting happiness of others is wrong."

The duke had coughed gruffly. "I should have taken a whip to the boy's backside five years ago," he had said.

And so the matter had been settled. The viscount and his estranged wife were both on their way to Hammond Park for Christmas, neither knowing that the other was to be there too.

They were late arriving and the last to arrive. Curiosity as to what would happen when the two met again grew as tea progressed in the drawing room. The driveway below the windows, at which many glanced covertly from time to time, remained empty.

Martha, seated behind the tea tray, quelled her anxiety with a silent prayer.

Perhaps we have interfered where we should not, she confessed to God. *But we meant well. We love them and want to see them happy with each other. Let it happen. This is Christmas, the season for love. Let them love again. Show them that only love matters.*

But I with they did not have to meet quite so publicly.

Keep them safe.

Where are they?

When the axle on the carriage broke, they were only three or four miles from Hammond Park. She was sure it could not be much farther than that. The landscape was beginning to look familiar.

Fortunately, they had been traveling up a slight incline and so at no great a pace. There was a sharp jolt and the carriage tipped to a precarious and unnatural angle and came to an abrupt halt. But no bodily harm was done despite the fact that Mollie screamed with ear-piercing terror and the coachman's exasperated and shockingly profane comments were clearly audible from within the carriage as soon as Mollie paused to draw breath.

June Nichols, Viscountess Garrett, shushed her maid, adjusted her position so that she could maintain her balance, shifted her bonnet so that it was straight on her head again, and waited for the coachman to leave off his swearing and come to their rescue. What rotten luck, she thought, when they were so close to their destination. But at least no one was hurt. She could hear the horses snorting. None of them sounded injured.

Five minutes later she was standing in the middle of the roadway, a sniveling Mollie and a glum coachman on either side of her. There was not a carriage or a person or a dwelling within sight. The only thing for it, the coachman said, was for him to ride back to the village they had passed through some time ago and bring help. He would be maybe an hour or two. He looked doubtfully at the viscountess and up at the sky. At least it was a mild and clear day, he said. The sun had even been breaking through the light cloud cover at times.

"I do believe we are closer to Hammond Park than to that village, Ben," her ladyship said. "Why do we not all walk there?"

Mollie sniveled audibly and Ben ventured respect-

315

fully to disagree with her ladyship. Hammond in the forward direction was *much* farther away than the village in the backward direction. And either distance was too far for ladies to walk. Riding bareback was out of the question for them.

June clucked her tongue. "It is early afternoon, the weather is delightful, Hammond is only a few miles away, and a walk is just the thing," she said. "Do *you* ride back to the village, Ben, if that is what you feel you must do. Mollie can wait here. *I* am for Hammond Park, on foot. If it is farther than I think, Ben, you may take me up as you pass me later, if there is a sound carriage for hire in the village. But I daresay someone else will come along before then. The Duke and Duchess of Dunsford are doubtless expecting the usual army of guests for Christmas."

No dire warnings of peril from Ben or tearful pleadings from Mollie would dissuade her. She pulled her cloak more warmly about her, thrust her hands deep inside her fur muff, and strode off in the direction of Hammond Park. She took with her only her money and her valuables, which were inside the reticule she carried over her arm. Mollie, she noticed when she stopped to look back after a couple of minutes, was riding up in front of Ben on one of the horses while he led the others. They were going in the opposite direction. Well, those two had fancied each other for some time now. They would probably welcome this disaster and her own absence from their company. It was a good thing she had brought her valuables with her.

Someone else would come along within minutes, she predicted confidently, though she almost wished no one would. The walk and the brisk, cool air felt good. And the delayed arrival at Hammond was no hardship to her. She hated Christmas, especially the Christmases she spent at Hammond. They were a mockery with their emphasis on love and peace and family harmony. A mockery of her own lone state and of the essential emptiness of her existence.

At every other time of the year she could mask both facts about herself. She had her own small house in the country, a home in which she took great pride, and she led a busy social life, doing the rounds of house parties during the summer and winter, taking in some of the pleasures of the Season in London during the spring whenever she could be assured that Elliott would not be there.

She had not set eyes on her husband in over five years.

Her jaw set harder for a moment and her stride lengthened. He did not matter to her any longer. She did not know why she so assiduously avoided him. She had been considering—for one and a half years, ever since her twenty-first birthday—taking a lover, filling the emptiness in her life as other women in her situation did. There were several candidates who would be only too ready to oblige her at the slightest encouragement. But she had still not solved in her own mind the problem of possible conception. She had not given Elliott a son. It was an unwritten law of Society that a married lady did not take a lover until she had presented her husband with a legitimate heir.

But this year, she decided, this spring, she was going to break that law regardless of the consequences. She was twenty-two years old. She was lonely. She had needs. She was bound by a marriage that had been arranged for her when she was barely seventeen— although at the time she had acquiesced in it gladly enough since Elliott had always been her hero, especially after he had gone off to fight in the Peninsula Wars and at Waterloo. Foolish girl—as if childhood memories and a dashing military uniform and the will of her father and stepmother had been a firm enough basis for a marriage.

This spring she was going to go to London and she was going to take a lover. She was going to be happy. She was going to be young again.

But she had loved him—Elliott. Once upon a time. A long, long time ago.

Her footsteps lagged and she looked up sharply suddenly, feeling disoriented. Where was she? She was at the top of the rise at last and could see for what seemed miles about in all directions. Hammond Park was nowhere in sight. It must be farther away than she had thought. Not that she was worried. There were hours of daylight left and anyway, someone was bound to come along soon.

But she frowned as her attention returned fully from the thoughts that had been directed deep inward. When had the sky clouded over so thickly? The clouds hung heavy and low. They looked for all the world like snow clouds. And although she had just reassured herself about the daylight, the afternoon had grown gray and gloomy. Even as she looked upward, a flake of what was unmistakably snow landed on her nose, and then she could see it on her muff and on her cloak and on the roadway ahead of her.

Bother, she thought crossly. This was all she needed. But where had it come from? The weather all day and until just a few minutes ago had been unseasonably fair and mild. And it had looked settled. She had noticed no buildup of clouds on the horizon even though she had looked for them before deciding to walk away from the carriage.

Well, she thought, striding onward, it was too late now to turn back. And to what would she go? A tipped up and cold carriage? Someone would be along soon. And yet the road behind her was almost ominously empty.

She walked for perhaps half an hour after that. The snow fell thicker and faster until she was wading in it and it was becoming increasingly difficult to see where exactly the road was. There were no hedgerows to help her keep her bearings. And she could not see far. At first she thought she could see a few yards ahead. Then she was sure it was only a few feet. The world all about her was frighteningly white and all of a sameness.

Oh, yes, she grew gradually more and more frightened. What was she to do? There seemed nothing *to* do except keep moving onward and hope she was still on the road. She could not remember snow that had come so quickly and with so little warning. Or snow that had settled quite so fast or quite so thickly.

And then, just when fright was beginning to escalate into terror, she saw a light. Or what seemed for a moment to be a light, glowing through the blinding whiteness of the snow and the gloomy grayness of the afternoon. She lost it and thought in a panic of desert mirages—where had she even *heard* of such things?

And then there it was again. Though it was not a light, she realized, but a human figure—a bulky figure all bundled up inside a gray cloak and a gray bonnet. How on earth had a figure so entirely gray appeared almost like lamplight for a moment? But she did not ask herself the question until much later. At that moment she only sobbed with relief though she had no evidence that the woman was not as lost and as frightened as she.

At least she was *human*. At least the terrifying sense of aloneness was gone.

"I thought there was someone there," the woman said in a voice that sounded reassuringly unlost and unfrightened. She clucked her tongue. "You had better come inside, dearie, where it is warm. There is a kettle boiling. I shall make you a nice cup of tea."

June could see behind her suddenly the darker gray bulk of a building—a small thatched cottage. The other woman took her by the arm and led her firmly toward it. The grandest mansion she had ever visited had never looked more welcome to June's eyes.

"Oh," she said as they stepped inside and the woman in gray shut the door firmly behind them. "Oh, thank you. However did you know I was out there? I might so easily have gone on by. I might not have seen your cottage at all. I dread to think what might have happened."

It looked cozier than any other building she had ever seen though the whole thing would have fit inside the bedchamber that was awaiting her at Hammond Park. The main part of the cottage was all one kitchen and living room. There was one room leading off it, probably a bedroom. A fire crackled cheerfully in the hearth and a kettle hummed merrily over it.

It was cozy and warm and somehow made June want to weep—with joy. She found herself doing just that, much to her embarrassment.

"There, dearie," the gray lady said, and she came in front of June to unfasten the strings of her bonnet and the buttons of her cloak just as if June were a child and could not do those things for herself. "You are safe now. All will be well now. Your wandering is at an end."

She felt safe. She felt happy despite distant and vague worries about Ben and Mollie and about what the family at Hammond would be thinking.

The gray lady had taken off her own cloak and bonnet to reveal a neat, unfashionable dress of gray wool and golden gray hair worn in a neat bun at the back of her head. She was plump and plain and of any possible age between forty and sixty, though her face was unlined. June, newly released from the terror of a near-death experience, thought that it was perhaps the most beautiful face she had ever seen.

"Thank you," she said again foolishly. And then she found herself seated beside the fire in a chair that felt more comfortable than any other she had ever sat on, a cup of tea in her hand and a slice of bread and butter on a plate at her elbow.

"Oh," she said, closing her eyes briefly, "tea has never tasted so good."

The plump lady, standing before the fire, beamed at her.

"I am June Nichols," the viscountess said. "I was on

my way to Hammond Park for Christmas when the axle of my carriage broke. And then the snow came. And now I have burdened you with my company and my family will be worrying. And my coachman and maid will have been caught in this too."

Her rescuer leaned forward and patted her shoulder. "Elsie Parkes," she said, introducing herself. "There is nothing to be anxious about, dearie. Those two will be safe. And no one will worry. All will be well."

They were meaningless words, of course. How could Mrs. Parkes know that Ben and Mollie would not go astray in the snow? And how could she know that everyone would not worry when they saw the storm and she did not arrive? And yet June found herself reassured. She relaxed. Totally.

This was such a peaceful place. The most peaceful place on earth. She lifted her cup to her lips again and smiled.

"Thank you," she said once more.

He found himself wondering where June spent her Christmases on alternate years, when he came to Hammond. She had no family beyond her father—and all of his family, of course, which had adopted her as one of their own when her father had married his aunt.

Where was she spending Christmas this year? It was her turn to come to Hammond, but she had plans, his grandmother had written, and he must come to Hammond himself. She had not said what June's plans were.

She had friends. He heard about her occasionally though he had not seen her for more than five years.

He had expected when she had requested, through his man of business who handled her affairs, that he finance a small home of her own, that she would live there quietly alone. He had worried about it. She had been barely twenty years old at the time. But it had not happened.

He was glad she had friends. He was glad that she had a life.

He wondered if she had lovers. There had never been any hint of scandal.

She was only two-and-twenty now. The age he had been when he married her. She had been just a child, a beautiful, innocent child—just what he had thought he needed after the horrors of the wars. He had longed for youth and innocence and beauty and peace. And so he had taken them when they were offered and had unwittingly destroyed them in less than three months. Oh, yes, less. She had stayed for three months before fleeing back to her father, but everything had been spoiled long before that.

He had not gone to fetch her back even though her father and stepmother, his uncle and aunt, had dutifully informed him that she was with them.

He had not seen her since.

And had no wish to see her, he told himself firmly. He wished he could set her free somehow, but there was no way. There was no cause for annulment and divorce was out of the question even if he had proof that she had been unfaithful to him. His own infidelities were no grounds.

The best he could do for her was to stay out of her sight. Out of her life. And the best for himself too. He felt a troubling guilt every time he thought about June. Sometimes he felt a certain hatred for her too—and that made him feel even more guilty.

He was driving his curricle to Hammond Park, even though it was winter. He disliked being cooped up inside a carriage and the weather had been unseasonably mild and settled for almost a week. He had left his carriage to come along after him, bringing his luggage and his valet.

And yet suddenly, jolted from his gloomy thoughts about the sorry state of his marriage, he was aware of something cold and wet landing on his face, beneath his beaver hat and above the multiple capes of his greatcoat, and he realized in some surprise that it was snow. He could see it speckled white on his coat and on the chestnut backs of his horses.

Snow?

He looked upward and all about him and noticed in some amazement that the sky had clouded over heavily without his having noticed it and that the world had grayed despite the fact that it was still just early afternoon.

Where the devil had such weather come from in such a hurry?

He was still six or seven miles from Hammond, he estimated. He had better quicken his pace if he wished to arrive there before snow made travel hazardous and the road difficult to see. He hoped that the rest of the family and guests had come even earlier than he.

But good fortune—and the unexpected weather—were against him, it seemed. Half an hour later his horses were wallowing almost knee deep in snow and he had got down from his high perch to lead them, afraid that they would slip and injure themselves. Snow fell all about him like a white blanket, obscuring everything that was farther than a few feet from his eyes. The road was obscured so that he could no longer be sure that he was on it. He was no longer even sure of the direction he took.

Damn and blast, he thought. He was lost within a few miles at the most of his grandparents' house. For all he knew he might be going about in circles. But he had to keep moving on, of course. One could not stand still and give up. The very thought sent a quick shaft of fear through him.

He had never seen anything like this. Where the devil had it come from?

And then, just as he had finished clucking a reassurance he did not feel to his horses—for surely the dozenth time—he thought he saw a light. A light in the middle of the afternoon? He strained his eyes to see it again. Well, why not? Anyone who had a lamp would be sensible to light it on such a day. But it was gone. He felt something very close to panic for a moment.

And then he saw a shape, a small gray shape that was nothing like a light. But the relief he felt was as strong as if the sun had been on the ground before him, because the shape was *human*. A moment ago the world had seemed vast and strangely empty of humankind. It was a boy he saw, a slight lad, dressed in warm and serviceable gray clothes, his hair and face half hidden beneath an enormous cap. It struck Elliott Nichols, Viscount Garrett, as strange that he had spotted such an insignificant little figure in such weather.

Much later it struck him as even stranger that he had at first thought it was a light he had seen.

"Ho, boy," he called. "Are you lost?"

Somehow it would be reassuring to have someone else's safety to look to beyond his own.

But the boy looked up at him, tipping his head back so that he could see beneath the absurd cap, and grinned at him with a cheeky and cheerful face.

"No," he called back. "But you are, mate. No longer, though. You are found. Follow me."

Elliott became aware then of the larger and grayer shadow of a building behind the boy. A thatched cottage, he saw as he led his snorting horses in its direction. But the lad took him first to a shed beside the house, a shed just large enough to house the horses. It was well supplied with fresh straw and hay though there was no sign of other animals. It was a relief to get inside out of the snow. An enormous relief. It was only as he tended the horses, with the boy's help, that he realized how close to death he might have been in another hour or so if no one had found him.

"What were you doing outside in weather like this?" he asked. "Did you hear me coming?"

The boy grinned cheekily and sweetly at him. He must be about eight years old, Elliott judged, with carrot red hair and the freckles that went along with it. His ears stood out like cup handles at either side of his head. All these features had been revealed when he took off his cap and hung it on a nail inside the shed.

"I knew you were coming," he said. "You are safe now, mate. All will be well now."

Elliott spared him a look of amusement. The child

spoke like a mother reassuring her frightened child. Well, he had been frightened too. Perhaps the boy had saved his life.

"Come inside," the boy said when they were finished, "and have a cup of tea. I don't suppose you fancy tea much, though."

Elliott grinned. "At the moment," he said, "tea would taste like the nectar of the gods."

He had the instant impression of smallness and warmth and coziness and—peace when he stepped inside the house. It was just a humble country cottage, its kitchen and living room combined in one, its floor-hardened dirt covered with a few woven rugs, its furniture of the most utilitarian. A fire burned in the hearth, giving warmth and cheerful light to the whole room.

It was, he thought foolishly, the loveliest house he had ever seen.

"Here he is, Gran," the boy said in a piping voice, stepping in behind him and closing the door firmly on the blizzard outside. "I brought the other one."

A plump and comfortable-looking woman of plain, even drab appearance and indeterminate years stood beside the fire. She looked across the room at Elliott and smiled in a manner that made her appear curiously beautiful.

"Gran!" she muttered softly and chuckled. "Well, so be it. Yes, I can see you have, Joss. Take off your hat and coat, sir, and come and make yourself comfortable by the fire. I will pour you a spot of tea. This makes two of you."

"Thank you," he said. "You are most kind, ma'am.

Your grandson has saved my life this afternoon, I do believe. The storm came from nowhere."

His hat and coat were off and the boy took them. Someone else must have been caught in the storm too, then, and had taken refuge in the cottage. She had been sitting on the chair at the near side of the fire when he came inside, her back to him. But she was rising now and turning to face him, her eyes wide with bewilderment and shock.

For a moment he did not recognize her. Or else his brain refused to accept what his eyes told him. It had been so long—more than five years. She had been little more than a girl then—only seventeen years old. And he had not expected to see her in this part of the world, only a few miles from his grandfather's house. She had had plans this year, his grandmother had written. Certainly she was the last person he had expected to encounter here in this country refuge. The coincidence was too mind numbing.

But here she was, still small, still slender yet shapely, her hair still abundant and richly auburn, her eyes still huge and green. A woman now. Still as beautiful as she had been as a girl. More so. Oh, yes, more beautiful.

He heard himself swallow.

"Elliott," she whispered.

"June." He was not sure the sound of her name got past his lips.

"Elliott and June," Joss's grandmother said kindly, breaking the spell. "You know each other, then. Come and sit down, Elliott. You may sit too, dearie, while I pour you another cup. You will both be warm soon.

How lovely, Joss. There will be people to keep the house warmer and more lived-in for Christmas."

Strangely—there was a very strange quality to this whole situation—they were both seated a minute later, he and June, one on either side of the fire, drinking tea and stealing curious glances at each other. And despite the intense discomfort and embarrassment that he knew she must be feeling and that he *should* be feeling, he felt seduced by the warmth of the fire and the coziness of the cottage and the smiling hospitality of Mrs. Parkes, who had introduced herself as he sat down. And by the sweetness of his little carrot-headed savior, who was seated cross-legged on the floor before him, his bright head almost resting against the viscount's knee.

He felt almost—happy.

For five years, he realized, admitting the truth at last, he had longed for a single glimpse of her and had punished himself by keeping himself well out of her sight.

Had she been on her way to Grandfather's after all? Had they been trying to matchmake, his grandparents? Or rather, trying to patch up a disaster of a long-dead marriage? If he had met her at Hammond, he would have ripped up at the lot of them and stormed out perhaps never to return. He was almost sure that was how he would have reacted. He would have been unbearably ashamed, meeting her before the curious eyes of all his family and hers and all the family friends.

"We are husband and wife," he found himself saying to Mrs. Parkes, who must be wondering at the strange coincidence of the fact that he and June had the same name. He noticed the slight flush of color that crept into June's cheeks at his words.

"Ah, yes," Mrs. Parkes said placidly, hiding the surprise she must have felt. "And you will be able to spend Christmas together after all. It is the best time of all to spend with loved ones."

He would not know. He had not spent a Christmas with June since she was a child and he a mere boy—before he had purchased his commission and gone off with his regiment to Spain. He had come home finally in July, 1815, after Waterloo, and married her almost immediately. By the beginning of October she had run away from him. And he had not gone after her. Loved ones? Love had died between them a long time ago.

"This will be the *best* Christmas," Joss said happily.

"He enjoys a spot of company more than just his old gran," Mrs. Parkes said with a chuckle.

The boy joined in her laughter. It was a happy sound. June was smiling, Elliott noticed when he glanced at her, though not at him. He was smiling too.

—*The best Christmas.*

Ah, if only!

It became quickly apparent that they were going to have to stay for the night. She supposed it had been clear from the start, but then she had been too relieved by the safety and warmth and comfort of the cottage to think about it.

It was still snowing heavily outside. The roads were obviously impassable. And soon it was dark. Oh, yes, they would have to stay for the night. And who knew what would happen tomorrow? Perhaps they would not be able to move on then either. Tomorrow was Christmas Eve. The day after tomorrow was Christmas Day.

They might be stuck in this isolated little cottage over Christmas. The prospect was unthinkable. And strangely beguiling.

Very strangely.

They sat around the table, the four of them, for an evening meal of thick vegetable stew and freshly baked bread. But before they ate they joined hands to give thanks. Normally June would have been embarrassed— she was used to a more sedate bowing of the head and a quickly muttered prayer. But the hands of Mrs. Parkes and Joss—fortunately she was seated opposite Elliott and did not have to touch him—clasped her own warmly and firmly and she felt the warmth and the comfort all the way up her arms and all the way through her being to the center of her heart.

It was a strange feeling, she thought, one that must have been aroused by her recent rescue from terror and possible death. A strange feeling of gratitude and joy and commitment to life.

What had he been doing on the road to Hammond? The question had been repeating itself in her mind ever since he had stepped into the cottage earlier in the afternoon. Though the answer had been as obvious then as it was now. He had been going to spend Christmas with the family. He must have known that it was her year to go, but he had been going anyway.

And by some strange, bizarre twist of fate they had both been stranded at this same cottage. Why had none of the other guests found their way here? Why just the two of them—she and Elliott?

She caught his eye across the table and lowered her gaze to her plate.

The peculiar thing was that she could not feel the alarm, the horror, the outrage that she would have expected to feel. Had he been on his way deliberately to Hammond—to see her? At last? She had never admitted to herself—and could scarcely do so now—that she had been waiting for longer than five years for him to come for her.

"It is going to be a blessed Christmas," Mrs. Parkes said, smiling kindly about the table.

"It is going to be fun, Gran," the little boy said, his freckled face aglow with the anticipation of it.

"I am afraid," Elliott said apologetically, "that this snow and your two unexpected guests are likely to spoil Christmas for you. Is the rest of your family any great distance away? How far away *is* the nearest habitation?"

"Our family is all here about the table," Mrs. Parkes said, picking up the basket of bread and offering it around again. "And all one needs at Christmastime is family. One's nearest and dearest."

Ah, there were just the two of them, then. Joss's parents must be dead. Just the two of them. It should be sad but was not. He seemed such a happy little boy. His eyes now glowed into his grandmother's.

"And these are the best guests," he said. "Aren't they, Gran? This will be the best Christmas."

—*The best Christmas.*

—*One's nearest and dearest.*

Ah, if only. June glanced at Elliott again and found his eyes on her, their expression unfathomable.

He had aged. Oh, not in any unpleasant way. Quite

the contrary, in fact. Physically he looked more solid. He had lost the thin, wiry, restless look he had had when he came back from the wars. And his dark eyes had lost the haunted, fanatical gleam that had progressively frightened her—among other things—during the three months following their marriage. His dark hair was still thick, but it was cut into a neater style than the one he had worn five and a half years ago. She had thought when she married him that he was as handsome as any man had a right to be. He was more handsome now.

"Tomorrow," the little boy said, drumming his heels against the crossbar of his chair and speaking in a high-pitched, excited voice, "you and I will go out, mate, to gather greenery and then we will decorate the house with it. And we will carve a Nativity scene out of wood from the shed and set it up by the window. And we will make a star and . . ."

"Wait a minute!" Elliott was holding up one hand and laughing. He was knee-weakeningly attractive when he laughed. "Tomorrow I shall be trying to get my curricle and my horses and my w—, my w-wife on the way to Hammond Park. My grandparents, the duke and duchess, will be expecting us. It will not be Christmas if we do not make it home to our family."

They were expecting him, then. They knew he was coming. It had been planned. But no one had thought to inform her.

"We will have to wait and see, Joss," his grandmother said gently. "Wait and see what tomorrow brings."

June supposed that having unexpected guests must add some excitement to the life of a young boy who lived alone with his grandmother in the country. Especially when one of those visitors was a youngish man, a sort of father figure, who might be willing to do things with him.

"Elliott was always carving wooden figures when he was a boy," she said, smiling at the child. "He was very talented."

"Yes," the child said, bright-eyed. Just as if he thought it impossible that his guest might *not* have the skill to carve a Nativity scene in the space of one day.

"And June would always create backgrounds for what I carved," Elliott said. "Meadows of moss for the sheep with pressed daisies. Trees made of twigs for the birds to perch in and a river of painted paper to flow beneath."

"When we were children," she said softly, feeling the ache of tears in the back of her throat. Since the breakup of her marriage she had stopped remembering the parts of her childhood that had been shared with him.

When dinner was over, she helped Mrs. Parkes to clear the table and wash the dishes while Elliott helped Joss bring in more wood and build up the fire. Then Elliott sat in the chair he had occupied before while the child sat at his feet, looked up, and asked him to tell the story of Christmas.

Glancing at them occasionally as she dried the dishes, June felt that ache of tears again. The child was looking up with rapt attention as he listened to the Christmas story, and Elliott looked back at him with a softened, almost affectionate expression.

He would have made a good father, she thought. He would . . . But she closed her eyes in sudden pain.

"All will be well, dearie," Mrs. Parkes said very quietly so as not to disturb the two at the fire. "I promise you all will be well."

She must have realized by now, of course, that she and Elliott were estranged. Her words were enormously comforting, though why they should be so June could not explain to herself. Could all be made well by a stranger merely through the power of goodwill?

"Ah, the angels," the boy said on a happy sigh. "Singing to the shepherds. I would like to have been one of them."

"With a long white gown and white wings?" Elliott chuckled and ruffled the boy's ginger hair.

The lad looked across the room to his grandmother, who paused in her task of wringing out the washcloth and looked back. June saw the look. It was one of rich and warm mirth, a strange look of equals more than one to be expected between grandmother and grandson.

"Wings!" Mrs. Parkes said before laughing so heartily that they all joined her, the boy more merrily than any of them. "As in all the pictures and sculptures, sir? How would they fly with them, pray? And why would they need them if they are spirit and can move at will?"

"Ah, but you must not spoil our romantic image of angels, Mrs. Parkes," Elliott said.

"Why would they not appear in the shape of a flower?" Mrs. Parkes said, still chuckling, "or a lamb or a—a boy with red hair and ears that stick out to catch the breeze?"

June glanced quickly at the child to see if he had been hurt by the description, but his face was bright with laughter. "Gran!" was all he said. "Careful now."

"Very well, then," Elliott said. "It was a heavenly host of Josses praising God and singing. But the shepherds mistook their ears for wings and so the story has come down the ages." He ruffled the child's hair again as they all laughed helplessly.

The evening passed very quickly. Or perhaps it was just that grandmother and grandson kept country hours and night seemed to rush up on them very fast.

There was a loft above the kitchen, where Joss presumably slept. When June's mind had touched upon sleeping arrangements during the evening, she had assumed that Elliott would share it with him tonight and that Mrs. Parkes would somehow make room for her in the bedchamber. But it seemed that matters were not to be so arranged after all.

"Come, dearie," Mrs. Parkes said to June when bed had been mentioned by a yawning Joss, "you will need to wash yourself and put on a nightgown I will find for you. I have one tucked away somewhere that will fit you. I shall sleep up with Joss tonight and probably tomorrow night too. You and your husband will be welcome to the bedroom."

But—she must realize that they were estranged!

June stiffened with shock. "I—I would not turn you out of your bed," she said.

But Mrs. Parkes smiled her warm, bright, strangely beautiful smile. "It is no trouble at all, dearie," she said. "I am only too happy."

The only real trouble was that it was difficult to argue against such kindness and—such love. It did seem almost, June thought foolishly, as if Mrs. Parkes *loved* her despite the shortness of their acquaintance.

She waited for Elliott to protest, to explain that he would be happy to share the loft with Joss. She waited for Joss to express excitement at the thought of sharing his space upstairs with his new friend.

Neither said a word.

"Thank you," June murmured, following Mrs. Parkes, first into the bedroom and then beyond it into the small, curtained-off washroom. "You are very kind."

Mrs. Parkes patted her on the shoulder. "All will be well, dearie," she said yet again. "Believe me, it will."

She was wearing a white linen nightgown that covered her to the neck and the wrists. She had let down and brushed out her hair. It hung straight and shining almost to her waist. She was sitting very upright on the edge of the far side of the bed, facing away from him. He had been banking up the fire and helping Joss set a guard about it for the night.

He stopped in the doorway and then set down his candle. Her shoulders hunched slightly.

"I will sleep on the floor," he said quietly. "I shall fetch my greatcoat. I will be quite warm and comfortable."

She said nothing for a moment as he turned back to the main room.

"No," she said, her voice stopping him. "The floor is hard and will be cold. It would be foolish."

He watched her get to her feet, pull back the bedclothes on her side of the bed, climb in, and pull them back up over herself, up to her ears. She did it all without turning fully to look at him. She was lying as close to the edge of the bed as possible.

He had known her for one month as a man knows his wife. Frequently. Constantly. Night and day. Until he had finally admitted to himself that the silent and half-hidden tears, the involuntary cringing were just not going to stop. And that he was unwilling to assert himself as her lord and master.

He had been so tired. So very weary. Of life. He had loved her deeply. And had then hated her just as passionately. Until he had turned the hatred against himself.

He wondered what she would do or say now if he suddenly blurted out that the day after she left him he had stood in his study for fifteen minutes, his pistol first to his temple and then—in order to hold it more steadily—in his mouth, trying to summon the courage to pull the trigger. And that afterward, after he had flung the gun away from him, he had cried for longer than fifteen minutes.

Would she move? Say anything? Think anything? Would she care?

He undressed slowly, sitting on the edge of the bed to pull off his boots. When he was wearing only his drawers, he blew out the candle, and lay down on his side of the bed. It was not like climbing into a winter bed. It was warm and unexpectedly comfortable. Could her body heat have warmed it already? He lay on his back, one arm over his eyes, trying to hear her breathing.

She was his wife. This beautiful stranger was his

wife of longer than five years. When his grandparents had suggested her as a bride on his return from Waterloo, he had remembered her as a pretty, happy child who had laughed a great deal and who had loved him and followed him about and tried to please him. And when he had seen her again, he had wanted her with an intense longing. She had been seventeen—beautiful, sweet, innocent. He had wanted her and everything she had to give him. Everything he had lost in years of fighting even though he had been only two-and-twenty when it was all over.

She had been able to give him nothing. And he had made her miserable—for those three months anyway. Perhaps she had recovered later, after she had left him.

He lay still, waiting for the old bitterness to wash over him and the old hatred and the old sense of guilt. But the bed was warm and comfortable. The room was warm even though it was separate from the kitchen and there was no fire in here. There was a clock ticking somewhere, a rhythmic, comforting sound.

He should be uncomfortably aware of June in the bed with him. He should be worried about tomorrow, about whether he was going to be able to get to Hammond Park or not. He should be worried about his family worrying about him—and about June.

But he felt warm and comfortable and sleepy. And strangely at peace. Peace was something with which he had little acquaintance. But he felt it now unaccountably yet unmistakably.

If he could live with her here forever, he thought as he sank closer to sleep, they could be happy together. They could be man and wife again. They could . . .

Viscount Garrett, who for years had suffered badly from insomnia, was asleep.

After she was awake, she wondered why she had woken. Usually in the winter it was because the bed or the room or both had grown cold. Or else it was because she was lying in an uncomfortable position or had had a troublesome dream. None of those things had woken her tonight. She knew instantly that she was in a strange bed in a strange house—not for a moment did she feel disoriented. But she did not believe she had ever felt more comfortable, more at peace in her life.

She was lying on her side, facing away from the doorway, as she had been when she lay down. Except that now she was in the middle of the bed. Her head was only partially on the pillow. Her neck was settled comfortably over a warm, firmly muscled arm. Her chin was resting on the same arm, which was bent beneath it. She could feel that the hand belonging to that arm was lightly clasping her shoulder. Her knees were drawn up. Behind them she could feel other knees. Along the backs of her thighs she could feel other legs. Around her bottom and along her back she could feel a warm, relaxed body. His cheek was against the back of her head. She could feel his breath warm on the side of her head, just above her ear.

Elliott!

She waited to feel outrage, panic.

She had worshiped him throughout childhood, the older, handsome, accomplished cousin who was really no blood relation at all. She had agonized over his safety during his years away at the wars. She had fallen headlong in love with him on his return. She had married him, fully expecting a glorious happily ever after.

And then she had been confronted with a dour, moody, incommunicative stranger for a husband. A man who seemed intent on ignoring her except in one capacity. A man who seemed almost to hate her and who resisted all her attempts at tenderness and all her conversational overtures. He had wanted only to do *that* to her, over and over again, night and day. He had been insatiable and terrifying to her in her naiveté. Always the swift, deep, merciless penetration of her body, followed by the fierce, painful pounding, and culminating in the sobbing of his release. She had felt robbed of personhood.

Yet she was not afraid now. Or outraged. Or even embarrassed. And she felt reluctant to edge away from him lest he himself wake and find them thus.

How strange it was, she thought. How very, very strange. Just a matter of hours ago she had been on her way to Hammond Park for Christmas. She had been thinking of how she would go to London for the Season and choose herself a lover at last. She would have been horrified if she had known that Elliott was at that very moment also on his way to his grandparents'. And then there had been that uncannily sudden snowstorm and both of them being rescued and brought here—only now did it strike her that she had not set eyes on Joss before he had arrived with Elliott. Where had he been for the half hour before that? Why had none of the rest of the family been stranded here?

But here they were, she and Elliott, stranded together at this little cottage. Having to share a bed. In close embrace in its center.

Yet she could feel no horror. Only deep comfort.

And then she realized something. His breathing was too quiet for sleep—and yet he was relaxed. And she realized something else too, something that was so beautiful and so sleep-inducing that she had not even noticed it at first. Mrs. Parkes was singing up in the loft, softly and sweetly. Infinitely sweetly. The child must be having trouble sleeping. She was singing a Christmas lullaby.

"Lully, lulla, thou little tiny child . . ."

But no—there were two voices, her own a soft contralto, the other the achingly pure voice of a boy soprano.

June could scarcely believe that she had not noticed the singing at first, though she knew that it had been there in her unconscious hearing since before she woke. She felt close to tears again, tears of—joy? What was there to feel joyful about?

"June?" His voice was soft and warm against her ear. "I do not want to die. I want to live." She heard him swallow. "I want you to live."

She did not know quite what his meaning was. Perhaps he had woken from a dream and had not yet shaken off its shreds. Perhaps he was remembering yesterday afternoon. And yet she felt deeper meaning than that. And she realized, though she did not fully understand even now, that those words had been a part of him since his return from the wars. He had wanted to live. That first dreadful month of their marriage had shown him grasping desperately at life—and had revealed her withdrawing from it in bewilderment and fright.

What had she done to him in her naiveté? What had he done to her in his pain? What had they done to each other?

She did what some rational part of her mind told her she ought not to do. She turned in his arms so that she was lying against him, front to front. There was the remembered feel of his body, firmly and splendidly masculine, though when she had known it before it had been only the weight of it on top of her as he performed the marriage act. And there was the remembered smell of him—soap and leather and sweat and masculinity. Smells that had always been part of her barely controlled panic.

Now he felt and smelled wonderful.

"They saved us, Elliott," she whispered. "It must have been for some reason, must it not? We are going to live."

She sensed that her words had more meaning than she understood even herself.

"Elliott," she whispered again. "How did they know we were out there? Why are they singing?"

He did not answer her first question. He drew her head to rest in the hollow between his neck and his shoulder and settled his cheek against the top of it.

"They are singing us a lullaby," he said.

The lullaby was for the infant Jesus. Or for Joss. And yet his words did not seem in any way absurd. None of this seemed absurd.

She sighed with deep contentment and slid back into sleep.

It had stopped snowing by the time they got up. But it must have snowed heavily all through the night. The sun, which had broken through the thin layer of clouds, sparkled off white oceans of snow. The branches of the trees were laden down with it. His curricle, which had had to be left outside the shed occupied by his horses, was a mere mound of snow, like a formless snowman without a head.

There was to be no possibility of travel today. Despite the sunshine, the air was cold and crisp. There was no hope of much melting.

He stood in the open doorway of the cottage, waiting for Joss to wind a long striped scarf about his neck and bury his head beneath yesterday's enormous cap so that they could go out to feed and water the horses. June was helping Mrs. Parkes set the table for breakfast, a voluminous white apron over the simple yet fashionable wool gown she had worn yesterday.

He doubted that she had ever helped with kitchen chores, just as he had never been forced to feed his own horses. And yet she looked cheerful and domesticated. As cheerful as he felt.

He realized something suddenly. Something strange. He had been almost holding his breath when he first opened the door, hoping that travel would be impossible.

Being stranded in a simple country cottage without his valet and most of his belongings—all he had with him was a bag with a change of shirt and handkerchief and his shaving kit—should have been nightmarish. Especially when he had been stranded with his estranged wife. And more especially when it was Christmas Eve. A Christmas without a large house party and piles of rich foods and liquor and without the endless entertainments was almost inconceivable.

And yet he had hoped, opening the door, that there would be enough snow to keep him stranded?

His hopes had certainly been realized.

"Ready, mate," Joss said with his cheerful, cheeky grin.

Elliott remembered the almost ethereal voice singing its lullaby last night. The memory seemed almost like a dream. But he knew it had not been. He had woken up this morning with June still in his arms. And incredibly they had smiled at each other before turning away without a word to get up on opposite sides of the bed. Oh, no, last night had been no dream.

The most incredible memory to him was that he had felt no real physical desire for her despite the close proximity of their bodies. Only a deep, warm affection.

It was what had been missing from the first months of their marriage—*one* of the things that had been missing. There had been only desire then. Though it had not been entirely a desire for sexual gratification. There had been more to it than that. It had been the desire for what she had and what he had desperately wanted—youth and innocence. He had never been able to put himself deeply enough into her body. He had never been able to put himself into *her*.

"Come, then, lad," he said, rubbing his hand over the top of the cap and inadvertently turning it slightly so that it was now worn at a jaunty angle.

"The porridge will be ready in a quarter of an hour,"

Mrs. Parkes called cheerfully after them. "Don't catch cold, Joss."

The child giggled happily as Elliott closed the door and they waded side by side toward the shed.

She was on her feet all morning and busy the whole time at unaccustomed chores—stirring the porridge, browning toast over the fire at the end of a long fork, washing breakfast dishes, making up the bed she and Elliott had shared, washing out the water jug and basin, helping to make mince pies, jam tarts, and small spicy currant cakes for Christmas, washing up more dishes, peeling and chopping vegetables for the evening meal.

She could not remember a happier day.

She could not remember her own mother. She liked to imagine as the day wore on that her mother was just like Mrs. Parkes. She felt the comfortable, loving sort of mother/daughter relationship that she had always dreamed of.

Elliott and the child were in and out all morning, fetching in wood and water, carrying in armfuls of bright-berried holly and ivy and pine boughs, bringing in the freshness of the outdoors and the wonder of Christmas with them. They decorated the house until it was laden with greenery, perching on chairs, balancing even on the corner of the table at one point. Elliott was down to his shirtsleeves before they had finished. And he was in the sort of lighthearted mood June remembered from his boyhood, a mood she had not glimpsed even once during the three months of their marriage.

He leaned around her at the table once in order to help himself to a currant cake fresh out of the oven. She slapped his hand without thinking and he grinned at her and told her she had flour on her nose. She retreated hastily to the small washroom and peered into the mirror hanging on the wall there. He had not been lying.

"Cook at your grandpapa's used to tell us that it was bad for the system to eat baked goodies when they were hot," she said, coming back into the kitchen with the flour gone. "She used to say that we would have severe cramps."

He clutched at his stomach and doubled over, groaning.

Mrs. Parkes and Joss laughed merrily. So merrily that, as usual, their laughter was infectious.

"Idiot," June said, giggling at her estranged husband. "Clown."

"The damage is done now," he said hoarsely. "I might as well try a mince pie too. Joss?" He tossed one across to the child, who caught it deftly and promptly ate it, and picked up another for himself.

"Do make yourself at home," June said in a tone that was meant to be chilling.

But he merely grinned again, dipped his finger in a pool of flour that had not yet been cleared from the table, and tapped his finger on her nose.

"That is better," he said, standing back and looking critically at her, his head tipped to one side.

They were behaving like a pair of silly children. Whatever would Mrs. Parkes think of them? But she was bent over the fire, placidly pouring boiling water from the kettle into the teapot. She was smiling. And so was Joss, his face strangely radiant as the firelight caught it.

June felt a totally irrational surging of warm joy. She was so *glad* that it had snowed heavily enough last night to strand them here for another day. How awful of her to feel that way. All the family at Hammond must be frantic with worry. And they were imposing upon the hospitality of people who were clearly not wealthy.

"Here," she said, picking up the tea towel and tossing it at Elliott. "There are more dishes for me to wash and Mrs. Parkes deserves a sit down with her tea."

He stood beside her, meekly drying dishes.

And then Mrs. Parkes noticed that for all the greenery that was draped about the house, there was not even a single sprig of mistletoe.

"There, dearie," she said to June. "You have earned some fresh air and exercise. You will go out with your husband to fetch some. Joss will stay inside to help me."

Joss laughed. "Yes, Gran," he said.

She chuckled with him. For some reason his calling her that always seemed to amuse the two of them.

It took a while to find mistletoe. Partly because the snow was so deep that they had to wade through it and were looking downward at their feet—or rather at their knees—more than up at the trees around them. And partly because they became very conscious of each other without the accompanying presence of Mrs. Parkes and Joss. And partly because, to mask any discomfort they might be feeling, he started a snowball fight.

He threw one at the back of her head and it landed perfectly—between the bottom of her bonnet and the neckline of her cloak. She shrieked and whirled around and the battle was on. He would have won handily if he had not been incautious enough to step too close. He realized too late that one slim little foot had encircled his ankle and wrecked his balance.

He could have taken her down with him, but a gentleman must be a gentleman. He lay sprawled back in the snow allowing her her moment of triumph. She giggled down at him, for all the world like the child he remembered from a long, long time ago.

He got up and stood with his back to her, slapping at the snow caking his greatcoat. Her giggles had died.

"I never meant to hurt you," he said quietly. "Truly I never meant it, June. I was—sick. Not physically. In other ways. I was—very sick."

"From the wars?" Her voice shook slightly. "You would not talk to me. You became morose or openly hostile whenever I tried to talk to you. All you wanted . . ."

He understood why she could not complete that thought. Yes, all he had wanted . . . And yet it was not quite what it had seemed, perhaps. That was not really all he had wanted.

"I wanted you," he said, turning his head to look at her. She was standing staring at him, her cloak speckled with the snow he had been hurling at her just a few moments before. "Not just your body, June, though that is how it must have appeared. You were so young, so innocent, so pure, so sweet. I wanted—I thought perhaps I could regain those things for myself through you. I wanted so desperately to be innocent again. Instead I became more guilty. I hurt you."

"Was it so very terrible?" she asked. "The war? Did you fear for your life every moment?"

"Yes," he said. "But being a man I could not admit it any more than any of the others could. And so there was all the swaggering and bravado, all the devil-may-care high spirits, all the—killing and pretending that those we killed deserved to die merely because they had been born French. I killed and killed and killed, June. Men who wanted to die as little as I did. Men who deserved to die as little as I did. Men with mothers and grandmothers and wives and sweethearts. I am sorry. I am so sorry to be talking about this now. This is Christmas." He turned abruptly and looked upward and saw—mistletoe.

"I thought you were a hero," she said. "I thought you had fought evil men. But I thought the fighting had made you a little arrogant and little—insensitive. I was very naive."

"No." He turned his head again. "Never blame yourself, June."

"Stepmama told me," she said, "that when a marriage breaks down, there are always at least two people to blame."

"She is wrong," he said.

"You were not insensitive," she said. "You were too sensitive. You had been hurt by the wars. You needed healing."

"I was selfish," he said. "I wanted and wanted. I took

and took. I gave nothing. I wanted to take from you. I wanted to take all that was you and make it part of myself. I thought I had nothing to give. Perhaps I was right. But I did not mean to hurt you, June. I loved you. A contradiction in terms, perhaps. Love gives. It does not take. I only took."

He both saw and heard her swallow.

"Mistletoe," he said, nodding in the direction of a nearby oak tree. "I had better get some for Mrs. Parkes."

"It looks rather high," she said, frowning. "Will you be safe?"

"If I fall," he said, grinning with some relief at the change of subject, "you can catch me."

But she did not need to do so. Men do not forget the tree-climbing skills they learn in boyhood, he discovered, though perhaps they are a little more concerned about the well-being of their pantaloons and Hessians and leather gloves.

She was standing a little way from the tree when he came back down. He turned to smile at her.

"Come," he said softly, knowing that he should not. She had probably healed her life in five years and a few months. He should not deliberately complicate it again. Perhaps she had a lover, though if she did, she must be very discreet. No word of it had ever reached his ears.

She came and stood, not only in front of him, but against him. She spread her hands over his chest, beneath the capes of his coat and lifted her face to him even before he raised the tangled bunch of mistletoe he held in his hand.

He had never before kissed with conscious intent.

He had always kissed to gain maximum pleasure. He liked to kiss with opened mouth and with his tongue. He liked kissing to be a prelude to full sexual contact.

He kissed June gently and tenderly with lips that were only slightly parted. He kissed her with no intention of pleasing himself but with the desire to make her feel his sorrow for what he had done to her in the past. He set his free arm loosely about her waist. She could pull away any time she chose.

She leaned her head back when the kiss was at an end, but she made no attempt to draw away from him. They gazed into each other's eyes.

"Elliott," she said at last, her voice almost a whisper, "why are we here?"

It was a strange question, perhaps. But he knew exactly what she meant. Unfortunately, he did not know the answer any more than she did.

"I do not know," he said slowly. "But I think it is good that we are here."

"Yes." It was a mere whisper of sound.

"We had better go back," he said. "Mrs. Parkes wants the mistletoe and Joss wants me to carve some sort of a Nativity scene."

They need us his words seemed to say. But he knew that really the opposite was true. Strangely true. He and June needed a very ordinary middle-aged cottage woman and her redheaded, freckle-faced grandson. And the cottage itself.

"Yes, let us go back." But she still did not move away from him for a moment. "Elliott," she said, "why is it so peaceful there? Why is there such happiness there?"

"Because it is filled with love," he said. He had felt

it yesterday as soon as he had stepped inside the house. Love had reached out to him and enveloped him—and June too. If he had met June anywhere else, there would have been nothing but awkwardness and hostility and stubborn silence between them. But in this cottage they had both been wrapped about with love.

He could explain it no better than that. Even all of that he could not put into words for June. But she understood. She looked into his eyes and read the words there.

"Yes," she said. "It is so simple really, is it not?"

He leaned down and kissed her again softly and briefly. And then they walked back to the cottage. Back in order to find out why they were there.

If anyone had told her that she would be doomed to spend the evening of Christmas Eve cooped up inside a small and simple cottage with a very ordinary country woman and a young child and—Elliott, she would have recoiled with horror. This was always the busiest and happiest evening at Hammond—and even at the other houses she visited for Christmas on alternate years.

At Hammond the evenings were so full of activities that they were dizzying. There was the concert, in which every member of the family down to the smallest child was required to participate and guests were strongly urged to do likewise. There was the children's Nativity play that always ended the concert. And then the village carolers, followed by church, all of them trudging the half mile to the village and enjoying the once-a-year most joyful service of all. And then the feasting afterward and the talking and laughing, and the parents trying to get overexcited and overtired children to bed and to sleep.

It was always at Christmas she most regretted that she had no children of her own—and never would.

Here, in Mrs. Parkes's cottage, there was only quietness. And yet it was a quietness of such contentment that at one time, when she thought about Hammond, she felt that she would not make the exchange even if she could. They were surrounded by the greenery and by the Christmas smells of the pine boughs—and of the mince pies.

Elliott was whittling away at the wood he and Joss had brought in from the shed after feeding the horses again. He had not lost the boyhood talent for carving wood into any shape he pleased. There was no time, as he explained, to make intricately detailed figures, but the simple, rugged shapes he created seemed more beautiful than anything June had seen before. There was a manger and a kneeling Mary and a stooping Joseph and a humble shepherd and a proud king. They came from his hands almost like magic.

Joss, seated on the floor before him so that he could sweep up the wood shavings, watched, his expression rapt and glowing. Mrs. Parkes, her day's work done, sat in an old rocking chair, moving slowly back and forth, her hands clasped loosely in her lap, her habitual kindly smile on her face.

June, at Mrs. Parkes's request, was telling the Christmas story again. But it took her a while to tell. When she reached the part at which the angel gave his message to the shepherds and was then joined by the heavenly host of angels praising God and singing, Joss wanted them to sing. And so they sang, the four of them, cheerfully and lustily yet reverently. It seemed rather surprising to June that the child knew all the Christmas songs either she or Elliott started. He knew every word of every verse and sang out joyfully in his lovely soprano voice.

"We would be going to church," June said rather wistfully when the story was at an end, "if we were at Hammond. If we were not snowed in."

"Ah, but church is where there are people, dearie," Mrs. Parkes said. "Where there are two or three—or four—gathered together and turning their minds to worship and fellowship."

And yes, of course she was right. June caught Elliott's eye as he looked up briefly from his work, and they exchanged a smile. Yes, this was church. They had worshiped together even if there was no altar and no clergyman and no Gothic architectural splendor.

A chubby little sleeping baby was taking shape in Elliott's hands. He was smiling down at it, his concentration fully on what he did.

"I have an idea." June got to her feet and hurried into the bedroom, where she had left her reticule. There was a lace-edged handkerchief inside it. She folded it until the lace was hidden. Lace would not do at all. And then she spotted the bundle of jewelry she had taken from the carriage before she left it. She set the bundle on the bed, opened it, and carefully selected the most precious piece, one she never wore because it had been a wedding gift from Elliott. It was a jewel-encrusted brooch in the shape of a six-pointed star.

Why had she brought it with her this year? She

never took it with her when she traveled. She never even looked at it. But this year she had brought it. She set it on the handkerchief and put the other pieces back inside the reticule.

"We must set up the Nativity Scene," she said as she went back into the main room.

"Familiar words," Elliott said with a smile. "June always had to set up my carvings into scenes."

She looked critically at the space below the window and at its faded blue curtains. "Hm," she said. "We need straw."

"I'll fetch some," Joss said, bounding to his feet and rushing across the room to snatch up his coat and hat. He was back from the shed before five minutes had passed, his arms loaded with straw, which he strewed liberally over the floor between the door and the window.

Mrs. Parkes clucked her tongue. "You make a clumsy little boy, Joss," she said.

Joss chose to be amused by the remark. But he picked up the mess he had made while June spread the straw carefully to make the stable floor.

She arranged all the carvings with great care, moving everything about, shifting angles until all was to her liking. Then she took the baby Jesus, wrapped him close in the handkerchief so that no lace showed, and set him carefully on the straw she had spread in the manger. She set him down as tenderly as if he were a real baby. Her own. Elliott, she noticed, was standing silently beside her.

But she had not quite finished. She took the brooch and pinned it to the curtain, directly above the manger

Immediately it caught light from the fire and the candles and shone down brightly on the stable of Bethlehem.

She sat back on her heels and Elliott came down on his haunches beside her. She turned her head to look at him, not even realizing that there were tears in her eyes until she found that his face was blurred. She reached out a hand without even realizing she did it, and his fingers touched hers even though their hands did not clasp.

"There," Mrs. Parkes said. "It is Christmas again. It works its magic every year. It was certainly His best idea."

His? June looked at Elliott, startled. But she could see that he had realized, as she had done, that Mrs. Parkes was referring to God. And yes, she was right again.

"One more piece for the scene," Elliott said, holding out his closed hand and opening back his fingers to reveal another carving. He was grinning. "Mrs. Parkes and Joss will approve. It is an angel without wings. To me he looks like a lad of eight or nine years with spiky hair, which is probably red, and ears that are not quite flush with his head. And freckles."

He opened the curtains back just a little so that he could place the impish angel on the edge of the windowsill. It appeared to be peering down at the scene below, well pleased with what it saw.

Joss had dissolved into peals of laughter. Mrs. Parkes was rocking in her chair, her apron thrown up over her face, her shoulders shaking with amusement.

It was growing late. Joss was beginning to yawn.

Mrs. Parkes set out some supper on the table, and they all sat down to sample the Christmas fare, though Elliott of course had done that during the morning, while it was still hot from the oven.

"Go on up," Elliott said when Joss's head began to nod down in the direction of the table. "Go with him, Mrs. Parkes. I will help June with the dishes and I will bank up the fire and set the guard about it and make sure the door is securely fastened. You have had a busy day."

They went, the two of them, without argument, and it seemed as if there were now only two occupants of the cottage, cozily playing house together. They did the tasks Elliott had listed without talking to each other, though the silence was curiously companionable.

She turned to go into the bedroom eventually, leaving the candle to him. But he was standing by the window, looking through the crack in the curtains, and he called to her.

"Don't go yet," he said. "Come and see this. No, better still, come to the door and see."

He shrugged on his greatcoat and wrapped her cloak about her himself. Then he opened the door and they stepped outside. He kept an arm tightly about her shoulders.

"You see?" he said.

It was almost like daylight. The sky was clear and star-studded. The light gleamed off the snow. But almost directly overhead was the brightest star of all. It seemed to beam down only on them. It seemed to bathe them in warmth as well as in light—a fanciful thought.

"Oh," she said, "it is the Bethlehem star."

"Yes," he said. "Yes, it is."

His head was tipped back, she saw when she looked at him, and his eyes were closed.

"Elliott," she said almost in a whisper, "what is happening?"

He opened his eyes and looked down at her. "I am trying not to ask myself the question," he said. "I am trying to be purely grateful that it *is* happening. Christmas and all its holy magic. And more than that. Christmas is for everyone. This seems to be just for you and me."

"For us." She closed her eyes as he had done a few moments before. "I did not believe there could ever again be an *us*. Can there?"

She wanted desperately for the answer to be yes. She ached for what had seemed quite impossible just a day and a half ago. She had always ached for it, she realized. All through those dangerous years when he was gone from England and she was little more than a child. All through those dreadful and bewildering months following their marriage. All through the months after she had left him, when she had expected that he would come to take her back. All through the dreary years since. Now.

"I am beginning," he said slowly, "to believe in miracles. And in second chances. June." He lowered his cheek to the top of her head. "June, will you come back to me? Will you give me a second chance to love you?"

For a moment, despite herself, there was terror. Inside the cottage there was a shared bed awaiting them. If she said yes now, they would not share it as they had done last night. If she said yes tonight, they would unite in the act that had only ever been terrifying to her.

But she had been a naive girl then. Then she had expected sweet romance, ethereal love. She had not expected the carnality of physical passion. She had been quite unable to cope with the needs of a man who was trying to escape the demons of warfare through the body of his bride.

She was a woman now. She understood that she was body and mind and spirit and that all parts of her being had to be nourished if she was to be happy and fulfilled. A marriage was between two people. Married love was not just a spiritual thing, not something of the emotions only. Married love was richer than that. It was of the body too.

She wanted her body united with his. She wanted him.

She wanted a marriage with him.

"I will be gentle, my love." There was doubt, the beginnings of misery in his voice. Her silence had been extended. "If you wish, we will be together only as we have been together yesterday and today. It has been good. We have been friends. It can be enough. If you wish."

"No." She nestled her head against his shoulder. "I cannot be enough, Elliott. There has to be everything between us or nothing. I would prefer everything please."

He did not move or say anything for a while. But she felt the breath shuddering out of him.

"Yes," he said at last. "Let us not ask what is happening or why, June. Not yet. Let us allow it to happen."

He turned and took her back into the warmth and peace of the little cottage.

His hands were trembling, he noticed, as was his mouth. He wanted so badly to be perfect. He had had dozens of women since the breakup of his marriage and dozens before his wedding. And yet he had never, he realized now, made love.

Even to June. Even to his wife, the love of his heart. He had tried desperately to take from her—so that he would have something to give back. He had believed that he had nothing to give that was of any value. Just hands reddened with blood and a heart hardened by familiarity with death and violence. And a soul that yearned for life but did not know where to look to find it except in her body, in her sweetness and innocence.

He had not realized at that time that he did have something to give. Something infinitely precious. The most precious gift of all. He had belittled even his love for her.

He knew now that he had that gift to give. He knew that somehow he had the power to make her happy— happy tonight and happy for the rest of their lives.

And yet now too he was overwhelmed by the immensity of the gift he had to give and the desire to give it perfectly. His hands and his lips trembled.

As did hers.

He came to her naked after blowing out the candle and he lifted away her nightgown and threw it over the side of the bed. They touched each other with trembling, wondering hands. They kissed each other with trembling, yearning mouths. They whispered to each other endearments that they had never used before.

"My love," she murmured, her voice throaty with desire. "Yes, come. I am no longer afraid. I am a woman now. Come, my love."

"Beloved," he whispered into her ear as he came on top of her. He kept his full weight off her, on his forearms. "There is no longer anything to fear. I have love to give. I have not come to take."

He mounted her slowly, careful not to jab inward in his need and cause the tense terror he had always felt before with her. But she tilted her hips when he was fully sheathed in her, inviting him deeper, and when he started to move, she twined her legs about his, tightened them, and moved tentatively until she had fit herself to his rhythm.

And he discovered something. He discovered that in giving he also received, that in loving he was also loved. He loved her for a long time so that she would learn that there could be pleasure, so that she would know that there need not be ugliness and pain and terror. He loved her long so that she would know herself adored. He took his time so that he might wipe from her mind and her body memories of desperate selfishness.

And he was rewarded in two ways. He felt her pleasure with every stroke into her body. He felt it grow to something beyond pleasure and realized finally and in some wonder that she was sexually aroused and would come to climax if he gave her the time. He gave it, moving steadily and firmly into her until he felt the cresting very near and held motionless deep inside her.

He knew that she was about to cry out and he covered her mouth with his own and absorbed the sound. The sound of his woman reaching the ultimate physical happiness.

He had not been in any way intent on his own pleasure. He had labored only for hers. But at the moment she cried out into his mouth he felt his own powerful release and spilled out his seed deep inside her. He sighed aloud into her mouth and knew as he descended with her into the oblivion beyond fulfillment that the gift they had shared came not just from the two of them but somehow from outside them too. From the whole house surrounding them. From Christmas. From the two people who had found them in the snowstorm and had saved them and brought them to this haven.

If he had been able to think consciously, he would have almost expected to be able to turn his head to find the two of them standing on either side of the bed, shining as they had seemed to shine through the blinding snow the previous day.

But not as people. As . . .

But he had fallen with his wife beyond ecstasy into sleep.

"Elliott?" She feathered kisses across his chest, which was warm and still damp from the exertions of lovemaking—they had slept deeply through the night but had woken together in the early morning, wanting each other again.

"Mm?" His chest expanded beneath her mouth as he breathed in deeply and then let the air out on a long sigh of lazy contentment.

"Elliott," she said, "it is Christmas morning."

"Mm," he said sleepily. "Happy Christmas, sweetheart."

"And we have no gifts," she said.

He chuckled softly. "The one you just gave me was priceless beyond measure," he said. "I cannot think of one I would value more unless it is more of the same tomorrow night—or do I mean tonight?—and in the coming nights."

"And the same goes for me," she said. "If I could have known what gift this Christmas had to offer me, I would have been too delirious to leave home to receive it."

He chuckled and his arms closed more warmly about her.

"I was thinking of Mrs. Parkes and Joss, though," she said. "We have nothing for them, Elliott. And Joss is a *child*. He ought to have presents. Do you think his grandmother has any for him?"

She had his full attention now. She could tell that he was no longer hovering between sleep and consciousness.

"Strange," he said. "He seems such a cheerful and contented lad that I had not thought of it. He cannot be more than eight years old. When I was eight I thought the sole purpose of Christmas was to provide me with gifts."

"I have money," she said unhappily. "But money makes such a dull gift for a child."

"What do you have with you that you could give to Mrs. Parkes?" he asked.

She thought for a while. She did not even have a

change of clothes with her. "The purse I keep my money in," she said. "It is silk and I embroidered the design on it myself only last month. It is new."

"Can you bear to part with it?" he asked.

"Of course," she said. "Oh, yes, it will be just the thing. It will be something personal. Something I made that she can remember me by."

He found her mouth with his and kissed her. "Yes, love," he said. "Problem solved."

"But what about Joss?" Her unhappiness was back.

"Let me see," he said and she gave him time to think. There was nothing she could give the boy. Her comb? Her little vial of perfume? Some of her jewels? There was nothing.

"There is my whittling knife," he said. "My father gave it to me when I was a lad and it has followed me about almost everywhere ever since. When Joss tried using it yesterday he looked very happy."

"He always looks happy," June said. "Have you ever seen brighter red hair, Elliott, or more prominent freckles? He is *such* a sweetheart. If he were mine . . ."

He kissed her again.

"Is it a safe gift?" she asked.

"I was nine years old when my father gave it to me," he said. "He trusted to my sense of responsibility with it. I have no doubt I can trust to Joss's."

"Of course," she said. "You are quite right. I think he will like it, Elliott, especially if you tell him how precious it is to you. I believe you are his hero. He scarcely takes his eyes off you and there is always such a brightness in his face."

"The same could be said of Mrs. Parkes and you," he

said. "I believe she sees you as a daughter figure, June. I wonder if it was Joss's mother or father who belonged to her. Neither of them has said."

"No."

They lapsed into silence. June was almost asleep when he spoke again. At the same moment he slid his arm out from beneath her head and rolled over to sit up on the side of the bed.

"I have an idea," he said. "There should be time. It must be very early. I probably have a couple of hours before Joss gets up. I am going out to the shed, June. I saw tools out there. If he does get up before I have finished, try to keep him away from the shed, will you, love?"

"What are you going to do?" She was not enjoying being deprived of his body heat.

But he merely leaned down and kissed her once more. She could see his grin in the dark.

"Secrets," he said. "Something for Joss. But the best gifts are always those that are a secret from everyone except the giver. Go back to sleep."

"Elliott," she said after he had dressed in the darkness and was in the doorway on his way to the other room and the outer door.

He paused and looked back at her.

"I love you," she said. "I love you so very much. I always have."

"Temptress," he said softly. "Say that again tonight when I am at liberty to reply suitably."

She smiled as she listened to him let himself quietly out of the house. Then she turned into the faint warmth he had left behind and went back to sleep.

* * *

Joss's cheeks and nose were as bright a red as his hair, but since they were a different shade entirely, they clashed horribly with it. Fortunately, perhaps, his hair was all but hidden beneath the capacious hat.

He would not hear of going inside even though June and his grandmother had decided to go in search of a hot cup of tea and a mince pie.

Joss was still shrieking and laughing and bounding about. He had all the exuberance that a young boy should have, Elliott thought, and then some. One would almost swear that the child had never played in his life and was now furiously making up for lost time.

The sled was not expertly made. There had not been enough time or quite the right tools. But it clearly delighted Joss beyond measure. The two of them had been outside—and Mrs. Parkes and June had been out too for well over an hour—since two minutes after the time the gift had been brought inside and revealed to a curious threesome who had been barred from the shed for almost an hour after they had risen and dressed.

Joss had been up every snowbank in sight at least two dozen times each and had screeched his way down to the bottom. He had made Elliott sample each hill. He had coaxed June into trying three of them. He had wheedled his grandmother and there had been a great deal of laughter between the two of them, but she had declined the treat.

Joss could not have been better pleased if he had been given the costliest toy fort with a whole army of tin soldiers—the great dream of most little boys. Not that Elliott would ever give such a gift to any son of his. Toy soldiers always looked rather too like real soldiers for his comfort.

Joss, who for all his sweetness, had never seemed quite like a typical child, now seemed to epitomize all the joy and exuberance and carefreeness of childhood.

Elliott stood and laughed at him and picked him up when he fell off his sled, as he inevitably did at least one out of every three times, and slapped the snow off him and sent him on his way again.

The child was inexhaustible.

But he was not the only one who was bubbling over with happiness. Elliott could have done some whooping and capering of his own if behaving so had been consistent with the dignity of his seven-and-twenty years. Just looking at June as she appeared when she stepped outside made his heart leap and his loins ache. Though it was not lust he felt for her but love pure and simple. For though there was definite physical desire in the feeling, there was far more to it than that. There was the knowledge that they were one in that indefinable way that husband and wife are supposed to be one—that they shared physical bonds and friendship and deep affection and a future.

He knew whenever their eyes met—as they frequently did—that she shared his thoughts and his feelings. They did not need words this morning. Or even privacy.

Even after she had gone inside he was warmed by his memories of last night and by the knowledge that from now on she was to be at his side, his wife in every possible way, that he would never again have to know loneliness or uncertainty.

Joss slid with an ear-piercing shriek to his feet and somersaulted into the snow in the opposite direction from his sled.

"You are going to have to make one of these for your own son, mate," he said breathlessly.

"I have no son," Elliott said, reaching out a helping hand.

Joss bounced to his feet. "But you will," he said. "You make him one of these. I had no idea they could be such fun."

Elliott chuckled as the boy raced off again. But the words had caused a certain somersaulting sensation in the region of his heart. He had not thought of that. Perhaps he would be able to put away the five-year belief that he would never have children of his own body.

Perhaps . . .

"Watch me!" Joss yelled and he launched himself and his sled off the highest bank in what looked to be a suicide dive.

Elliott laughed and strode to the rescue.

"This has been so pleasant." June sipped on her tea and leaned back in her chair. She smiled at Mrs. Parkes. "The most wonderful Christmas ever. I hope we have not been too much of an imposition on you."

"Christmas is for love, dearie," Mrs. Parkes said. "Indeed, life is for love, but sometimes we forget. Christmas helps us remember."

She ran her fingers over the silk purse she held on her lap and over the even silkier surface of the embroidered design. She had actually shed a few tears when June had given it to her earlier.

"All will be well now, dearie." Her face glowed with her own unique brand of happiness.

"You have said that a number of times," June said. "Is it your philosophy of life?"

The older woman rocked gently in her chair and folded her hands across the purse. "Neither of you must blame yourselves any longer for what is past," she said. "You were too young. You knew too little of life. And he was too old for his years and knew too much of life. It was too soon for the two of you. Now is the right time."

June stared at her fixedly. "Elliott has been telling you about us?" she asked. Or was it just a lucky guess given the fact that their estrangement must have been obvious at first?

Mrs. Parkes continued to rock, the picture of contentment and quiet wisdom. "Now is the right time," she said again. "All will be well now. It will be a son."

"*What* will be a son?" June's eyes widened.

"Your firstborn," Mrs. Parkes said. "Conceived at Christmas. A good time to conceive, dearie."

June felt dizzy. And horribly embarrassed. They had been *heard* last night. The bed springs had not seemed squeaky but then perhaps on both occasions she had been too intent on other matters to notice. And she could remember that the first time Elliott had covered her mouth with his own—just as she was crying out with the wonder of what was happening. They had been heard.

"I am so sorry," she said. She could feel her cheeks flaming. "Was it very tasteless? It was just that—"

But Mrs. Parkes was smiling her comfortable, almost

radiant smile. "Love is never tasteless," she said. "Not in any way it may show itself."

But she did know. She clearly knew that they had made love here in this cottage, in her bed, last night. June sipped on her tea again, though for a moment it seemed too hot. But her embarrassment gradually receded. *Love is never tasteless,* Mrs. Parkes had said.

Mrs. Parkes thought June had conceived last night. She thought they were going to have a son. She could not possibly know, of course. It was purely conjecture. But the very possibility of it washed over June. It was something she had not really thought of. She had been so intent on the wonder of their reconciliation and the discovery that intimacy with Elliott was no longer a fearful thing but something of infinite beauty that she had not considered the possibility that she might be conceiving.

But she could remember both times she felt the warm gush of his seed inside her. What if . . . Oh, what if they were to have a child? A baby. A son. It would not matter whether it was a son or a daughter except that he would have his heir if they had a son.

A baby.

Perhaps she had conceived last night.

She laughed softly. "Now I know how Mary felt," she said, glancing at the carvings beneath the window. "Being told by the angel that she was going to have a son even before she knew it herself. How do you fancy yourself as an angel, Mrs. Parkes?"

She expected the other woman to laugh heartily. Instead, she merely rocked in her chair and smiled gently. Something deep inside June turned over.

And then the outer door opened and a draft of fresh air came inside with Elliott and Joss. Elliott looked quite as boyish as the child, June thought, turning to look at them. He was grinning and bright-eyed. He was carrying the child up on his shoulders. Joss was ducking his head so that he would not bump it on the door frame.

"Gran," he called in his eager, piping voice, "I never knew what fun it was to be a little boy."

They were endearing, rather sad words to June, but they set Mrs. Parkes off into gales of laughter. Joss, in the process of being swung down from Elliott's shoulders, joined her. The mingled sound of their merriment was pure joy.

"I thought I had better bring him inside, ma'am," Elliott said, "before he turned into a block of ice." He took off his gloves and hat and greatcoat and came over to the fire to warm his hands. But he set them first flat against June's cheeks and grinned at her when she winced from the shock of the cold. And since Mrs. Parkes had got up to fill the kettle and Joss was already examining his new whittling knife, Elliott bent his head to hers and kissed her swiftly and openmouthed.

"Hello, my love," he whispered.

She could feel herself blushing again. She felt all the world like a new bride.

He was sitting at the kitchen table with Joss, giving him some instruction on wood carving and watching his efforts. The child's tongue had appeared out of one corner of his mouth and a line of concentration had formed between his brows. He kept tossing back an errant lock of hair that had a habit of hanging down in his line of vision.

He loved the child dearly, Elliott realized. And he realized too that he wanted a child of his own. Children. Today the longing was a pleasant thing because his marriage had begun again last night and would continue into the coming days and weeks and years. In all probability they would have children.

But he would always love Joss. He must keep in touch with the child. Perhaps he could do something for his future.

June was sitting at the table too, quietly watching until she got up, went into the bedroom, and came back with her comb in hand. She combed the lock of bright red hair back from Joss's brow in such a way that it would not fall forward again and then she bent and kissed the boy's bare forehead.

"My hair is in my eyes too," Elliott complained, and with a smile she did the same for him, even down to the kiss on the forehead. She was blushing like a girl, he noticed with interest.

Mrs. Parkes was standing by the window, looking out.

When he was first married, Elliott thought, all he had wanted was to take his wife to bed, to bury his pain and his guilt and his knowledge in the pure innocence of her body. Now it was different. The thought of the coming night was pleasurable anticipation, it was true, but he was content just to be close to her, sitting quietly with her, though they were not alone and were not talking a great deal.

She felt like the peaceful, other half of himself that

had been missing all his life. He was feeling incredibly happy though this was a very untypical Christmas Day.

"The snow is melting," Mrs. Parkes said.

"Good." Elliott looked up. "We will be able to be on our way by tomorrow then, perhaps." It was not an entirely pleasurable thought although part of him was eager to take his wife back into the world they knew so that they could begin the life together that they had tried to begin more than five years ago.

June got up to stand beside Mrs. Parkes. They were both silent for a while.

"It is incredible, Elliott," June said at last. "The laneway seems perfectly clear already and I can see where it joins the road. The road looks clear too. It seems not even to be muddy."

That could not possibly be. He got to his feet and joined them at the window. The snow was as thick everywhere as it had been for two days. Except on the laneway and the road, quite visible in the distance, to one side of the cottage. And June was right. There appeared to be no mud.

"I believe," Mrs. Parkes said quietly, "that your family will be expecting you for Christmas dinner. It is a pity for families not to be together for the most joyful feast of the year."

She had her arm about June's waist, Elliott noticed at the same moment as he felt a small hand creep into his. He squeezed it and looked down at the child.

"I will sweep the snow off your curricle while you get the horses ready, mate," Joss said.

It was only the middle of the afternoon. Even if they were farther from Hammond Park than he had thought when the snow came—and they must be or he would have recognized both the cottage and its inhabitants— they would still arrive there in plenty of time for dinner and for the ball that always followed it in the evening. If the guests could travel through all this snow, of course.

How could the snow have disappeared so fast from the road and how could the road have even dried? It was a strange mystery. But there was work to be done. He shrugged into his greatcoat again while June went through to the bedroom to pack his shaving things and fold up his spare shirt.

Less than half an hour later they were taking their leave of the two who had saved their lives and opened up their home so cheerfully to strangers. It was not an easy thing to do. He shook hands with Mrs. Parkes and kissed her cheek while June was hugging and kissing Joss, and then he stooped down on his haunches and drew the child into his arms, into a bear hug. He felt very close to tears.

"I'll come back, lad," he said. "I'll make sure that you never want for anything. I'll make sure you have school- ing and that when you grow up you have the chance to do something interesting and fulfilling with your life. I promise. I'll never forget you."

The child's arms tightened about his neck. "You are all right, mate," he said in his high little voice. "For a while I thought you would not be, but you are. I am happy. I am always happy. Always. Forever and ever."

The innocence of childhood, Elliott thought, closing his eyes and hugging the child even closer to him. Children believed that happiness could last forever. But happiness could be worked on. And love could be worked on so that neither need ever be totally lost even during the inevitable hard times of life.

He kissed the child's soft, freckled cheek and got to his feet. His eyes were swimming with tears. June, he saw, was clasped in Mrs. Parkes's arms and was openly sobbing.

"I'll come back," she was saying. "I promise I will come back. You have been so good. I love you so dearly."

And then finally they were on their way, seated side by side on the high seat of his curricle, both looking back as much as they could and for as long as they could until they had turned onto the road and the cottage and the two waving figures of their hosts had disappeared from sight.

"Elliott." He was guiding the horses with one hand. His other hand was clasped tightly in hers. She rested her cheek against his shoulder. "How is it possible to feel so deliriously happy and so wretchedly miserable all at once?"

He could give no answer. He could only turn his head for a moment and kiss her briefly.

"It was strange," she said a short while later. "Very strange. It *is* strange. What was the meaning of it all?"

He could offer no explanation. But he knew she was referring not only to the events of the past two days but to the strange happenings of this afternoon too. The snow clearing from the road like that was somewhat uncanny. So was the fact that almost instantly he began to recognize landmarks, as he was sure she did too. They were no farther than two or three miles from

Hammond. And yet the cottage and its immediate surroundings had looked quite unfamiliar. Only two or three miles—and yet within that space and the time it took to travel it in his curricle the snow got less and less until by the time they passed through the village and through the gates into the park and onto the driveway it had disappeared altogether. Without a trace.

Within two or three miles? In less than an hour of travel?

The thing was, he was beginning to *feel* the meaning of it all even if he could not yet translate feeling into thoughts or words.

"I think this was the meaning," he said, lifting their clasped hands to his lips and kissing the back of hers.

"Yes," she said quietly, and he knew that for her too there was intuition but no full understanding yet.

It seemed to June that everyone must have gathered in the hall. It was crowded with family members and family friends and even the children—it was Christmas Day after all.

The duke was there, rubbing his hands together as if he were washing them. And the duchess was beside him, her hands clasped to her bosom. June's papa and stepmama were there, her arm drawn through his, his free hand covering hers. *Everyone* was there. Aunt Martha was there too, a little removed from most of the others, though she did have two children hanging off each arm.

They all wore identical expressions with the possible exception of the children. Expressions of bright expectation mingled perhaps with a little anxiety. They looked as if they were all holding their collective breaths.

None of them looked frantic with worry, though.

She and Elliott stood hand in hand in the doorway for a moment and then stepped inside the hall.

And noise ensued.

Everyone spoke at once. Everyone talked loudly in an effort to be heard above everyone else. Everyone was trying to kiss them or shake their hands or slap them on the back or do all three at once. There was a great deal of laughter. Children, delirious with exuberance, were darting about amongst legs and skirts.

The duke finally made himself heard while the noise level subsided to a mere loud murmur. He held their clasped hands in both of his and patted them. Yet he appeared not to have a great deal to say after all.

"Well, my boy and my girl," he said. "Well. This was certainly worth waiting for. It was indeed."

"Dear Elliott. Dear June." The duchess sniffed against a lace handkerchief. "This is the best Christmas gift of them all. Not that I am belittling any of the wonderful gifts I have been blessed with this day. But this is better than all."

"This was worth waiting for," the duke said, to be original.

"We are so very sorry to have worried you all," Elliott said, including the whole gathering in his glance. "You must have realized that we had been delayed, though no one else seems to have been. But you must have been worried even so. There was just no way of getting word to you."

"But there was word," the duke said above a swell of

protesting sound around him. "There was a note from Mrs. Parkes. Do you not remember asking her to send a note, my boy?" He shook his head. "Your mind must have been preoccupied with other matters."

There was a gust of laughter. Some of it, especially from the male members of the family, sounded suspiciously bawdy.

"From Mrs. Parkes?" It was Elliott who spoke. June's mouth opened but no sound came out.

"She wrote to say you had decided to stay at her guest house until this afternoon," the duke said. "That you had decided to try to settle your differences before coming home."

The duchess was dabbing at her eyes. June could see that her stepmama was biting her upper lip.

"She wrote?" Elliott's voice was faint. "When?"

"The afternoon before last," the duke said. "Her letter arrived just after teatime and just before your valet and June's maid. So of course we did not worry, my boy. But we have all eagerly awaited your arrival today. One look at your faces has given us the answer we have all awaited. And clasped hands, my boy. Not the thing at all, you know." He coughed and then laughed heartily, together with the rest of his family and guests.

"The afternoon before last." Elliott exchanged looks with June. "But who was the messenger? And how did he get through all the snow? Unless he came before the snow fell. But how could they have known then . . ."

June felt her head swimming. She felt herself take one more dizzying step forward to understanding.

"The snow?" the duchess said, puzzled.

"The snow?" Other voices, loud with merriment, took up the question.

"Where were you, Elliott, m'lad? The North Pole?"

"Never peeped out of your bedroom window, did you, Elliott, to see what the weather was doing?"

"Imagined yourself marooned by blizzards, did you?"

"We have never had a drier, milder Christmas," the duchess said. "Much to the children's disappointment." She clapped her hands. "Upstairs everyone for tea. It is half an hour late already. If we do not eat soon, none of us will have appetites for the Christmas goose."

There were loud protests as everyone surged in the direction of the grand staircase.

Elliott and June looked at each other, their hands clasped almost painfully. She could see from his expression that, like her, bewilderment was mingled with the dawning of incredible understanding.

Lady Martha, standing alone now in the shadows of the hall, watched them with shining, tear-filled eyes and then looked upward to the high ceiling and beyond it in spirit to give silent thanks.

Strangely reluctant as he had been to leave the cottage where he and June had spent two days, Elliott rejoiced at being back with his family to celebrate the end of Christmas Day. This year the family gathering was complete. This year he had his wife with him.

And so this year was the most blessed Christmas of all.

The good wishes of his family, the sentimental tears of the ladies, and the hearty and often risqué congratulations of the men should have embarrassed him. But he felt the warmth behind the good wishes and he felt fully for the first time the wonder of family—the wider family of grandparents and aunts and uncles and cousins as well as the smaller family of two, formed by his wife and himself.

They feasted on goose and Christmas pudding and all the trimmings until they were fit to burst. And they danced through the evening and on into the night until their feet were ready to drop off. It was no formal ball, for which Elliott was profoundly thankful. He danced at least half the sets with his wife.

And then, late as it was when they went to bed, and tired as they were, they stayed awake almost until dawn, making love and talking alternately.

One thing they were agreed upon. On the afternoon of the day preceding Christmas Eve, they had both stepped outside the bounds of reality into some shared yet unreal experience.

"It should be frightening to think about," June said, curled warmly against his chest. "But it is not."

"We should wonder about our sanity," he said, kissing the top of her head. "But I have never felt more sane."

"There was no snow," she said.

"Mrs. Parkes sent a message," he said.

"They knew we were coming, Elliott. They were waiting for us."

"And they planned for us to come home this afternoon. The road cleared for us."

"Whatever it was," she said, "it was good. It had to be good, Elliott. It felt good. There was a feeling there. I could have stayed there forever except I knew that I had to come back, that this is where we must live. In the real world."

"It had to be good," he said. "Three days ago, June, I hated the thought of you. You hated the thought of me." He swallowed and tightened his hold of her. "It had to be good. It had to be, my beloved."

"Elliott." She raised her head and kissed his lips. "Elliott, nobody recognized our description of them even though they live only a few miles away. And no one knows of any such cottage."

"Except for the derelict one that has not been lived in for twenty years or more," he said.

She sighed. It was not altogether a sad sound.

"Yes," he said, just as if she had spoken. "Yes, my love. Tomorrow. We will go back there tomorrow."

"Elliott," she said, "I love them so very, very much. My heart aches with love for them. For near strangers. *Are* they strangers?"

"He said a peculiar thing this morning—yesterday morning," Elliott said. "He said I was all right. That he had not been sure I would be but was certain now. To what was he referring? I did not really think about it at the time."

"She told me that when we married it was the wrong time," June said. "That now was the right time. She did not even know us five years ago. Did she?"

He kissed her—deeply. "When I first saw Joss," he said, "I thought he was a light."

"And so did I," she whispered, "when I first saw Mrs. Parkes."

He lifted her over him to lie on top of him and tucked the blankets and his arms about her. She snuggled her head into his shoulder and sighed once again.

They did not talk anymore—or make love. They lay in quiet happiness and wonder until they fell asleep.

The cottage and the shed beside it were very derelict indeed. It was clearly many years since either had been used. The faded thatch had gaping holes in it. The door of the house hung at a crazy angle from its hinges. The door of the shed was missing altogether. The house held nothing but leaves and assorted rubble inside.

There was not a trace of snow.

"But it is undoubtedly the place," Elliott said quietly.

"Yes," she said. "Oh, yes, it is."

They had dismounted from their horses and stood hand in hand just outside the door of the cottage.

"Shall we go in?" he asked.

She closed her eyes. She felt afraid. Afraid of the unknown, the supernatural. Afraid to dabble in it again now that she knew it for what it was. For what it must be.

But with her eyes closed and her hand clasped in Elliott's, she could feel only a sense of almost overwhelming peace.

"Yes," she said.

There was nothing in there, of course. Only a sense of aching nostalgia. And yet there was something after all.

"It had to be good," Elliott said, echoing her own thoughts. "It is still here, that feeling. Contentment, peace. Love. Even though everything else is gone."

"Who were they?" she asked. "Elliott, were they—?" She found it almost impossible to say the word. "Or did we imagine them?"

But he was drawing her across the room toward the window even as she spoke. He reached out his free hand and touched something on the windowsill and then picked it up. He held it out on the palm of his hand to show her without saying a word.

A roughly carved but cheeky-looking little angel without wings—but with definite freckles and protruding ears—lay on his palm.

"Oh, Elliott." She turned her face in to his shoulder. She felt his forehead come down to rest against the side of her head.

"Mrs. Parkes," she said, "you are there, are you not? You are always there. Though I do not suppose that is your name. Thank you. Oh, thank you. I do love you so."

"Joss, you little rascal," he said, naked affection in his voice. "You little rascal. You must come back again and try swimming or tree-climbing or bareback riding. It *is* fun to be a little boy."

It was surely imagination this time, that echo of joyous and merry laughter.

"Elliott." She turned to stand against him and wrapped her arms about his waist. She looked up into his face. "She said we were going to have a child. A son. Conceived at Christmas."

They stood gazing into each other's eyes and smiling slowly and tearfully.

"While we were guarded by angels," he said.

He had put it into words at last.

"Yes," she said. It was all she could say.

He kissed her.